Stella

"No One Will Ever Know."

So he had said and so he had provided. Angel's head fell back and she smiled up at him in gratitude. But what she saw in his face resembled no friendly protectiveness. His half-lidded eyes burned into hers and swept below as he caught his breath and clutched her arms. Inhaling mightily, he slid her along his virile body. . . .

"You are this Devil's damnedest temptation," he rasped as trembling hands crushed her nakedness to him. Again, she felt the iron evidence of his desire for her. Breathless, she arched to yield him more. . . .

"You are gloriously wanton," he growled, and laid them both down to the cushions. His hand covered one breast, his thumb and fingers circling, then feathering the begging crest.

"More," was all she could think of.

"Aye, anything you want." He slid his hand along her bare body, his reverent fingers squeezing, shaping, claiming ribs and waist and thigh. "God"—he said it like an invocation—"you're everything I want. . . ."

Praise for Jo-Ann Power's *Angel of Midnight*

"Rich in historical detail, this great lusty romp through medieval England will keep you turning the pages, rooting for Angel and her Devil. Wonderful to the very end."
—Diane Haeger, author of *Angel Bride*

Nationwide Bookseller Praise for Jo-Ann Power and Her Latest Romance *You and No Other*

"An excellent story . . . wonderful characters . . . I hated to see it end."

—Annie Oakley, Waldenbooks

"You and No Other starts with humor and ends with love. The [wedding] ring symbolizes all. Terrific."

—Jackie Skimson, Pages Etc.

"Full of action . . . *You and No Other* is a wonderful story . . . a winner! Medieval romance at its best."

—Kevin Beard, Journey's End Bookstore

"This is a fantastic tale, fast-paced . . . Matt [is] the love of every woman's dreams."

—Elaine Martin, Book Nook

"You and No Other is a great story, sweet, tender, and moving. Jo-Ann Power is an author to look forward to reading again."

—Linda Schnelbach, Linda's Used Books

Books by Jo-Ann Power

You and No Other
Angel of Midnight

Published by POCKET BOOKS

For orders other than by individual consumers, Pocket Books grants a discount on the purchase of **10 or more** copies of single titles for special markets or premium use. For further details, please write to the Vice-President of Special Markets, Pocket Books, 1230 Avenue of the Americas, New York, NY 10020.

For information on how individual consumers can place orders, please write to Mail Order Department, Paramount Publishing, 200 Old Tappan Road, Old Tappan, NJ 07675.

Jo-Ann Power
ANGEL OF MIDNIGHT

POCKET BOOKS

New York   London   Toronto   Sydney   Tokyo   Singapore

This book is a work of fiction. Names, characters, places and
incidents are products of the author's imagination or are used
fictitiously. Any resemblance to actual events or locales or persons,
living or dead, is entirely coincidental.

An *Original* Publication of POCKET BOOKS

POCKET BOOKS, a division of Simon & Schuster Inc.
1230 Avenue of the Americas, New York, NY 10020

ISBN: 1-4165-0711-6

This Pocket Books paperback printing September 2004

10 9 8 7 6 5 4 3 2 1

POCKET and colophon are registered trademarks of
Simon & Schuster Inc.

Cover art by Brent Watkinson

Printed in the U.S.A.

Great thanks to two writing buddies who keep me fueled with laughter and great suggestions: Dawn Miller and Susan King

Chapter

1

❧

Prayers came true.

Her first glimpse of him as they rolled him from the winnowing sheet showed her he was the answer to her problems. Her hope manifested in one magnificent body.

He was a huge man. A virile man.

But bound and gagged as he was, a furious one.

She closed her eyes in thankfulness and then listened as her three servants disentangled the canvas from his swaddled body and laid him on his side upon the carpet before her searing solar fire. But her eyes flew open at the sound of a tussle. For quick as her captive was freed of the cloth, he contorted his tied body in an acrobat's lashing attempt to kick her men with both feet. They neatly sidestepped his lunges.

Neither ropes nor a blindfold nor failure deterred him.

Angel shivered in the confirmation of all her expectations.

1

Worthy of his notorious legend, her prisoner struggled within the inescapable clutch of the triple hemp cordons that fettered his hands, his thighs and ankles. True to his reputed strength, he had already frayed one rope at his wrists and had his captors panting and perspiring, though they had just entered with their burden from the frigid November night.

Her steward, Peter, flung back his cowl and shook his head as he avoided another attempted kick. "I tell you he lives up to his name! We have had a rough night's work taking this brute!"

Beneath his gag, the man muttered a menacing retort.

Peter bent to him. "Now, now, brigand, I told you there is no need to fight us so."

Peter was right. Though their prisoner might not have had the opportunity tonight to view her steward, Peter—true to his biblical namesake—had been fashioned by His Maker as a gentle man if a big one. In fact, Angel had never seen his equal.

Until now. Until this man who struggled before her.

Without taking her eyes from him within her reach, she ordered her steward, "Help him up, Peter."

Her captive stilled. He waited, an animal taken, deterred, unbroken, unbowed. Ever more dangerous in thrall to another.

"Milady, we must have a care. This man is a worthy opponent in any colosseum. I swear to you, we must needs pour a goblet or two of good strong wine down his throat before we bring him to his feet."

"Aye," agreed her auditor, Edwin. "He almost broke my arm when we fell upon him near the waterfall. I'll gladly empty a flagon into him if it means he'll quiet."

2

He would soon enough. For she could not bear to see a man yoked like a beast. It reminded her too much of her own bonds, her own terrors. She would not see any man or woman suffer as she had. Certainly, if she were to enlist the aid of this man, she could not show him the very enslavement from which she sought to free herself.

She strode toward him, rubbing her hands together, surveying her trophy. Her bound, gagged, blindfolded prize.

"I beg you, sir, cease your struggles."

His face, sleek cheek to her bare floor, jerked toward her. His brow furrowed as if he would peer through the black cloth to view her face.

Peter chuckled. "That's more like it."

"Help him up," Angel insisted.

"No, milady, that's not—"

Their prisoner grunted his approval.

"Peter, do as I say."

"Aye, milady." Peter hooked his meaty forearms beneath those of the tied man and hefted him to his knees.

Even in this pose, her captive appeared Herculean. For she, whom many declared too tall for troubadours' tales of total acclaim, could stand before him, and still his head leveled near her heart. With him upon his knees like Samson in homage to Delilah, she could admire his every arresting feature.

No wonder 'twas said few gazed upon this man's face, for his every aspect declared the rightness of his outlaw's name. Black hair the color of Hades's depths flowed in glossy waves to his nape. The sooty color repeated in his clothes, his laced black silk tunic and marten fur vest across his incomparably broad muscular chest, and to his sculpted legs in molded braies and hose. The measured way he breathed drew her eyes and prodded her imagination toward the successful accomplishment of the task he might perform for her. Freedom spread before her, all the sweeter a paradise because she saw in this man's pervasive might a sign that God favored her with an advantage to overcome her enemies. This one perfect, powerful man might very well free her from her personal prison. Her hell on earth.

Catching her wayward gaze and thoughts, she trained her eyes up to his face. Square, arrogant in acutely chiseled proportions, his strong visage surprisingly amended her ideal of handsomeness. Perhaps feeling her scrutiny, he raised his countenance for her perusal. Ebony-winged brows took flight over what would be, without the blinding black cloth, expressive eyes. Even with the gag drawing at his mouth, Angel could imagine when he spoke, men—and women—certainly listened. Else, how had the man won so many to his cause in so brief a time? And how had he attracted even her attention—enough to do this dastardly deed?

Angel suppressed her own remorse at the robbery she committed upon him. For outlaw or not, no man or woman deserved such pillage of their rights. Not for any reason.

Ever aware of her, he turned his head left and right, inhaling the air in an attempt to absorb his surroundings, as if he could with his infamous unearthly senses divine the nature of the room to which he had so ruthlessly been hauled. She knew he also sought from the surrounding elements some indication of her size, her demeanor, and her intent.

4

She smiled at his intelligence and daring. She had been right to want him. For she had need of both his qualities. If she could but persuade him to her ends . . .

"Remove his gag and blind, Peter."

Her steward's blue eyes flared, but years of acceding to his lady's will had him stepping to her wish. "I hope you are prepared for this," he murmured.

Angel squared her back. Of course, she was prepared for this, for *him*. She had ordered this. She had arranged this. Planned it. Nurtured the idea in her mind and heart, until . . . until there was no rest from it, no redemption save through the commission of this crime, this sin. For if this man would not help redeem her, she could find no other.

"Remove them," she whispered.

Peter shook his head and strode forward. His two friends, Edwin and Leon, shuffled their feet as the steward unknotted the first cloth.

Peter's hands moved nimbly. The gag fell away first and the mouth Angel had predicted would be appealing flexed away the stiffness. Then firm lips bared, flashing white teeth in silent promise of a threat. The mouth pursed, adding a mute savagery that screamed of retribution.

Angel raised both brows in rebuff. Tied and so totally within her power as he was, she told herself she had nothing to fear from this man's threats. Others were more menacing. It was said that this man made no invectives where they were not merited. Was not his famous sense of justice the very reason she had chosen him and him alone to do this service for her? If she could ever excuse herself on infirm grounds of morals equal to those with whom she kept company,

5

here she was guilty of no more than he did day in and night out. Like him, she had *stolen* . . . albeit his person. Unlike him, she would return to her victim that which she took. She would reward him with his freedom and allow him resumption of his former life, if only he would consider becoming part of hers for a brief time and give her the independence she had once so briefly possessed.

Amazingly, while Peter worked at the well-knotted band about his eyes, her captive said nothing. She knew that with his other senses, he assessed every condition within this room, all the better to deal with them once he could see them.

She appreciated that he held his tongue. For what could harsh words gain him? He probably concluded that they could buy him nothing. And rightfully so. Tonight, no matter his name, his band of friends, or his renown, he belonged to her. Though words might ultimately free him, they would never be his.

She reveled that she could for once in her life hold such power over a man. She prayed God she would use it skillfully, wisely.

At the last knot, Peter hesitated and looked up at her. "You know what they say happens when one gazes into the eyes of this man?"

She smiled at her worried servant with more serenity than she felt. True, she had looked upon many men. Some she found amusing, others dense as stone. A few she thought intellectually stimulating. But many men failed to reciprocate to discover if she possessed similar mental acuities. In fact, she found to her unending dismay that most men merely pretended to enjoy a female's conversation. They pursued her

6

either for an hour's fleeting dalliance or a lifetime's permanent obedience.

Whereas she, unlike her only sister who had accepted her lot, had never contented herself with those two alternatives. When Angel realized she was to marry, she had ultimately yielded to the idea, hoping to wed a man whom she could love and care for, honor, and cherish. She had even convinced herself—long before circumstances intervened to teach her otherwise—that she could, by the very act of loving a man, transform him. In her two husbands she had hoped to encounter one who incorporated all those hallowed traits a woman wished for in a mate and the father of her children, but she had never found one willing to love, eager to change into anything endearing to her. The result was that she never wanted any man because she saw such a lack of quality. Even this man she wanted for two traits only—his heathen's strong body and his spirit—and *those* she would not cringe before, but welcome with her whole heart for a temporary yet judicious arrangement.

"Aye, Peter, I have heard the tales of what his eyes can do, especially to women." She waved her hand for Peter to release the cloth. "Unveil him and his fabled eyes. I am not afraid of curses."

She should have been.

His eyes—oh, sweet heaven—his eyes blinked, focused, and then burned like twin pokers into her own soul. He transfixed her with his golden gaze. Pinned her to her spot with the hot shock of how wickedly handsome he was. How spellbinding. How damnably appealing.

She ceased to breathe, think, needing only to view him more closely, and drawn, she went to him.

7

The wide-winged brows shot to his darkly dipping waves as he examined every inch of her. From her hair, unbound at such an hour of the night, to her cheeks and parted mouth, he outlined her features with two eyes so flaming with ferocity Angel began to melt to the bone in his firestorm. Far from finished, he poured his liquid gold outrage over her chainse and the miniver bed throw, scalding her breasts, her hips, and the length of her legs to her bare toes. His wizard's eyes darted up to hers, hurling her up to a heaven she'd barely glimpsed before casting her down into the boiling cauldron of his loathing. Bewildered, she found herself drowning not in fear but in her own bubbling indecision. The very state she so abhorred, particularly when in the presence of powerful men.

Restraining her reaction to that weakness within herself, she met his potent stare with one of her own. She had oft wondered what it would be like to fail to keep God's commandments here on earth and be sent crashing to the pits of degradation to view the devil in his lair. Now she knew.

She could control her destiny with him. She *would*. After all, what was he?

This so-called Devil was merely a mortal from her forests, her coves, her coasts. A human of marvelous sinewy flesh and long, strong bone. A man whom some affirmed had hailed from the dead King Richard's crusading retinue and others said had emerged from the back door of a monastery, defrocked. Angel even heard it conjectured that he was a lowly merchant, lately dispossessed of his business in Venice or Alexandria. Whatever he had been, wherever he had come from, only God knew for certain. The people of York—young and old, firm and not—cared not for the facts of his past, only those of his present. They claimed him as their own. Named him for his diabolic speed, his agility, his utter devotion to disrupting King John of England's every move in their shire. For his foiling of John's fleet, his harassment of John's tax collectors, and his cunning nature to attack his prey in the deep of night, the people of York baptized their brigand the Devil of Midnight. Though for more than two years he remained a cipher to many, tonight he knelt before her, totally within her power and, she acknowledged by his demonic good looks, completely worthy of his calling and his name.

Angel folded her hands at her waist, a natural mode long retained from her years in the nunnery. If the reverend mother could only glimpse this man, what hours she would spend upon her knees praying for his eternal soul! Of course, that venerable woman would pray for anyone's soul if it meant she could avoid her share of the long hours with the sickle and plow. Why, one look at this fiend and the whole order might follow their leader, take to their knees, and slowly starve!

Angel cleared her throat to stifle a chuckle. "Peter, you may leave us."

"Nay, madam! I will not go. Heaven preserve us from this Devil's wrath."

"Oh, Peter. He is bound, even at the knees. He can get no further than my solar door in any case, for I would have you stand just outside it."

The Devil's eyes went wide with surprise. Then they traveled once more down her form. Wherever they roamed, Angel felt he perceived more of her than she herself had ever seen. She warmed when he swirled his eyes atop the rise of her breasts and flamed when he

9

rested his narrowing gaze upon her loins. Clearly, he thought she intended some mischief. Ha! If a woman desired a man so badly she would send her villeins repeatedly into the forest to trap an outrageous Devil, then the woman required a good purgative for her overactive imagination—and a restorative to boost her underdeveloped sense of right.

"But milady, I trust him not."

"I do."

"He could kill you with one blow of his hand."

"He could." Angel settled her eyes into incredulous gold ones. "But he will not."

"How can you—"

"Be certain? I have only to look at him." That was a lie. She was actually relying upon logic that a man with such a reputation of saving the oppressed from the oppressor would find something noble to uphold and someone downtrodden to protect within her sorry story. Besides, if she were to secure his aid, she must sound as just as she ever strived to be. Furthermore, she needed to do it quickly before he formed irrevocable opinions of her behavior that had less to do with reality and more with necessity.

"Thank you, Peter. You three may await me outside the door." She nodded benevolently and followed them to hasten their egress. When she shut the heavy oak against her men, she turned to find her captive tensely poised, his face turned in sharp profile to her.

On his knees with his sculpted body bound in tight relief from the winding ropes, she let her eyes wander down his broad back and lean hips to his sturdy thighs. Even in so suppliant a position, he was a man beyond all others in virile form and potent grace. She delighted in his severe features, his stoic demeanor, his attentive study of her every movement.

She circled him to her window seat and her large table with its vessel of red wine. Without asking him, she poured a hefty draught of it into a pottery goblet. Her motions calm and deliberate as her years in the convent had taught her, she nonetheless felt a quivering in her stomach as his eyes traced her. When she turned to him and met his gaze boldly, he did not hide his interest—or his surprise when she came to stand before him and tip the cup to his lips.

Wordlessly, she gave and he took. And when she knew he had sipped enough, she withdrew it to watch him lick his bottom lip with a languid tongue. His action fascinated her, ravaging her purpose for an uncharted moment. "I would give you more, dear sir, if you would give me your promise to be kind should I free your hands."

His head fell back. His eyes probed hers. He nodded his agreement. She returned to the table, replaced the goblet and, from beneath her alcove seat cushion, removed her small jewel-handled dagger that no one knew she possessed.

Air hissed between his teeth.

Her gaze flew to his. "Nay, dear sir, this is to loose your ropes, not hurt you."

His golden eyes debated her veracity.

"Please, sir, I would that you believe me. I brought you here because I need you alive and well. This dagger does me the same service it does you. It frees us both."

He stilled as she approached and knelt. The miniver bed throw dropped to the floor, leaving her bare throat and arms prey to his scourging eyes. Her fingers went to his wrists, bound one atop the other. His hands were decidedly cool. His long fingers were elegantly proportioned, and for all his years of living in the forests and marauding along her coasts, his nails were clean and cut blunt. On the right hand he wore a thick gold ring that spanned to his knuckle. The object looked beyond price, scored as it was with some mystic script and encrusted with one onyx and a dozen or more perfect pearls. This element of great charm seemed an absurd counterpoint to the calluses that dotted his palms. Along the rise of his thumb one predominated and she trailed one fingertip over its crown.

He jumped.

Startled, she made quick work of cutting the cords. Never had she touched a man so . . . intimately. She knew she blushed and knew she shouldn't. Shutting her eyes to suppress her fear of letting him see her maidenly and flustered, she found the composure to gather the miniver about her shoulders again and rise to face him.

He splayed his long fingers and fisted them. Deliberately, he rolled his massive shoulders and stretched his colossal arms full length to his side and before him. Swift as a thunderbolt, he swept her to the floor. In testament to his agile might, she never knew he tucked her beneath him until she felt his total possession, breast to belly, to hip and thigh.

The wind knocked from her, she lost the knife as well and gasped, "Sir, you—!"

He swallowed up her words with his mouth. Yet she registered that his lips were feather soft and his breath sweet with mint and rich with the wine she had offered. His actions were as smooth as his body. But far from a kiss, his claiming of her mouth was no more than a ploy to absorb her sound so that the others might not take alarm.

Pressed flush, he murmured, "You have said enough, madam." His gruff whisper brushed her senses along her spine to her thrashing legs. "Nay!" he commanded and seized her hand, which reached for the fallen dagger. He threaded his fingers through hers and spread her arms as if she were an offering upon a cross. "I have listened to you. Now you shall hear me." He grinned, a demon's gleaming-eyed triumph, then rearranged his contours more comfortably along the hills and valleys of hers. She turned to stone. One black eyebrow took flight in glee. "By all the saints' bones, you feel good. Whose wife are you, lady, that the demented man should allow you about to play rough games with your three stout fellows?"

She frowned. "You think I am a wife?"

"You are independent enough, old enough," proclaimed her captor as his eyes skimmed her bare throat and thinly clad breasts. "And ripe enough."

"I am *not* old, but merely twenty."

"Twenty, eh? Old enough to be a wife and mother many times over. But still young enough for sport. And that, I would assume, is what you seek. Well, I tell you, lady, bed sport is welcomed by me"— his golden eyes turned hard as coins of the realm—"but *not* when you send out three madmen to truss me like a stag, haul me about in a filthy winnowing sack, then dump me on a hard floor in some unknown solar."

This close to him, Angel could see how angry he was. But worse, she could feel how very lethal he could be. She suddenly knew he had earned his name

13

by deeds more than false attribution. If only she could make him see her total purpose and understand her just cause, he need not be so exacting with her.

"I promise you I meant not for my men to hurt you. I simply wanted you to listen to me. Un—uninterrupted." *Undetected* was more to the truth.

He bathed her with gleeful glinting eyes while his mouth twitched in humor. "You could have asked about, invited me properly to sup with you."

She hooted. "Oh, certainly! I could have posted missives on the church door, is that it? 'To the bandit who lives in my forests and harasses my fishermen, please come forth. I have a wager to make.'" She blew a strand of hair away from her nose. "I suppose you would have presented yourself without a moment's hesitation."

A ghost of a smile toyed with his slashing mouth. "You could have told me how good you feel beneath me and I would have come instantly."

That made her cheeks burn brightly.

"Blush wildly as berries, do you not?" He was laughing, softly but more deeply with each chuckle. His vibrant voice made her own blood course with a righteous indignation—and a curious delight that tones so textured, so luxurious could resonate so comfortably, heart to heart.

"*This* is not humorous!" She wanted to pound the floor, but with her hand pinned beneath his terrifyingly pleasurable weight she could only tap the floorboards with her knuckles.

"I agree! But you, I think, have the full of it, as I do not. And so, my dear, rash lady, whoever you are, I bid you come and sit. Tell me why we are here in these most indelicate circumstances."

At that, he sat up and, never freeing her, plunked her on his lap as he braced himself against the sturdy legs of one of her solar chairs.

"Sir! I tell you—" She pushed at his chest to achieve only a tiny distance and a modicum of propriety. The way his body touched her along a thousand points made her mind whirl. Enjoying the heady sensation, she rued the distraction.

"And I tell you," he purred as one hand clamped her wrist and the other trailed her hair behind her ear and down her shoulder, "you will sit like this with me until I have heard the whole of your story."

She would deny till her death her enjoyment of his fingers' endearing caress. "You cannot force me. My men—"

"I know, but I do wish to live for many long years. And yet should I try to leave, your men—clever and opportune as they were—might win again over me with the strength of their numbers. Alas, dear lady, ultimately you cannot force me, either, and yet you say you desire my help. What better way to secure it than to treat me as I seek to be treated?"

She ceased her struggle, allowing herself the novel charm his hard hands worked upon her. "I am a gentlewoman and you must release me."

His brows arched. "I am a free man and you must release me."

He said it with such certitude and pleasantry, she marveled that he was not angry any longer. Since anger was an emotion she knew not how to debate, she felt the expectation of that challenge rise like the mist from a poisonous humor. She smiled despite her need to set herself far from his compelling grasp. She had enjoyed nothing as much in so very long a time. She

15

had forgotten what joy could do for a body, a mind, a searching lonely soul.

His eyes sparkled with teasing delights. "You like many sports, I wager."

She grinned broadly while her eyes negated everything he implied. He was being rude, even bawdy—and yet she could not find the will to act haughty. She, after all, had abducted him and brought him here. She had no right to judge his behavior, only the need to set him straight in his opinion of her. "Not those you think."

"No?" His finely etched brows danced. "There should be no harm in a woman's declaration that she loves to love."

She sucked in air and stared at him. "Bed sport is not love."

He sighed. "It can be. It should be."

"What would this world come to if women thought so?"

"Some do. If more did, then we might witness an end to wars as men stayed at home to taste the fruits God has bestowed upon his creatures."

She shifted, making herself all too aware of his solid flesh beneath her thighs.

His eyes narrowed and wended over her once more. Again Angel knew that probing torch that burned her clothes, her resolve, and her reason to ashes. "Who are you, my lady, that you should seem so sweet—nay, naive—and yet send out three brutes into the dead of night to seize a man?"

"Oh, but I have sent them out for ten nights."

He snorted. "I cannot decide whether to be honored, intimidated, or insulted."

"Be honored," she said, imploring him with her

eyes. "Please know that I simply wanted you, only you."

"That is terribly complimentary, I *think*. Dare I say, I *hope*? For I do not wish to be handed over to the sheriff in exchange for a bag of gold."

"Nay, I have no need of money." She considered her hands in her lap. "I have need of your person."

"Interesting. I must hear more, my lady."

She could not raise her eyes to his, but threaded her fingers together in desperation for her cause.

He stopped her fidgeting by covering her hands. His own had become warm with regard and gentleness. "What can be so awful that the very idea makes your blood run cold?"

She swallowed hard the terror that had stalked her night and day for over a fortnight. Unable to recount the horrible facts impelling her to this hideous abduction of him, she shook her head and squeezed out fat tears.

With one tender touch beneath her chin, he raised her face. "Nay, you cannot hide such misery from me. Look at me. Tell me who you are and what you wish of me so that I might see your celestial smile again."

His words coupled with his expression to let her spirit slip free of its broodings, if only for a moment. "I do have need of you."

"I *am* honored. And intrigued." He met her eyes in sympathy. "I am not easy to capture and have never come close, though the king's men would seek me out in every cove and glen from here to the Kentish coast. But now that you have me and I am yours so completely . . ." He brushed away a falling tear with his thumb. "I wish to know how I may be of service to you."

She bit her lower lip, praying for reason and help from her God for this ordeal. "I need you."

His handsome brows quirked in a thousand finite exclamations and innumerable questions.

She wrung her hands.

He stilled them by grasping both and bringing them to his marvelous mouth for two chivalrous kisses. "I am here, no matter the means. Whatever your pain, tell me. 'Tis why you brought me to you. 'Tis why I am still here." She tried to express her gratitude but failed, and he smiled. "Tell me, lovely lady, how may the Devil of Midnight aid you in your hour of need?"

She wanted to have done with this now, to inform him quickly and begin the bargaining so that they might reach an accord and order her universe for once in her life. "I am Lady Angelica Forrester."

He repeated her name without sound, until finally he glanced about the solar and returned, a knowing light within his startled eyes. "The countess of Windom?"

"The dowager countess of Windom."

"And of Carlisle?"

"Aye, that too."

"And we are where, milady? Surely not Windom Castle, for this solar seems too small for the grand dimensions of that noble fort."

"Nay. This is Montrose Manor Castle, that which I brought with me as dowry land when I married the Windom heir five years ago. By all rights, it is only mine."

She lowered her lashes, waiting for his cry of indignation. His repugnance. For surely word of her and her sinister nature had spread beyond her castle walls to unknown forests and farther shores than she could fathom. But when he sat unmoving and his eyes delved into hers with infinite acceptance and patience, she reminded herself he was outside the law. This man seemed more noble than to accuse her of criminal behavior when he himself suffered the same condemnation.

Yet, eternities passed while he considered her revelations. Then in a slow motion during which she swore she could have copied ancient tomes, he lifted her chin and whispered, "Now, really look at me, Countess. Aye. Meet me with those grass green eyes and realize I have not run from you—in spirit or truth. Nay, for I am here despite who and what others say you are. Just as you have brought me here despite—or perhaps because of—my accursed reputation. I am still here and find you, dear Countess, as angelic as your name and just as sweet. So unlike what is said about you."

That brought forth tears once more. This time, she could not halt the cascade. Nor could she fight the temptation to accept the solace he offered when he pulled her down to his massive chest and let her weep into his soft, silky tunic.

His lips nestled into her hair. His voice wove consolation into the fabric of her remorse, and she quieted. "It seems we are alike, you and I." His hands bound her closer, stroked her back more purposely. "I gather then that what is said of you is not so."

"Aye!" She spoke against the strong column of his throat. "None of it is true."

He hugged her nearer, more securely to the wall of his chest. "Much of what is spread abroad is never even half the truth." He combed her hair with his fingers, his lips a gossamer touch against her temple.

"Please tell me how I might help you, my lady. I will do whatever I can, for injustice is my sole enemy. Ever. Always."

She sniffled and pushed away to view him through the facets of her tears. She would say this, try this, cast herself upon his mercy. For he and he alone embodied her only hope of salvation. "I wish you to become my husband."

Chapter

2

Her sorrowful eyes told him her proposal was no jest. No ruse designed to trap him, ease his worries, lull him while she sent for the sheriff to ransom him to the Crown's warped justice. Nay. Her tears, her torments, her tender pleas rung with the chime of truth—impossible and illogical as it sounded.

She waited like a doomed man at the end of a sword, ready to be run through. For the life of him, he could not find the heart to refuse her. Verily, she embodied every fine characteristic her name denoted. By her every move and word she also negated the recent rumor cast round concerning her.

Everything—and nothing—they had ever said about her was true.

She was devastatingly beautiful. Enchanting. Beneficent. Aye, God's angel. From far and wide, this mortal Angel of Windom and Carlisle was lauded as the comeliest creature in the shire. He affirmed with his own two eyes and his own straining, throbbing body that she deserved much more than this hollow praise. Her beauty inspired songs of homage beyond human intonation.

Had she not instantly imprisoned his mind when her men removed the blindfold? Christ in His grave, she appeared to him like a shining vision—a goddess with swirling white gold hair, pearl-kissed skin, and large, artless green eyes. Vivacious, untouchable.

More, she moved like a dream. Elegant, though taller than most women, ethereal despite ripe lips and breasts many women would rue, she carried herself as regally as if she were the queen. But the grace of her body offered up faint accolades to the glory of her face. Round with well-curved eyebrows and straight nose, her face held such even proportions that he longed to trace the symmetry with his fingertips. She was in the flesh far more lovely than the tales told of her. Her features, her demeanor spoke eloquently of her name.

She was, in truth, the shire's Angel. But in the past few days, he had come to hear how she might actually be more a devil in disguise. For her to seize him suddenly and request marriage from him seemed uncharacteristic of the lady who he knew was charitable and considerate.

Now he understood she was blamed for the foulest of deeds. Unspeakably lovely, she certainly appeared to form the substance of any man's fondest fantasy. But was she devil or angel? And why would he, how could he *marry* her?

"How can I, my lady? Your husband, the Earl Carlisle, is dead two weeks, if I do hear correctly. His soul has not yet passed the gates of Heaven." *What kinder way can I find to excuse myself without blatant-*

22

ly accusing her of the perfidious act that forms the crux of the vile rumor? "You must still be grieving and—"

She clutched his hand, her nails gouging him with an intensity that made him wonder at the strength of such a porcelain beauty. "Aye. I grieve. I miss him. Chretian was . . . my friend, my bulwark, my barrier against those who would rather see me elsewhere than at his side as wife. But Chretian is gone from me now, completely, finally, and I . . ." She pulled away from him, her expression desolate as her eyes scanned the room. "I need another man who will serve as my dead lord once did. I cannot face his men alone." Her gaze again locked on his. The verdant green of her eyes glistened like new dew-laced grass of springtime.

He raised both hands to cup her delicate chin, his thumbs tracing the perfection of her cheeks. "Have Carlisle's retainers not sworn to protect you after the death of their lord? You are his only heir, I do believe. 'Tis the custom for them to do so, and I have heard they were faithful to him."

"They were very dutiful to my lord Carlisle." She curled her shoulders together in defense. "They will not give me their allegiance just yet."

"Why not?" He knew, or thought he did, and had to broach the hideous subject with her. Her reaction would tell him much. His years with men and women of every calling from here to the Great Khan's palace in Karakoram had made him the master assessor of humanity's true nature. His own survival depended upon the accuracy of his perception, then and now. From the first moment when she had spoken, he had perceived her nature to be kind. She had wanted him cared for, released from his bonds. She was courageous, too. Asking her man Peter to remove his gag and blindfold, serving him wine, then cutting the cords from his hands while alone with him showed him the tenderhearted nature of this angel who sat here on his lap and twisted her fingers to white knots.

But he had also learned caution from his years of captivity. It was a state he abhorred and, until this hour, one he had managed to avoid. To curb his anger and quell his nagging sense of unease in any situation where he could not use his body's strength to complement his mind's, he required facts. He needed evidence to substantiate what his instinct declared was true. For in addition to her kindness, her grace, her inordinate splendor, she was a woman. And women, no matter their age or culture, could play at games beyond his reckoning. Had not one done so and conspired to rob him of all that he treasured?

Without more understanding of her problem, he could not comfort her in word or deed. For if the act of which she was accused had been committed by her, he would have to leave her to her dead husband's men and any others who sought to bring her to justice.

She crossed her arms to stop her violent tremors. "They say I am not worthy. That my honor is suspect. That I—" Her eyes went wide with horror. Her soft body froze to ice. She left his arms with the speed of a desert wind.

In whirling agitation, she paced the room. Clutching at the white miniver-lined bed throw draped about her shoulders, she appeared entranced, seeing nothing, no one, except some heinous knowledge. Her translucent linen chainse clung to her curves as she moved, revealing more of the body that incited his

24

mind to fervent fabrications and made him chastise himself for his base considerations. But she was a lady, a noblewoman, and she required—aye, deserved—more. He wished he could have risen to contain her trembling torso, restrain her clenching hands. But still tied at the legs and ankles, he could only wait for a story she struggled with some inner demon to communicate.

Presently, she stood before her roaring fire. She set her jaw. Resolution transformed her visage to a mask of glowing courage. Silently applauding her, he felt his heart cleave, one half of him reaching out to her with confidence, the other weeping for her agony.

"They accuse me of a most horrendous deed. I have no doubt rumor has done much—and nothing—to serve the truth of my real predicament these past few days. I have no means to stop such tales. You yourself know any efforts in that regard are useless wastes of time and hope. You have made your own reputation by use of wagging tongues."

She stole a look at him. "But my quandary is much different than yours in that I never wished a reputation to aid my ends. I wished only peace. I enjoyed it once in my life for a few years and then, suddenly, it was torn from me. I calmed my sorrows by telling myself I was being obedient to my father and his brothers. Thinking I might find tranquility and joy in marriage, I invested hope and discovered . . ."

She bit her lip and found no means to go on.

"My lady, I pray you, tell me in plain language what has happened to you. Aye, I have heard of you. The Angel of York is renowned for her concern and generosity." *And her haste to remarry.* "I can recite

25

tales of you. I know the aged tanner in Windom's woods who praises your effective remedy for his aching legs. And I have discussed with the women of Carlisle Manor your gifts of scented candles for the parish altar. I give you these unpolished examples of acts that I have heard you have committed in good heart. You have no reason to be coy with me. For who am I to judge you?"

That drew a relaxation of her features, a softening of her incomparable green eyes. "Very well. But though you have heard well of me, Devil, lately I do think wicked streams of rumors turn into rivers of lies."

He did not wish to hurt her, but he could not properly assess her guilt or innocence by coddling her. So he chose the tactful but unkind path and said, "Nay, my lady. Not rivers. Oceans."

"Aye." Her eyes closed. "So wide and turbulent are they that a man or woman may drown in their fury."

"No lie should be so potent that an innocent person should die from it."

"Ahh," she smiled humorlessly, "that is my irony, Devil. I am hedonist enough to wish to live. Though I have seen such evil on earth from which many would cower, I believe I was meant for more than . . . what many wish to do to me."

When she could not continue, he did. "What do many wish to do to you?"

"Use me again, for a third time—or perhaps, for the last time to gain their fondest desires."

"A third time?" It was the only phrase in her litany of woes that made any sense. That of which rumor declared this lady had possessed two—and of which

rumor declared she would now acquire the third—
was a husband. But the probable candidates never
included him. No one should ever want to marry the
Devil of Midnight. Not even an Angel in peril.

"Aye, a third time. A divine ordinal, is it not? A
magic number." Her sarcasm shattered, exposing
once again her pain. "The number which brings me to
my knees and makes me sit upon my pile of ashes like
a confused Job, who asked his God why tragedies
came upon him when he had only been faithful to his
Maker." Her head fell back, her eyes traveled the
ceiling, and her hands dragged the miniver higher.

"You see, my Devil, I am beset by those who do not
care if I grieve in solitude for my last husband, my
most noble Chretian. Those about me—and those
hastening to me in my hour of darkness—wish more
to see their own needs served. At their insistence, I am
simply required to do one thing. Marry." She cast an
outraged look upon him. "I am required to marry. For
a third time. Meanwhile, my second husband,
Chretian, is not yet—as you say—past his inquisition
at the Gates of Paradise."

"Aye, my lady. I know the improper timing of it all.
I also have heard that there are many prospective
bridegrooms. Who are they, then? All idiots or slaver-
ing brutes? They must be awful men if you would trap
a Devil and propose to him rather than seek your
peaceful life within one of their embraces."

She laughed.

He blinked.

She lifted her face and chuckled to the heavens.
"What jest! What absurdity!" Her hilarity sank to
silence that made her head drop to her chest. When

she finally spoke, he could barely hear the mournful voice he knew had plucked the strings of his compassion. "For the next husband to the dowager countess of Windom and Carlisle, I will have presented to me three eager candidates. Each is a perfect age for me. Neither too young, as was my first husband, a boy of ten to my fifteen years—nor too old, as was my second lord, who was considered by many to best be dubbed my grandsire, not my husband. Furthermore, each current candidate is also my match in station. None of the three is less than an earl. Therefore, I need not fear that any of these men who seek to walk into my home are not fully qualified to stand next to me—or rule me. Yet I cannot, I will not take any one of them."

Under any other circumstances, he might have pointed out the tenuous position of a woman—especially such a landed woman—living alone and widowed. But the two of them had come so far in this conversation and she had wept too bitterly for him to find an iota of anything but remorse in her story. Yet, while bitter cries might soothe the soul for moments, she had greater problems than tears could ever salve. He needed to know more so that he might help her heal and seek that goal of peace she so desired.

"My lady, you mean to say that of these three, none of them bears any noble qualities by which you might come to care for them? Ah, ah." He put up a hand. "I know it is scarce two weeks since your husband departed this life, but even if your period of grieving had been observed, are you saying that not one among them is worthy of you?"

She stiffened. "Sir, I am not vain. 'Tis a sin to be so

self-proud that you look down upon another. Nay. I do not reject these three men because I think them beneath me and my supposed grand status. I assure you that I feel no great power or glory from my position as countess or even from my wealth, accumulated by the untimely death of my two husbands."

He had not known her first husband, the young heir to the previous earl of Windom. But he had oft seen this Chretian Forrester, the earl of Carlisle, her last husband. Appearing a gentle man, Forrester was known as a proud baron whose loyalty to the Crown was unquestioned. Indeed, he had served with great praise and greater reward both King Richard the Lionheart and now his brother King John. Through the past decade, Forrester gained a reputation for his loyalty and discretion. He appeared a quiet man who had never married until a few months ago, when at the decree of King John, he took this young dowager countess of Windom to his bosom and his bed. This well-liked, simple man Chretian Forrester died much mourned, it seemed. His death was untimely only in that, according to rumor, it was not God who had chosen the time of the earl's death, but perhaps some earthly hand that had snuffed out his candle of life.

"Forgive me, my lady. I meant no insult. I merely wished to imply your second lord was well advanced in age."

She shivered. "He would have been five and fifty this week. We were to have a celebration. Now we have dirges instead. He was healthy, I tell you. Healthy!"

As hale and hearty as you? He could not stop the war that raged between his propriety and his compulsion once more to assess her long, lush body. With a stifled groan, he acknowledged how her nearness stimulated him in ways he reluctantly admitted was lust. Not only he, but any man would remain vigorous—aye, rigorous—merely to know that this woman awaited him in his chambers. Her impressive assets would draw a man from any preoccupation, even a flirtation with Death. For what temptations could everlasting life offer to compare with the bounteous pleasures a flesh-and-blood man could discover within this woman's arms?

He seized his wayward senses and tutored them to logic's necessity. Emotion had ever been his downfall.

"Your husband must have died from old age," he said, hoping it sounded like the appropriate conclusion instead of the leading question he meant it to become.

"Ah, Devil, how I wish that were so."

He could not breathe. He stared instead.

She did not disappoint him, but came to kneel before him. Like a sinner seeking absolution or a believer in search of revelation, she beseeched him with shining green eyes. "He died an untimely death, my Devil. I know and will attest that my husband Chretian did go to his Lord unshriven two weeks ago in the dead of night."

He dared not touch her, this immaculate angel with the beginnings of the most horrible of confessions upon her luscious lips.

A knowing smile curled her mouth. "You will not ask the obvious, will you, Devil? For somewhere in your own sojourn on this earth, you, too, have found as I have that the paths we desire to take are hardly ever those we watch ourselves walk. Very well. You shall hear the truth as I know it to be. Whether you perceive it as truth will be your decision." She sought his soul with her glorious stare. "I did not kill my husband."

He narrowed his eyes at her. In his head, loud bells rang with her honesty.

"I did not kill my husband. But someone did. Aye, someone did." Her head lowered. "And though I did discover him and weep and call Chretian's chamberlain to me to investigate, I am now in sore distress." Her head snapped up and her eyes caught his. "My husband's men held an immediate council and they say—" She licked her lips. "They attest I killed Chretian." She laid her warm palm to his chest and his heart missed beats in an attempt to leap its confines. "I swear by all that is holy, I did not commit this murder."

He gazed down at her hand. Had not other women appealed to him with their bodies for what their minds crafted as necessary? He could not be deterred from truth, and fastened his eyes to hers. "I must know who did."

"Aye," she whispered and took her hand away. "So must I. I have no clues."

"Describe to me what happened, then." Perhaps within her recounting of events he might find the core of fact.

"Two weeks ago this night, I was sewing in my solar in Windom Castle when the hour grew very late. I wished to go to bed and so I put my sewing down."

He frowned. "You *sew* in the dark of night?"

"Aye. I use many candles. I am not blind."

"'Tis costly to burn good tallow after the sun sets."

31

"I am rich, sir. Have not you heard how wealthy the twice-widowed countess of Windom and Carlisle is?"

The way she tossed her brilliant head in a show of defiance struck him as sweet—and too damnably provocative for his comfort. "Aye. I have heard. And now I have seen this widow is stalwart as well. Continue, I pray you."

"I left the solar, opened the door to my lord's bedchamber—"

"You sleep together, then?"

Her eyelashes fluttered. He could have sworn he saw her heart take wing. "Aye. It was my husband's wish. Besides, I cannot seek a bed in the women's chamber because Chretian's retainers now sleep there."

He crossed his arms. "I see. What did you do then?"

She glanced at her hands. "I disrobed and approached the bed. I climbed upon it. Usually when I come to bed, Chretian lies awake. This night he did not notice."

Any sane man would note the addition of this woman to his bed.

"Chretian is—was a light sleeper and a . . . courteous one. He never snored or"—she swallowed —"or took more space than he should. Usually he would murmur something to me about my having stayed up too long and ruining my health for love of the mending. But I—well, I would end his fears with my own declarations that I preferred to remain awake at night. I like the night." She averted her face of a sudden, then shook back her hair, waves of it cascading like ivory silk over her shoulders. "I like the peace. The quiet." She brought herself back to this place from some horror she had glimpsed. She contemplated her hands. "In any case, I sank beneath the coverlet and furs and, as is regular for me, I lay awake still."

Probably waiting for her mate to perform his husbandly duties which, of course, the man would do immediately for such a spellbinding bride.

"Most times, Chretian reaches out to me and . . . and—"

Does what to you? Caresses your breasts? Weighs their fullness? Laves your nipples to tight buds or blossoming satin petals? Which is it?

"He massages my arms or turns me on my side to knead my back, if I still seem stiff."

Stiff? By Buddha's bones, I am gone to granite just imagining how a man might please you and thus discover his own nirvana.

He froze, uneasy with an uncontrollable desire for her. Control over his mind and body was the asset he had learned long ago. He could not lose it now. Anxious, angry, he waved a hand. "But this night, your husband did not reach out to you. What did he do then?" *Tell me anything other than that he brought you rapture. For I am jealous of what he had and what I will never savor in any bed with any loving wife of my own.*

"Nothing. He remained on his back, an odd position for him to rest in. But on his back, nonetheless. So—as is my wont—I reached out to him."

"And?" *Did what?*

"I touched his shoulder. He was cold. I thought him ill. I told him so. He did not reply. 'Twas then I rose—so surprised by his lack of response that I went to him."

He conjured a vision of her naked, and fisted his hands.

"I lit a candle and bent to him. His eyes were open. His one hand thrust above his head, which was twisted to one side. I—" Her lips trembled. "I brought his face up to me and then I knew." She gulped. "I knew he was dead. I have seen death so often of late. Too often. My first husband and his parents died less than a year ago. I remember too well the startled look of death upon their faces."

He waited.

"I felt for his breath. There was none. I felt his heart. There was no beat. 'Twas then I began to cry, I think. I was so shocked, so wild! I called for help. No one came. No one heard because the walls are so thick. I remember I found the sanity to reach for my gown and opened the chamber door. Guards came. I babbled something. They rushed to him and confirmed my knowledge. Chretian was surely dead. Gone from me in his own bed as I sewed in my solar."

"How do you know he died in his bed? And as you sewed? He might have been elsewhere when he was killed and then placed in your bed."

"I knew when he came to bed that night because he opened my solar door to tell me so. He was attired only in his tunic and his feet were bare. He looked tired, spent." She shuddered on the last word and gnawed on her lower lip. "He told me he was retiring."

"He did this as a practice?"

"Every night."

"So when he announced this, it was his signal that he wished you to join him."

"Nay."

34

"I am confused."

"Chretian would come to my solar door to announce he would retire, but by this he did not necessarily indicate that he wished me to go to him." She fidgeted with the edge of the miniver throw. "That was a decision he left to me. He . . . was courteous and . . . considerate of my need to sew and keep some solitude."

She liked her husband, praised him. Yet when he called, she did not run to him. Why? Few answers sufficed. "You are long at your prayers, then."

"Aye."

His brows rose in question.

"Chretian was not a husband who demanded anything. Not of me, leastways. He honored me, my needs and foibles."

"Truly, a paragon of a man."

"In many ways."

"What happened after the guards came to you and confirmed your husband was dead?"

She sagged. "They talked among themselves and concluded he died by suffocation. They said one of the pillows had been the means by which he departed this life."

That was what rumor declared had been Carlisle's cause of death. "And what do you think?"

"I think it might be so. I have no way to know." She spread her hands wide in bewilderment. "He might have died of a failure of the heart or a seizure of some sort. Death looks the same no matter the means by which it comes."

"True." Though death by foul means often left hints of the perpetrator's methods, if not motivations.

"'Twas then my husband's retainers made their accusation. Three of them, led by his chamberlain Eugene Demere, emerged from their little circle by the fire to confront me with their conclusion." She bit her lower lip white. "They say I put the pillow to my husband's face. That I killed him. That only I had opportunity."

"Is that true?"

"I cannot say for certain! Our bedchamber door is never guarded and—"

"Why not?"

"Chretian declared he trusted his people."

"Well, someone abused his trust."

"Aye, anyone could have entered there or . . ."

Her vehemence told him much of her fear and her innocence in this matter. "Or?"

"Through a corridor which connects to my guarderobe and which few know of . . . if any do."

"To what does this corridor connect?"

"I know not. 'Tis an awful place of cobwebs, insects, and . . . other things I could not see. I never found an exit, though I would say it runs toward the curtain wall."

"I see. And of your accusers, what motive do they say you have for killing him?"

She blanched. "My desire to be free of any man."

"Is it true?"

She flung her hands open, her words bursting forth like a shower of stars. "That I wish no other men as husband? Aye! That I wish to be free to live in peace? Aye! That I wish no man harm and would seek my solitude with no hurt to anyone? Aye, 'tis true. True! But I swear to you, I would not kill to gain this life I seek." She grabbed his hand. "I swear I would not. You must believe me."

How could he? And how could he not? She was so adamant, so fervent in countenance and declaration. "What is this life you seek that your face does light with the love of it?"

He could tell by the way her eyes searched his that she saw his question form, saw her last enemy array in battle. She sallied forth to meet and defeat it. "Dear Devil, I would not kill a man, any man, to gain my freedom from him. I am not fashioned in that manner. I seek no other husbands. Never again will I marry. I have had two husbands, one young and one old. One father-in-law, who was unprincipled enough to try to take that which was his son's. Aye . . . I tell you true, for you are in need of all facts here, and I will put my hand to any Bible that this attempt at my virtue by the earl of Windom did occur. I have also had as father a man who tore me from my convent just as I was about to take my vows and become a bride of Christ. Not hearing my pleas, this sire of mine did marry me to my dead sister's betrothed, the Windom heir. He had the support of his own two brothers doing it. Then, when my young husband and his father and mother died of plague, my father and uncles came to me again and told me I must marry a baron of good repute. This was Chretian, and he alone of all men I have ever known has treated me well.

"I tell you, Devil, I seek no other husband. I seek to live as a woman alone. A woman praising God. I seek, sir, to rule over my estates alone and until I die, to live with a vow of celibacy."

Her passion and her disclosure drowned any doubt

of her innocence. Her desire to become celibate made him mourn the sweet loss of her to any man who might find joy beside her. His sympathy flowed over him and out to her like a river of regret. From its depths, his desire to aid her rose like an armed avenging god. "I do believe you, Lady Carlisle."

"You are the fourth who does believe. Only the three men who captured you do proclaim my innocence. Peter, the burly man who led the band, and who is my steward, and Edwin, my auditor, plus his brother Leon, my wood ward, are loyal enough to me to know of the charges of Chretian's retainers and still do my will."

"They must love you well, my lady, to take such risks. For it is well known Lord Chretian's men are quite the opposite of your dead lord in temperament and are . . . shall we say, not the most tolerant of men."

To put it baldly, Chretian Forrester's retinue roamed the earth like a pack of wolves. Plundering the homes of villeins or raping village women, the earl of Carlisle's men were roundly hated by the Windom villagers. Angelica Windom had married Chretian Forrester only four months ago, but to many in these climes the time seemed like years of mistreatment since the Carlisle contingent had come to Windom Castle.

Only last week, he himself had called forth his loyal disciples to extricate a woman from one of Carlisle men's ravening clutches. They had hung the rapist by his tied tunic sleeves over the only gargoyle on the Windom village chapel rafters. The cur did repent his sin immediately and promised to leave Windom if he could be cut from his punishment. They granted his wish, and soon after, he disappeared along the road north.

Lady Carlisle shook her head. "It confounded me, this dichotomy between the nature of my good lord and his eight men. Yet when I would ask about this, Chretian would turn from me and excuse them their excesses because they had their appetites trained and fed by fighting in the Orient on crusade."

He snorted. "Such pillage and rape no man or woman should ever see or feel. It smites the joy of life and robs the soul of hope." He had seen such foul deeds done too often, from the shores of Venice and Constantinople past the sands of Samarkand to the steppes of Karakoram. "That excuse pardons nothing."

"Service to God and king and country are often equated to service to self."

"My lady, I have seen men ride to the Holy Land with hope of reward far more temporal than divine."

"I know. Or . . . at least, because no one has ever seen your face or identified you, rumors multiply about your past. One says you have been a crusader. Another says you have been robbed of that which is rightfully yours here in England."

"'Tis a rare rumor which is true."

"Is this one?"

For a reason he could not name, he felt compelled to tell her what few others knew. "I have been denied my estates, my titles, and my heritage."

"By the king?"

"He sanctioned the actions of another. Or I should say, two others."

"And there is no recourse save to take to the coasts and the woods in brigandage?"

"It is the course I have chosen." He stared her down.

She did not flinch, but returned his look until she glanced at the floor, picked up the dagger, and freed his legs in two strokes.

He flexed his cramped thighs and calves. Watching his every move, she made another appendage of his stir to life, higher and harder than before. She lifted her eyes to his and he found they were half-lidded with a desire she blinked away. How could such a beauty consider celibacy? It was a sin. Some man's eternal loss.

He could not leave her, though by her severing of the ropes he knew he could do so freely. Instead, he crossed his arms and waited until she told him what he needed to know.

"I chose you because I assumed you would help me, another person in need of freedom from tyranny. Your reputation tells me I might ask this of you, as I might not of any other man. But I need you for other things. I need your courage. In this ordeal ahead of me, I need to emulate more stoutheartedness than I think I possess."

Was it not also arguable that she needed him because of other assets unique to a phantom, an outlaw? "I would hear the whole of your proposal. Aye, I know the absurd portion, this marriage portion. But you cannot kneel here before me—a lady in all your finery and grace—and confirm you wish to truly marry such a man as me, only to let me return to the woods so that you might seek your celibacy. I am no fool, my lady Carlisle. Nor do *I* truly wish to marry. I may be beyond the law in some respects, but I am not beyond God's law. I cannot, will not wed, for I would not make any woman a valid mate. Even for a cause, noble or otherwise."

"I understand and did predict you would say so. Therefore, I thought we would return to Windom Castle with the marriage declared as done and consummated."

"How can that be?" A greater problem made his hair stand at the back of his neck. "Who else is in this manor castle with you?"

"Only my maid and the head of the guard, Michael Ross, both of whom support the accusations of Chretian's chamberlain, Eugene Demere. They watch over me, restricting me if they can. If they dare." At his probing look, she explained. "Chretian always allowed his chamberlain liberties that stunned others. With such power, Demere flaunts himself. Three days ago, Demere took three of his men and left Windom to fetch his candidate for husband. I took his departure as my chance to come here, where I hoped Peter might smuggle you inside to me more easily. I feigned a greater sorrow for Chretian than I felt and Ross believed me. I hoped that by giving Ross and Nell the run of the wine stores these past two nights they might drink themselves into an oblivion in which my three loyal men might bring you to me. Praise God, Peter and the others found you when they did. The wine went low. And this night was my last to remain here."

He scrutinized her features for long moments as he assessed their condition. "Have you not thought that Demere will ask for the marriage documents?"

"Aye. I have created some by my own hand, using the form of my last two agreements."

She used her intelligence to all ends. From the pale looks of her, she was also distressed by her dishonest action.

"Hear me, Devil. I do not believe the end justifies the means, but in this case, I am willing to lie to save myself from yet another marriage which—" She halted. "Another arranged marriage."

"What of a priest? Have you one who will claim he married us?"

"Nay. Documents will serve."

He fought down a Saracen curse. "My lady, these men have threatened you. Do you think they will take your *word* that you are married? They will want proof."

"If necessary, I am able to pay a person to pretend he is a priest."

"And risk the chance this mummer will fall prey to a bigger bribe offered by the Carlisle men? Nay. That will not work." But he knew of some means that would. If only he could persuade the man to lie. . . .

"Well then, will you marry for certain? I can compensate you. I have gold, jewels, land. God above, I have a king's ransom of things I will *never* use. They can be yours! Then you might cease robbing! I will never ask anything of you. You might disappear into the night and—"

He took both her hands in his and though his grasp was gentle, he made it as firm as his voice. "Stop. Listen to me. We need not marry truthfully. I have an idea. Among my men is one who was a priest."

She cocked a brow. "You?"

He roared in laughter. "Where did you get that idea? Lord in His heaven! I am not nor ever was a priest. But my friend was one. He joined me in protest

42

of King John's base treatment of his order when the monks supported the Pope more than John in a religious argument."

"And this man of yours will lie and say he married us?"

"Samuel knows the rituals and the words. He can assist us, I have no doubts. He does look formidable as well as pious. No one would dare to disbelieve this man." He grinned and chucked her under the chin. "We can have your men seek him out, for I know how to bring him to us without capture."

She smiled, tremulously at first and then broadly. "You will help me."

He laughed lightly. "I think it justice a fallen angel should assist one who should not be condemned." With more resolution than readiness, he rolled to his feet. His cramped muscles screamed in protest. His body took fire as he gazed down at the nymph who peered up at him, her tempting mouth open, her eyes admiring every inch of him from hips to chest to throat and mouth and hair. His loins tightened in his hose.

"You are much bigger than your legend," she whispered wondrously. "Larger than I ever thought a man could be."

Ah, and you know not the half of how unbearably huge you make me. He offered his hand. "I am at your service, my lady. Come up to me and let me see how impressive this angel really is."

She placed herself in his care and he tugged her up. The crown of her radiant head reached the base of his throat. She froze, examining his contours closely. Unable to bear her scrutiny, he put a finger beneath her chin and raised her face. From this vantage he could kiss her lips easily, trace her curves copiously, raise her a few inches and be inside her, worshiping at the altar of her inner beauty. He strained to say something that belied his wayward mind's imaginings. "You and I will make quite a pair."

She swallowed, looking flustered. "Aye, daunting I should think. I had hoped it would be so, and now I know 'tis true. No man has ever towered above me. It is a comforting aspect, or so my older sister told me often as men came to court her."

He smoothed her hair behind her exquisite ears. "I pay your beauty court, my lady. More, I will see you comforted and protected in all ways. If my height serves a purpose, I will not dissuade you from admiring it. I like your stature as well."

She tilted her head. It made his hands cease their stroking and cup her cheeks instead. "Most men dislike big women."

"You are not *big,* my lady. You are merely tall. With long limbs and slim neck, you are as elegant as a swan."

Her fawn-colored lashes lowered, but he could see how the pearlescent sheen of her skin grew pink and so appealing he longed to put his lips to every inch of her perfection. She dragged in a ragged breath. "I am honored you think me suitable to you. I . . . I would hope I may please you in substance as well as in form."

He scowled. What was she implying and fearing? "You are a lovely woman, and you please me, but— look at me."

She would not. "You have not named your price for this service you do me."

"What was your idea of how I might be compensated?"

Her eyes flashed to his. "Name your reward. It is yours without quarrel."

Clearly, by her looks and words, she thought he might ask a physical expression of her gratitude. "You think me such a demon that I would demand of you many things I have no right to take." He sighed and gazed above her head. "I suppose I deserve that. It is a logical conclusion, given my past." He lowered his eyes to her fearful ones. "I will ask of you many things. Not one will be *that*." Sorrow wrung his heart for what he could never ask of her or give her. "But I will require that you pretend to be my loving wife. For as you do, you will prove beyond others' doubts that you met me, instantly loved me, and hastily wedded me for very palpable reasons. Do you see the wisdom here? Good. Second, you must allow me"—*God help me*—"to display the same abundant affection to you. I pledge you it will be a show, a sham for those in your household. Say you agree."

"Aye, to anything. I want to drive these men of Chretian's far away from me and quickly."

"So shall it be."

"You have not yet named your compensation."

"Gold will be but one reward. And quite a bit of it, I predict. Gold I find useful. Gold I can dispense to those who have been disenfranchised by King John and his friends. It will be a goodly sum to keep them warm and fed."

"No jewels? Furs?"

"Nay. Jewels I do not desire, for I can put my hands on any and all I wish with the snap of my fingers." He winked. "And as for furs—" Of their own accord, his fingers dug into the depths of the miniver she wore and drew her nearer. "I see we have enough here for a warm night's rest or to adorn the beauty of the lady of the castle."

"Land, then."

"Land," he mused. "Nay, not land as most would give it and receive it, for I could never keep it. But land—Windom and Carlisle land—as only you may give it to a brigand such as I. I shall request from you safety from the king's law within your boundaries. You will never seek me or any of my band within your domain. Neither will you ever conspire with the king's men to take me before his ill-named courts of justice. What say you to these stipulations?"

"Done. Cooperation, affection, and protection are my vows to you." Her eyes twinkled. "What more could I as your 'wife' offer you, my 'husband'?"

"Little else could the world hold for a true mate."

"And for this, you will stay to rid me of these men, both Chretian's and my three suitors."

He smiled and dragged the miniver up her shoulders, as much to keep her warm as to hide the line of her neck and collarbone from his need to stroke her skin. "Aye. Who are they, these three who would compete for you?"

"My father and two uncles bring forth a man whose name I do not yet know. They have sent word they will visit me within days to present this man to me."

"Ah. So then your sire will be surprised you have a man to husband you already."

"So will the new earl of Windom who arrives tomorrow. He comes to pay me court and hopefully marry me, returning to his family's care the third of the Windom estates that came to me as my dower portion at my first husband's death."

"And the third candidate? Who might that unlucky fellow be?"

Her eyes fell to his throat. "The man proposed by Chretian's chamberlain Demere as the one I must marry—or else they will tell the king I have killed Chretian."

He lifted her chin, which quivered with her fear. "Distress yourself no longer, my lady. Whoever he is, he is no equal to the Devil of Midnight."

"He is a friend of the king's and until last year, he was sheriff in Hereford Shire. His name is Roger Bartlett. The earl of Swansdown."

"Swansdown. From across the river. Christ's tears . . ."

She grasped his wrist. "You know him?"

His mind traveled backward to ageless crimes perpetrated against those he loved. "Aye."

Her green eyes took on the color of the Aegean Sea in turbulent times. "From the way you set your jaw, you know him well . . . and he is terrible!"

Unable to stop himself, he took her to him. He almost voiced his appreciation of her firm lushness against his rock-hard need. He nuzzled her rose-scented tresses. "Do not fret, my Angel. I know the man. But he is no match for me." *Never again will he be a match for me. For I have sworn such revenge, God's justice will seem like the kiss of peace compared to my fury.* "I promise you we will see him to his horse and never will he bother you again. At the end of our journey together, I will see you free of all men who would invade and rule your life." He pulled her away to admire her lovely eyes. "Say you believe me."

"Aye!" She threw her arms about his neck and pressed into him with desperate joy. "I do believe in you as I have never believed in any other man."

He held her like that for he knew not how long. Perhaps until his joy of her enthusiasm transformed into his lust of her. Perhaps until his need to comfort her transcended his desire and brought him a sanity and peace that had eluded him for decades. "Come. We will summon your men. We will keep one at this door and—"

"You will not leave me, will you?" She dug her fingers into his arms.

"Nay, my Angel. Never will I leave you. But time is short. We must move like the wind. I will send two of your men to my band's newest settlement and the means by which they will be accepted without question. Peter will take this ring, which never leaves my finger save for such a signal to assist me. That way we will quickly have our priest—and our wedding." He skimmed her cheek with the tender caress of his knuckles, then turned for the door.

She caught his sleeve. Her eyes danced in delight, her cares gone from her if only for a moment. "What is the name of this man I would marry?"

He grinned. He'd give her truth, but for the safety of them both, he'd offer only half of it. Accustomed to lies and diversions as he had been for more than half his life, he'd cover the truth of his first name with the lie of a family name that would strike bewilderment into her foes.

"I would say this new husband of yours is a minor baron from the northern borders where John's arm seems not so long or strong. This bridegroom comes from the family Forrester, cousin to Chretian. That should make the men who carry your late husband's standard think twice before nay-saying me."

"And what of your given name, my good sir?"

"You may call me Nicholas."

"Nicholas," she said like a new prayer, then beamed. "Nicholas is the saint who protects children."

He traced a finger down her nose and tapped the upturned end. "And angels."

"This must be a divine sign that bodes well for my pact with my Devil."

Her outlandish joy radiated to her every glowing feature. He longed to kiss her to seal their bargain, but knew in his heart—and in other vital parts of him that rose to demand attention from her—he could not, should not.

But as he strode toward the door, he admitted that he knew one thing for certain. One of them was destined to discover raging torment in this bargain. And most likely that person was not God's Angel but heaven and earth's outlaw Devil.

Chapter
3

~

Her husband became more silent, more sullen by the moment. Apart from the others in their party, Nicholas sat his huge black mount in the gathering doom of a frosty, wind-bitten morn, waiting for a friend so that they might enter Windom castle with a greater numerical advantage. But as the morn wore on, she began to feel a chill from her Devil she had not marked in those first satisfying hours when he had committed himself to her.

"He is alone often," came a strong and distinctive voice from behind her.

She recognized the resonant bass of the priest who had married them—or rather, pretended to. Turning, she offered a small smile to the rotund man who perched on his aged sorrel. "He has many cares."

"Aye." The priest nodded for them to ride together far from the earshot of others. When they were well away, he lowered his voice and said, "My deafness in this left ear makes me speak louder than I should. And you and I must talk in plain language." He considered the bleak terrain. "The Devil is far different from what the common folk would tell of him—that he is a blithe and laughing creature. Far from it. He leads us, all strong men who would follow him to the ends of the earth. We eat well, live warm and dry, while we are safe and perform the noblest duty God could grant a man—to harass a true devil—King John. Our Devil makes this so with the great care he puts in everything. He takes all his responsibilities to heart." He nailed her with watery aqua eyes. "Especially this one."

"I felt it to be so," she admitted.

"He has rescued women before."

"Aye, I have heard of a Lady Abbeville—"

"Ah, the famous tale of a lady's capture from the king, who would marry her off for political reasons. That was a successful escapade. But this is a complicated ruse and I fear it."

"You are not alone."

"The Devil is too valuable to be trapped and taken. Many barons who hate John rely upon their Devil to help them in their subterfuge. They need a man who can ride with the night, disappear into the forests, and make John gnash his teeth."

"I will require your Devil for only a while."

"Time matters not so much to me as content."

"Are you saying you have a problem lying that you married us?"

He chuckled, his jowls jiggling. "Not at all! To lie to defeat John and his minions appeals to my soul's sense of justice." The humor drained from his florid face as he put up a forefinger. "Mark my words, though, you should make this deception appear real. John is a crafty bugger. So, too, his ghouls, like Swansdown."

Jo-Ann Power

"'Twill be easy to say I am married to this man," she said in truth. "I wonder . . . if you were examined by King John, would you have as easy a time?"

"Madam, to aid this Devil I would lie to God Himself."

Despite the fact that this priest dressed like one and spoke like one, she could hear in his voice an unholy resentment against John. Such rabid emotions did not come lightly. "You owe Nicholas that much?"

"When I was young, John went into one of his notorious fits and confiscated my family's properties in payment for taxes and scutage. Then last year, because my order opposed his quarrel with the pope, John set fire to my monastery. In the middle of the night, John's men killed my friends and left me for dead. The Devil found me, gave me health, home, friends—and a purpose. I can never compensate him for that. Vengeance may be God's, but on my lips it tastes very sweet."

To instruct a priest amounted to irreverence, but in the interest of truth she did not balk. "Such evil motivation could eat away at whatever good you might perform."

"I'll worry over that after John is dead."

"And if you go to your reward before the king?"

"I'll die a happy man."

"Albeit one in purgatory."

"A small price."

"You *do* hate viciously, Father. I shall never cross you," she said with the ghost of a smile.

"Wise. Go now. Talk with your new husband. The others wonder why the new bride has so much to say to the fat priest. You need to put performance to the show."

She kneed her horse toward her husband.

"Are you warm enough?" Nicholas asked presently, reaching out a hand to pull her hood higher over her hair. "These clouds will soon bring forth a frigid snow. Before that happens, we must be firmly ensconced inside Windom." His gold eyes cast out over the clearing to her home on the far ridge.

"Let me go forth and hail the gatekeeper," she pleaded yet again. "He will recognize me and raise the main portcullis."

"I will not chance it. Before he finished, we would have to assemble before the moat. At such close range, he could easily see you have one more man accompanying you home than with whom you left for Montrose. He could call us in and cut us dead within the barbican before we drew another breath. Nay, we await my friend and ally, Lord Gainsbridge. That way, I appear a member of his party."

Gainsbridge was Windom's northern neighbor. As such, this noble had visited here twice, though truth to tell he was more a friend of the rebellious barons who made King John sign the great charter last June than he was of Chretian Forrester. Still, her second husband, ever hospitable—and ever curious about the man's activities so that he could send news to King John—had welcomed Gainsbridge whenever he traveled. Thus did the Windom gatekeeper know him as one who could cross their moat with impunity. Now she also knew Gainsbridge as one who crossed other lines to befriend outlaws.

"Odd how little we know of each other," she murmured while her palfrey stomped in agitation at the interminable wait. Angel soothed her with a few pats.

Nicholas frowned at Windom's sand-colored walls through the gloom. "How little we know of ourselves until we must summon some new quality to a new challenge."

"Like patience?" she ventured.

"Aye," he gave her a rueful smile. "It is at least midmorn and we have waited here too long. If Gainsbridge does not arrive soon, we will need to seek some better shelter than this copse."

Angel knew also without her new husband proclaiming it that if Gainsbridge did not come at all, they would need to devise some means not only to get this party inside Windom but also to survive in there without numerous allies to balance or best the Carlisle numbers.

Chilled to the marrow, Angel surveyed the group of seven others beneath the secluded canopy of tangled trees. Angel's three loyal servants sat their horses uneasily, gazing at Michael Ross and Nell. Both of them still showed an anger at their own laxity, which had permitted the opportunity for their mistress suddenly to remarry. The presence of the priest—stentorian Father Samuel—killed whatever objections they might have voiced. The stunned Michael Ross, who could reasonably assume this homecoming might be no welcome one, had found the will only to exclaim how he wished an end to sitting here in this chilling weather. Meanwhile, Nell, who had ceased her senseless mutterings soon after the very convincing marriage ceremony, cast baleful looks at both Angel and Nicholas.

Nell was a wily witch with a thundercloud of storm black hair, eyes as silver blue as lightning, and a body she moved with arrogantly. The combination made her the source of the ribald attention of many of Windom's and Carlisle's men. It also brought her, Angel had no doubts, to the bed of Chretian's chamberlain, Eugene Demere. In fact, there was only one man whom Nell's charms did not interest: Michael Ross.

That pockmarked bear found her utterly distasteful. Even now, whenever his bleak hazel eyes left Windom's walls, he viewed Nell with a sneer. Certainly, he had more things to occupy his mind than her. He showed it, too. Shifting often in his saddle, he awaited the moment he must cross the moat and face those men he had controlled, but now would no longer, as captain of the guard. Even without Demere there to elicit the story, Ross would have to tell the tale of how he had drunk himself into a daze last night, and by his negligence thus permitted the countess to open her manor castle to a stranger and then to summarily marry the man.

Angel had questioned Nicholas about the need and wisdom of bringing Ross back to Windom. As they left her chapel and the false ceremony that made them husband and wife to all the world, she had walked with him to the stables and asked why Nicholas had not sent Ross and Nell to captivity.

"Surely," she said, "you could have sent both of them with Ibn Said." That odd little nut brown man, who was a Devil's disciple and who had left immediately after assuring himself his young Devil was safe and sound, could have carted these two away to the forest in chains and soothed some of her fears.

"Aye, my Angel, I wish I could leave Ross and Nell behind. But we need them. Their absence from your returning party would raise an alarm, if indeed we ever make it inside. And we must gain entry in a natural manner and not arouse their suspicions of our cause. Only then can we walk the castle and try to discover who and why and how these servants could attempt to murder your husband and make you marry another man. We seek to make you a power, not hand your inheritance to others. Trust me."

"I do."

Her admission had made him turn, narrow his eyes at her, and sear her with sweet gilded fires.

It was the last time this morning he had looked on her with such fervor. And she acknowledged how she enjoyed his glances and ached for more.

Even now, preoccupied as he was, her mouth watered at the sight of him. Certainly, dressed in hell's black as he had been when Peter rolled him from the sheet, her Devil had appeared formidable, frighteningly appealing. But now, attired in the ruby wool cowled cloak with emerald green tunic and darker braies and hose beneath, she admitted to herself how impressive this man would be to anyone anywhere on earth or perhaps in realms beyond. She smiled at the way the colors complemented his swarthy handsomeness and remembered how the tunic had spanned his incredible chest and how the braies had molded to his lean hips and oaklike thighs.

And Nicholas had been so impressed with his garments, she teased him. "I sewed these garments the past ten nights since Chretian's death to clothe a new mate whom I assumed would be a threadbare brigand."

"Outlaw I may be, but I am hardly impoverished. Though I declare to you, none of my clothes compares to the crafting of these."

She had admired them, too. Rich fabric, fashioned by her, but sized and cut to proportions her wood ward Leon continually insisted were accurate . . . Leon . . .

Leon, who also with great foresight had restrained the Devil's horse from galloping away when they had seized him. Leon, who surprisingly brought the huge black beast forward when they needed to journey to Windom.

How could Leon, her lifelong friend, predict the need to tether the unruly animal . . . or know enough about measurements to clothe a Devil?

"Lord Forrester!"

Angel snapped from her reverie to see Nell step before Nicholas's huge horse.

For him and Angel, loathing lit her blue eyes. "I wish to relieve myself. This waiting causes me pain."

Nicholas lifted his chin. "Go with her, Peter. See she does not run off."

Nell swiped a lock of black hair from her eyes. "I won't have him coming with me!"

Nicholas leaned forward in his saddle. "Though it is a little late for correct behavior from you, Nell, there is no woman to guard you. Go."

Peter gripped her arm, but she yanked it from him as she spat at Nicholas. "You fiend."

He moved not a muscle.

"You should kill me now." She spun to Peter when Nicholas did not respond. "Why does he not slay us now, eh? He should. If he takes us inside, he has two more to worry will attack him." She halted in her tracks so that the silent Peter had to pull her forward to the only thicket which could best serve the purpose of some privacy.

"Mayhap he cares more for his eternal soul than you do for yours, Nell. Have you not heard? Killing is still a sin."

"Pah! What need have we to fear death? 'Tis life which brings torment." And then she wrenched herself from his hand to tromp behind the bushes, murmuring of the ills of her day-to-day existence.

Nicholas turned to Angel. "I will relegate Nell to the kitchen. I don't want her so near you anymore."

She beamed in gratitude. "Thank you. I had not the power to issue such an order myself. Chretian's chamberlain would not have permitted it. He used her to spy on me." She bit her lip and her eyes drifted away.

She had often wondered what Nell knew of her relationship with Chretian. The maid had frequently intruded on her and her husband's intimacy. All the more reason for Nell not to be able to carry tales of this new husband—and this bedtime activity. The very fact that there would be nothing to report would declare the reality of this wedding today.

Nothing.

Was that so?

Surely, for all her inexperience in the matters between men and women, what she felt when this man looked at her, touched her . . . or kissed her as he had this morning at the door of her chapel . . . was something new and terrifyingly exciting.

But the exhilaration twined with a disappointment that had her dismounting and tethering her horse to a tree.

Since dawn, all here—save the portly, nearly deaf Father Samuel—could swear on any Bible she belonged to Nicholas Forrester. Lady Angelica Forrester. His, yet not. A lie that ironically was truth.

From all she could say of the ceremony Samuel had performed for them, the marriage appeared real enough. They had stood before the chapel door, the wind whipping high with a dim winter's sun fighting steely rain clouds. Samuel had asked—with his loud, grating bass—if there were any impediments. When no one objected, Samuel had then asked—in ear-splitting bellows—what dower Nicholas would provide his bride, and he, in that feigned but hallowed moment, had spoken words at which she marveled.

"I give her rights to inherit all my worldly goods, without reservation or restriction. Also all rights to the profit from my efforts, in England and abroad."

Smiling at the question that surfaced in her eyes, he had placed on her fourth finger the heavy gold and pearl ring that the priest had returned when Peter brought him to Montrose's solar before dawn.

Recalling the recitation of their vows inside the chapel, she thought the ceremony so valid that she wondered exactly where the priest had omitted portions to make the marriage false. Certainly, no one there appeared to challenge it as other than gospel.

For if anyone had any doubts at the end of Samuel's celebration of the nuptial mass, the kiss Nicholas and Angel had shared at the door would kill any question. He must have planned it so, knowing he must add the show of lust to a marriage that seemed too fortuitous, too convenient.

So like the Fallen One whose name he claimed, Nicholas took advantage of the lie he would live with her—and demonstrated his wild affection for her.

Gathering her into his arms, he boldly fit her body's curves to the endless planes of his and cupped her face with one hand.

"Kiss me," he had demanded in a gruff whisper. "Really kiss me."

What she had never known he taught her in that brightly blinding moment. He showed her how a man's mouth could top her own with precise delight. How he would touch her with one reverent hand pressed to her waist and another thrust into her hair. How he could catch his breath and slant his lips across hers, and murmur something sweet-sounding in a language she knew as mystic and compelling, and take more nibbling tastes of her. What she never knew was how he could take his lips away so slowly and too soon to make her stare at him and wonder if the universe had stilled as had her heart.

She skimmed her fingertips across her mouth now, imitating none of the euphoria she knew at the glide of his skin along hers.

How had he done that?

And when might she hope for more?

Answers eluded her.

Shivers consumed her.

And suddenly she remembered what else brought such tremors. Her fear of men. Other men.

Only her motivation to be free of those who would use her and abuse her assailed her.

Still, close behind stood the newly pervasive feeling that this man—this husband—was very different from all others.

"Angel?" Nicholas beckoned softly and grasped her shoulders to turn her to him.

He gazed down at her hand upon his forearm,

where through her ivory wool glove they viewed the shape of the onyx and pearl ring that proclaimed that she was his.

He surveyed her expression. "You are sorrowful of a sudden. Do you have doubts? You must not."

"Nay. I thought . . . perhaps 'twas you who had the doubts. You seemed so distant from me these last hours."

He bit his upper lip and shook his head.

"What then troubles you? If I have done something—"

"Nothing," he spoke sharply, then tried to soothe her. "I have lived a rough existence most of my life, my lady. I have forgotten manners which many would say make a lout a gentle man. Father Samuel can vouch for some of those years. Ibn Said for more than twelve of them."

Ibn Said was the other member of this Devil's disciples whom she had met that winter's morn. This stoic little man who said little or nothing to anyone had appeared with the priest and shattered her assumptions of what a Devil's cohort might be. As tall as her shoulder, the wiry fellow's appearance duplicated those of which she had heard in tales of the exotic Orient. Dressed in vermilion silk from the turban atop his ice white hair to the laced tunic caught into the gathered waist of a voluminous pair of breeches, he had worn a cropped black fur vest, much like the one his leader had worn. But unlike her Devil, the tiny man had a body that was a tight, thin rope corded by crinkled leather skin of aging earthy brown. His watery eyes resembled black pools that swirled around her and engulfed her as if seeking some surrender of the secret nature she shrouded from others. At her returned stare, he spread his thin mouth indulgently. Then he bowed from the waist, gracefully, tactfully, for she knew he took assessment of her and found her wanting in some quality he would, in deference to his Devil, not dare describe unless required by dire necessity.

"Gracious lady," he had intoned in his native dialect, which curled his tongue and shaped his lips with sibilant sounds foreign to her ear, "I am here to do your will, my Devil's and Allah's."

She had nodded, unable to do more for this new surprise that cramped her heart. Her Devil had infidels in his band? She had heard much of his companions, but never that.

Fearing now she might breach the bounds of privacy, she nonetheless asked, "What could Ibn Said tell me of a Devil who is now my husband?"

"That he has been with me since I was a boy of fifteen. That he has been much to me. Counselor, teacher, surrogate father. He is a remnant of my tattered past. Just like the priest and the twelve others who have joined my band, Ibn is a boon companion to the troubles of my days and the aspirations of my nights. Each knows me completely, and together we fight John and all the forces of his evil. Ibn is no stranger to such a struggle. He came to me when once I sat in solitude inside a sultan's suffocating cage. Ibn and I were prisoners, you see."

She did, shuddering at a memory of one such captivity of her own. Nicholas drew her closer in his arms.

"Still, amid that horror, Ibn and I became friends. Whereas Father Samuel and I are different. We share a history only a few years old, but nonetheless important. This priest and I count not as many days together as we do sympathies. For the poor, the oppressed, the dispossessed of King John of England's domain, Father Samuel and I share the same zeal. It is our mutual desire to see our monarch bedeviled in his tracks. We wish that those barons who so rightfully made the king sign the great charter at Runnymede six months ago would wrest the final power to dispel him who fouls our land with his rapaciousness."

"And the others who have joined you? Do they have the same motivations?"

"Aye. One or another variation, but most the same. They wish to fight a man who would take another's God-given rights." He lifted her chin and smiled into her eyes. "That is why they will gladly come to your rescue as well."

"Can I meet them?"

He raised his nose into the air, inhaling. "They are here," he whispered. "Ibn has told them and they have come to watch over us."

With wide eyes, she scanned the horizon. She saw nothing, heard only the vacuous silence of the land before a fall of snow. Only one bird circled overhead and it called mercilessly into the turbulent winds before it darted and dipped to the valley near Windom's moat.

It was an extraordinary fowl. Huge. Ivory against the gray clouds. With the graceful wings of a gyrfalcon.

She focused on her husband and the matter of his men. "How long have they been with us?"

"Since we left Montrose. Aye." His mouth hitched up in a lopsided grin. "They are talented. They have much practice at it, fortunately and not."

"And you?"

He paled. "I have many years' experience. Too many for my taste. But then, John lives long."

His bitterness ate at her like acid on her skin and she itched to soothe his agony. A hand to his cheek, she exulted when she felt him bury his lips in her palm and close his eyes.

In the next moment she melted to him. The long, strong length of him was just as she remembered at the chapel door. It was the feeling she had wanted again—nay, craved.

"Nicholas," she whispered. "I would not see you hurt."

"Angel, my Angel," he chanted, his firm lips warming hers. "How did God imagine such a lovely creature as you?"

She flowed nearer. His hands pressed her frantically closer. "I adore your mouth. 'Twas meant to be kissed." He ran his nose across her cheek to outline her ear. "All of you was meant to be worshiped with body and soul."

She vibrated with feverish need and tilted back her head. He ran his tongue along the seam of her lips. Moaning, she opened for him. He swirled his mouth atop hers, paused . . . and then retreated.

Confused by what would have been, Angel felt herself flush. She spun to leave him, but he seized her and tenderly drew her back against him, her body burning for more than the touch of his palm to her waist, more than the fit of her to his body's declarations of his desire for her.

"Angel, listen to me. I must take an oath."

Wounded vanity replaced feminine fluster. While her body traitorously yearned to be embraced, heart-to-heart, face-to-face, propriety demanded she scold him—and warn herself of unknown consequences. "My lord, of necessity, you have already taken vows today that mean nothing. Now you issue an oath. You should fear for your immortal soul."

"I seek to save yours, my sweet. Mine is already lost. But this . . . *this* which almost occurred between us will not happen again."

"Before our marriage, you said a show of affection would convince them of our love and need to wed." She inclined her head in the direction of the others, some of whom stood gaping at the sight they had just witnessed. "They believe we are meant for each other. What happened at the church door and here now confirm it."

"Aye, that wedding kiss was one few ever know and many dream about. Still, we breach the bounds of courtliness with more of them. It will not happen again. I give you my pledge. And my humblest apologies."

Her back stiffened. "You need give me nothing more, Nicholas. Of this . . . this kiss, I know not why or how it happened. . . ." She ran a hand shakily across her brow. "I was to blame, too."

"We will see this quest through to the end. I will secure you your freedom, Angel. And I promise you I will take nothing from you that is not mine to have."

She jerked away from him and faced him, her eyes declaring only her sadness. "Thank you, my Devil. You are truly an honorable man to pledge such to me."

"I am not so selfless in this, my lady. I want to subdue these men, distract them, for my own reasons. Not all of them are noble ones. Aye, I seek to nettle

John. I would also deter your father and the new earl of Windom from coercing you. But that is nothing to my desire to see this earl of Swansdown defeated."

"So you have a personal issue to press in this. Good. I can expect a supreme effort on your part. But that gives me no leave to probe your motivations."

"The very fact that you do not leads me to offer you everything else I can lay before you. Especially my promise that I will act honorably with you."

She felt bold again and tossed her hair back to stare at him. "Let me offer my matching promise then, my husband. I will give you nothing that I will not give freely. Nothing. Then at the end of our time together, I will assure you your freedom. We will both be satisfied, won't we?"

She raised her chin, defying him to answer. When he did not, she grew solemn. All glory gone, she looked at him, this handsome, tormented Devil she called her own. "Aye," she breathed, "we will each have what we want. But now I do wonder at what price."

She spun from him.

Wild, denied, empty, she plodded down the mountainside.

Let him think on that. Let him ponder.

Let him.

Meanwhile, she could do the same. She could try to understand why she found delight in looking at him, how she discovered serenity in talking with him. . . . She could try to determine when she had first wanted his smile to heat her and his words to woo her. . . . She could try. . . .

She walked through tangled brush and brambled trees. The ground cover crackled with crisp deadwood. The earth was packed, ready for the season's first layer of snow. Just as she, too, must become hard, toughening her resolve into a new armor for the fight ahead.

She pushed aside an ancient rotting limb. Her foot stuck in a hole and slipped. The ground gave way. She shot out a hand, stumbled forward, and came nose-to-nose with a man's meaty face—and his gleaming dagger.

Chapter
4

A pearl of great value.

From the moment they had rolled him from the winnowing sheet, Nicholas had known she was precious. Brave and resourceful. Every element he admired in men and never dared hope to find in a woman.

He watched her walk from him into the forest and cursed his past, his lack of a future. She was everything a man could want. Everything he could desire.

If he were a normal man.

His own man.

He longed for the kiss they should have shared minutes ago and remembered the one they had enjoyed when they were first married. He tensed in his saddle at the memory of how she had come to him at the church door. All sweet surrender and soft surprise. Her hands winding in his hair. Her breath sighing into his. Her lips molding to his own. Her breasts crushing the clothes he longed to strip from both their bodies so that he might put his lips on her throat where her pulse pounded and where the miniver had once feathered and teased his imagination. He wanted to discover what awaited any husband of hers beneath her gown, all those wonders he had glimpsed in the firelight and knew a man would live to adore and die to protect. And she had let him kiss her to prove the lie, keeping her eyes shut as he tore himself away, trailing her tongue over her lower lip to savor what they had both barely sampled.

He had fantasized taking her there in the open, before his Maker, and later in the church, before his renegade priest. He had wanted to lie down with her there, anywhere he could put his eyes and mouth and hands to the test of praising her. Hell, he simply wanted to learn her, know her, as Adam had known Eve and all other men had known their women, their wives. To wed her, in fact or fiction, only heightened his desire for her, his need to become the man they now proclaimed he was—and he knew both showed starkly on his face. To her loyal servants, who coughed in embarrassment, and to her disloyal ones, who glared and groaned in disbelief.

What would he have given at that moment to be a real man, unfettered by the past and free to grasp his rightful future? Christ in His grave, he would have given years of his wretched life to have one with her. For in those short days, he'd transport her every night to a heaven he'd fashion for her. He would caress her and kiss her and endow her with such riches that no man after him would dare to rob her, threaten her, touch her, or take her to paradise.

So what delusion was this?

He jammed a hand through his hair and turned his

horse from the one vision he wished to view till his eyes went blind.

What was he thinking of?

He could not want a woman! Could not claim one. Least of all, this one.

She came to you to save her, St. Cyr, not turn her need upon the rack of your own. Still, when Bartlett arrives, your goal will be stretched upon the same device as hers.

The duality of his purpose manifested itself in all its hideous diversity.

And was it also duplicity?

By advancing his own revenge was he tainting the purity of the fight he took up in her name? And by such blemish was he inviting defeat for her cause?

That he could never allow.

Ah, Christ.

He cantered back to the rest of his party. He prowled the forest's edge. For insidious minutes, he scowled at Windom Castle, its drawbridge down, assessing all its challenges that would soon bow to his will—and his Angel's . . . if only he could get in easily with friends to protect those remaining who had plotted against her and the murdered Chretian.

He considered the path from the north.

Where on God's green earth was Gainsbridge?

They had been circling this clearing far too long. Over an hour. Even his gyrfalcon grew weary of the wait, defining her celestial territory with ever smaller circumferences of the sky, eyeing him pitilessly from an occasional perch. Soon, too, dinner would be carried to Angel's great hall and the complete castle guard would assemble for its first full meal of the day. He wished not to enter at such an hour.

No enemy was ever to be overcome if he were interrupted at his repast. The Great Khan had taught him that military precept. The second one he had learned at that master warrior's knee was that no foe should be allowed to assemble in strength if he could be cut to pieces before he expected confrontation.

That was why he needed Gainsbridge, damn it. As a man well known in this northern clime and a past visitor to Carlisle, Gainsbridge could enter here with impunity. Once inside, the man and his retainers could guard this new husband's back, advance his cause, and collect information inside where and when he could not. He could help him outnumber the three Carlisle men-at-arms left within the walls and discover if the remaining four of Windom's men sided with their Carlisle brethren.

Of course, if Gainsbridge did not come soon, he knew he would have to consider the only alternative of dressing half of his twelve disciples in the attire of men-at-arms and so insinuate himself into his wife's stronghold. It was not the most sophisticated ploy, and it would leave fewer to guard Carlisle Castle from the outside, should King John take it into his head to send an army to enforce his will.

But inside or out, his band could intimidate any foe. Ibn Said, with his taut Saracen body, his menacing ivory grin, and his gaily colored clothes that concealed a mongoose's ferocity. Tall Vic, the tailor's son. Almost able to look Nicholas in the eye and best him with a sword, as no one else had ever done. And James, the baker's boy from Swansdown across the river. A runaway, loyal to his lord since youth. And then the one who remained loyal to another, but stayed at his post to spy for the Devil and his disciples. Leon, whom he needed to scold and instruct . . .

A woman's scream curdled his blood.

He stood in the saddle.

Angel?

He dug his spurs into his horse and the beast churned earth to do his master's will.

At the point where he had left her, he slid from his seat and crept into the brush. Emulating the panther that had once been his pet, Nicholas circled the path he had seen her take. Tall Vic and James stood across the clearing and turned in synchrony with him, all slithering their daggers from their sheaths. Avoiding the snap of twigs and crush of brush, Nicholas made out a line of trees beyond which he saw a man apply a shining blade to Angel's throat. With her back bent to him, she spoke softly to him. The man urged her up the hill. Toward her horse.

The bastard would never make it. With the speed of a predator, Nicholas skipped silently between trees to gain on the fiend. At a steep climb where Angel stumbled, he took his opportunity, darted around a thick oak, and lunged for the man's legs.

In one swoop he had him down. Free, Angel tumbled forward and spun to the two who wrestled before her.

Nicholas discovered instantly the man had more nerve than strength and pressed his hands back to the dirt, one knee to the culprit's throat. His knife settled at the man's ear. "To your reward!"

"Nay, Nicholas!" Fine fingers bit into his wrist. "He is a Windom guard!"

Nicholas eyed the man with new interest. "How

inconvenient. You chose the wrong time and place to yet again treat your lady badly."

"Nay!" Angel pleaded. "He never did. Though he was captain of the guard before Ross was appointed by Demere, this man never did hurt me. He was my father-in-law's friend. And kind, Nicholas, to *me.*"

"If so, why put a knife to your throat now, Angel?"

"Because I wanted her horse!" the man blurted. "I had to get away!"

Really? "What is your name?"

Vic and James, witness to this at the edge of a bramble bush, sank to the shadows, still waiting, watching.

When the captive made no response, Nicholas twisted his cloak collar. His beefy neck reddened and he choked.

"Who did you say you were? Speak up. I cannot hear you, man. Or perhaps you'd like a better taste of this knife to loosen your tongue."

"Tom Carter," he spit out.

Angel skittered closer. "He has been one of Windom's men-at-arms since he was a boy, isn't that right, Tom?"

Nicholas calculated the man's anger and shame at being caught. If he had been Windom's man, was he now loyal to Demere? Could someone in the castle suspect that Angel had abducted a man last night and this morning married him at Montrose? Knowing, could they have sent out a man to spy on the couple or kill them before they arrived? Nicholas could not imagine how such information could have traveled here. But many things were possible in heaven and on earth that this Devil had not reasoned. "Why are you out here this cold morning, Carter?"

The man's reluctance manifested in a flexing of his shoulders.

"If you need persuasion—"

Carter's savage black eyes met Nicholas's, then shot to Angel, where they softened. "I was leaving Windom," he told her more than Nicholas.

"Bound for where?" she asked.

To summon Demere to a wedding feast?

Coughing, the man stared at his captor. "Anywhere away from there."

"Why?" Nicholas persisted.

Carter shook his head, his gaze once more to the sky.

"Why would you leave?" It was Angel who repeated the question with a sweeter tone, an empathetic one.

"I couldn't stay there. I heard what Demere was doing to you and others and I knew. . . . I just knew I had to go or lose my own soul." His head shot up, his eyes swimming in terror. "I couldn't help you and I had to help myself. I wouldn't be a party to their devilry anymore."

Nicholas glanced up to see Peter and Edwin managing to descend the steep hill to assist him. From the corner of his eye, he noted how Vic and James drifted away. His attention remained on the guard.

"Carter, we know that you ran from Windom, but not what you ran toward." He arched a brow.

Carter worried his lips as though he tasted a foul flavor. "Anything was better than . . . that."

"What is the nature of that which you despise so, Tom?" Nicholas asked, but was not surprised when the man blanched and turned his eyes away again.

Whatever evil lived inside Windom, Nicholas now knew two things about it. The first was that all did not share a penchant for it. And second, some knew what it was and could not bring themselves to name it. His skin crawled with the supposition of what few sins could cause such virulence.

"Very well, we shall ask that again. At a later time. I will return instead to the question I asked before. What exactly do you run toward, Carter?"

The man shook his head, weary and regretful.

"Nothing?" A sound idea formed in Nicholas's brain and forced him to a half-smile. "What would you do for your Lady Forrester if, say, you were allowed to return to Windom—with her?"

Carter's jaw clenched. "I swear I love her and honor her. She has been good as any of them in that place allowed her to be. But I am full of sorrow, madam, for I cannot return there—not even to try to protect you."

"We understand your remorse, Tom. But we are speaking of something slightly different than you might anticipate." At the man's frown, Nicholas went on. "You could return with us to Windom Castle and, once inside, resume your duties as head of the guard."

"Nay, what trick is this?" he growled. "I saw Ross with you. You offer that, but Ross sits there beside you, free as the air! You can't fool me, whoever you are."

Angel came even nearer. "He is my new husband, Tom. Bound to me this morning, vowing to rid Windom of its woes."

"Bah! That's trying to rid Egypt of locusts! It can't happen."

"It may not—unless you help us," Nicholas wagered that truth might help persuade this troubled man. "I need to go inside, and unless I have a means to lull the gatekeeper into thinking I belong to this party, nothing will ever be right in that castle." Nicholas peered into the man's bleak black eyes and took the stakes higher. "Would you abandon all inside Windom to the whims of Demere and Ross?"

Carter's broad nostrils flared. "What prevents Ross from shouting out the truth and all of you being cut to the quick and dropped in the moat to rot?"

Nicholas smiled, remembering the expression on Ross's face when Angel had opened her solar door to the man to reveal a priest and a candidate for husband. The captain of the guard had laughed, incredulous. But as Ross's hazel eyes slitted, Nicholas had seen how he understood the enormity of his failure to guard the wealthy widow of Windom and Carlisle. Ross had acquiesced, his only recourse being captivity —or perhaps death. "I tell you, Carter, Michael Ross is that ever-artful lizard that changes his skin to the color of his surroundings. Survival is the only thing Ross understands—and he will pay any price, serve any master to do so. Until he sees another way out."

Carter took in Angel's fervent expectation. "So then if I return, I increase the odds in your favor. Inside, three of Windom's guards suffer under the tyranny of three of Demere's loyal men. They did not think it more than my good nature that I volunteered to do the morning duty on the gatehouse." His round face crumpled into a grin. "Aye, I *do* like these odds. Perhaps they have not missed me yet. I would love to try for you."

Nicholas released his grip. "Splendid. Come." He helped him up. "Peter, Edwin, we have a new ally."

Neither man looked too happy at the prospect, nor did they argue.

Only Peter spoke and softly. "My lord, your friend and his men approach. We saw them from the ridge."

"Good. We can proceed, then. Give this man a dagger, Peter, and let us see to Gainsbridge." Taking Angel's hand, he helped her up the slope.

At the top of the hill, Allen Gainsbridge dismounted to greet Nicholas with open arms and a polite salutation to Angel. Risking no errors, Nicholas led Allen to a clearing where they might speak privately.

"I must say, Nick, I'm glad I found you, but surprised as hell you remain here in this frigid weather! Tell me," his large gray eyes crinkled in concentration as they traveled to Angel, "did Ibn summon me with a true excuse? Have I come to celebrate a wedding?"

Nicholas nodded at the lean nobleman who asked questions with a familiarity born of years of mutual support. "Only this morning was the service performed."

"Ah, my friend, I can understand the reason for your fervor—and your haste. This Angel is divine. I know, for I have visited here often and enjoyed her conversation, her music. She is as accomplished in person as her station indicates. But I swear to you, this Angel will be a terror to protect from all those who would control her."

"Ibn told you everything, then. Good."

"Aye. I am astounded old Samuel agreed to the lie."

"He says John is the Antichrist." Nicholas said, chuckling. "To lie to him is therefore sacred duty."

"Well, Nick, I wish I had been there to see it, for

never did I believe you would wed anyone—even in falsehood."

Alone, Allen Gainsbridge knew the reasons marriage was so impossible for Nicholas. Allen, who had been pledged with him as squire when they were ten years old, had remained Nicholas's only friend in England during all the years when he had been imprisoned, ransomed to another. All the years when he sought only to survive to another day so that he might return, seek his revenge, and take his retribution on those who had stolen his inheritance and his honor.

Aye, Allen understood Nicholas had nothing to give a wife. Not name or home, or even hope.

But he could give her himself. "The greater terror is what would happen to her if I did not come to her service."

Allen stared, his voice edging upward. "Did you not understand my inference? This ruse cannot work."

"Have you ever known me to fail?"

Allen plunked his hands on his hips. "Of course not, but—"

"Will you not assist me?"

"That answer you already know."

"What then is your issue, Allen? You think I cannot play the part of a nobleman? That I have been too long a creature of the forest?"

"Nay! I remember what you did last summer for the Lady Abbeville." He chuckled and scratched his bearded chin. "Her abduction, dare I use the term, so that she might marry Somerset's heir instead of that grizzled earl of Weston was a divinely inspired ploy. But that was simple compared to this. The lady had only one foe to foil. Her father. This—*this* charade bears more complications!"

At Nicholas's arched brow, Allen paced. "I understand your compassion for Lady Angelica's plight. I, too, sorrow for her. But to pretend a marriage, to live inside her castle walls with the likes of Demere? Nay. Even if I and my four men go in with you, we could be easily outnumbered."

"For a short time the advantage is with us. Demere is gone with three of his men-at-arms. But he will return within days. Meanwhile, we have allied with us the former captain of the guard, namely one Tom Carter, the man you saw walk up the hill beside me. Carter bears Demere no allegiance, nor does he favor the captain of the guard, a Michael Ross. That man is the rugged bear who sits the chestnut stallion. Now, with Carter's control of the six guards who remain, we need not fear Ross as much. Without Demere, he is less powerful."

"Still, Nicholas, you must realize that ultimately this plan is folly! You cannot go inside Windom and expect to fight Demere! I know 'tis a grand dream to rid the place of those who would rob Lady Carlisle, but lovely as she is, she is but a pawn to the problems and allegiances engendered by her late husband. She is too rich in land for John to allow her to wed just anyone, especially a knight he knows not. With John's eternal need for money and allies in a land beset by rebellious barons, the king must know she, her wealth, and her villeins are safely allied with him. What better way to do that than to legally bind her to him with marriage to someone he trusts. Rest assured, he and his men will come ready at their lances to fight over her and all she possesses. For you to enter the contest in this way may be your undoing. I beg you, can we not find another way? I would hate to see you inside, outnumbered, perhaps captured. So would our friends. You are too important to our cause."

"There is no other way, Allen. The fight against John's injustice will go on until the man is dead. We know that now, since the signing of the charter at Runnymede in June. Despite it he still flaunts his rule, taxing us beyond our power to pay, selling women— Jesus wept, even his own wife—for gold! He'd barter his soul to control a kingdom he sucks dry with his sloth and lechery."

"But Nick, you cannot risk what you have built to take yourself inside that castle and believe that you can make a difference there!"

"We struggle against the odds in every fight with John. At least you and I have each other and our friends throughout England who counter the king at every move. Angel has no one. She never had. Now she has enlisted me. If I do not try to help her, there will be no one who will."

Gainsbridge sighed, huddling against the wind, which whipped higher. "That I concede."

"And still you say me nay?"

"I say you will have the devil's own time to counter what ails Carlisle's guards. They are a ravenous lot whom Chretian Forrester had not the ability to tame by word or deed. I felt it—whatever it was—seething over the men, crawling over them like maggots on meat."

"Chretian kept them, unruly or not. That took some evil glue. Enough to send Tom Carter in flight for his

80

soul into a winter morn. Enough to make him readily align himself with us, of whom he knows nothing except that we are the countess of Carlisle's new husband and his retinue."

"Aye, and what of the maid whose eyes shoot arrows at your lady? She is her chambermaid, if I do remember correctly."

"She will now work in the kitchen."

"And put poison in your food?"

Nicholas's lips curled in a wicked smile. "We'll have her test each dish before we eat it."

"Ah, such royal practices from the king of the underworld. You make my heart sing."

"And are you appreciative enough to come with me?"

"Of course. I will remain with you to put good quality to the show. I hope we can ward off the suitors and her father with ease. But what of Bartlett? When Demere returns with him, you will need to gird yourself for your fight with him."

"I welcome it. For the first time in seventeen years we will face each other."

"And he may recognize you."

"I doubt it. I was thirteen when I escaped him and his mother. They knew a lanky boy with sorrow in his soul."

"The boy has grown, but his soul still yearns for what was stolen from him." Gainsbridge stepped into Nicholas's line of vision. "You tell me you do this for Angel out of noble rectitude and I believe you. But if you allow your anger at Bartlett to color your quest, you may fail. I do not wish you slaughtered here, my friend."

"The issue between Roger Bartlett and me will not interfere. I will not allow it."

Gainsbridge shuffled his feet, winced at the sky, and shot Nicholas a wary look. "Beatrice is not worth it."

"Beatrice is dead almost ten years, Allen. I do not do this in revenge for her. Once Beatrice was pledged to me, but she was forced to do her father's will and marry Bartlett after I was gone and declared dead. But if she sits in hell for those acts, I know not. Nor do I care anymore." Instead of this topic, Nicholas ventured, "Shall we to our feast, my friend? It is not every day the Devil takes a bride."

Allen grinned and rubbed his hands together in glee. "Nor every place that boasts such lures as this den of iniquity. Hardly what I wanted on a damnable November morn. Let us to the gate, then. When we approach the guard and perchance he asks if I know you, I will vouch for you. We'll prompt this Tom Carter to bluster with all his authority, have the portcullis drawn high, and"—he made a flourish with his hand—"we will be in. God knows, I would it were done quickly," he said as he drew his cloak about him in the wind. Then he winked. "I must divest my men of a certain Devil's accoutrements of clothes and gold and jewels that Ibn brought to me. I also have a blessing to give to the new bride and groom—and a sumptuous bride's gift Ibn did entrust to me." He wiggled his brows. "I would view your lady's eyes when she sees it."

"Lord above, I never knew you to be such a romantic!"

"A ploy to get me inside to dinner. I am famished."

"Aye, I think to have as the main course a Carlisle villein or two." Nicholas surveyed the walls of Windom with a zealot's eyes. "Here's to the hope my lady stocked a goodly supply of strong wine to put them more in the mood for carousing than killing!"

Chapter 5

⤳

At Angel's approach, the newly affirmed earl of Windom, Geoffrey Devereaux, ceased his pacing before the fire in her great hall. Tall, with curls of chestnut hair, he was a passably handsome man, but also a worried one.

His concern showed in his eyes as he surveyed her and her large group. More concerned were his two knights-companion, who snapped to attention and drew closer to their lord.

All others in the hall froze. One kitchen maid who scurried about the long tables to place saltcellars and goblets stopped midstride. Three of the castle's men-at-arms who had come to assemble for dinner paused.

With the richly attired dark giant by Angel's side and a strange nobleman close behind, all stared at the procession that trailed Peter, Edwin, and Leon plus Gainsbridge's four men and a Dominican priest. Angel felt her vassals' scrutiny and accepted their strained greetings with a normality that surpassed even her own understanding.

Thus had it been with the two Windom guards at the gatehouse. Seeing their captain Ross within her retinue and then Gainsbridge, those men asked no questions but lifted the portcullis. Accepting their friend Tom Carter's excuse that he sought the clandestine company of a certain lady in the village, and leading as he was their lady, they took no note of anything amiss. Nor did they see the knife Leon held to Ross's back as Tom Carter bid them good morning. Only after Angel, her Devil, and his friends were safely inside did Ross have an opportunity to cast mean glances at his Windom guardsmen for their failure to perceive that in so welcoming these newcomers they displeased him mightily.

She had promptly dismissed Ross, degrading him before the men he had once ruled with an iron fist. When he appeared loath to leave she had won the day by the mere flick of an eye. With like courage, she sent Nell to her new post as kitchen maid.

Angel had no delusions, however, that both Ross and Nell would have fought her—and perhaps even won—had she stood alone, without the fearsomeness of her devilish husband close behind her.

Having come this far into her castle so easily, Angel girded herself for this first display of her grand lie. Her eyes on the distant claimant to the title and lands of Windom, she summarily dismissed all her servants while she registered Geoffrey Devereaux's resentment that he had been kept waiting.

"Lady Carlisle." He inclined his head in homage, while his brown eyes took in her and the man who towered above them all but who kept so near to her. "I am ever your servant."

"Thank you, Lord Devereaux. I was delighted when

my guard informed me you and your men had arrived." *Delighted to meet you, confront you, have done with one aspirant to my bower and my body.* She gave a small sign of welcome to the two knights who stood braced at the earl's side but did not do her chatelaine's duty to introduce her party to Devereaux. Such a breach of etiquette had him tilting his head at her in question. But she gave no quarter. Having held so few advantages over the years, she valued those she clutched this morning. She'd wait to see this man's intent before she offered any glimpse of her own.

"I hope I have not inconvenienced you by my eagerness to visit so soon upon the death of your lord and husband. I know your mourning period for Lord Carlisle is far from over, but I hastened here to put forth my hopes in person. Such urgency, I felt, was necessary because of the rumors of other suitors, and I could do naught but see for myself if you were in need of any aid." He lifted a brow slightly as if to ask how she fared with this titan at her right hand and the others surrounding her.

His sentiment about aiding her rang true, despite whatever self-interest he might have had in hurrying here to marry her himself. She offered him a pleasanter look and words that would kill any hope he might harbor of taking her to him as his wife.

"I thank you for your interest and your help, my lord. I know stories did circulate about my prospects for marriage. It is true that many men have an interest in my future. But allow me to tell you one new fact that will change much about your visit to us here. Let me introduce to you Sir Nicholas Forrester, cousin to my late lord, and the man who this morning became my husband."

If Angel had thought anger or hatred might evidence itself on Geoffrey Devereaux's features, she was wrong. Astonishment came, of course. But some other emotion surfaced in his eyes. For a man who had come to wed her to reclaim the dowered lands she controlled that should remain with any Windom entail, Angel swore she saw relief that such would never now be so. Even as she welcomed his reaction, she wondered why it was at odds with his stated intent.

"Your husband?" he mused. "And so quickly, too. How did this happen?"

Nicholas gazed down at Geoffrey, his ungodly gold eyes assessing the man mercilessly. "I traveled last night amid that gathering rainstorm to pay my respects to my cousin's widow. When I became weary and my horse grew tired, I feared he might turn lame. We sought rest in Montrose Castle and this good lady obliged me. We met and loved instantly. Hours ago, my confessor heard our vows at her chapel door and performed the nuptial mass."

Geoffrey's tight-lipped mouth told how he believed not a word. His dark eyes sought more information from Angel.

She gave the only thing she would. "I am grateful you are here and hope you might remain for our celebration."

"A *charivari?*" Curling his mouth up and frowning, he obviously thought the very idea ridiculous.

Nicholas nodded. "Small, given the recent passing of my lady's last husband, but adequate. I want our marriage noted with all the ritual we can bring to it."

"Aye, my lord. I am certain you would. 'Tis good you did this two days before Advent after which no marriages—or consummations—may occur. Otherwise, many men would challenge your right to take this lady as your wife."

"Do *you* challenge me, Lord Devereaux?"

"I could. For I have never heard of you, my Lord Forrester. And though I do suspect you come from the border lands where Forresters abound, I must admit when last I heard of that clan, I understood all of their men were elderly, *feeble*. You are far from that, my lord. And so, perhaps my information lacked certain"—he waved a hand—"facts."

Angel watched with bated breath as Nicholas narrowed his eyes at this intruder from the south who pried at the layers of truth. "I would say it did lack that."

"Why then do you not carry the red hair and blue eyes as the other Forresters?"

"My father's Scots traits were colored by my mother's darker stock. Will my looks keep you from acclaiming me as this lady's husband, Devereaux?"

Angel did not miss the challenge in his voice, and neither did Geoffrey Devereaux.

Instead, Devereaux glanced at a complacent Father Samuel and then at Gainsbridge and his armed men. "I see such would be a waste of breath. You have documents, I assume?"

"Aye."

"Well then, who am I to counter you?"

"You are the man who wishes to have my Lady Carlisle's Windom dower lands rejoined to yours."

"True. But I tell you, Forrester, if I cannot have them peaceably, I will not try to take them in any other way. From what I have heard, this good woman has many who say she cannot keep what is hers now."

"You could ally yourself with them and if they win, take what spoils you can."

"I could. But I have no stomach for such conflicts. I have enough troubles of my own. My Devereaux family boundaries are contested by another knight, who sees them as prime target for his own expansion. I shall have a fight on my hands to protect myself from that intervention."

Allen Gainsbridge came abreast of Angel and Nicholas to examine Geoffrey Devereaux with compassionate eyes. "I had heard that might be so."

"And I know it is," said Nicholas.

Bewilderment hit Angel. "How might that be, my Lord Forrester?"

His golden eyes twinkled like stars into hers. "I have my ways, as you can imagine. I know from a good source that Lord Devereaux was challenged by Roger Bartlett, the earl of Swansdown."

Angel felt revulsion. This Bartlett sought to take not only her lands but others'.

"Aye," Geoffrey affirmed in wonder as he searched Nicholas's expression. "How would you know this, my lord?" He stepped closer, his hands on his hips in defiance even though Nicholas bested him by at least six inches.

As the man approached, Nicholas's fingers bit into her waist. His whole body filled with a stiff ferocity. "Does it matter *how* I know as that I *do?*"

"Perhaps not. But yet I wonder who you are."

"And so I ask you—does it matter *who* I am so much as that your plight is so well known even a cipher such as I might make some sense from it?"

Devereaux, still suspicious and still unwon, rocked forward. "Pray tell me, my Lord Forrester, what sense can you make of this Bartlett's need to gobble more and more land, none of which was his, nor ever should have been?"

"Bartlett is greedy, my Lord Devereaux. Eager for all which he can control. Therefore, it appears you stand in his way. Or to be precise, your land does. If he can wrest your land from you, he can control the entire eastern shore of England from The Wash to the Humber River." Nicholas turned to Angel, his face a study in harsh misery as his jaw flexed in anger. "And if he had been able to claim more north of the Humber by sacrificing this lady on his altar, he would have. That would have made him the foremost power in England next to our most unrighteous King John."

So that was Bartlett's full intent! Angel recoiled at the perversity of it and marveled at Nicholas's skill to gather all raw facts and make such sense of them.

Close in the wake of that thought came the question of how Nicholas could know this Bartlett so well. Was this the result of the Devil's disciples harassing Bartlett as they did so many other nobles who supported John? And if so, would a band of robbers understand the politics of one lord so well? Better than she, his neighbor? A man of whom before recent weeks she had heard little?

Devereaux swept a hand back from his brow. "Christ's agony. You think Bartlett becomes a power with or without John?"

Angel crossed her arms. "And if John falls to the rebellious barons, Bartlett can spring up in his place."

"Aye," said Nicholas as he pulled her closer to his side. "Not as king, certainly. For his blood is not royal. But with such a base, he will be a landed baron with whom John's young son Henry must deal, whether Bartlett comes as regent or something slightly less."

"Absurd!" shouted Devereaux. "He has no experience to hold such sway. That cannot be!"

"Ah, but it can, my Lord Devereaux," said Gainsbridge. "I have met this Bartlett. I know him. He is a cunning cur who will serve whichever master feeds him. And at the moment, the master who fills his dish is John. Tomorrow, that could be King Philip of France. Who can say?"

Angel shivered, settling sad eyes on Devereaux. "And in the meantime, the one he seeks to rob is you."

"Aye, my lady, and you."

Nicholas squeezed her to him, the consoling embrace a declaration for all within the walls to note. "I dare him to try."

Devereaux stared at her, his features softening with concern. "I am most glad this Bartlett cannot add you to his list of possessions."

Angel's Devil frowned. "What would you give to be sure he did not add you and yours either, Devereaux?" Before the man could scarce get out a grunt, Nicholas continued, "What if I told you you could help us and thus deter this Bartlett and his master John from taking your lands and your rights?"

"I would be thrilled and more than grateful. My lands are not extensive, but they are rich and green. My villeins live a full life and bless my father and his fathers for their good management. I would continue that for them and for the next generations. I have seen what this king can do and seek to see his power curtailed." He surveyed Nicholas now with a new light in his dark brown eyes. "What would you require of me, Lord Forrester?"

"Your allegiance here. Help us show John exactly how much power this Bartlett really desires. The king resents all men's flagrant greed, ensuring only his own will survive."

"I do not seek to build up John's power, but to make him a king bent more on peace and justice."

Nicholas pondered and then shook his head. "We, too, would take that, if we could get it. What say you? Will you join with us?"

"How can I know you will help me in this? We are strangers. What chance have you for success?"

"I can give you nothing more than my word."

"Why should I take only that?"

"Is that not all a man—any man—may ever give another?"

Angel intervened. "My Lord Devereaux, this man's word was enough for me."

Hard brown eyes turned softer. "And from what I have heard of your virtue, my lady, I should proclaim my allegiance to this man instantly."

"Thank you, Lord Devereaux. I thought my reputation completely lost to me these last few weeks since my husband's death."

"I did not believe you could have killed a person. May you enjoy this man much longer than either your first or last husband, my lady."

She bristled with the remembrance that she had never enjoyed them at all.

Gainsbridge leaned forward with the only sign they were attending a supposed happy event. "If we do not put the revelry to order, she may never launch this marriage, Devereaux. What say you we set ourselves to the task of ordering up the wine from the cellars? Your men and mine look famished and I am parched from long hours in that wind. Come, Devereaux. We now have the opportunity to harass the Carlisle guards who have so much bothered yours and mine these last months, eh?"

Once all others had gone, Nicholas turned Angel into his arms. "We have transformed one suitor into an ally."

She pressed a palm to his warm heart. "Thanks to you."

He traced her jaw with the backs of his fingers, smiling as if there were no more foes. "God is with us in this." And he nestled her close, his lips to her hair.

Yet, she closed her eyes to shudder at the idea of the coming of her father and her uncles—and this man Bartlett, who sounded more devil than the one she embraced.

As dinner began, Nicholas surveyed the six guards with an eagle's scrutiny. Three guards sat with Tom Carter at one table and conversed quietly. But from the looks of the three others whom Nicholas assumed were Carlisle retainers, Nicholas would say they slavered to have one of their new visitors for their carving. Only logic—and lack of their leader, Demere—stayed their hand.

Michael Ross certainly didn't qualify, nor did it appear he could substitute. Indeed, they shunned him. They chose instead to sit together at the end of one long table and assess in silence the allied group of new Forresters, Gainsbridges, and Devereauxs. Even when

Nell and the other kitchen maid, Kate, brought the wine and laid the trenchers, they obviously wished more to fill their bellies than to have them slit.

The wiser choice. For though they had heard their lady's announcement of her marriage with surprise and deference, they must be conspiring, Nicholas knew, to set this aright before Demere returned to Windom.

Nicholas turned to Angel, who sat next to him at the high table where Chretian Forrester had so recently presided. Even she saw their hatred, so blatantly did they eye her as they swilled wine quickly.

"A surly looking lot, aren't they?" asked Angel, as she followed his gaze out over the hall, whose rafters vibrated with the beginnings of a raucous wedding feast.

His heart turned over that she should witness such a sight as these rough men. "Aye, my sweet, they are sorely impressive. Large beasts, aren't they? 'Tis to our benefit they are divided. We can overtake them more easily."

"Aye, but like any pack of wolves, these animals are lost without their savage leader." She took a sip of her own wine and struggled to swallow it.

From the depths of the hall, the three huddled together to gossip and become boisterous about their lady's newest husband and the bawdy time that man could have with so often wed a matron. Angel heard, for her delicate cheeks flamed with the crudeness.

"These three are different from the three Windom guards and Tom Carter. Though my first husband's father was not honorable with me, to his men he must have been noble enough to engender some respect."

"Have you no ideas what made them turn their loyalties?"

"I would say it was money and power that fed fear. Carlisle came, tagging behind him the authority not only of my father and uncles, but also that of King John. The Windom retainers, afraid for their lives, had to choose. Two requested to leave. One guard simply disappeared. These others turned with the tide."

"And left you alone on the shore of desperation."

Her mellow eyes searched his and he covered her hand with his. "God, I am glad you sent for me."

"So am I," she admitted with a smile that he knew the others would take for a bride's look of admiration for her new groom. "They know power when they see it."

"Fortunately, they also love to drink, don't they?"

"I purchased twice the supply days after Chretian died, saying it was for the period of the funeral."

He considered her with even greater esteem. "You did plan this wedding for a long time, did you not?"

"It was either this or . . ." Her voice dropped. "I know not what."

Her despair made his heart pound. Few possibilities offered hope of deliverance.

She picked at the crust of her trencher. "You don't know what it is to be taken and used."

Her sorrowful words skewered him. Perspiration broke on his brow as he remembered how it felt to be chained, whipped, hung inside a bamboo cage, and poked at, jeered, and taunted. He swallowed bile and forced himself to speak. "But I know quite well."

"How can a man understand what it is to be

bartered, sold, handed from one man to another as chattel—?" She turned her face away from him.

He brought her around with two fingers to her chin. "Think you that such things happen only to women and happen here in England? Nay, injustice can occur with men as well as women. Evil can live anywhere, my sweet."

"You say this with such certitude."

"Aye."

"But how can that be?"

He could reveal his past to her, but never here or now. It was too obscene a tale to tell a darling woman who needed to hear scintillating stories of the world's enchantments. Never its nightmares.

She sat spellbound. "Shame cannot be the reason you have taken to the forests. I swear I cannot see it of you, for you are so very stalwart and so—"

"The reason I live there is because I seek to live a free man. Free of John. Free of rules."

She stared at him. "If I were free of my restraints, I would be free of heartache."

"Perhaps it seems that way now, my Angel. But God does not put us on this earth to offer only paradise."

"Once it was so."

One side of his mouth hitched into a half-smile. "That was before Adam ate from the tree of knowledge."

"Aye, and now Adam's descendants live with the pain of that loss."

He retreated to old memories.

Her voice came to him, distant, sad. "So, then, you lost a woman whom you loved?"

Her question gave him pause. What truth was in her query? He had not loved Beatrice. He had wanted her as any boy would want the pretty child his father picked for him. But that was all. He had not known what it could be to love. He had never known. Only had he loved the usual things—his father, his land, his heritage. Always had he known what joy sexual pleasure with a woman could bring. But never had he loved. Never had he allowed it. Never had he asked himself if he turned from women because one had turned from him. And another had turned on him.

"I did not love her." He lowered his voice. "I assure you, Angel, I would take a wife in certain if I could."

She flowed closer. "You live without restriction from church or state. You could take a wife if you saw fit."

He chuckled lightly. "Aye, my sweet. I could have taken a wife long before this morn. But I did not and would not, for I have naught to give a lady save sorrow and deprivation. That is no life for a woman."

"Many women live in the richest of castles and still abide in sadness," she said, her eyes cast down, bitterness in each word.

"Tell me, dear heart, what did Carlisle do to you?"

"Chretian? Oh, Nicholas, he did nothing. Honestly. Never did he raise his hand against me."

"But others did."

"Aye. Chretian alone showed me respect . . . and left me to my own devices."

"Who were these others? Are they here? Now? Where may I find them?"

"Nay. Not here. Not yet. But they will come. For they are predators to the kill. Demere. My uncles. My father."

"What did they do to you, my Angel?"

"When my sister died and left the engagement to

97

the young earl of Windom open, my father did take me from my convent. He brought me home and told me that in one week's time I would take my sister's place at the church door in a wedding ceremony. I refused. He . . . he would not take my answer as a sacred one. I tried to plead and show him how I wished to make the church my life, but he laughed. He said I needed to learn respect and my place in the order of things."

Nicholas's heart wrenched to hear repeated the very same words one man once spoke to him. "So much evil is justified by more evil."

Her eyes met his, wild now with remembrance of scenes she thought she alone could see. But through the veil of his own, he could see her sorrow, feel her pain, know her loss. "My father told me I would wed this Windom boy-child for reasons of land and wealth. I told him that meant naught to me for I sought to live my days contemplating a land of heavenly wealth and joy. He . . . he only scoffed at me. When I refused again, he had his bailiff take me by the arm and lock me in the women's quarters."

"Alone?" He remembered what a group of Saracen women had once done to a girl who would not conform. With their sultan's blessing, they had beaten her until her skin grew black with bruises and her mind grew forever dim with torment.

"Aye. I was alone." She broke off portions of the day-old bread in great jagged hunks.

He caught her trembling hands and lifted them to his lips. With the warm breath of life, he pressed soft kisses to her palms and sought to bring her from the hideous reverie that he feared might fracture her mind here before him. "You are no longer alone, my blessed

Angel. And he cannot hurt you. Tell me what he did and then let us cast out this demon who hurt you."

Cold, she stared straight ahead. "He starved me."

"Mother of God."

"To this day, I love all things sweet and savory. Creamed sauces and sugared pears." She swallowed, ashamed and seeking some haven not accessible in this great teeming hall. "When I grow old, I think I shall be quite fat for all the sinful dishes I constantly desire."

Compassion and outrage filled his chest to the breaking point. With one move, he reached over and swept her to his lap. "You are safe and sound here with me, my Angel. And no one will say you nay to stews or puddings or any sugared pears. I think, in fact, I'll have my men bring you a supply of lemon drops from Antioch and candied apricots from Egypt."

Her gentle hand drifted from his cheek into his hair. "My husband, from such delicacies, I will soon be gumming my food."

"Nay. For have you ever seen a painting on a chapel wall of an angel grinning and toothless?"

That made her laugh. The way she threw her head back to do it told him much of how she hardly ever found such joy and how she deserved to, how she needed to and might not unless he provided such assistance.

"You are so very good for me, my husband."

"And you for me, my wife." He rubbed his thumb across the fullness of her lower lip. "I will make you laugh more often now that I know the way."

"I would have much more of this, but then . . ." Shadows crossed her eyes. "What will I do when you are gone?"

He sobered, but only for an instant. "Remember me and how it's done. Then you can imagine what I would say and you can smile at any time."

"I enjoy making you smile. Tell me, my lord, do you like music? I play a harp."

"Then, by all means, my wife, do. Where is it?"

She raised her hand to Nell who all this while had sat at the end of one long table with the Carlisle three, hand to chin in sullen watchfulness. When the maid approached, Angel sent her to her solar to fetch the harp. Then, winding her arms about his neck, Angel settled more securely and intimately to his flesh. Between her clothes and his, he could feel against his thighs her plush feminine petals pressing innocently near.

He barely breathed. If she knew she planted riper ideas with the seed of her proximity, she gave no sign.

On the contrary, she spoke of her expertise. "I have not played in many weeks."

He chuckled and shifted her in his arms to a position that he hoped would offer more relief to him, and instead provided more tantalizing impressions of the flower garden he wished to plow and sow and reap a harvest of succulent fruit. He swallowed painfully. "Perhaps, my sweet. But from the looks of this wedding party, they will not notice if you are proficient."

"You will."

"Aye, my Angel. I am not drunk." *Not besotted save at the sight of you smiling. Of you clapping your hands in a glee all too absent from your life until now.* "But I know good music when I hear it." He lifted his goblet to toast her.

"And good wine when you taste it?"

"Mmm. And the most lovely of all women now that I have found her."

She tilted her head, looking charmed and enchanting. "Think you I am that woman?" she asked breathlessly.

"I know you are."

"You are kind. Chivalrous." She was recovering enough to flush, her pearlescent skin taking on the blush of rarest gems.

"I am no more than declaring God's truth."

"No one has ever told me so before."

"Though they should have, I am pleased to be the first." He wended one long pale tress behind her ear. His fingers of their own accord slipped along her jaw and down her elegant throat to cup her shoulder. "You tremble."

"Aye."

His eyes shot from her heaving breast to her incomparable green eyes. "But you are not afraid of me."

She shook her head. Then grinned and glanced away. "I feel a fear which is a new one, but a welcome one. I know I am not afraid of you, but . . . because of you." Courageous once again, she faced him and whispered, "How can that be, my lord?"

"You like me. As I do you, my sweet Angel. Such does happen between some men and women."

"I have never known it to be so with any man. I have only ever known what horror men can inflict, as you said to your men this morning. Yet, I met you only a few hours ago and still I see that you are different."

"Of that I am very happy and most honored."

"And you do not see me as a widow of wealth and lands."

"Nay, you are far more than that. You are a woman of courage and grace and intelligence. A lamb sacrificed to others."

"You are a righteous man."

He smiled slowly as his arms tightened in possession. "Nay. But I am your man."

"As surely as if you were pledged to me by knightly vows as well as marital ones. I am most grateful, Nicholas."

"Aye, sweet lady." He saw Nell approach and raised his voice to feed the woman's curiosity. "Show me how much, will you? Here is Nell with your harp. Sing me a song of joy to suit this occasion."

Nell snorted indelicately. Pushing her black hair from her eyes, she gave her mistress and her new lord a withering look before she stomped away to resume her seat.

"Better than that, my Angel," Nicholas's golden eyes flashed like royal coins, "sing me a song of love requited, will you, my dearest? I do believe old Nell needs to have more bones stuck in her craw before your rich wine can bring her a good night's sleep."

Angel gave a trilling laugh. "For you I will do anything. For Nell?" She leaned over conspiratorially. "I'm sad to say nothing will make her laugh. So, in lieu of that, we'll see she gets deliriously sodden."

With that, she strummed the strings, flexing her fingers in anticipation and then in brief practice.

Suddenly, she struck a few chords and all turned. Those silent quickest were the Carlisle contingent. The visitors were also the most awestruck.

Save for Nicholas himself. He watched her, this Angel of his life, this heavenly woman who belonged to that phantom, the Devil of Midnight. And he marveled at her. Her fingers, plucking the strings of the harp with deftness. Her voice, the delicate chords rising from her throat. Her mouth, the perfect bow whose lush contours shaped such pretty sounds now —but uttered such hideous tales of murder, deceit, and base abuse. This lovely woman had been tortured by her father, accosted by her father-in-law, acknowledged by her first husband but only befriended by her second. Through it all, she had survived. She had retained her inner self, her sense of right and wrong, her integrity. And only then to come to the point where her own servants banded against her to accuse her of murder and thus wrestle from her the rights to her lands and wealth.

Aye, he had been correct this morn. Men did commit gross evils against women. In the name of power or money. Or just plain lust.

This woman had suffered and endured all those ills. For no man had ever treated this woman with justice.

But he could. He would.

He drained his cup and listened to her more closely as she sang of requited love between a man and his wife. Unbidden, the thought came that no man had ever treated this Angel with love.

Only he had come close.

Of a sudden, he knew he could come closer. If he permitted himself the pleasure. The luxury. But what good would it bring either of them? Pleasure.

And pain.

More sorrow than her heart was meant to hold.

And more agony than he had told himself he would ever allow himself. For certainly, he would never cause this Angel more anguish than she had already known.

But he could make the days sweeter. For both of them.

And the nights?

He worried the inner flesh of his cheek on that.

What of the nights, oh noble Devil? For sleep with her you must. And embrace her you will.

Nay.

Be not so fast to declare your honorable intentions. For these men will seek proof she is yours. Even now, that vermin Ross douses his sorrows in the wine and discusses something with his cohort, a Carlisle, which bodes no good for you. Think you he will let this marriage pass unchallenged? Unproven?

He would not dare.

Of course, he would. He will. You can rely upon it as you may predict the sun will rise tomorrow. He cannot let your victory over him go so easily. Here . . . See? Your wife has ceased her music. And Ross rises with his man. He comes. Wanting retribution.

Nicholas applauded Angel's efforts and ignored the weaving Ross as he approached the dais. Finally, when the man's bloated red-blotched face appeared below his, Nicholas arched a brow. "Ross, you may retire."

"Nay, my lord. We are your guests and cannot seek our beds until we know you and your lady wife have taken yours."

The swine.

Nicholas felt Angel stiffen, while Gainsbridge cocked an ear and leaned near. "Ross, my wife and I are not ready."

"Oh, do come, my Lord Forrester," said Gainsbridge with an encouraging light in his gray eyes.

"We are all exhausted from this day's events and cannot get our rest without you taking yours. Come, humor us, good sir."

Nicholas glanced down the table to see Geoffrey Devereaux nodding and Father Samuel yawning. Even the kitchen maid and two small squires at the far ends of the tables blinked from the need for sleep.

"Very well. Come, Angel."

Nell, who had stood just behind Ross, circled like a crow. "Do come with me, my lady. I will see you to—"

"Nay!"

All eyes shot to Nicholas as he sprang from his chair.

"My wife stays with me," he said more calmly as he fought back fear of what Nell might do to Angel if she had her alone. "Always." He could hear some snicker at this bridegroom's possessive nature. Ignoring it, he stepped toward Angel and scooped her high into his embrace. "Hold to me, my lady, and tell me where your rooms lie."

Curling her arms about his neck, she nodded, "Up the main stairs and to the left, my lord."

The diverse elements of the household followed, becoming more a unit in their effort to see the married couple bedded. Some guffawed at their own ribald jokes.

"Do not listen to them, my Angel," he crooned into her ear as he took the stone stairs.

"Nicholas, I have heard these songs before, you know."

He frowned. "You have?"

"Aye. Not when I married my first husband, of

course. He was too young to have any bedding ceremony, but naturally, with Chretian, I did."

"I see," he said, none too happy to be reminded that
once she had belonged to another.

"You need not be jealous, though."

"I needn't?" God, what was the matter with him?
Suddenly, he was carrying his wife to bed and he was
blathering.

"He never carried me off this way, but I prefer this."

"Is that so." He was now fuming, even if his wife
did like this show of brute strength. "Well, this is not
the custom, my sweet. But I won't let them have the
chance to remain with you alone. I can't."

"I know," she said as she planted a kiss on his cheek
and he muttered at the pliant appeal of her lips.
"What is the matter, Nicholas? Am I too heavy?"

"Nay. Just . . ." He stopped at the portal some
servant had flung open. "Is this your bedchamber?"
he asked Angel, and when she nodded, he spun to
glare at those who had crowded him on the stairs. "We
thank you for your kind assistance to this door. I
know you seek to enter here and do the usual stripping
and bedding. But that won't be so tonight or any
night, I tell you. For I need no help with that." He
evidently had given enough credence to that because
the crowd murmured in agreement. Even Ross nodded, grudgingly ready to leave these two to their lust.
"We bid you all good night."

He would have turned but for a hand to his sleeve.

"Nicholas, wait."

As others departed, Allen Gainsbridge pressed
something slick into his hand. "Here," he murmured.
"I almost forgot to give it you. Ibn gave me this this
morning. He said it was from your private store and

that you had asked him to bring it. I dare say it matches other beauties." He smiled serenely at Angel.

Nicholas smiled in thanks. "You and Devereaux have split the sentry duty here and on the wall walk?"

"Aye, Nick. Rest easy here. One of my men guards this door. Devereaux's men will change the shift with me and mine. No one will enter Windom who is not loyal to us and you, my friend. Sleep secure."

"My thanks and best wishes for a silent night, Allen."

When they entered her bedchamber and sealed out the world, Angel squirmed to see what was in his hand and couldn't. "Well? What did he give you?"

Nicholas felt some measure of safety as he had not known all day and sank against the door to grin. "Have you always been so greedy?"

"Nay!" she feigned, shaking her long hair back and smiling at him with such delight he thought he'd have to kiss those glorious lips or die. "Did Gainsbridge bring you something you intend to give to me?"

"Stop wiggling like that or I'll drop you!"

Her green eyes glistened like a cat's sensing cream. "No you won't. What do you have, my lord husband?"

"Close your eyes."

She did instantly. "You are a brigand."

"Aye, and do not forget it."

"Where are we going?" she asked as he passed her solar door to the larger bedchamber, where stood the massive curtained bed she had once shared with Chretian and would now retire to with him.

He set her on her knees. "Keep your eyes closed."

"What? What else?" Her face was a study in anxious delight. Her fingers danced along his forearms.

"My God, woman! Has no one ever given you a present?"

"Once. My mother gave me a silver cross to take to the convent. Are you giving me a present, Nicholas? Are you?"

He chuckled at her unabashed enthusiasm. Keeping one arm around her tiny waist, he let the item drop from his fingertips to its full length. It had been years since he'd looked at it. Eons since he'd ever thought he'd use it for more than an extravagant ransom. Odd. In a way, these priceless nuggets were buying someone freedom. How appropriate that the Devil could buy his Angel her rights.

She mashed her lovely lips together. "What are you doing? Oo-o-o, you are torturing me! Can I open my eyes now? What *have* you got?"

"Silence, my wife. What a little shrew you can become. Remind me never to bring you gifts again." *Every hour they'd arrive, by God.*

"Oh, Nicholas!" she groaned, "what is it that you have? You must tell me, for I—"

He placed a forefinger over her alluring mouth to still her words. "For you, my Angel, I have a bride's gift fit for a heavenly being." He took the necklace, draped it over her waterfall of hair and watched as it rippled over her shoulders and between her incredible full breasts to dangle at her waist. "Open your eyes, darling."

"Oh, Nicholas," she breathed, her hands spreading wide. Her long fingers twined into the rope of perfect white beads.

"They are priceless pearls which cannot match the beauty that you are, inside and out."

A cascade of silent words of wonder flowed from her lips as she gathered the length of pearls and stroked each one. She called his name. "How could you find such as these? Have such as these?" She let them fall and stretched up to frame his face with her two elegant hands. "They are so lovely. I have seen a few pearls, but smaller, less round, grayer and . . . Oh, Nicholas, they are too rich for me. I am not your wife. You must save them for the woman who—"

He gripped her arms. "You *are* my wife. Remember that. Take these. I will never have a better use for them than to offer them to the only perfection I've known that holds more grace than these poor bits will e'er possess."

Struck, she swayed to him as she stared into his eyes. "You would not speak a lie to me, would you?"

"Never, if I could tell you the truth."

"And . . . and these things you say are . . ."

"God's law, my Angel. I swear it."

Tears sprang to her lovely eyes and her misery sliced him. He wrapped her closer. "Darling, don't cry. Please, don't. There is much in the world over which to shed tears, but never over a compliment to your beauty. Don't."

He kissed her fine brows. "Don't."

He trailed his mouth down her soft cheeks where her sorrow had wet a path. "Don't."

He found her open mouth. Her responsive lips. "Oh, Angel, don't."

He crushed her close and sent his tongue into the savory recesses of her mouth. He bent her over his arm, noting how breast fit to chest and belly to loins. Running one hand over the curving arc of her hip, he moaned and molded her supple splendor to him with ravenous hands and body that needed only her to sate his hunger.

Her arms clutched him nearer as she murmured mindless things. Beseeching things. Mad things.

None of which could ever be.

He dragged himself away and held her at arm's length. Drawn to him by some invisible force, she swayed toward him and he caught her close again. "God help me, I love holding you."

She swallowed so hard he felt the convulsion down the length of his torso. She shook and he knew enough to name it ecstasy.

"That was a very different kiss from those this morning, wasn't it?" she said, her face to his chest.

He choked on his nigh-to-bursting frustration. "Aye. Our wedding kiss was one of discovery."

"And in the clearing, it was more . . ."

"Passion, aye. Call it what it was," he said and wished he could lie about it and thus deny its power. He stroked her hair.

"But this one was comfort." She looked at him in wonder. "There are more, aren't there?"

He avoided her dreamy eyes. "More a husband has a right to give a wife. But you are not mine."

He pulled her away from his chest and felt the cold reality of the winter's night seep into his bones. One look into her desolate eyes told him he needed to end this quickly. "For now we will to this bed for our much-needed rest. You to this side. And me to that. And in the morning, we shall rise to ferret out more clues of your late lord's death and put off others of your suitors."

Wordless, she turned and slipped away from him off

the bed. With downcast heart and disappointed body, he watched her walk around the corner to her solar where she might disrobe in solitude.

He wanted to say a thousand things. Point out the reasons why they could not kiss, at least not privately, not even publicly as they had just now. He wanted to bring her back, resurrect the laughing woman whom he held in his arms only moments ago. But he knew he could not.

Such talk would be superfluous. His Angel was a brilliant woman who needed no reminding of her terrible situation and the coil they must unravel together. He would not insult her by restating the obvious. And yet, to see her so dejected ripped at the fabric of his sanity and made him yearn to once more be a normal man, instead of the illustrious, elusive Devil of Midnight

But that course he had long ago ceased to consider feasible. And to explain all to her would only tempt more demons to dance on the grave of his hope.

Cursing, he turned to consider the bed. He would lie in it, God damn it, and he would sleep in it! He would keep his hands to himself and his mind focused on his task!

And as for your heart, Devil? What fate awaits that portion of your anatomy, lord of the dark?

Long into the night as icy blasts hit the castle walls, he lay flat on his back beside his silent, rigid Angel and asked himself the question for which he found determination as an answer. But no peace.

Chapter
6

Sobs roused him from a fitful sleep.

Gasps brought him bolt upright.

Angel was gone.

Heart racing, he threw the fur mantles from the bed.

A wavering amber light upon the stone wall told him a candle flickered in her solar.

Digging out the dagger that he had placed beneath his pillow, he crept forward.

If anyone so much as touched a hair on her head, he'd pin their testicles to—

Good Christ.

She sat, her ivory hair about her shoulders, one hand to her mouth, rocking back and forth and crying as if tomorrow would never come. No one accosted her, hurt her. He checked the corners of the solar. No one threatened her.

"Angel," he murmured as he dropped the dagger, went to her, and knelt. "Darling." He ran his hands through her silken tresses and the wealth defied his efforts, sliding over his hands as he drew her near. She shuddered, her tears flowing heavier than before. He gathered her to him, crooning nonsense all meant to bring her from whatever horror made her night a misery.

She came willingly, desperately. Her arms bound him hungrily and she buried her wet face against his bare chest. Still, she cried with no remittance.

Frantic, he felt her back. Through the thin linen of her chainse, he detected the sculptured flow of her muscles. All tensed. He ran his hands along her side to hear her whimper. In panic that she was in some mortal pain, he drew her away and she flexed her shoulders as if soon she would flee from him.

"Oh, Nicholas, let me go!"

"Look at me."

She shook her head.

"Sweeting, what ails you?" He dragged one hand through the veil of her hair and drew her face up as he pulled her close to his heart. His lips went to her cheek and to the corners of her eyes. "You must not cry," he told her and warned himself how he would not kiss her as he had scant hours before. "Tell me what is amiss. I want to help you."

"You can't," she got out on a shaking breath. "I wish you could. But no one can."

That terrified him. He gripped her with iron resolution. "What is it? A malady? I know many remedies. I have cures for headaches and back pains. Restoratives for—"

She placed two fingers over his mouth. "What ills I have not you, or anyone, can cure with a potion." She sniffed, her tears less copious, her misery as alive in her dear eyes as any he had seen in those possessed of evil spirits.

"What is it, then? You *must* tell me." He wiped her cheek with his thumb. "And why are you awake at this unholy hour of the night?"

"I was sewing."

"Sewing?" He winced, stupefied by an answer that made no sense to his alarmed brain.

She nodded and recovered enough to straighten. "I sew at night. I told you that. Or had you forgotten? No matter, I do it. Every night, in fact."

He now began to feel the effects of rising with such speed. "I am at a loss, Angel. Why would you sew tonight? I am here and Gainsbridge brought me my clothes to fashion me in the image of a knight. You need not awaken after such a day as we have had to do this." He picked up a length of black velvet that she had trimmed in gold braid. He dropped it to the stool.

"I did not awaken." She blinked and nodded at the confusion in his eyes. "I was awake. I hardly ever sleep, you see. I—" She bit her lip. "I sew at night to keep the dreams at bay. I cannot sleep for fear of the nightmares I shall surely have if I sleep before dawn. Only tonight, sewing did not help."

She rose from him and walked to the dying solar fire she must have lit. Its red embered glow cast enough light to make her body shine in profile through the sheer fabric.

Christ, she was created by a god who understood how mortal man might wish a woman crafted. Artless in her innocence, she made his mouth go dry. His tongue rolled around his cheeks, sucking on the taste of creamy skin, a cherry-tipped breast, and the very idea that beneath the frothy mound that curved her gown at the apex of her luscious legs awaited a peach of paradise, ready to be opened, licked, honeyed with his hunger for her.

He closed his eyes. He clenched his hands. To see her thus, and have her not, raised a siege of his desire to win a battle over his honor. He ignored the fight by focusing his forces to the cold issue of import. "I am afraid I do not understand."

She swirled to face him, hands behind her back. He caught a groan as it rumbled from his groin. Now he was presented with the complete if translucent sight of large blossomed nipples, willow waist, and the dark crescent that garlanded her womanhood. He had never grown this high and hard this fast. With his manhood straining his breeches, he shifted in his chair only to hum at the rub of fabric to taut skin. He forced his eyes to her ravaged face.

She did not let him suffer but began another litany that mystified him. "I have nightmares. Usually every night. No matter"—she licked her lips—"no matter where I sleep or with whom. I keep the demons away by sewing. I have become quite excellent at it and many of my serfs—whether Windom or Carlisle— will tell you I have done them proud with what they wear." She smiled valiantly, sadly. "Tonight, after you kissed me, I thought for a fleeting moment I would not dream. I caught a glimpse of some surcease I might claim and I . . ." She caught a ragged breath.

"I was wrong, though. I tried to fall asleep, but fear came strongly in me, as it always does at night. My heart pounded and my eyes glazed and I could not rest. I noted you did not either for the longest time and that brought comfort. But when you finally did close your eyes, I saw my evil ones come for me. I had to rise." She clenched her hands to white-knuckled fists.

"I had to sew. But I was not as agile as I usually am." She grimaced, even that show of distress not able to mar her extraordinary loveliness. "I kept pricking myself and so I made myself cry more from the pain of the needle than from the white-hot poker of my nightmares."

"What are these dreams then, that they can bring you such distress night after night?"

"They are hideous."

"Of that, I am certain." He went to her, a pain to move with so hot a need to have her, but a joy to take the few steps toward her and run his hands down her thinly clad shoulders. "Tell me what they are."

She shook back her hair, the act reminiscent of her gaiety when they had entered her chambers and she was effervescent in her delight at a possible gift. He would make her laugh that way again. He swore to God he would. But first, he would exorcise the devils who made her walk her floor every night. He told his body to desist and show her comfort.

With one hand to the small of her slim waist, he brought her enticing body securely to his own. With the other, he sent tender fingers splaying into her hair to cup her head. With a whisper, he urged her, "Tell me what haunts you. Often if you share a horror, it loses its power. Share yours with me and I will not disappoint you. For I have promised to support you in all things."

Her eyes drifted closed and she writhed a bit, seeming to savor the feel of his hands on her and his body against hers. Suddenly, her eyes opened and he saw she had surrendered to his will. "My Devil, those vows you spoke today were not real ones. Though I would wish they were, you need not do more than rid me of my current foes. My past ones you would have a hellish time subduing."

"You cannot know until you test my mettle, darling."

She surveyed his eyes. "You are so very kind. How could anyone rob you of what was yours and justify it? The hosts of heaven would scream in outrage."

"My Angel, you and I both know much injustice goes unresolved. Mine is one of those. Yours are not. Not the matter of your marriage and not this older ill. Describe it to me now, sweeting, for I would know all your cares and take them from you."

That brought forth trembling again, but also a torrent of words. "I dream horrible things which are, in fact, all true. Each one has to do with marriage." She caught the look in his eye and laughed sorrowfully. "I know 'tis ironic, but nonetheless a fact. These things I see at night I saw when I was fifteen and later . . . years later. The story I told you at dinner about how my father obtained my agreement to marry the heir to Windom? Aye. Well, 'tis so, but not the total story. For you see, I almost died from starvation. Know you what it is like to want for food?"

He nodded, remembering the gnawing of a thousand insects in his stomach for want of a morsel, recalling the parched need for a drop of water as he was left to burn in the desert, alone without hope of meeting another soul save in heaven.

"I cried. Locked up in that women's quarters, I became a madwoman. Weak and mewling. Wanting only to live and wishing I could die."

She shuddered so badly, he could no longer hold her

or stop the fear that mounted in his mind for what she meant to tell him. In one bold move, he bent and scooped her into his arms, striding to the alcove seat appointed with lush velvet cushions and thick hanging drapes. Here, he sat down and nestled her into his arms, arranging her cold limbs, one hand about his neck, the other in his own firm grasp. She settled there as if she had forever done so.

"How did you leave?"

"I was weak. Finally, craving release, I begged for it. For food and drink. I promised I would marry young Windom. I was so hungry, I would have promised anything that night for, you see, the first of my terrors had visited me. I saw visions of creatures too far from real. Winged beasts, black as sin, breathing vermilion flames."

"Beasts of hell," he offered from memories of his own.

"Aye." She pressed closer to him, her hand along his tensing jaw. "You have seen them?"

"When the mind is deprived of the staff of life, the body begins to provide other kinds of sustenance, none of it conducive to good sense."

"Nicholas," she mourned, and he turned to kiss her caressing hand.

"Give me the rest of your troubles, darling." He smiled sweetly into her large green eyes.

"I married Windom and, as you might imagine, because he was still a boy, I never slept in his chamber with him. 'Twas a godsend that I not disturb a child with my nightmares. For I was troubled by my memory of that winged beast long after I saw him. Especially at night. Then, to add to that, other things began to occur in the night. Other incidents as awful that made me fear men. Drinking, fistfights, brawls in the great hall. Arguments between the earl of Windom and his wife or son. One night, after such a dispute, my young husband ran to my rooms seeking refuge from his father, who meant to beat him for some misconduct. My father-in-law told me he would consider my protection of the boy if I agreed to do my father-in-law's will. I agreed, of course. The boy went free and then my father-in-law said he would return upon the following evening." She halted.

"And did he?"

She clamped her eyes shut and lowered her head.

Nicholas took her to his heart, his lips to her forehead. "Let it all come out, will you, Angel of mine? What did the man do?"

"He came to initiate me into the act of love," she whispered, and then buried her shame by hiding her face against his throat. "He said it was his price for saving his son. He came close. Laughing. I surprised him. I fought him. I had my needles, you see, and I used them in my own defense. He called me mad. I was, I know. I told him he must never come again to me, for if I did not tear him that night, I would one day when he would never guess I came upon him. He believed me and left me, never to darken my chamber door again."

Nicholas filled his lungs with air he had failed to draw as she spoke. "You were right to stop him thus. He was a madman himself to try to take that which was his son's. I see now why you would so loathe the night."

"Aye. But my tale does not end. There is more. It is similar . . . and worse."

If he could absorb her pain, he would have at that

moment. He bound her closer, as near as flesh could yield, and buried his lips in her floral-fragrant hair.

"When my husband and his parents fell ill and subsequently died, I was beside myself. Not so much with grief for the earl who had tried to take his son's rights, but for the boy who died so young and for his mother, who had tried to be kind to me. I thought their deaths a judgment on the entire house of Windom and felt perhaps I had not scourged some awful fault from my character, and thus could be responsible for their deaths."

"Nay, that kind of ecclesiastic teaching fails the test of logic, my sweet. Each man and woman is responsible for his or her own failures. No one else."

"I was more devout than reasonable then. Now I know better."

"Good. What changed your thinking?"

"What happened next did make my life . . . different." She gazed into her lap where their hands entwined, and where she began to trace the outline of his finger with one of hers. "After the dirges were sung for the Windoms and I did give alms to all for the repose of their souls, my father and two uncles came here. They were . . . solicitous. Kind. I had known so little of that, and none from men, that this new attitude on their parts amazed me and comforted me. I was thrilled. They asked me to come home for a while. To recover, my father said, from my grief. I took him at his word and went home to Lancaster with him. I was there two months in which he was kind and sweet to me. Then, one night he called me to his solar and told me what I must do."

She halted, her chest rising and falling with rapidity.

"What did he say?"

"He told me I was to wed again. I think my mind snapped. I told him he was crazed to think I would ever consider taking another man to me. He told me I would do as he desired—and immediately, too. I turned on my heel and left him, headed for the door, my horse, and my freedom. No man, I yelled at him, would ever take me to wife again. He had his men-at-arms seize me before I made the barbican. And then he—" She broke and would have jumped from his arms had he not clamped her to him with all the ferocity five years of living with Genghis Khan's army had taught him.

"Tell me all, dear heart. Tell it now. And fast. We'll cut this disease from you so that you never cry in pain again."

"Oh, *God,* Nicholas! He sent me to his dungeon!"
Jesus wept.

"He had his men take me, one for my hands, two others for my legs. They put me in one cell, a pit. Ancient. Filthy. With no torch. No food. Again, *again,* I starved. But this time, in addition, he let the worms and spiders come to test my strength of mind."

Her nails clawed at him. Her gorgeous eyes went wide, white horror showing more than the innocent green.

"He would open the trapdoor once a day. Telling me as he held the only candle I would ever see in that hellish place that he would set me free when I agreed to marry this new friend of his, this Chretian Forrester. I told him to go to hell. He told me I was in it. And he left me to my crawling, sordid state. I was . . . far from what you see me now. I was ragged and raving. Starving and eaten alive with the nibblings of a thousand tiny creatures who came to feast on my flesh."

His gorge rose. He wanted to shout *no more, no more,* but knew she had never told a living soul of this, her degradation. And he understood that to rid herself of the obsession of her nights, she had to tell it all, reveal it now or never live a peaceful day.

"How did you manage to survive?"

"I know not, fully. But I will say to you, whether 'twas hallucination or fact, I thought I saw a vision appear. An angel I would call her. My own watchman, I could surmise."

She smiled. "She came to me, this talisman, and told me I was meant for happiness and great love. That I was meant for more than this cruel treatment and that if I persevered, if I gathered hope, much joy awaited me. I know not now if I believed her, but I do know I asked myself then if I could just simply die. Do you know what I learned, Nicholas?

"I learned in that filthy stinking pit that I loved life, what little I had seen of it to enjoy. I loved the sunrise and the rustle of tree leaves in a spring rain. I loved to go hawking and to sew. I wanted to know more of that, though I had no one ever to call my friend to share them with, save a god who often turned his face from me. I could not will myself to die, so I chose to live. I told my angelic visitor I would marry this Chretian and hope for better than I had received. I called for my father and he came, accepted my word I would marry, and led me to the man.

"The odd thing was marrying Chretian *was* better than the last union. He was kind and considerate to me. He was more of a friend than I have ever known. No one came to me threatening to rob Chretian of his marital rights. No arguments or brawls occurred. Certainly, I had heard from the villagers about the ruthlessness of Chretian's men, but I had no power to deter them. I was a woman only. A wife, merely. Oh, I was wealthy, a widow of Windom, but that was all. And then one night, just as I thought the joy I was promised by my heavenly visitor was that which I shared with Chretian, he died. Worse, he was murdered in his bed. And Eugene Demere accused me, and his other men supported him. And more nightmares began that pervaded my days."

She stared at Nicholas, her eyes seeing far beyond him. "You understand now why I hate the night. I cannot sleep. All things morose and evil come to me then."

"Aye, my darling. I know now, and while I am appalled, I will tell you this. You need to rest. You cannot go through your life without some balm for your days' cares. You will sleep now. I will see to it. For now, for as long as it takes to rid you of your demons of day and night, I will be here for you. Trust me to make it so."

She considered his eyes, his mouth. "I believe in you as I have never believed in anyone, my Devil."

He crushed her to his heart. "Think you that you will come to bed now, sweet? I will but hold you and the night will pass to dawn."

"And would you also kiss me?"

He tipped his head down and gazed into her yearning eyes. "Ah, Angel mine, if I kiss you, there is so much beyond it I do crave. I may be the Devil of Midnight to many, but here with you, I am merely a man."

"Then what if I kiss you?" Before he could object,

she elaborated. "I would learn if what I saw before when you kissed me was imaginary or real. And then, too, if I initiate the act, you need not fear to break your code of honor."

"To kiss you is heaven, Angel, but also hell. You are a widow and you know kisses are the prelude to the act of love between a man and woman."

Searching his features, she suddenly went lax. Unutterably sad, she turned, slid away and, with shaking hands, took up her needle and the length of black velvet from the stool.

Pain severed him from his resolve. Logic was vanquished as well. After all, would it not be simple to fill her requirement? He had learned long ago and far away to control his baser instincts and offer up the refined act of bliss.

He reached for her two cold hands and stilled them, uncurling the delicate fingers from their artful attempts. Shielding her hands in his giant ones, he brought them to his mouth, and with his eyes consoling hers, he placed tender kisses in her palms. If he could only kiss away one of her sorrows, one of her awful memories, he'd do it.

He wound her hands around his neck, gathered her back in his arms where she belonged, and sat with her cuddled in his lap. She watched and waited, barely breathing.

His fingertips descended to her jaw and raised her face. Her two lips parted, their glossy pink allure promising delights untold. He cupped her chin and let his thumbs graze the lower line of her lip. She quivered like a little bird, her thighs clamping in his lap. He wondered if she understood the message she gave him with that move. She wanted him as completely, as badly as he wished for her.

Kissing her might seem a simple event to her, an exploration to find this nirvana she had but glimpsed last time their mouths met. But to him, this blending would yield a thousand new joys and, he feared, a foretaste of the greater banquet she could lay before him. He knew it as surely as he knew the stars shone or the moon glowed.

He knew it, and God help him, he ignored it. For to please her now meant more to him than his own peace in body or mind. To aid her offered more earthly reward for him than any denial might have won him in heavenly merit. Aye, he'd kiss her—but he'd sip every drop of joy from her mouth a mortal man could covet.

He put his thumbs to the two corners of her mouth and made her open wider. "You are the most beautiful woman. Your mouth is a flower made for a man to tend and admire."

She stilled, enchantment filling her features.

He ran the pad of his finger along the rise of her lower lip. "Your skin is soft, too. Finer than the sheerest silk from the grand rivers of the Chinese realm."

She vibrated.

"Aye," he murmured and ran one hand into her hair while he noted how she fluttered her lashes in desire. "There, beyond the land of a thousand breezes, they spin silk threads which, woven, cling like supple skin to a woman's body and tear the fabric of any fair-minded man's intentions. Like you do to me, my Angel."

He brought her face inexorably closer to his own and felt her sighing hot breath escape her. "You give me your air of life and so now take mine." He hovered above her, his mouth not touching but imparting. She trembled but inhaled his gift. As reward, he placed his lips on hers so briefly, so fleetingly, he imitated a silk moth's caress.

She called his name in a long tone of need.

"Aye, darling," he spoke atop her quivering lips. "You wanted a kiss and so you have one unheralded one, my sweet Angel. Any pleasure delayed is ecstasy magnified."

Her voice reached him like muffled bells of deep desire. "I did not know I could yearn this much."

"Nor I, pretty peony. Open your pink petals wider. Show all your hidden secrets to me. Aye, like that." And when he knew she would have expected him to devour her, he skimmed his lips across her cheek to her fragile ear.

She moaned in protest. Her fingers plucked at his bare shoulders while he rubbed the tip of his nose around the leafy perfection of her ear, only to bite the tip and make her buck within his arms.

It was then he swirled her down to the cushions, secured her beneath him, and framed her lovely face with his two reverent hands.

Beneath his pulsing body she writhed, exultant and eager with the ardent agony they aroused each in the other.

"Tell me how you want me now, my Angel."

She licked her lips and cut the last thread of his iron will. "I throb. I burn. I'll die for lack of you."

Groaning, he took them both from their tantalizing starvation and fit his mouth to hers.

The meeting was a mating that brought a harmonious cry from each of them. He reveled in it, in her, in the gossamer essence of her lips and the smoothness of her tongue as he touched the tip of his to hers, heard her purr, and then sucked her, sound and all, into his mouth.

She grabbed fistfuls of his hair.

God, she knew how to kiss, how to receive, how to give.

She opened wider for him.

He came inside willingly, sweeping the tip of his tongue along the roof of her sweet mouth and down along her plush cheeks. He drank her ardor's succulent juices like a thirsting man's fondest libation.

He had never drunk at such a revel. Never known such instant intoxication. She had no equal. She soared above all those other women whose essences he had tasted in the gush of eager youth and sated older age. This meeting of his mouth to this Angel's came like the discovery of a new land, opening up new vistas for delight.

He crushed her closer. *"Cara mia,"* he caught himself calling in his mother's language and in his own euphoria. The shock of that reality intruded on this interlude, which had so quickly surpassed all understanding.

He hesitated.

She clung.

He had to end this . . . or spend the night repeating this delight and teaching her others. He trembled at the loss, but she kissed him wildly. Captured, enraptured, he explored her mouth and then paused, a second skin to the contours of her own. Withdrawing, he caressed her almond eyes, her crescent brows. Her fawn-colored lashes drifted open and shut, her green gaze serene and misty as her hands smoothed his shoulders and her fingers threaded through the hair on his chest. He schooled himself to inhale the musky perfume her body yielded to the air about them. If she could want this badly with only a kiss, she would surrender greater celestial wonders in the supreme act of love. And he admitted he would even bargain with his faithless God to be the one to instruct her in the delicacies of delayed joy, endless unions, boundless human ecstasies.

Aye, it was a temptation for a saint. But thanks be to the God who had not deserted her, this Devil was a mortal man who had been trained in self-control, even unto the ancient erotic arts of mating *yin* with *yang*. He could take her, slake her desire and his, but then, he would once more have to face his own lack of honor. To kiss her thus had to be enough. It must be all there was to this affair he called his marriage, his heaven and his hell on earth. He would see it so. He *would*.

Eternities passed before he shifted, lifted her, and sat with her, his fingers tangled in her heavy hair, her arms entwined with his, her head upon his shoulder, her mouth against his throat.

She reached up to kiss him briefly and he tasted traces of the elixir they had brewed together. "I think I was correct about what visions I saw when you kissed me."

He gazed at her serenely and smiled. "What did you find with this kiss?"

"No beasts. Only fields of peace." She placed a hand against his cheek. "If I could see only that, I could sleep forever."

"One night is sufficient for now."

"I will try."

He grinned at her as he rose, strapping her to him with arms aching to possess all her charms always. "I'll put you in your bed then, so that we can test this method of inducing sleep in tireless young women."

She laughed lightly as he placed her in her spot and tucked her beneath the covers. When he did not climb next to her, she began to object.

But he dragged one of her chairs near the bed and sat in it, facing her.

"Nay, my Angel. I will not share the bed." She was no virgin, but nonetheless a widow to revere. "'Tis too dangerous to your virtue and my honor that I do so. I will instead stay here. And you will close your eyes and dream of a golden land of quietude and freedom."

"You will not leave?"

"Never."

When she awoke, amazed she had discovered sleep so easily, she found him in the very same spot. His hands steepled before him, he narrowed his eyes at her in delight.

She struggled up on an elbow. "You did not leave me."

He grinned, a slow and glorious dawn to a new day when she might trust a man to keep his word.

She gazed toward the solar where hazy sunlight cast a few bleak rays. "Is it past the time for morning prayers?"

"Almost time for dinner, my slumbering Angel." He cocked a brow, ready to laugh outright.

"Oh, they will all wonder if we're ill!"

"I would say that hours ago they did conclude we exhaust ourselves to celebrate our union as man and wife."

She wanted to say they had. But she knew, of course, they had taken only one small step along a path of ecstasy. Her body pulsed at the memory of the forceful touch of him, the titanic feel of him, the tender sound of him speaking such words of praise as she had never suspected a man could surrender to a woman.

She went up on her knees, her scope taking in the well-tended chamber fire, the black cloak that draped his broad, naked shoulders and his dark-shadowed precious eyes. "Did you sleep?"

"I watched over an angel."

She returned his gentle smile. "May I return the favor and protect a guardian devil as he rests?"

"Nay. I need no more, for I have found my repose in your respite from your nightmares."

She blazed to full awareness at his sweet admission. "You are far kinder than anyone I have ever known."

"And you are far more worthy of that consideration than anyone I have ever met."

"Not so, my Devil. Have you not seen, heard? I have lied, cheated, manipulated, and loved life more than an honorable death. My saints above, I even abducted you to gain my wishes!"

Totally unaffected, he stood, drew near with his pervasive presence, and lifted her chin to stare into her eyes. "Listen to me, my heavenly one. What you have done you did for good and proper reasons. Even seizing me. I see your motives and I wipe your ledger clean of sin. Do you hear me? I'll have no more talk of what you are and what you've done or not. We will instead have baths drawn and prepare ourselves to meet your most unnatural father and his brothers. Then, too, should your common chamberlain show his face this day, I have a thing or two to take up with that lout. Rise up, my darling, and prepare yourself for another day in your journey to freedom. No one will waylay you. For you are allied with an avenging devil, and husband or not, I will see to it no one will ever hurt you again."

Chapter
7

But no one came that morn.

No one could. The frozen rain of yesterday had turned overnight to an ice storm that trapped the land in a taut silver sheet. No creature moved over it. An occasional bird flew above it. One large white fowl in particular circled and darted for the castle walls, only to return to the forests.

Intrigued by the familiar bird that she had seen yesterday in her forest, Angel sat gazing at it through the crystals glazed to her solar glass. As it sailed toward her forests once again, she turned to watch two servants enter with a tub, followed by none other than Nell.

Angel wrapped her chamber robe about her more securely, her heart tripping over the presumption of the woman. The servant woman hastened in, giving instructions to the men who set the tub before the roaring fire and filled it with hot water for the new lord's bath, then put other buckets aside for Angel's later use.

Nell had always been arrogant, even with Chretian, who was stern with her, but for some inscrutable reason he tolerated her unruliness. For Nell to come here with this kitchen crew this morning displayed a greater measure of her vain valor, especially since Nicholas had shown such avid distaste of her. Certainly the servant came to ferret out any morsel of information she could take below and save until Demere's return. She would do anything to get that, even pretend to accept this marriage of her mistress. But more, Angel knew the woman came to test the resolve of the new lord of Windom Castle. She came head held high, breasts bobbing, and hips swaying as she set down protective sheets upon the floor and tested the temperature of the water with two fingers, which she licked, gazing at Nicholas.

He did not appear to notice. Angel thanked her God for that. She wished her Devil to never see another woman, save this woman he called his wife. Never want another woman, except her. Never kiss another woman as he had her last night. For what had happened then may have sent her to sleep, but the euphoria had spun through her dreams and curled through her every conscious thought of him for the past hour of her waking day. Aye, her lips had tasted the elixir of a devil. And she thirsted for more.

Unaware, Nicholas continued to pore over Demere's ledgers as he had since long minutes ago, when he had ordered Michael Ross to bring them from Demere's chambers. Ross had loudly objected but succumbed, no other recourse open to him without Demere to protect him.

Nicholas looked up at the three. "All of you may go."

The two men bowed themselves out the chamber door.

Nell sauntered to the bed, plumping pillows, straightening sheets, and pulling the covers high. She crossed the room, then loitered at the steaming tub, her gaze darting to Angel, who made no sign to assist her husband into the bath and thereby do her chatelaine's duty.

"Nell?" Nicholas called.

The woman smiled at Angel, her red lips spread in satisfaction at the sound of the Devil's soft question. "Aye, my lord!" Clearly, from the way she preened and narrowed her eyes at Angel, Nell thought she might be called to substitute for the new master's wife, and she whirled to come face-to-chest with him.

"I said *all* may leave. That does include you." He pursued her backward to the door. "Do not bother to return. For if I see you in this chamber again, I will demote you again. This time you may not expect the niceties of cooking and washing, or even the charms of cleaning the guarderobe pit. Next time I will turn you out to the cold world beyond. Get you gone. *Now.*"

Nell needed no more.

Watching until the woman closed the door, Angel sighed in relief. She wished no other woman to experience the same untamed appreciation she herself had found for this broad-shouldered, lean-hipped giant, whose mouth and hands brought her rampaging pleasure. Desire, sharp as her dagger, pricked her conscience. For beneath that layer of rectitude stood a ribald truth she could not deny.

She wanted his naked body exposed to her alone.

Heat flared in her cheeks at the very idea. She put

her hands to her face to cover her erotic thoughts and turned to her solar. But her husband followed her and lifted her chin with his fist.

"Nell needs someone to put her in her place."

"You do it well, my lord."

"You can do it just as well and better."

"Most here—save for Peter, Edwin, and Leon—are either Windom's or Carlisle's. I am a Montrose. None would give allegiance to me."

"Of course, they would. They will."

"I have not your commanding presence, my Devil."

"You have better, my Angel. You possess the right to rule them. You have inherited it—and if we are truly to win here, you must grasp the power that is yours and use it so that you may keep it long after I am gone."

Regretting the day that would come, she sank to her alcove seat. "I admit I am at a loss, good sir."

One knee to her cushions, he leaned over her. "Look into my eyes, my Angel, and tell me that the woman who managed to escape this castle and capture the bandit who has roamed this shire for two years is not capable of seizing control of a few vassals."

"You may twinkle those sweet eyes at me, sir, but I have no experience in controlling people, especially men."

He examined her mouth. "I know one man you sway with any smile."

Words eluded her. Elation made her vision hazy, her hope view a clearer possibility of happiness with a man.

He blinked.

The moment died, but her mind's eye fixed her sights on new possibilities. Nicholas had other ideas to which she forced her consideration.

"Power comes when you have shown those you lead that you not only demand it, but will use it to all ends. Continued control comes because you are considerate, moderate but decisive. You can be all of those and more. I have seen it. Have you ever adjudicated a matter here at Windom?"

"Chretian did that. Before him, it was my first husband's father who presided in his own leet court. No woman I ever knew has ruled over such matters, only over her kitchen staff."

"I know many women who take control of more. A dowager countess in Lincoln who cows her knights and vassals with her knowledge of iron-working. She owns a foundry. Another lady of my acquaintance leases her lands yearly instead of perpetuity, and so has built a treasury the pope would shamelessly steal."

A wicked whisper in her head asked how and why he knew so many women. Ghosts of other faceless, nameless fortunate women who had talked, laughed, and kissed him floated before her, taunting her. Stricken that he was hers for a small space of time, she shook her head adamantly. "I know nothing of iron-crafting, nor have I the ability to change the perpetual leases here to annual ones. 'Tis written in the entail how Windom lands and Carlisle's can be rented."

"But you possess something else more valuable."

"And pray tell what would that be, good sir?"

"You know injustice when you see it, smell it. For you have suffered at its hands and can empathize with those who know its misrule."

"You are right. But I can think of nothing which needs adjudication here and now. Especially with Demere away to fetch Bartlett, all seems quiet. In fact, whenever that man is gone, peace reigns."

"Is that so? And does Demere leave Windom often?"

She thought on that. "Once or twice a month."

"And does he tell you where he goes?"

"Not me. Once Chretian told me Demere went south to visit Bartlett. Once he took a gift from Chretian to King John on the birthday of one of the king's children." She noted how Nicholas ground his teeth at the mention of the two he meant to defeat here with her. "I wish I knew more."

"You have learned much in the four months you were married to Chretian."

"Ah, but not enough about Demere to thwart him."

"Perhaps we can change that. The accounts that Demere keeps are interesting reading." He inclined his head toward the leather-bound pages on the table. "How did he take them from your Peter's care?"

"He came to Chretian one day and said he had heard complaints of inconsistencies in fees charged for cutting trees and in selling surplus goods at market. Chretian believed him and took the auditor's responsibility of charging them from Edwin and the responsibility of recording them from Peter."

"And Chretian did this without questioning Peter or Edwin?"

"Without even asking Leon, who knows everything which occurs in our forests, including . . ."

The idea struck her that Leon knew her forests, from each sapling to its thousand soaring crows. Reared at the edge of Montrose's northern glen, he had found favor with her father for his innate knowledge of all who walked their woods. The reason Leon came with her retinue to Windom years ago was because her father had wished to preserve some of his power within her Montrose dowered lands. And her wood ward had proven faithful and diligent, just as Peter and Edwin had. But now Angel wondered if Leon had other interests. If he had not merely observed, but perhaps even tolerated the existence of the brigand called the Devil of Midnight and his disciples in her forests.

"Including what?" Nicholas prodded.

She examined her Devil's deftly carved good looks, his colossal chest, strong hands, and sturdy thighs. "Including the fact that Leon knew how big and broad a Devil would measure so that I might sew the creature a guise to fit a husband." She cocked a brow, confused—and not.

"'Tis easy to fit a man like me." He lifted his hands to display them for her. "Simply imagine twice the size of any other man."

She smacked her lips and wobbled her head from side to side. "You think to deflect my question with such silliness?"

Molten gold swirled in the depths of his amused and appreciative eyes. He bent so near again she felt the cauldron of his body heat. "Tell me you have seen a man my like."

His proximity stole her humor, replacing it with a desire so palpable she dug her fingers into her palms. His question robbed her of good sense. Honesty came blurting out. "Never, my lord. 'Twould be a sin for me to lie and say I have ever met your match."

She could have sworn before Almighty God he

138

meant to kiss her then. His lips came close. Her breath drew his. Here and gone in the flicker of the candle that burned at the altar of her desire for him, he put distance between them, yet took her hand and smiled as if they were friends.

"Come. Take your bath."

She forced herself to think of everyday things like baths and formalities. "You should be first and I should wash you. 'Tis my duty."

As if hit by an ax, his control split before her eyes. *"Nay,"* he ground out. "You will not touch me thus. Nor will I stay to tempt myself with the nearness of you. I have a task to do. While you enjoy those soothing waters, I will take a candle and search this corridor you spoke of yesterday morn. I need to find its outlet and get word to Ibn, if indeed he and my others have not found the entrance themselves. Meanwhile, Devereaux's men are on guard, so you should have no fear anyone will enter."

His eyes ran down her chainse. He drank in every contour of her body. His hands clenched. "Take your bath. In privacy."

He was gone for interminable minutes. But not long enough to miss what he had taken such pains to avoid. She was stepping over the rim of the tub when he emerged from his exploration in the tunnel. Brushing cobwebs from his glossy hair, he rounded the corner from the guarderobe. His candle sputtered, then took the air and burned higher, brighter. His eyes flashed as he took one glance at her—her hair piled high but dripping ringlets from the steamy bath, her nude body sluiced with water, her nipples rising, hardening to the touch of his golden flames—and he halted.

Like a sleepwalker, she took a towel to her chest.

With her gaze only for him, she felt how the material barely covered any portion of her anatomy adequately. Every inch exposed to him, he savored. Then, followed one large drop as it wended from throat to breast and below the towel.

She shivered.

His eyes flew to hers. Hell's torment lived within his gaze and she would not see him suffer.

Modesty exiled for curiosity's sake, she took two steps forward. So did he. She took his hand.

Her touch made him wince. He spun—and gutted the candle with a rough pinch of finger and thumb.

He made for the chamber fire, rubbing his hands together and glowering into the flames. "Now I can understand why you could not find the corridor's exit. 'Tis a hideous maze, ancient as a pharaoh's tomb."

She took up a larger towel and forced her mind to this matter. "Did you find the door in the curtain wall?"

"Nay. I did find a surprising passage to the wall walk. Only one of Devereaux's men was on duty. It is too blustery to mount a full watch. It was fortunate, for I was able to receive a message from Ibn, who sits in your forest."

"How could that be? Does he write in the sky?"

"In a sense, you might say that." He opened his palm. "These came from the heavens for you. I think they will make a wonderful adornment to a hair comb."

Towel clutched securely about her breasts, she took three steps to view his prize. Two small stones of pale, true green sat in his hand.

"Gorgeous," she said as she fingered one smooth surface. "What are they?"

"Jade."

"How could you acquire these?" Her eyes met his laughing ones. He recovered while she still hungered for things she could not have.

"Get dressed and I will show you."

"Upon the wall walk?"

"Of course."

"You are too smug. What secrets do you know?"

He twitched a dark brow over golden eyes that swirled down her body in all the sensuous fury a woman could crave from a man. He straightened and cleared his throat. "For that you must come with me, my Angel. Besides, I would have you know how to send a message to Ibn."

He did not say why, but she knew he meant her to be capable of everything and anything to save her and him if perchance he could not. . . . Nay, the idea was past bearing.

"What of the direction of the tunnel?" she asked him, her mind seeking other subjects except his nearness. "That is another possibility of escape . . . if I can ever brave it."

Compassion lit his gaze. Desire supplanted it. Still, he spoke of the corridor. "I would say you were correct that it runs to the curtain wall. I'll find it tomorrow."

She drew close to him, her towel firmly in place over her breasts and her body dried more by the embers she'd seen flash in his eyes than by the fire that blazed on their hearth. On thread of a sound, she asked, "You will go again?"

"Of course." He drew back and she knew he made his eyes very carefully go to her own and nowhere else.

"I need to know if there is an escape route from here if things begin to go badly for us."

"You mean if someone feels threatened by us enough to kill us."

He did not need to nod. He simply stared into her eyes.

She licked her lips. "Aye. I thought so."

"Did you think this corridor could be the escape route of others?"

"The person who killed Chretian? Aye." She gripped the towel defensively. "Fantastical as it sounds."

"Mayhap you think that no one else could bring themselves to enter it because you dislike such dark and dreary places so."

She pressed her lips inside her mouth. "Possibly." She had feared others would know and might come to take her life as they had Chretian's. She did not want to die, but live—and perhaps now, live with other hopes lighting the bleakness of her days.

Nicholas had frozen as if he had heard her fears, her hopes. "Have you ever heard others speak of its existence?"

"Nay. Not servants, who usually know such things. Nor Lord or Lady Windom, who shared this chamber before I came here to occupy this room as widow to their son."

"How then did you discover it?"

She curled a shoulder. "One night I was awake and it was very late. I walked the floors"—she checked his compassionate eyes—"as usual. I thought I heard scurrying. Footsteps. I Thought I was going mad. For these walls are thick and solid, and never have I had one inkling of the activities beyond a chamber. I followed the origin of the noise . . . and there," she pointed to the right-angled convolution in the wall that led to the guarderobe, "I put my hands upon the stone and with a touch, it yielded. I took a candle, anxious to prove to myself that I was not mad . . . but I found nothing. I could not." She sank dejected to her solar seat. "I became too frightened of those things I felt—and of those I remembered, rather than of those things I thought I heard."

Somehow his hands had circled her and his fingers traced her backbone. Her cheek was pressed to his chest, and her arms, of their own accord, went round his waist. When he spoke again, he nestled his lips atop the crown of her hair and whispered, "That was natural. But you need not fear. No one will hurt you now."

So he had said and so he had provided. Her head fell back and she smiled up at him in gratitude.

But what she saw in his face resembled no friendly protectiveness. His half-lidded eyes burned into hers and swept below where he caught his breath and clutched her arms. Inhaling mightily, he brought her up in a slow slide along his virile body. With the scrape of his wool tunic against her bare skin, her breasts tingled, sensitized by this new delight to add to the litany of the wonders she continually found in his embrace.

"You are this Devil's damnedest temptation," he rasped as trembling hands crushed her to him and she felt elation at his closeness and soaring hope that he might once more kiss her. His hands traveled her spine, cupped her derriere, and lifted her to him.

Again, she felt the iron evidence of his desire for her. And though she had learned long ago with the old earl of Windom how such display might strike terror into her soul, this did the opposite. She rejoiced and knew her vision of joy with a man was but a lifeless icon compared to the reality of delights with this one made of sinew and hot blood.

Her head fell back. She stared at the beauty of this virile man who craved her. Her naked nether parts shamelessly fused to his.

She only wanted more.

His hands kneaded her willing flesh. He hitched her legs up around his hips and, grinding his teeth, raised her higher. She felt her velvet drapes against her back as he supported her against the alcove wall. He gripped her, his hands convulsive, as he dipped his head and drew one begging nipple into his mouth with one long, dark pull to rapture.

Breathless, she arched to yield him more. The branding shock of his suckling turned her bones to tallow, her will to his. He stroked her with his demanding tongue, shaping her with little dexterous licks into a burning cone of need.

"Your breasts are exquisite as your mouth," he rasped as he sought the other nipple, and she helped him by twisting her body to offer him access. He kissed this yearning aureole and then drew her taut into his mouth. She felt her nipple bloom inside his scorching velvet cavern. Resembling the ardent ministrations she remembered he had given to her mouth last night, this laving brought her one wild new delight.

Holding her with his lips, he caressed her nipple with the soft underside of his tongue. A joyful cry erupted from her as she evaporated in his hands.

"You are gloriously wanton," he growled and laid

them both down to the cushions. Lighter than clouds as she was, she marveled that she felt the wonders of his lips as he took an intricate journey along her jaw, her throat. His hand covered one breast, his thumb and fingers circling, then feathering the crest.

"More," was all she could think of.

"Aye, anything you want." He slid his hand along her bare body, his reverent fingers squeezing, shaping, claiming ribs and waist and thigh. "God," he said like an invocation. "You're everything *I* want."

The affirmation worked miracles, but his lips once more on her breast sent her to heaven. He kissed her and laved her, then sucked her into the fiery core of his mouth and let her go. At this sorcery, she offered up nonsensical hosannas to his wizardry.

"You like this. And what of this?" He lightly took the peak of her other breast between his teeth and lifted her.

She shot back in a bow's arc.

"Ah, my own Angel, so appreciative, so ready. What of this, darling? What of this?" While his mouth held her captive, his hand went in search of her hip and belly and found her woman's mound. His fingers dipped into her curls and pressed.

His discovery became her own.

He cupped her with a searing palm, holding her for endless moments as she felt herself swell into his care. With infinite grace, he slid one long finger along her lips. His mouth brushed hers as another finger parted her and his thumb touched a point that made her jolt. "A pearl of infinite value. So round and smooth. Hard. But I can make it harder, my giving Angel, larger and wetter with your own sweet polish."

She thought she'd fly apart when his fingers sluiced

along her lips and she heard liquid part. But he caught her to him. "I'll make you soar, sweeting. Let me anoint you with your own desire." He bathed her. All along her yearning, burning lips, he stroked her, opening her enough to please her but tease her to want more. Gathering her essences with reverent fingertips, he caressed and petted her, then swirled the jewel he brought to pleasured throbbing with the salve of her body and his fingers and his unholy care.

"Nicholas . . ." She dug her nails into his chest and felt a ferocious power invade her loins.

"Soar, Angel. I'll be here, darling." He took her mouth and offered paradise. Suddenly, her lower body swelled, burst, rocketed to the heavens in tempo with his rhythmic fingers. She moaned, panted, shuddered, and clung, wanting him to offer more sustenance to fill the spasmed emptiness of her body, her heart, her life.

But he merely held her and crooned to her, taking her from the blinding, pulsing ecstasy of heaven back to earth.

Her eyes drifted open and met his.

In that instant, she knew he wouldn't venture with her any further. Sadness dwelled within the gilded depths of his gaze. His eyes went to her own mouth, open and needing his.

He shook his head in denial, but his eyes traveled to her breast and stroked her with his eyes. He reached to the floor for her towel.

She stopped him with a hand to his wrist.

He would not look at her. "Nay. You are divine, my darling. But we must end this. I cannot take you here."

Oblivious, mutely arguing her own point, she rose to spread nibbling kisses along his square jaw.

His head dropped back, exposing the corded column of his throat. "Christ's agony, I can't take you anywhere."

She tasted on his skin the moist torment of his admission. She sought to give the only consolation her lips might bring him. Amid the turmoil, she identified the flavors of his passion. Like pepper and spice from some far-off land, he tasted like incense, mysterious and addictive.

"Angel." It was a prayer, a plea, an agony. "Darling, no more kisses."

She felt him peel her from him, the rush of reality too frigid for such a morn. She closed her eyes, treasuring what had been and wishing she could have enjoyed more. But he was setting her to her feet and wrapping the towel about her. Tightly. "You will dress and I will take my bath. We have matters to settle and none of them can wait."

And what of this matter between us, my special Devil?

She bit back her retort, saw he was determined, and spun away to dress.

Minutes later, within the cozy nook of her cushioned and curtained solar, she sewed steadily, but not calmly, while she listened to him at his bath.

With every stitch she took, her ears tuned to the hectic splashings of the water. He was disturbed, tempted, sad. The same as she. She envisioned how he looked, his bold face with square jaw clamped against his needs, the water drops clinging to the ebony hair across his classic chest and dribbling to his ribs and farther below, where during their embraces she had pressed against his massive sword of steel.

She felt the hollowness the lack of him had caused. Even the tremors he inspired in her before brought forth an ache to have him again, completely. In all her married years, she had known this throbbing fulfillment only this once. And though she surmised today's experience was only partial marital joy, she dared to compare her human reaction to that she had seen of animals when they mated. No ecstasy ever crossed their expressions. Yet her novel bliss formed enough experience to tell an intelligent woman what her body understood.

She wanted him. In all ways, sacred and profane.

She jabbed the needle into the cloth.

From disappointment's void, one pattern now manifested before her in full fashion.

With each new stitch, she sewed together the two fabrics of her need of him. The one, her request of the Devil of Midnight, a renegade who would deliver her from her accusers, her oppressors. The other, her desire for an extraordinary man who could offer her kisses, caresses—and naught beyond them. The first made her heart sing, the second her body. Between the two, the thread of her mind wove a romance for which she found no moral, no resolution, and certainly no happy ending.

Chapter

8

~~~

Geoffrey Devereaux raked his hair, waiting until Kate the kitchen maid had departed and the four of them were alone in the great hall. "I tell you, Lord Forrester, Bartlett is hefty game. He is too long with John to counter easily. We must have a plan for when he arrives. This ice may have saved us today, but could melt tomorrow. With it can come disaster." He downed a hefty draught of his wine and frowned into the roaring fire.

His dejected mood fit not only that of Allen Gainsbridge, but was surpassed by the tenseness Nicholas showed—had displayed since this morning. Watching him, Angel sat in a chair amid the three men, tasting her own wine with little relish as they discussed their predicament.

Absently, she fingered the pearls she'd worn for all to see the generosity of her new mate and to confirm so close to her skin his concern for her. Aye, to affirm his care of her that made him act the loving husband in word and deed before all here, but compelled him to avoid her eyes.

She suffered in her own pit of rejection, but looked at Geoffrey. "Aye, my lord. Add to that the fact that when my father comes, he will trail his two brothers and all the power of the northwestern lords of England. John needs my father, because he is the largest landowner from the Midlands to the Welsh marches. John needs him—as much as my father says he needs to keep me within his sphere."

Nicholas gazed at her without change of expression. Indeed, he had worn the same one of malcontent since this morning, when he had ended for her and himself the pleasure that surged between them.

Even now whenever his eyes chanced hers or flowed like molten gold over her tingling breasts and loins and legs, she felt her senses ring like tiny, tinkling bells of joy—and need. He'd lick his lips, cast his glance away, clear his throat—but she knew his thoughts, his wandering mind's turn of every corner in their mutual journey to an unknown destiny.

In the black velvet tunic trimmed in gold—the very one she had finished for him today—he created an appealing, if bewitching, portrait. To look at him was not half as satisfying as the sinfully delightful and yet roiling knowledge that once this supper was ended, he would once more repair with her to her chamber. Then again, this man would share her bed. And she knew with aching heart that not tonight or any night he lay beside her would she find any quick or adequate rest. Still, she would never ask him to do other than continue his noble, moral course.

He was so right. They could not take the pretense of a marriage further than they had. It would cause such pain to her—and now she thought herself correct to say—to him as well. The very idea that a man could care for her with tenderness, and not greed or some other self-serving motive, gratified her. Excited her. Saddened her.

She had to find a way to save her and him from the misery and tension of sleeping beside him—and never having more of each other than they had so blissfully but incompletely shared.

Allen Gainsbridge rubbed his beard. "I will say I would have felt better if we had more men. By tomorrow two more of mine could be here. Shall I send for them, Nick?"

"Aye. But then we'd be one man less. With your four, and Geoffrey's other two, we should have the advantage when Demere returns."

"Thank God for your gyrfalcon," breathed Geoffrey.

Angel smiled. The fowl had been the means by which much was saved this day. Peace of mind for all of them when they watched the trained bird land at Nicholas's side upon the parapet. Joy when Nicholas unrolled a parchment message from his men who patrolled the woods and told of no sojourners upon the ice-locked land. Satisfaction when she learned from Nicholas that the two jade stones were ones her Devil had requested of his wiry little Saracen for her just this morning as he called the circling bird from the sky and sent a message back tied to his leg.

"I have never heard of a bird able to track his trainer without the hunt for prey," said Geoffrey, as he watched the gyrfalcon soar into the air, back to her base somewhere in the glistening trees.

Allen had scratched his beard and raised a skeptical eye to Nicholas.

Nicholas replied with what Angel felt was half an explanation. "This bird is one of four that I own and have trained to do this. 'Tis a trick of which my father told me. He learned of it on crusade with King Richard years ago and knew how the infidels use birds for more than the hunt. Across the steppes of the Orient, falcons are used by Mongol tribes to obtain fast information of friends and foes."

Geoffrey asked then how one might train a bird in this manner, and Nicholas, taking them all down to dinner with his explanation, had amused and instructed the man well past the dining. So had he also managed to include Angel in the discussion but circumvented the need to speak with her directly. But as Nell and Kate cleaned away the remains of the meal, Angel stood, able no longer to sit, yearning for his full attention.

At her first movement, her husband had circled her wrist. "Wherever you wish to go, madam, there I am also."

"I must discuss with the cook her plans for the Advent feasting," she said more sharply than she should. "I have not seen to the preparations. Though we have had a funeral here, I would that much be in order for this season since we have two squires recently come to us. They are young boys who miss their families. For them, and my kitchen staff who have always been good to me, I would prepare a good array of foods for the season."

Nicholas rose then and excused himself from Allen and Geoffrey to walk with her down to the bowels of the castle and be introduced to the kindly cook, her husband, and two lingering young lads, who looked at Nicholas with more trepidation than Angel thought justified. As she led Nicholas away to give him an introductory tour of Windom, he mentioned the boys' fear of him. Angel said she had seen it, too, but could put only one reason to their reaction.

"Perhaps they wonder if you will resemble Chretian in manner or if you will be more like Demere, who tends to bellow at them."

Nicholas's brows had knit at that, but then he told her he would watch over the boys so that Demere did not intimidate them.

Later, when he called each of the six guards to him to interview them—and test their temperament and turn of mind to support him and Angel—he asked leading questions about the squires. The three Windom guards proclaimed the boys good lads. The three Carlisle men muttered their displeasure with the children's laxity and impertinence.

After the three Carlisle men had left the hall, Angel told Nicholas how she agreed with the Windom guards and not the Carlisles.

Now tonight, as Kate and Nell entered the hall with linen for the head table and saltcellars for all, so did the two youths.

Nicholas, a frown never far from his face this day, turned his attention to them. Smiling serenely and nodding at the boys' quick sign of greeting, Nicholas surveyed their every move. They knew it and grew wary as they went about their duties, eyeing the giant in the corner.

It was later, as supper began and Nicholas filled her cup with more wine, that he leaned over and spoke low to her. By his tone, he clearly had relegated his bad humor to a farther corner. "Tell me more about these two lads. When did they come here?"

"Two weeks before Chretian's death. They are cousins, come from Hereford Shire. Their fathers served with Chretian, and thus King Richard, on crusade."

"What are their family names?"

This fact she had omitted in the introductions this morning. "The blond boy is Gil Landover and the redhead, Jack Pelletier. Their mothers—"

"Are sisters. Aye. I know their fathers." At her questioning look, he added, "Good men who fight as valiantly for justice as for the Holy Land. Gil's father almost died at Antioch. He must be near sixty-five now. The same age my own father would have been. . . ."

He drifted off to memories that made him gnaw the insides of his cheeks.

She put a hand to his velvet sleeve and the warmth of him sent a geyser of pleasure through her. He felt it as comfort, for he covered her hand with his own and traced the wedding ring she wore.

"How long ago did your father die?"

"I was thirteen, about to marry." He widened his eyes and sighed. "Seventeen years ago and I remember him still. He was a kind man. Black hair and eyes. With a voice I used to liken to God's. And a heart as bounteous. And big? *Huge.* Taller than I!" He shot a glance at her and chuckled through what she thought might be the glistening of tears. "I know that might be difficult to believe, but it is true. We St. C—" He broke off, horrified at what he'd almost revealed.

Her heart slammed to a stop. *Saint S-s-s . . .* what?

He mashed his lips together. "I do not make mistakes like that."

Her eyes held his.

He tore his own to the room, the gathering crowd, his golden cup, her hand and ring.

"Aside from Allen," she asked low, "who else knows your true identity?"

"None." He followed her eyes out to one table where Peter, Edwin, and Leon sat.

All three had been so loyal to her. Ever since her father had given her the dower lands, these men had been better to her than her own family. Peter supervised her personal household of Windom Castle. Edwin oversaw her peasants and the well-being of their crops. Meanwhile, Leon lived in her rich woodlands, so full of ancient firs and myriad animals . . . and an infamous band of Devil's disciples. Conceivably, Leon had opportunity to catch sight of such outlaws, mayhaps even their leader. So had he proclaimed to her when first she confided to her three servants how she wished she could bring a Devil to her rescue.

"Allow me to try to find him, my lady," Leon had pleaded.

And so had she permitted it, because to do aught would have been to accept the only alternative— nothing. Truly, Leon might know where to look for the Devil of Midnight, but once there, how had he proceeded to bring the outlaw to her?

She examined Nicholas for clues to many secrets. "Are you here with me because you were captured or asked to come?"

"Captured, I assure you."

"How do you explain that? No one has ever taken you or your men before this."

"I have not had the opportunity to discover why that is so. But I will. Whatever the means, I am here."

"And would you have come if you were asked?"

He met her eyes. Fires of his regard for her flamed higher.

She warmed at the heat. "You will not tell me the whole of it, will you?"

"I would not endanger you."

"Is your crime so heinous?"

"Like yours, my offense is that I fell into a web of deceit from which I knew not how to extricate myself. I was too young, innocent of the ploys used against me."

"And now? Can you not address those wrongs?"

"My foes are very powerful, entrenched. I can but fight as I do. From afar"—he squeezed her fingers—"for those to whom I can restore some justice and a measure of their dignity."

Desperate to have him happy, she pleaded, "There must be some hope. You have taught me that."

He traced her jaw with feathering fingers. "Have I? God, I'm glad."

"Why could you not remain here with me? After this is done and all my suitors retire, if you return to the forests, I will have to send forth news my husband has disappeared or . . . or died. You could certainly continue the ruse. I would not mind if you left occasionally." *I think now I will die if you go permanently.* "And I would never reveal your secret."

His mouth twitched in joy and sorrow. "Nay, my adorable and adoring wife. You know I could not do that."

"Tell me why not."

"Oh, Angel." He sat back, shook his head and blew a gust of air to the rafters. Running his arm across the back of her chair, he put his mouth close to her ear. "You think I could stay with you and pretend to have a normal life? I cannot bear to be with you *now*—Nay! You asked this and you will listen to the bald response! I want you naked, wet, writhing like this morning, coming to me, coming *with* me, in that big, broad bed upstairs."

Her mouth watered at his harsh adamance, his gruff admission that made her breasts stiffen and her toes curl. Inside her stomach, the desire that had slumbered since this morning uncoiled and stretched to every little nook within her yearning body.

She watched his throat convulse as he narrowed his eyes at her and said, "I am tired, tense, *sore* from need of you—and we have been wed only two days. What think you would happen if I lay beside you for the rest of my life? Christ above, my sweet, I'd have you on your back, on the floor, in your solar, in a chair, every hour of the night and most of the day as well. We'd have children because I would not be able to stop myself from taking every inch of you. But they'd be bastards with nothing to inherit from me, not even my name. Think you I could do that to you, to them? And what, dear heart, of your desire never to have another man rule you again?"

Tears veiled her eyes, not so much from disappointment at his rejection, but from utter joy at his sensuous words. He wanted her. He needed her. He only meant to save her from herself and him. And in light of that, what of this goal of hers to keep from any man and his jurisdiction?

"I doubt you would ever breach the bounds of justice, Nicholas. With you, I would be mistress of my own domain."

He offered a wobbly smile of misery. "Aye. And what would I become? Your stag in rut?"

That repulsed her in word and thought.

He saw it and she knew he considered a softer approach, but she waylaid him. "You are right. Of course. I was foolish to think of such. I simply—" Could she reveal the crux of her problem and her desire? "I find that what I feel when I am in your embrace is nothing like anything else I have ever known. Like a person who has glimpsed a glorious horizon, I would see the whole panorama. And I offer you my apologies for such simple behavior." She sat back, allowing Gil to place her trencher before her and move on to do the same for Nicholas. "My suggestion was a rash solution."

Dismal, he stared into his cup for long minutes, and while the servants brought forth the courses he said no word, made no move toward her.

Her heart ached, pounded with the need to seek solace somewhere. She could not eat. And surely tonight, she would not sleep.

Meanwhile, Nicholas transformed, becoming the epitome of the jovial, besotted bridegroom. His attitude became more sweet than the lure of roast goose and a blancmange of chicken. Far more intoxicating than the mulled wine with which he constantly refilled her cup.

"Do you not care for the turnips, my wife?"

She glanced up into his concerned features. "I am not hungry."

"Wash them down with the wine, if you must, but you should eat the turnips."

She wrinkled her nose. "Why? They are not manna for the gods, sir."

"Turnips, whether baked or boiled, are good for your liver." He popped a piece into his mouth and relished it.

She made a face.

"And these," he hoisted a platter of oatcakes, "will improve your blood flow."

She grimaced, refusing to take one. Already her blood pounded fierce enough to leave her veins, leaping at the merest husk of his voice. She sought to tame it, ignore it, forget it.

"Here." He reached for another platter near Devereaux and the priest. "Open your mouth," he demanded and when she did, he plopped in a morsel of something strange.

She swallowed fitfully. "Was *that*—?" she managed around the squishy stuff.

He wiggled his brows in imitation of his wicked reputation. "Mushrooms. Increases . . . well, all sorts of bodily fluids."

"I hate them. I would rather have sugared orange peels and glazed walnuts." *Anything. Everything. Nothing of your concern and all of your heart and body.*

The meal went on and could have consisted of rocks for all she cared or ate of it.

Gil and Jack brought forth candied pears and apples with a repressed glee only two eight-year-olds could hold for sweets. Their smiles at Angel elicited small ones of her own.

"Here, good lady," said towheaded Gilbert Landover as he set the platter before her. "I beg you pick the best ones quickly so that we may feed these brutes and send them off to bed with more of your fine red wine. Last night and this morn, they left Jack and me alone because they were so drunk."

Nicholas chuckled. "We should have more feasts here, eh, son?"

"Aye, my lord. With you about, I'd say each night will be a celebration for Jack and me."

Angel wrestled with a grin—and despair. "Well then, Gil, there is more than enough wine for this. Bring it forth with liberty, if it means you and Jack can rest later each morn on your pallets." This would benefit them all to see the Demere faction continuously disadvantaged by overindulgence.

"Thank you, milady. I'll say a prayer for you each day you keep them so pickled."

She saw Nicholas halt at the tone of this child. She herself heard some chord of distress. But what caused it?

She had always known the two boys stayed far from the Demere crowd, but never in the few weeks the boys had been here had they given any hint that it might be more than mere dislike. Or had she simply not had the time to look? Was she too preoccupied with the terrors of murder and extortion to protect two young boys from . . . what?

Nicholas bent near the child to whisper, "Thank you, Gil. I'll count on you to bring my lady and me word the night they do not retire to their beds with more than a full skin of wine."

Gil scrutinized Nicholas with youth's sagacity. "Aye, my Lord Forrester. You may rely on me. 'Tis worth it to me to see them flap like fish on the riverbank."

Nicholas gave the child a pat on his arm. "Off with that platter and quickly to your fishing, then." After the boy began his rounds of feeding the minions, Nicholas shot a look at Angel. With a slight shake of her head, she told him she knew not the source of such intense hatred.

He picked up a pear, then put it down. "I fear I smell something foul. Have you any ideas what ails those lads?"

"I know Gil and Jack have oft worked longer hours than ever I saw pages do in my father's house."

"There is more to that child's hatred than the resentment of hard work."

She searched her mind for clues. "They tend to keep to themselves, though they have been kind to me. They have not been pleased to be here, and I have feared that Demere's men have tried to corrupt them with gaming."

"Gil fears something more than chastisement for gambling. What could it be that a young boy would find them . . . repulsive?" He turned to her, sorrow swirling in his eyes. "Tomorrow we will summon him to us and learn what troubles he and his friend encounter. For now, I wish to see you devour that pear."

She picked up his lighter attitude, if only for one sad moment. "You care not if I become rotund."

"I simply mean to keep you jolly, madam."

She thought her good humor, even so recently pricked by the needle of the squires' situation—and Nicholas's rejection—could never return.

Nicholas saw it. "You test me mightily, my sweet wife."

With a clap of his hands, he demanded some revelry to suit the hour and the coming Christmas season. He began by asking Angel to take up her harp and sing. Fire in his golden eyes, he kissed her cheek, told her no heavenly seraphim matched her skills, and moved her chair closer by his side. Afterward, with a hand to hers, he made his friend Gainsbridge recite a ballad from a French romance, and when the crowd, in the flowing wisdom of their wine, thought that superb, Devereaux offered a bawdier tune. The evening soon became an exhibition, which with more inebriated people became a bacchanal.

"Well, now, that seems enough for us to witness," Nicholas said as he bid her rise and led her to the stairs. "They'll all sleep dead as stones this night. And so, my dear, will you." He pulled her close with a hand to her waist.

She noticed he did not sweep her up to his arms as he had last night. "I doubt very seriously that you ever have been thwarted, my good sir. But I tell you, sleep will be difficult for me to find," she offered as he flung open their bedchamber door and hastened her inside.

"Not after you hear my plans for the evening," he warned as he nodded to the Devereaux guard, then barred the chamber door.

"Plans?" She vibrated at the very expectation.

"Do your ablutions and don the chainse you sleep in, my lady. I have tales to tell which will put you in the mood for sleep in a thrice."

She went to her solar to disrobe, while he in all good courtesy left her in privacy to walk toward their chamber fire.

She divested herself of the shining pearls and layers of clothing to put on the linen tunic she'd slept in with Chretian—and now with this new husband. For never would she sleep with Nicholas sans all clothes. Such was left for normal lives, usual practices for unassailed people.

Without hope, she called to him, "Whatever your plans, I will not wager on your success."

"Challenge me, will you?" He chuckled.

How could he laugh when she was so disconsolate? "Always."

"'Tis not a good idea."

She rounded the corner and walked to him. "I would hear these stories you think will make my defenses fall so easily." *I would hear why you are so suddenly happy, and I am drawn to your good nature beyond my own good sense.*

"You make a grown man weep with your stubbornness. Very well, then, I'll show you." He hauled her over his shoulder like a sack of wheat.

She whooped and beat his back with her hands, and all the while he strode back to her solar, she choked on laughter. Upended on a whoosh, she landed in his lap.

He grinned at her. "Now, at last, I see respect in your features. Do you not understand when the Devil tells you to do something, you must or suffer at his hands?"

She grasped his and examined them. "I have not suffered at *these* hands, my Lord Devil. Tell me something else which will make me quake."

All levity drained from his face. Too soon he covered his expression—and her breath caught at what for one sublime moment she had glimpsed on his stark features.

"What will you tell me, my lord?" *Tales of women you have loved? Hearts you have stolen? Lips you have kissed as deliciously as you have mine?*

His gold eyes glazed. "You think I cannot capture your mind?"

"Nay."

He stared at her in pain.

"You have already done so, my lord of midnight."

He inhaled, flaring his chest wider in the torment of which she caught only a hint. "You *must* listen to me. You must not be so kind to me."

"I could say the same to you, but that is folly. For kind is what you are, what God made you."

"You think I can live as I do and be *kind?*"

"Ever have I heard it to be so. Otherwise, why would I have given orders to capture you?"

"I was your only hope."

"And now you have become my only joy." She could not help herself but stroked his cheeks.

He seized her hand. "Nay, no caresses. Listen to me! We will not—*I* will not do as I did yesterday and this morning. I was wrong to kiss you, no matter your request or need. Such delights are meant for a man to his rightful wife—and lest our play be so apt we forget ourselves, we must remember this marriage is not valid."

Dejection such as she had felt last night and this morning shadowed the moment. With firm resolve, she ignored it. Such joy as his companionship had given her last night beckoned brightly.

"My lord, I do not castigate you for what happened last night or this morning. For I *did* sleep much better than I ever have in my life. If I am not critical of your behavior, why are you?"

"Because such kisses lead to others."

"Yet you controlled all the kisses and caresses. I felt it and knew your boundless abilities."

He grumbled. "Aye, I controlled much and not enough. Don't you understand, Angel? A man, no matter his attempt at self-control with a woman, can sometimes reach beyond the boundaries he sets himself. No matter that the man tells himself he has years of practice. Surely you suspect this from your past knowledge of men with Chretian."

She let that pass and took the other topic. "You have enjoyed many women, then?"

He brushed her lips with two of his fingers. "I enjoyed many women in my youth. And I was taught in my youth how to please a woman. The education was an integral part of my life. But I cannot practice with you. You seek not me nor what pleasures I can give you, only what joys you may attain as a free woman. But while I am here with you, I promised you protection. Even from me. And so, turning to the matter of your nightmares and your sleeplessness, I have a hope to help you find a cure. I thought I would tell stories."

She settled into his lap and folded her hands. This went much better now that he was over his bout of remorse—and she knew he cared for her still. "Very well. I am ready. I love stories. What kind of stories do you have, good sir?" She rolled her eyes playfully.

He exhaled, surrendering to her with a rueful twitch of his handsome lips. "Suppose I tell you tales of lands beyond the rising sun?"

"Do you fantasize these stories or are they real?"

"Real. From places I have lived."

"Will you tell me when and why you lived there?"

"Perhaps." His eyes twinkled at her, but she knew he covered reluctance with teasing.

"Good. I wish to hear them."

He wet his lips and eyed her. "They are odd stories."

"I should like to hear the nicest ones first and then, if I can bear to hear of more evil in the world, you may progress to the awful ones."

He slowly smiled and arranged her chainse more securely about her legs. "So shall it be. This land I speak of is endless compared to England. Its boundaries could encompass one hundred Englands."

She pursed her lips. "You *do* tell an amazing story."

"Mmm. But true. I swear it. This kingdom, walled for thousands of miles to its west, faces east to a great ocean and marches south to vast scorching jungles and north as far as the ice which lies over the land year round."

"Like ours outside?"

"I am afraid so."

"I wouldn't like that—unless, of course, it kept away my father and Demere forever."

"I'm sure. Within this land are a thousand rivers, all flowing to the great ocean. Some of the rivers are so wide, no one may see across to the opposite bank. One stone bridge crossing one river is a marvel. It can support eight chariots of two horses abreast. Great carvings of their temple gods line the way. But at other rivers, sometimes great floods occur, sweeping all away for hundreds of miles. Many homes are lost and people die."

She waved a hand in dismissal. "I do not wish to hear this. I want the better tales."

"Aye, and so I promised. Suppose I tell you that this kingdom is ruled over by a fat and silly man who has four hundred wives and six hundred children? At least, when I left he did."

"Good heavens, does the man think it his responsibility to people his kingdom by himself?"

That made Nicholas throw back his head and roar. "Nay, my Angel, although now that you say it, it does seem so."

She settled more comfortably in his care. "And how can he keep all his wives' names correct? Certainly, he cannot even visit their beds once a year if he has so many!"

The solar filled with both their laughter.

Nicholas took her by the waist and pressed her down against his shoulder.

Angel much preferred this vantage and curled against his chest. Beneath his warm velvet tunic, his heart picked up a beat.

"The emperor loves no one, so I suppose it does not matter that he cannot remember his wives' names. He cares for only himself. He is unequaled in all the earth and calls himself the Son of Heaven. And he sits upon a giant golden throne within a gold-leafed palace atop a mountain facing east. This throne is decorated with more gems than you and I have ever imagined could exist in all the world."

"Is that where you acquired my pearls and the jade?"

"Aye. When I left this empire as agent for another king, I was given many jewels as tokens of appreciation. These pearls and jade are only the top of a treasure trove I have sequestered. And I think I shall bring you more. Ever would such poor stones be honored to adorn such grace and beauty." He kissed her palm.

He stole her breath, and quietly she asked, "How could such an emperor own so much wealth?"

"This empire is so ancient even Babylon was young when this kingdom grew mature." He settled her back against his arm.

She sighed. "I should like to see this land and these people. How does one travel there?"

He traced her eyebrows with a gentle finger. "Over deserts of parched sands and mountains with passes no wider than your foot. Through years of endless walking and riding great beasts with humps on their backs."

She stared at him. "May women go there?"

"Aye. Women travel across these routes. Usually they are princesses pledged to men of power. Otherwise, no woman would want the suffering of these journeys."

"But you did this." When he nodded, averting his eyes, she brought his gaze back with a hand to his square jaw. "Why?"

He flexed his shoulders. "I was forced to. At first. Then, years went by and I . . . I learned how to obtain respect until one day, I gained my freedom. I vowed no one would ever take mine from me again. Nor, if I could help it, would anyone rob someone else of their God-given right to walk the earth in freedom."

Her heart grew sore, and at the same time she exulted that he should have such a care not only for himself but for those others who shared a similar fate as he once had. "No wonder you work against King

John." *No surprise that you should become my champion.*

"John robs us all liberally. But what he cannot see is that ultimately he robs himself. He values not the finer aspects of his kingdom—his people. In that, he bears similarities to the Son of Heaven, who is greedy and self-centered. Like John's subjects, this emperor's people say heaven has turned from him and will soon replace him with a more able ruler."

"And will it be so, do you think?"

"I do, my Angel. For though I know not the Son of Heaven, I do know that man who would seize his power from him—and such an able leader, such a scourge of God, you have never seen the like."

"He sounds fearsome."

"He is. He obtained his power among his people by his decisiveness. He won his empire by swift use of his cavalry and merciless armies. He rules by might alone with no mercy for his enemies whom he annihilates, and with no tolerance for his supporters who counter him. But to those who serve him well, he can be kind. He tries to be just, unlike our John, who knows neither kindness nor justice but tries to administer his realm in any case."

She shook her head. "Let us not speak of John. Nor of this usurper whom you know. I would instead know more of this Son of Heaven and his domain."

"Ah, well, a wise choice, for it is a more pleasant tale," he affirmed and began to stroke his fingers through her hair. "I can tell you stories of how he uses not gold, but paper for money."

"Nay!" She jerked up, but he smiled and nodded, pressing her more securely to his care. "Aye. I have seen them make it. They take the pulp of mulberry trees and press it into sheets, which they dye and cut. The emperor long ago confiscated all the gold coins and made his subjects use the paper instead."

"Wondrous. And they use this to purchase anything?" When he grinned, she asked, "What else do they have in this kingdom?"

"The ability to put printing on this paper with the use of wooden blocks. This way thousands of the same message can be produced and sent to each government official in each province. The emperor controls his subjects by written decrees which all may see posted all over his domain at one and the same time."

"No monks sit for decades copying edicts or texts?"

"Nay, some monks contemplate the state of the universe—or in some cases, the lack of it."

At the tilt of her head, he told her of religious men and women who followed a holy man named Buddha, and how, as in Christianity, the factions grew as did the interpretations of Buddha's true word.

She sucked in her breath. "You do not lie."

"Never to you."

"What else is there in this land?"

"These Chinese have the ability to light a powder that fills the sky with a thousand colored stars which burst and sprinkle to the ground. Fabulous bells of all sizes which ring in every temple in every corner of the cities. Some are long as battering rams and others so small, dancing girls can fit them on their toes."

"And what a glorious sound they must make."

"Ah, but none of them sounds as sweet as your voice."

"I prefer the sound of you." She put a hand to his chest. "Your voice resonates through the halls. Everyone stops to know the sound of power."

He smiled, covered her hand with his own, and considered her mouth. "You can sound the same so that everyone may know who has rule here."

"I wish to know—" Compelled, she drifted closer.

He whispered, "What would you learn, my lovely?"

"In this land, do men marry women for land?"

"Land not so much as wealth. 'Tis true the world over that marriage seals many arrangements which have little to do with how a man and woman regard each other personally."

"How does a husband in this land treat his wife?" she asked, and moved to rub her lips across his cheek as he had done to her this morn. "Does he love her?" she asked against his ear. "Can he cherish her?"

He brought her mouth near his. "A man takes his wife and vows to adore her. And so that she may want him only evermore, he initiates her slowly into the joys of the five desires." He trailed his tongue across her lower lip.

She spoke, a breath from him. "What are these five desires, my lord?"

"Ways . . . five ways a woman shows she wants a man."

She moaned and he captured her mouth to his, taking a long, sweet, undulating kiss. "Like this," he said as he turned her under him and settled her to the luxury of her cushions. His fluid muscles molded to her rigid, burning body. "A husband knows his wife shows the first desire if she bates her breath and restrains her body. As you do, sweeting. As you have done all day whenever you looked at me." He breathed into her ear and nuzzled beneath it to place a wet openmouthed kiss there.

She gasped and shivered.

"She shows the second desire when she pants for air and shudders. And so—oh, God, I love you like this—if he is wise and tender, he offers something like the feel of this." He wended his way down her throat to the base where her blood pounded frantically.

Her hands sought his chest, his shoulders, his throat.

"Her third desire comes upon her when she draws him near . . . ah, my darling . . . as you do me." He sent one hand down along her body to find and lift one breast. Through the chainse, she felt his palm as he measured her fullness and massaged her. He rubbed his thumb across her nipple. His head descended and suddenly his mouth closed over her peak, pulling her in, leading her on to a breezy haven. Some wild sound rose from the essence of her soul.

She felt the want uncoil and arched her back, plunging her hands into his silken hair. He shifted to give the same attention to her other breast, and she felt his arm circle her waist and arch her up so that he could love her better, longer with his talented mouth.

Suddenly, he left her and she writhed, her feet pushing at the cushions. "Nicholas, oh, Nicholas, come back. I would have more." Her eyes met his bleak ones. His hands bit into her flesh.

"Nay, no more. The fifth sign of your desire is too near, and if a woman is denied at that point, the ancient masters of the mystic grotto warn of dire consequences. These wise ones say a woman can go mad if she is not fulfilled then. And though I burn to have you, kiss you till you are open to me, I would never harm you. This love-play is too poignant to me also for me to continue to lead us both along a path we should never travel."

She buried her face in his throat. "I have never felt like this."

"Sweet woman," he murmured, "it makes me thrill to hear you say it. For what your Chretian showed you is all there must be. I can never savor you."

She bit her lip to hold back tears and words that would declare the basic fact, the horrific lie, beneath this whole affair. She glanced away, sought any object on which to focus her despair. But it was unavoidable —this one real fact—that she had never been any true wife to Chretian Forrester. But she had suppressed these words because they would be the legal means by which anyone could deny her more of her rights. And that she would never do.

Those natural rights had been violated by every man she had ever known—save this darling Devil. And it was ripe irony—base agony—that the one man whom she wished to take her along nature's path to human ecstasy should also be the only man who refused to breach the barrier of all those other rights which had been shredded by lesser principled men.

But to this man, her integrity as a woman implied also her sanctity. And that became a sanctuary that he, of all men, would not invade.

And in that moment, she knew she loved him madly. Beyond reason and hope. She saw new earths and heavens open before her and she reached to kiss him.

But with shaking hands, he pulled her away from his chest. "My Angel, I am tempted to take you, show you each joy of love from every land in all the world. But I have no right to do that. 'Twould be divine to love you till time ended, but 'twould not make it less a sin."

"Sin?" She said the word as if she'd never understood such condemnation. "The Devil is concerned with sin?"

Rejected, she rose, trilled a laugh, and knew she sounded demented. And she concluded she must be, for what she declared next. "You deny this truth which sits between us. Three times now have you put it by. Refusing to acknowledge to yourself and me what pleasures we enjoy when we are together, you do us both a disservice, my lord husband, my very own Devil. What's more, you *lie!* So *do* it then!" She flung out her hand. "Ignore me and this we have between us! Take up your post in that bed, in this household— but touch me not, lure me not, and call me not from my nightly occupations. This is *my* castle, my home, my solar, and you, sir, are sitting on my sewing!" She yanked it from beneath him and threw it at him, filled with the rage of true angels. "Damn you! Damn you to hell."

He paled.

She was swirling from him, leaving, dying when he grabbed her, one arm about her waist.

"Get you gone from me!"

Drawing air like a mighty beast, he tried to turn her.

She fought like one possessed. Kicking, writhing, beating her hands.

He cursed in some heathen language and it was then

174

she felt the unequaled power of the Devil unleashed. He spun her in his arms, crushed the air from her, and captured her jaw. *"Nay!* No escape from the Devil now, my darling. For this is what you want. What I want. This is desire as you and I shall never find in heaven or in hell!"

Chapter

9

⁓

"'Tis past time for that."

His wicked eyes gleamed at her in defiance. Then in a lightning flash, he bent her backward along his powerful arm and fastened his mouth to hers with all the raging fires of hell's forge.

She took flame.

He ravaged her mouth, pillaged her will, took her air, and built the fire higher, stroking her tongue and the inner flesh of her cheeks, claiming every essence of her, inside and out.

She gave everything she was and disintegrated in the cauldron. Ashes in the inferno of his rapture.

Floating on the winds of desire, she pulled away and grasped her only misery. "You lead me on, give me joy, then walk away!"

"No more. For now, for all the nights my arms can hold you, you belong to me. Your mouth." He took it tenderly. "Your swanlike throat." He paid homage with the branding trail of his tongue. "Your beautiful full breasts." He gathered her chainse at the neck, and in one tear ripped it from her shoulders to leave her utterly at his mercy.

She could not move, dared not go, wished to know what came next.

Half-lidded, his eyes traveled down her bare body. She squeezed her thighs together and could scarce stand. He eased one leg around her own to secure her as he took her left breast in one hand and lifted it. Stroking it with the palm of his other hand, he caressed her with that husky voice of his. "I mean to have you in my mouth again, like this." His fingers stroked her to a peak so that his lips might follow. He laved her with a warm, wet need. She rocked with the rhythm he composed and drove her hands into his hair. His teeth nipped, his mouth suckled avidly.

Her knees buckled.

He bent and scooped her up to stride across the chamber. Upon the furs, he laid her on the bed, followed her to it, straddled her hips with his corded thighs, and covered her with his hot body.

Scarce understanding what was expected of her, she blinked at the ferocious sight of an endearing Devil devouring her with his eyes. His hand came up to tuck her hair away from her cheek. "You possess me."

His hands elaborated, sliding along her fevered skin, smoothing every muscle, each crevice until he cupped her core. She arched. He laced his fingers in her hair, delving to spread her lips with gentle fervor. She closed her eyes to the blinding fires of his touch.

"Christ, if I were a man who yet believed there was a God, I would say you were the answer to my every prayer. Angel mine," he slid one long finger along her cleft as he kissed one nipple with cherubic delicacy, "I mean to make a feast of passion for you and me. This night is ours, though I will swear you must not fear I will leave you with any evidence that I have ever known you."

Wanting, needing, she shook her head. "I do not understand."

"From this ecstasy, there will be no child. I will see to it. I know how to prevent it, circumvent it." He gave her a sad smile. "I know the ways to make our nights a joy divine. One thing my past has granted me is a knowledge of how to please a woman and myself without the chains of permanence to bind us. None of the women I have ever known has borne a child from our encounters. Neither shall you. Though God does know, I would want a baby of mine from your body, my darling. You are so rare, unique from any other."

Her heart flooded, the dam of her sorrow burst. "Others?" was all she could imagine in her jealousy.

Eyes wild, he crushed her to him, his mouth on her cheek. "I never said I loved them, darling. I didn't. I never loved anyone . . . Never." He gave her a little hug. "How could I when I had not yet met you?" He arched a brow, sweetly, wickedly, as he leaned back. His hands circled her waist, brushed her ribs and breasts, and skimmed her arms to spread them wide. His eyes glowed down at her like a million suns and just as warm. "My bewitching angel. How shall I proceed to teach you the ancient art of erotic love?"

She bit her trembling lips. "Teach me anything. Everything. For I know . . . little."

His eyes went limpid. "Tender woman, Chretian Forrester showed you his bed, but not the mysteries a husband can unfold for his woman. How sad for him. How frustrating for you. How glorious a present for me." He definitely took on the look of his name.

"How you shall quake and fly in my arms. I am near undone before I start, the idea is so delicious."

She shuddered at his words. "You make me want."

"Aye, I see it. Your cheeks flush. Your green eyes burn. Your skin grows moist." He palmed both breasts. "Your pretty nipples ask for more of me. Shall I offer them reward?"

For answer, she bit her lower lip and nodded.

His thumbs topped the tips of her nipples. That simple touch sent her tumbling in a world of pulsing delights. In her nether parts a furious firestorm whirled, gathering strength. She knew its power from this morn.

Her hands went to his waist, her nails gouging him. "What diabolical power can you have over me that you merely speak to me and my body takes flight from my control?"

"No power. Only my care for you. My desire to enjoy all, share everything with an angel who deserves it." He leaned over to sample her mouth and whisper, "This morning when you shattered at my kiss, you showed me how sweet a partner in the exotic skills of love you could be. I thrilled to learn it. Now, let me instruct you. 'Twill be a lesson all the saints would pant to impart to you, my Angel. But you must make some promises."

Aye.

"You will not wrest control."

Nay.

"You will not leave."

She rose and kissed his mouth, his word upon her own. *"Never."*

He smiled with narrowed eyes. "You are mine in thought and deed."

"Always."

"Though heaven and earth pass away."

"Beyond eternity."

He kissed her madly to seal their bargain. Then, he slid down her body to rise and divest himself of all his clothes.

The sight of him as God in His infinite wisdom had fashioned him caused her mouth to open and close. His marvelous chest she had admired before. So, too, his hips. His massive legs. But here stood long, hard evidence all those other attributes had merely suggested.

He was a man. Proud, bold. A man she needed to taste, feel . . .

"Breathe, will you, darling? 'Tis not as large as it looks. Here." He climbed to straddle her hips again and took her two limp hands in his. "Feel how big it truly is." He placed her fingers around him and sighed at her touch.

He was longer than her hand. Hotter than her mind. Soft red silk sliding over a sheath of sleek steel. "God made Adam in your image, my Devil, for you are"— she shook her head, incredulous—"truly beautiful."

"Angel, sweeting," he swallowed and rearranged her hands, "stroke me slowly, will you? I have not made love to a woman in a long time and I must proceed with care lest I negate that promise I made you."

"You're perspiring."

"I know," he blurted and snorted, taking a few moments to close his eyes and arch his back. Finally, he gazed down at her, her reverent hands on him, her breasts awaiting him. "I will have a wonderful time making love to you, my darling. Even without my hands on you, your body rises to my voice. Your rosy nipples pucker, and your mouth opens. Do other parts of you blossom for me? Hmmm? Shall we see?"

She could scarcely move in such anticipation. He meant to touch her *there*.

But in one smooth maneuver, he rolled her over and his hands massaged her back, while his lips nestled in her hair near her ear. "I mean to touch every inch of you," he crooned as he pressed his fingertips into the hair at her nape and sent his big hands plunging over her scalp. "You are lush as Eden." His hands trailed down her back, her arms to her fingertips, back up along her shoulders, ribs, and finally her buttocks. He molded, parted, pressed, and then kissed them until her embarrassment grew so keen she hid her face in her pillow. He murmured words of praise for her perfection and squeezed her inner thighs. She heard her heartbeat, erratic in her body, as his teasing fingers feathered the cleft of the part of her that needed him most. For surely, he would stroke her there *now*.

But he went lower, to kiss her calves, circle her ankles, and lift her feet. With bared teeth, he nipped her toes and made her writhe just short of objecting.

He chuckled, the fiend.

And with a tender tug, he put her to her back again. "You liked that, I can tell. And what of this, my Angel?"

He pressed two thumb pads to two points beneath each breast, then two above. His mouth followed, blessing each with avid joy until he gave wet homage to her waist, her navel, her hipbones, and her nest of hair.

"My darling, you are fragile, exquisite, even here.

Pale hair as silky as that above, but covering a wondrous landscape. A grotto meant for a new explorer. Open your gates, Angel of mine. I think you burn within and need refreshment only this devil can supply."

She ground her teeth at his words, but did as he required. He bent.

He kissed the crown of her womanhood, nuzzling her hair and putting two sets of fingers to either portal of her gate. His fingers opened her and he sank, his tongue gliding along her inner lips. She swirled, at sea in this delirium he concocted with long sweeping caresses of his warm, slick tongue.

"You taste better than any nectar, *cara mia*. Sweeter." She lost his voice and then all consciousness as his tongue darted into the center of her and his skillful fingers spread her wider so that he might plump her and suck her into his mouth. She cried out in exaltation.

She clutched for him, grabbed for this new heaven he showed her while he kissed her as if he were a butterfly tasting dew-laced flowers.

"Oh, Nicholas, Nicholas. What are you doing to me?"

"Loving you, my heart." He rose up, glorious, naked, hers, and grasped her to rearrange her just so. "Like this," he murmured as he raised her legs, bent her knees, spread her wider and gazed down at the center of her he had just devoured. "Christ, you are a giving woman—and *mine.*" He grasped his manhood in one hand and stared at her. "Listen to me, *cara*. You want me now. You are swollen and"—he narrowed his eyes and licked his lower lip—"milky. For this next, you will not move. You must promise."

"I swear it," she said but would have given him the moon and stars.

He grinned, his golden eyes praising her, his hands placing her own on his hips. "Here, darling," he slid the tip of his body along the lips of her center, "is the joy I mean to share with you."

His glide made her head shoot back.

"Lovely, *cara*. You are so wet for me. Is it as wonderful for you as you are heaven to me?"

"Aye," she choked out. "Aye." Her entire being focused there where he served her, pleasured her with long strokes to paradise.

He lifted her buttocks, settling her thighs to his hips. "Let heaven come now, darling. Let it come."

Pressing and sliding along the cleft and tiny nub which once his mouth and tongue had treasured, he took her to a new and startling place, where she throbbed and pounded with a joy divine. She whimpered for more. More. More of his body completely inside her. But she knew he couldn't, wouldn't, and she beat the mattress.

He pinned her arms and she wanted to shout *please* and knew she had promised to follow, not lead. She moaned in misery and joy as his fingers found the pearl he had polished this morning.

She arched. "Aye. That. This. Anything!" she cried.

His fingers sank between her lips, enough to make her sigh, but not enough to fill her growing need of something greater. But at his circling touch, she began to vibrate with the sounds of passion roaring in her ears.

"My angel, you are so small," he growled, his eyes clamped shut, his fingers gently, hotly, ever so shallowly moving in and out. He growled and pulled away.

"No!" she shouted, clutching at his arms.

Stronger, swifter, he sank to her, parted her, and fastened his mouth to the jewel he had adored before. This time, he loved her with lips and tongue and teeth. She shouted to the world as shocks of lightning fired through her, shattering her universe and scattering her to others.

But he was there to capture her close and put order to the sublime chaos. "My darling," he murmured. "How giving you are, my desire."

She drifted weightless through expanses of light and time. Her only reality was the knowledge that he waited for her, his all-encompassing arms holding her, his sweet voice praising her and proclaiming his pride in her.

Languid, she kissed his cheek. "I never thought mating between a man and woman was like that," she confessed as he stroked her hair and took her back to the pillows with him.

She felt him smile against her forehead. "There is more. This we enjoyed was but one small example, *cara mia.*"

"I shall savor each one." She tilted her head back to assess how well he had fared in this encounter. He looked as happy as she felt. "What is this you call me and in what language?"

For a split second, he looked distressed. *"Cara mia,* my dear. From the language of my mother's land, Venice."

"Does she still live there? Does she know you live as you do here in England with no—"

He rose from the bed and gathered the fur mantle to secure about her. Naked, he strode to their chamber fire and idly threw in a log, then stared into its crackling depths. "My mother is dead. She knows not what has happened to me."

"And your father—?"

"Dead, as well. Long ago. Two years after her. He tried to live without her, forget her, replace her, and he could not. He told me before he died she was his very air." He spun to her as if some novel and tragic thought occurred to him. "He called her his angel."

She went up on her knees, the cover pooling. "Come back to bed, my Devil. 'Tis so cold and I would warm you." Her eyes drifted down to see how hot the night and their encounter still kept him rigidly fired.

"I must cool lest I find your sweet body a haven for more of mine."

"I meant nothing—" She groped for proper words. "Sexual?"

"Aye. I meant more of comfort than of coupling."

He raked the black hair she longed to comb with her own fingers. "You must sleep, my Angel."

"And so should you, my lord."

He closed his eyes. "If I wake in the night and find you beside me, I fear I will want you again."

"Then you must have me."

"Nay, I—"

"How could I deny you anything, my lord of night and day? You have shown me such ecstasies as dreams are made of and you think I would not want you again, now, here?"

His eyes swept to her breasts and he nodded. "Even from so far, I can see your evidence."

"Come then," she beseeched him in a fervent prayer. "I want to sleep in your arms."

This time he did not deny her.

He returned to their bed and took her tenderly into his embrace. He kissed her temple, secured her to his warm form, then hummed a little tune until her eyes closed and she slept like the sated.

As dawn rouged their room, he watched her in her innocent repose. Her white gold hair fanned upon the linen sheets, her fawn-colored lashes brushing the blush of her skin, her rosy mouth so tempting even as she slumbered. She had not dreamed that night, or walked the floor, or sewn.

Instead, when once she had awakened, he had taken her to his care to caress her until they had both required more. Enchanted with her spontaneous passion for him, he found himself unable to resist her need, and in his own, he had pressed her to the sheets and shown her more artistic delights. She had kept her promise to let him lead, though he knew if she were less honorable and he were less controlled, his desire to project himself fully inside her torrid gates to paradise would conquer all—even good sense.

He grew high and hard just gazing at her. Her round face turned to his, her lush lips begging to be licked, her beautiful, large pink nipples teasing him to come closer and suckle, her lean supple thighs open and inviting a taste. . . .

With reverent fingers he parted her, the musky aroma of her previous ardor for him appealing to his violent need to please her—and himself—once more. For as long as he was here, he would take her, sample her, savor her. She still flowed with her body's own milk and honey—and unquenchable desire for him. Even in her sleep, she undulated, rolling up her hips to give him what he craved. He tenderly exposed her pearl to kiss and nibble it. She moaned. He spiraled his tongue around her cream-drenched flesh and she groaned, her hands fluttering upon his skin.

Drugged with passion, she came not so much awake as alive to him, responding to his erotic drive to please her with a nubile grace. Husky with desire, she murmured nonsense as she floated in her euphoria and then shuddered in her repletion. Thrilled to have her so fulfilled, he used his years of training to restrain his own tremors and stop his seed. Though he knew it mounted in a reservoir he prayed had greater depths than he'd yet tested, he consoled his body's urge to love her completely with the fact that his mission here would never be to make a child, but to adore an angel. His Angel.

Shaken by a memory, he clutched her close and let her drift to sleep, then paced the floor. Nagging at his mind was how well his father had likened his mother to a redeeming angel.

"Before I met your mother," James St. Cyr had gasped hours before he went to his last rest, "I was dead. With her, I became all the things . . . *all* things a man should be. Yet, I never lived a normal life with her. After she was gone from me, my heart and soul withered. I never knew another her like. I have mourned her greatly. Now, praise a merciful God, I meet her soon in heaven."

Nicholas's recollection had sent shivers down his spine and compelled him to seek his own Angel, for truly she was that to him. Haunted by the ghosts of his past, he kissed her hair, her elegant throat, her velvet nipples. She stirred. This time, he loved her longer and with more skill. Watching her convulse not once but endlessly, he praised her capacity to give and cursed his need to keep such tight rein over his own body and soul.

Sleep came swiftly to **her but not at** all to him.

He settled her to the pillows, rolled to his back, ran a tortured hand through his hair, and considered the day before him.

If he could only have all of her and take her to wife in truth, he would acknowledge the God who had turned on him and whom he himself had spurned in anger. But was it not another of God's follies against him to place in his path that which he could not have? A woman to love and offer no way to keep her in the manner that a wife of his should expect to live her days?

Of course!

It was his punishment for only God knew what.

He left their bed to meet the morn. Another day to love her and to not.

Another day to save her for a life without him.

But when he left their chamber and put Gainsbridge's guard on notice to protect Angel, Nicholas opened the door to the wall walk and saw snow packed the land that morn. Fresh precipitation froze the land further so that no visitors would come that day.

Only his gyrfalcon came, and within minutes. With two leg bands. One with a ruby brooch he meant to adorn his wife's gowns. The other with a message that Demere was still at Swansdown, but Angel's father and two uncles paused in their journey and rested one day's ride from Windom.

So then once this snow melted, he'd encounter her sire and that man's brothers.

No matter, it gave him respite to go to the kitchen. There, he found Angel with the cook, discussing the meals for Advent. He took the opportunity to speak with the two young squires and see them stammer over the conditions of their tenure. But they seemed reticent to speak with him, and as he turned to take up conversation with the cook, his sweet Angel's questions turned the quest into a winning siege.

"We'll need dates from the cellar. Lots of them, so do bring them up for Cook. I thought we'd make a pudding with dates and oranges for our supper." Angel waited for their reaction as she sat across from them.

"I like that even better than any mummers," said Jack.

"Me, too," mused Gil. "The band of mummers who came to us at Landover last year were"—he wrinkled his nose—"not kind to me."

Nicholas spied Jack kick Gil under the table. He turned from Cook, one shoulder to the wall, listening, watching.

The blond boy blinked at his friend. "'Tis true."

"What did they do?" Angel asked Gil.

He shrugged and wiggled his feet. "Oh, played songs and did pantomimes."

"You don't like those entertainments?"

"I do, my lady. If we didn't have us in mourning for our late lord, I'd say I'd like a band of mummers here for Advent."

Jack folded his arms across his small chest. "Well, I wouldn't. We have enough men here to serve. We don't need more."

Angel reached over to smooth a shock of red hair

from Jack's brow. "With Lord Devereaux's and Gainsbridge's men here, I know your duties have multiplied. What can I do to ease your burden?"

The boys checked each other's eyes and then gazed at the floor.

"Someday, you realize," Angel began wistfully, "I may have a child."

Nicholas's heart skidded to a halt and paused at the precipice of a joy he'd never envisioned.

"Until that day," she went on, "I would like to think you two boys could substitute for those I lack. I'd like to make your service easier, kinder. I know that my last lord, the earl of Carlisle, was friendly and I seek to be not just concerned with your welfare but devoted to it. Whatever troubles you, I wish to know. Whatever needs correction, I will see it done."

Gil and Jack eyed Nicholas.

"And what of your newest husband?" asked Gil with pluck. "Rumor says he will rule this castle soon."

Angel's serene green eyes flowed to Nicholas and back to the children. "My husband knows I hold sway here. He is my bulwark, my support. Not my master."

Gil shook his head. "I don't believe it. My mother told me few husbands treat their wives as well as my father does her. She says some men beat their women, even while they carry a babe. How do we know—" He stopped, his tiny Adam's apple bobbing with the tension of venturing this far into impropriety. "How do we know if your new Lord Forrester will not hurt you and bring more men like the last Lord Forrester did?"

Obviously, Gil and Jack expected Nicholas to answer that, and nailed their eyes to his. When Nicholas looked to Angel for response, he smiled tenderly.

"This husband is good and kind to me, I swear it here and in any church. Have you not seen it to be so? He brings no men-at-arms, save a priest. He brings only friends like Lord Gainsbridge, whose men have been polite, have they not?"

"Aye, my lady," Jack said, hanging his head in shame.

"And normal," murmured Gil so lightly they would have missed it had anyone so much as moved a muscle.

But hear it they did.

Angel, Nicholas—even the aged Cook—froze.

Angel left her chair to kneel before Gil, who tried to hide his face in his shoulder. She would not allow it, but put fingers to his chin and brought his tear-filled eyes to meet hers.

"How are they not normal, Gil?" When the child whimpered, she persisted, gently. "They eat heartily, drink overmuch, I know. They have taken from villagers, I do hear, and I promise you that will end."

"One man raped a woman in the village not long ago!" spat Gil. "The Devil of Midnight and his men caught him and punished him! That serves 'em right."

"Now they try others," mourned Jack.

"Who?" urged Angel.

"Cook's kitchen maid, Kate, for one."

The next obvious question hung in the air, thick and fetid.

Gil bolted.

Nicholas caught him and gently returned him to his chair. "Let me go, let me go," he chanted.

Nicholas looked at Angel and waited.

She understood and put her hand to Gil's. "Tell me. I cannot correct that of which I know nothing."

"Of late, since days ago when you left for Montrose and Demere went for Swansdown, the three who are left here have . . . touched Jack and me . . . in unnatural ways."

So this was the vileness Tom Carter wished to escape.

Angel sank back against Nicholas, but squeezed Gil's hand. "Were there any besides these three who did this?"

In misery, Gil shook his head.

"You need no longer worry." She rose, her back straight, her body filled with a righteousness Nicholas knew no man could thwart.

"Oh, my lady!" Gil shot to his feet, grabbing for her hand. "You must not say I told you! They said they would kill me if I told! I don't want to die."

Miserable, Jack followed suit. "What are you going to do? They won't like it that we told! My father would not want to know this. You will not say, will you, my lady?"

"Nay, dear hearts." She drew both close with a tug at their hands. Her eyes caressed their terrified ones. "Fear not. For your secret is mine, my husband's, and Cook's. No one will ever know. Not even your aggressors. You must go now and fetch those dates Cook needs for the supper dish."

"You have not told us what you will do, my lady," Gil asked once more.

"I borrow another's words which I have heard most recently. Vengeance is mine." She smiled no smile. "Go now."

After they departed, she spun to Nicholas, tears in her eyes. With terrible determination she blinked them away and bit her trembling lips.

The bond they'd forged between them conveyed the

192

message of his heart. *Whatever you will, my darling wife, say but the word and I am yours to assist you in any way.*

He rejoiced when she nodded and whirled for the door, the great hall, her chair, and a regal implacability he'd always known she possessed. Hell had no fury like her.

Within minutes, she had Tom Carter, Peter, and Edwin escort the three Demere men-at-arms before her. Close behind came an outraged Michael Ross, whom she quieted with a look that could kill. Within seconds, she had the three draped in chains for molesting children.

"As soon as the snow and ice are cleared, you will be cast out," she told them without explanation as their former captain stepped forward. *"Silence,* Ross! *My* will shall be done here, not yours or theirs again. Speak and you can share their fate, I dare you." He did not and she glared at the three defilers. "Now hear me. Should I or my husband ever see you near my lands again, we will hold no court, but on that spot hang you to the nearest tree. Get you from my sight."

Gaping, they recovered enough of their senses by the time they hit the stairs to threaten her.

She stared at them, her silence her answer.

From the back of the room, Nicholas rose and strode to her. Her hands were freezing, her body cold as death.

Wordlessly, he led her to their chambers. There, he built the fire higher, took her in his arms, and cuddled her to him in her sumptuous solar nook. He stroked her back, kissed her cheek, hugged her close, and let her terror recede while his own mind whirled.

He forced back bile that someone would do such to

children. But in addition, someone in this house had committed murder and placed the blame on Angel. One act was as vile as the others. And were they in any way connected?

He had no answer, only less and less time to find one. More opponents on their way and an ever-increasing love for this woman who grew in power and might. An ever-growing desire to have her, all of her, for now, for any small space in time she might be his.

He stood with her in his embrace and walked to the bed, yanking back the rich black bed hangings. "I have a need for rest before the supper hour."

Ripe, rewarding sexuality was what he craved and what he gave her.

And she was contented. Lying in his arms afterward, she ran a hand down his chest and marveled at him. "You amaze me, Nicholas. You give me all of this and yet I suspect that this enchantment you show me provides less for you."

"I seek to show you how pleasure soothes the wounds of everyday life. Tell me, do I please you?"

She blushed. "You show me the clouds, the light of heaven."

"Your joy is my very air."

"Is it? At moments when I am blinded by what you give me, I want you with me, completely inside me."

"Nay. You know that way a child might come. To fill you thus would tempt my control."

"Do you ever lose control? Don't you want—or—need—"

"You give me all I desire." He kissed her passion-swollen lips. "I promised you you would never need to worry that I had given you a child. That means I must

194

continue to go to the brink, let you fly, watch you soar, and not follow."

"But you—"

"I can enjoy what you give me, sweeting. It is enough."

Of course, that was fast becoming the greatest lie he had ever told.

Chapter
10

~

She took more power with ease. Like one born to it, bred to it, he saw her size, cut, fit, and fashion it to her purpose, her personality. And Nicholas smiled to himself that he witnessed an angel testing her wings.

And perform wondrous works she did.

She surveyed the books Demere had taken to his keeping and found many errors in that man's addition.

She confiscated all other estate records from his rooms and piled them high in their bedchamber.

"I think I'll make a bonfire," she mused, and burst out laughing as she threw her arms about Nicholas and kissed his cheek. "I know, I know. I promise I won't burn them. I need them to figure the rents. But, oh, I would love to make a show of how he has failed."

"Mayhap Demere has not purposely made mistakes," he argued with amusement. "He might not possess the skill to cipher accurately, you realize."

"And pigs fly."

"I didn't think so."

When the kitchen maid revealed later that day that the wine stores were more depleted than she originally tallied, Angel asked for an accounting. Soon after, the maid reported that Demere had ordered four casks reserved from the funeral allotment. Angel rescinded the order and had the casks tapped for the supper hour.

And all through the day, Gil and Jack walked the castle with surer gait and smiles. The cook, evidently, had spread word of some—but true to the pact they had made, not all—of the reasons why the three Demere men-at-arms sat in the dungeon.

At supper, Nicholas strolled about the group and overheard Kate and the three Windom guards sympathize with the boys. They conjectured that Demere's men had bullied innocents once too often—and their good lady, who now had power, took it to protect children. They speculated as to whether she might be able to save them from Demere and his other three men. Michael Ross, who sat at one end of the table alone, glared and said nothing.

Nicholas, pleased at this progress, resumed his chair next to his wife, who spoke with Father Samuel, Allen, and Geoffrey about the coming Christmastime revels. Over that, Nicholas could hear Tom Carter at the table before him. The new captain of the house guard added his accolades to his lady's actions, telling his three men how he now thought they might be able to find some peace and quiet.

"Since we have sequestered some of those who have oppressed us most, I wonder if we might not make a bond in supporting the one to whom we owe the most—our good countess of Windom and Carlisle."

But one of Tom's men shook his head. "She may seem to be ours now, but she is also this new Lord Forrester's. And what do we know of him, eh?"

Tom Carter had an answer. "From what I saw this morning, I'll bet he stays his hand and lets her rule this household."

Undeterred, the challenger scoffed, "Aye, and how long will that last?"

"He is a different man from Chretian Forrester."

"I'll say!" said another. "That man could scarcely control his own chamberlain. This Nicholas Forrester, I swear, controls even the weather!"

Guffaws came from that remark. One even said that with the way the couple gazed at each other, he'd bet the groom showed his bride no control in their marriage bed. Another stated it was Advent and unheard of that a man should take a wife to bed against the rules of church.

"Pity's sake, let him love her," said the third man. "She had little of it from Lord Chretian. And none from her first husband. Hell, she deserves a little joy. Meanwhile, I don't mind it if this man makes her happy. He gives her other things as well. He could remain here for eternity if by his presence he keeps Demere's dogs of hell at bay. I say we could have more snow on us till next Michaelmas, I wouldn't care. I'll take this lord over either Windom or Carlisle."

During his discourse, Nell had emerged from the stairs with a filled jug of wine and heard them. As she plunked it on the table, she sneered at them. "Drink it, you swine. When Demere returns he'll not take any rashness from you, you can count on that."

"As long as he takes all from you, right, eh, Nell?" said the first man. "Ugh. Women. She sleeps with him and she thinks he can do no wrong. And some say men think with their cocks! Bah. A woman can be seduced by sex, too."

That made Nicholas silently agree but pause to consider the depths of his wine. He took a hefty draught, but could not ignore the whispers of his conscience. He put his head in one hand and rubbed his temples.

Did he lure her unjustly?

Nay.

He persuaded her to no point of view, supported her in no rash endeavor. He encouraged her to become the mistress of her own castle. To take what was rightfully hers. And cast out those who would disabuse her of her power.

He did not seduce her or control her for his own ends. He sought to help her perform her own duties. He sought to do her will, not his. And if in the bargain they had struck together he found her enchanting, was that sinful?

You know the logic here, Devil.

Aye, it was not a sin to want her, but the greater evil done to her to have her night and day, to know she meant never to take another man to her, and to understand that this ecstasy they both tasted could not, would not endure. For she had a life to live minus him.

And he had no life to offer her.

Nay! That was not true! Could he not remain as she had suggested last night? Could he not pretend to be this man and keep her at his side, safe, loving her?

You argue with the same rigid portion of your anatomy that guard does cite. Use your brains!

He had claimed a mission before he saw her and accepted her quest as his own. That would never change. No one knew who he really was, not even Angel. What prohibited him from remaining here, administering his men and their tasks from Windom . . . ?

Power drains from those who do not use it. Could you stay here, in her bed, in her arms, and not adhere to the domesticity she brings? Could you leave her often and for long periods of time without warning or explanation? Would she accept it easily? What of the day you would have to choose between the needs of your wife and your home—or your children—for the requirements of your other identity, your friends, and your mutual dedications? What then, after all those years and sacrifices, you were taken—and she and your children had to share your punishment? How then would you argue? What of your need to fight John and his eternal perfidy then, lord of the night? Does that die for your love of an Angel?

Never!

The same word you use as pledge to her. The same you used to your men who walk in the woods beyond this castle, keeping watch over you and her. Would you desert them for a comfortable existence, when they have denied themselves the same comforts to follow you? Be reasonable. Should you stay here, you might well rue the day you chose passion over honor.

'Tis not passion. But love.

Prove it, then. Make her happy. Help her become bold. But leave her to her life. Without you, she will endure, perhaps prosper.

And flower for another man.

She seeks no other.

When we met—was it days ago or perhaps eternities?—she declared she wanted to become celibate, take no man to her ever again.

With good reasons.

Yet she comes to me.

Because she enjoys what you do for her. If you continue here with her, she may recant her hope to remain alone. And though that satisfies your man's heart, it condemns your soul. For at the end of this illicit romance with her she will hate you for your duplicity, your double identity made triple for her. And to what joy? What peace?

Can you give her love with one hand and take it back with the other? Look at her. She smiles at you with her woman's heart in her eyes. She worries over you. Leave her to heaven, Devil. She needs no other man to bring her pain. Least of all you.

"Nicholas," she surveyed him with those grass green eyes and sent her hands to his, "are you ill?"

He squeezed her fingers, drew her up. "Nay. I want only the sight of you, the feel of you."

She flushed rosy, her joy at his admission warring with her embarrassment others might hear. "Nicholas, I—"

He pulled her from the table and the dais, across the room until at the corner of the stairs, when he could no longer bear the lack of her, he pressed her back against the wall. One hand on either side of her face, he towered over her, his lips descending. "Kiss me. I thirst for the taste of you now and always."

He need never have commanded. She came like flowing wine into his hands. The intoxication she brought made him vibrate with anger at himself, and with little finesse or patience he picked her up to carry her to their bed.

Still she did not flinch from him, not even as he shut the door and stripped her to her opalescent skin. He spread her wide upon their bed and savored every inch of her.

Wet from his mouth, her body slid over his fevered one and she rolled atop him. With her soft voice and hands, she claimed him. "Tell me what bothers you, my Devil. I would share your burdens." She kissed his jaw and throat, and worked her own black magic on his nipples, his navel, and below.

He shuddered to have her there. And reached out a hand to stay her.

She paused, a beatific smile upon her lips, her breasts teasing him, her hair hanging like an ivory silken curtain around his hips, and said, "How is it that you may pleasure me this way and I may not for you? 'Tis not fair and ever have you declared I should seek my own power."

His breath soughed loudly as she took him in her mouth and, surrounding him, stroked him hotly from point to hilt.

Sweet Jesus. "You're going to kill me."

She nipped him with sharp little teeth and chuckled when he could bear no more and tucked her beneath him.

Winding her hair around his wrists, he peered at her. *"Now* who is the devil here?"

She rolled wicked eyes at him.

"I'll show you what happens when you tempt a demon!"

She pursed her mouth in a tiny *oooo*. "Do that."

"You are my sin."

And then he showed her just how great a one that was. He pulled her to the edge of the bed and bent above her, ever careful, always watchful that he dared not open her gates too far. Thus, he slid along the portals to her ecstasy, offering her the only joy his manhood could ever give her.

For her, it was sublime. She clenched the sheets, arched, flew to the vistas he opened for her at liberty.

For him, it was hell. Perspiration beaded from his every pore. Instinct—and love—drove him faster, made him harder. And still he could not have her. He stopped, breathed deeply, forced his attention to the bed hangings, the urn—*Christ, anything!*—to take his mind from the one consuming thought his body and mind confessed. He desired all of her.

His fingers went inside her instead. Never too far to fully possess her, never too little to deny them both what they wanted, he claimed her. Her flower's nectar filled her, as he knew it would. Her petals closed about him, swelling, pulsing, driving him to lunacy for the need to replace his fingers with that other errant part of him. Grinding his teeth, he took his hand from her and put space between his body and hers.

She dug her nails into his hips. "I want you back."

He flung his head up. Counted stones within the wall. Traced the edges of the pillows with burning eyes. And still, control came unmercifully slowly. This time, his fingers circled, smoothed her sweet pearl and brought her to quick ecstasy.

As she shuddered beneath him, he wrapped her fiercely to him until her tremors finally ceased. *I love you so,* his heart begged to tell her. *I am so wrong to have you thus and want you all the more.*

203

As if she'd heard him, she outlined his lips and placed an angel's kiss there.

All through the night he held her. Upon the wall where the firelight danced, he saw the shadows within his soul and he beseeched a God who had so long ago rejected him. *Anything I will give—penance, alms, praise—if You will set her world aright, help me beat off those who would use her and oppress her. Then help me to leave her. Finally and forever. For she is Yours, as I can never be again.*

After morning prayers, he understood her God's first response when the road to Windom cleared enough that she banished the three Carlisle guards, just as she had said she would.

Before dinner, Nicholas saw her God's second response when Dunstan Montrose stood before Windom's great hall fire, his two formidable brothers to his right side. Another, slighter man stood at the other. As she and Nicholas had planned with Gainsbridge and Devereaux the moment they had seen them from the wall walk, these four stood alone.

Immediately upon entering the gatehouse, the two Montrose men-at-arms who had accompanied them had been shown to the kitchen in a sign of Angel's hospitality. Thus separating the noblemen from their only defense, Angel had ordered Tom Carter to show them to the great hall. Carter had offered the greatest courtesy and no hint of what was to come.

When Angel made no sign of welcome—and no one else usurped her right to make such a decision—a confused and nonplussed Dunstan stepped into the breach.

"Rumor runs into the countryside," he said, as he

trained his eyes on Nicholas, who stood close by her side, "that I should congratulate you on the occasion of your marriage to my daughter. I bring you my felicitations."

Nicholas arched a brow and glanced down at his wife.

"I don't believe you," she told her father quietly.

His eyes, as green as hers but glassy, widened with surprise at her effrontery. "Do as you wish, Daughter. I speak with this man. I want to know how this came to pass. I would see the priest. I need to see the papers that make this union a fact."

Nicholas smiled smoothly.

Angel cast her eyes to a far corner from whence came forth Father Samuel.

Hands tucked high up into his trailing black robes, Samuel glared at Angel's kinsmen with rheumy eyes. "Then you wish to examine me, my lord. For I did marry them."

"You know this man?" Dunstan pointed a finger at Nicholas.

Samuel's mouth hitched up to one corner. "Aye, my lord. I have been in his service for more than a year. And well he does by me, too. May he forgive you your transgressions against his wife and take you to his good care as he has me. You will not sorrow, I vouchsafe for that."

"I wish to know how you could marry without banns! Without my consent! And without the king's!"

"With just cause, I have the power to waive banns as can any priest, my lord. Come, come, try not to show us you are stupid, sir, when we know you for better. You have controlled this good lady in two marriages and felt your own power over her twice."

Confronted by a man of God speaking truth, Dunstan had the temerity to demur. "I have arranged two suitable matches for her—and she honors me not for them."

"Ahhh. Would you, if you were she? Would you wed a child, sir, and then an old man, and then praise the man who made you do it?" Samuel placed his considerable bulk squarely in front of Dunstan so that her father had to look the priest in the eye. "Look at my good lord standing here, sir. If you were bent on grandchildren to inherit, I'd say I'd take this man to create them rather than the two you previously chose for your daughter. Or do you not care if your line breeds sickly babes, imbeciles . . . or worse?"

"Enough! Of course, I care. But now I care more for what the king will think. In that provision in the great charter he signed at Runnymede, he said he would not force a widow to wed, but he must approve any marriage she does make."

Angel felt a frisson climb her spine. "John has too much to worry over at the moment to fret over my marriage."

Dunstan scoffed. "You hope."

"No matter," said Father Samuel. "Whatever John thinks of the marriage, 'tis done. The vows taken, the contracts signed."

"The consummation performed?" Dunstan asked.

Nicholas looked as if he might kill him with a glance, yet did he remain silent.

Dunstan stared at Angel. *You* decide whether I stay or go?" He could not decide if he should believe his ears and eyes.

"Conclude what you will," she told him, and gave a nod at Tom Carter at the stairs.

From there came forth a party of Windom's four guards, Gainsbridge and his four, and Devereaux and his two. Swords drawn, daggers poised, they spread in a malicious circle, all the more ominous for their opponents' lack of any arms.

Montrose surveyed them like a smart man and, if he were not prudent, a dead one. "Clearly, Daughter, you also decide whether I live or die."

"As you once did with me. But I have no wish to taint my soul to punish you. Therefore, you and your party may stay the night." Imperious in her power, she eyed the man who had once tortured her and then cast a look at the stranger among them.

He came forward. Tall as she, he met her with a nervous look of condolence. "I am Hugh Lambert, my lady. And I must say," he inhaled mightily, "I am relieved you are already married."

"Is that so." She said it calmly, but Nicholas could feel the tension in her muscles. "Why is that, Lord Lambert?"

"I wish to wed another, madam, and came only because my father bade me do so."

"I see. 'Tis no way to begin a union, is it, my lord?" Her eyes shot to her father's. "To be made to use your body to do some other person's will."

Nicholas took her words as a third sign—a confirmation—from her God that the Devil of Midnight must ultimately leave his Angel to her own happiness.

When she closed their chamber door, she fretted. "I was too harsh with him."

"He needed every word," Nicholas said as he led her to a chair. He lifted her chin with a finger. "You are such a just and wise person that you wish to grant him forgiveness, I know. But he will never value it unless first he performs his penance. Let him. He will respect you the more for it. And I will love to see him suffer."

She smiled at his wicked words and innocent golden eyes. "You would see no one suffer, my Devil."

"Least of all you."

"You are so good to me."

"No one has ever meant as much to me."

She waited for more. Yet, to ask was not wise. Someday he must go and she would yearn ever after for his smile, his touch, his laughter and logic. Why did she have to come alive with the one man who was forbidden to her?

She took a taste of his lips and savored the sweetness of his kindness and the bitterness of their situation. Without an answer for their personal quandary, she ignored her need to speak of their relationship for the necessity of their current problem.

She rose to pace before him. "We have seen Devereaux join us for political reasons and my father succumb to the wisdom of a priest and the power of sheer numbers. Will Demere withdraw as easily?"

"He is outnumbered, even though he returns with his three guards. And with what we have to say about his handling of the books, I think he will leave us quickly."

"Pray God that Bartlett brings no guard of his own and retires as easily."

"Once we show Bartlett your marriage papers and let Father Samuel at him, I doubt we'll have any problems."

"Would that I may cast out Bartlett and Demere

before they have the chance to accuse me in public of killing Chretian."

Nicholas grew pensive.

She knew he contemplated their greatest problem and she stared at the rafters. "If only we knew who killed Chretian."

"We know not, sweeting," Nicholas snapped from his reveries, "but we will." He began to strip himself of his sapphire blue brocade tunic, and from her wooden chest where he stored his rich and wonderful clothes, he extracted one of many sleek black silk garments such as he'd worn the night she captured him. She knew he preferred these odd items to the gaudier ones he wore for the consumption of her household and guests.

"Why do you wear these?" she ventured.

"I lived in them for so long, I like the feel of them. The warmth and strength. The warriors of the Scourge of the Steppes wear them to ensure no arrows pierce them in battle. And in the company of other princes who are supposedly at peace, they wear them to assure no dagger makes a mortal point." At her gasp, he shook his head and smiled. "Nay, my darling, I doubt anyone will take a dagger to me inside these walls. But when one is accustomed to such garb, it is difficult to break the habits of a lifetime."

"Was it? A lifetime?"

He paused and she saw visions of his past shadow his eyes. "Most of mine. I was sold, held prisoner, but only when this Scourge of God bought me seven years ago did I find equality and fair treatment."

"Why would anyone *buy* a man?"

"He purchased me because I knew the Holy Land and the desert near Samarkand. He needed an informant who could speak their languages and remembered their landscapes, their fortifications, and the tactics of their armies. I knew all of that, you see, because when I was fourteen I was sold into slavery." He spun away, ostensibly to finish dressing, but she knew better.

She put her arms about him, and pressed her cheek to his strong back. Though she burned to know who he really was, she would not ask for more of this that tortured him and his pride. "Who is this man then, who redeemed you?"

"Genghis Khan. That one I told you of who would rule the Middle Kingdom and take it from the Son of Heaven. Genghis is a nomad, a fierce warrior who has conquered most of the world. The lord of all the realms beyond our imagination. Whose armies number hundreds of thousands and move upon the earth with the speed of demons on black steeds. Whose mercy is none. And whose word is absolute law." He turned in her arms and ran a hand up into her hair.

"I was his emissary to his minions, and for that he rewarded me with much. Until one day I was able to buy my freedom. He could have kept me, beat me, or chained me to his will, as was most likely with him when someone displeased him. Barring that, he could have killed me for such impertinence as to want to leave the Great One of the World. But amazingly, he let me go. 'Tis the greatest sign of respect to allow someone you value to leave you."

She felt her heart contract, knowing he told her another reason of why the Khan had freed him. *Was not this gift of freedom also a sign of love?*

Nicholas spoke no word of it. Instead, he grit his teeth against it, snatched up a fat candle, and headed for the tunnel to which he had not yet found an exit. "'Twould help us in our search for a murderer if I could find some beginning or end to this corridor."

Ignoring her dejection at his failure to speak of his care for her, but grabbing another kind of courage with both hands, she halted him. "I want to come."

"'Tis not necessary."

"To me it is."

He grinned and pressed her body flush to his, his lips to her temple. "Perhaps you will remember something useful."

She licked her lips and let her head fall back to peer into his absurdly wonderful eyes. "And forget something horrid."

He kissed her deeply, quickly. Then took up another candle and her hand.

It was worse and not as bad as she remembered. Worse because it was hell-dark, damp, and fetid. But not as awful as her first exposure to such a void. For now, not only did she have her beloved near her to befriend her in such depths, but she also had those other qualities he bid her nurture. And in that black hole she paused, blinded by the knowledge that she loved him. Loved him simply, completely. Whoever he was. Wherever he had come from. Aye, she loved him. For *what* he was. Humorous even after seizure in a winnowing sheet. Logical before friend and foe alike. Considerate in her house, in her bed, with her body.

She quivered with remembered joy.

He took it as fright and instantly wrapped his arms about her. It was like being enfolded by the night, a mantle of smooth, sinuous care encompassing her within the mysteries of the universe. She absorbed joy from him as once she had taken encouragement and support.

"I am not afraid," she whispered to his ear and kissed him there. "Let us continue."

As if the sun had pierced the darkness, she could tell he smiled at her. Hugging her, he turned and they took more steps into oblivion.

"I have come this way before," he told her. "It merited me nothing. We go this way."

Edging along a moldy wall, they turned left and left again. Their toes stubbed on steps. With Nicholas in the lead, they rose two steps to walk another length and turn left again. A small arrow of light pierced the doom. Giving her hand a tiny squeeze, he urged them toward it and bent. He peered into it, then muffled a curse. With no second for thought, he pivoted and would have tugged her with him.

But she stood her ground.

He had to pause.

She bent.

Good God in heaven. She felt a chill no damp corridor of Hades could create. Through this hole one could view her bedchamber, her bed, *their* bed—hers and Nicholas's.

But the next flash of lightning made her bones melt.

This was her bed and Chretian's.

She clamped a hand over her mouth. She felt ill. Sick of this labyrinth of lies. Of perversity. Deceit and murder. *Where did it end?*

Her sweet husband understood. He gathered her into his arms and molded her to his care. With only kisses in her hair, he told her much. How he sorrowed for this latest evidence of treachery within her midst. How he wished it were not so. How he would help her, as he always had, find a way out to freedom. But nestling his lips to her ear, he mouthed, *Come. There may be more.*

There was none.

They wove this way and that, and at a blank wall where she would have wailed in frustration, she hit the stones with the flat of her hand . . . and found it gave with a creak. She shrank back into Nicholas's arms. He put her behind him, and as the wall fell open they saw it led to a guarderobe. Just as her entrance did.

Thanking God, she saw no one sat there. She froze, praying no one heard. Dousing his candle, Nicholas handed it to her and took his dagger from his belt. In the waning light, she saw him put a finger to his lips, touch hers in a kiss, and disappear round the corner.

In a blink, he was back. Closing the door. Grasping her hand. Leading them down the tunnels of this purgatory, back to their chamber, her solar, and the heaven of his arms.

He held her for the longest time. She let him, confused, content to let his love seep into the horror that was her life here. But soon, she knew it was not enough. For she might find surcease here with him, but beyond his arms—as ever—lay a world in wait for her. And she could not fail to meet it in her own way—or find herself cut by others' specifications. And that she would no longer allow. For her sin had been one of omission. Now, whatever sin she committed would be a conscious act.

He left her, poured a large goblet of wine from their urn, and bade her drink it. "All of it."

She tried, but in the end she shared it with him.

He offered what she needed. "That chamber belongs to the guard. Carlisle's six. I can tell because it is devoid of any activity, what with the three cast out this morning and the other three gone with Demere."

"So any one of them . . ." She retched with the idea. "All of them could have used the squint hole to see us." She fell to his chest in shame.

He cupped her face. "What we have done is no disgrace. We have loved as a man and woman do. That is all and everything, my darling."

She groaned. Tears threatened as they had not in days. "What I share with you is sacred. I wish no one to laugh or scoff at what you are to me, what you bring to me."

He caressed her mouth with a gentle thumb. "We do not *know* anyone saw us. Perhaps no one knows of the squint."

"But perhaps the squint is the means by which someone knew Chretian was alone that night he died."

Her Devil could not deny it.

"And what," she dropped her voice to a whisper, "if someone can hear what is said here, too?"

"I doubt it. The walls are too thick. But I shall test it. I'll return and you come into the chamber and speak in normal tones."

He left. She conversed like an idiot to herself. When he returned, he shook his head. "Nothing. We are safe from that exposure."

A knock came at the outer bedchamber door and Angel jumped, then called to let them enter.

"Milady, milord." Kate came round the solar door and curtsied. "Nell sent me to get the bed linens for the weekly wash."

When the girl had departed with her arms full of the sheets and toweling, Nicholas stood and said, "Let us go up to the wall walk. I must signal my gyrfalcon and relieve her of the daily message."

"Aye," Angel sorrowed, "focused on our enemies within, I have forgotten those without."

Minutes later, as Nicholas unrolled the tiny parchment from his fowl's leg band he stared at her. His breathing slowed and his body tensed. "Roger Bartlett comes with Demere. Tonight. Probably by suppertime."

That news killed any delight she may have found in the delicately wrought gold chain bracelet that fell from the bird's other leg band.

Chapter

11

~~

Wondering about the man whom she resembled most of his two children, and who had twice used her to his will, Angel gazed at her father as he faced her allies, her husband, and her in her great hall. She measured Dunstan's power—and found it permanently shortened. By her own.

"I tell you, my Lord Forrester, my motives are not all bad." Dunstan said it without a hint of remorse.

Nicholas glared at him from his chair.

"I simply wanted my daughter married to a man who would honor me as his father-in-law and not encroach on my lands. You see, we three," he indicated his two brothers in their chairs with a nod, "equally divided at my father's death what was once his great domain. Because Alex is widowered and Graham has not yet married, we worry over the future. We decided long ago to ensure that, thus seemingly separate as we are in land, we never are in spirit. That way we maintain our influence over affairs in the northwestern part of England."

"A diplomatic maneuver," declared Nicholas as he swirled the wine in his cup. His mood was no lighter than this morning, nor made brighter by her father's attempt at reason.

"Especially in light of John's continuing troubles with some barons and now with the invasion of French armies."

Angel knew their fish had bitten on the bait. For a long time this afternoon had she, Nicholas, Gainsbridge, and Devereaux debated the worm they might use to lure her family to their cause. With the subject appearing this early in the conversation, she folded her hands together in hope.

Nicholas looked her father in the eye. "Aye, useful with John. But not one which you may use ever again to abuse your daughter, her lands—or our children and their entitlements."

Angel stilled. For Nicholas to discuss the children they would never have made her heart ache. She wanted them. But more, she wanted him. She desired his tender caresses, his wild expressions of a regard that went beyond the bargain they had struck, further into the desire they had found, and into a rapture she wished to claim more fully. She knew Nicholas failed to cross the boundaries to protect her. But she also knew his control crumbled before the siege of their senses on the growing love they bore each other. For he did love her, didn't he? Unseasoned with any caring man before this, she had only her heart to rely upon for answer. Her head certainly told her she was mad even to ask.

She took a drink of her wine and stared into her goblet.

"Are there?" snapped her father as he peered at Nicholas and her. "Children?"

"Sire!" Angel seethed, disgusted, as Nicholas cursed. "My lord and I have been wed less than a week."

"Aye, but last night we did have open to us the hospitality of the castle of Tremaine. That good lord was the one to tell us of your marriage, Daughter. He also said that rumors have it you and your newest husband here knew each other before the death of your last husband."

"'Tis a lie," she whispered, then wondered if he had also heard the rumor that she had killed Chretian. Her gaze went to Nicholas, who saw her question and gave a silent answer she understood as one of watch and wait.

"A lie, eh?" Dunstan nodded his white-blond head continually at Nicholas. "*How* can that be? Not only at Tremaine, where rumor reigns, but here, where more fact must dwell, I have heard how you have taken her to wife so quickly and made a potent display of how you care for my child." At her glare, he demurred. "Perhaps, no longer that. But what of yours? Are there any from this union?"

She choked on his arrogance.

Nicholas cupped her shoulder with a strong hand. "If there were, we would tell you last, Montrose. You have never had a care for her modesty or propriety." He scanned Allen Gainsbridge's and Geoffrey Devereaux's distress for Angel at her father's crudeness. "You have never had a care for her at all before this. Why now?"

"I did. She never saw it thus."

"How could she when you threw her in a dungeon?"

"She was impertinent!"

"She was terrorized, starved!"

"She is my only heir! Since the death of her older sister, Angelica is my sole concern. And because my brothers have no heirs, she is most important to us. So would you also wish to know the paternity of the one who would own your lands, Lord Forrester. So if she is with child—and it is Chretian's—"

Angel straightened. "I was married to Chretian only four months, Sire." She swallowed, unable to go on and say why such a pregnancy could never be. To declare such truth about her relationship to Chretian would give her enemies reason to argue her legitimacy as his wife and even depose her. It would give her power away, power she had only lately taken unto herself—and without which she could not rule here nor perhaps even survive.

"Once is enough to—"

Nicholas growled. "My wife, as you might well expect, does not wish to discuss the intimate details of her last marriage. Even if she owed you the courtesy of such knowledge, I would never think it seemly. As it is, you do not deserve such."

Dunstan's round face wizened with lines of age and worry. He picked at his tunic hem, reflective. "I have done many things she may not have found—"

"Oh, please." Angel had had enough of this. "Do *not* try to justify what you did to me."

"'Tis done and over. Your first husband dead. All of this yours. Then Carlisle, too. And though Carlisle is a smaller domain, I would surmise its addition makes you the landowner of the largest domain in northeast England."

"Next to the earl of Swansdown," added Geoffrey.

Allen Gainsbridge chortled and combed his beard with his fingers. "And thus she is the only major threat to King John in these climes."

Her father checked the expressions of his two brothers. "So that leads us to the next most important question. . . ." He spun to Nicholas. "What do you bring to this union, Lord Forrester?" His eyes scanned Angel's wedding ring, bracelet, and string of pearls.

Nicholas smiled sardonically. "Wealth."

"Gold?"

"Aye."

Angel heard the chime of truth in her husband's voice and stared at him. He had given her these things, told her how he had been granted them or bought them, conjuring ideas in her head of a few baubles he had accumulated. But this simple affirmation created illusions of more. Much more.

Her father, not sure to believe his ears, grew crass. "How much?"

Nicholas grinned. "Bars of it as long as your finger and end to end, equal to the circumference of this castle."

Alex, Graham, and Geoffrey grew more attentive while Dunstan leaned forward. "Jewels?"

"Which do you prefer?"

Loving this, Angel trailed her hand down the length of her pearls and watched her father gape, confounded.

When finally he spoke, it was another question. "Spices?"

"A practical man. Coriander? Cinnamon? Ginseng. Lotus root. Tiger's teeth. Dragon's bones."

"You go too far, Forrester." Her father fell back in

his chair. "This is not jest. I want to know how you will provide for my daughter and your children."

Nicholas narrowed his eyes at Dunstan, and Angel knew the control he showed her in his loving arms was as expert as this he used against his enemies. "If you think, Montrose, Angel will ever need to come to you for anything, I vow she'll never see your face. She will have whatever she needs—gold, gems, spices, silks— till I lie cold in my grave, and decades afterward when I am dust."

"Aha! You admit, then, you bring no land!"

"Not in any way that would matter to you."

For a man who based all his actions on the retention of his land, that was so much babble to Dunstan. "What's the basis of this match, then?"

"'Tis none you'd understand or value, Montrose. But one of our own making."

"For lust," he snorted.

"Or power," Nicholas replied coolly, and Angel knew he implied *hers*. "Believe what you will, Montrose. I care not. My wife is mine and I am hers, for better and worse, rich and poor. You cannot change it. You could accept it more than you have, though, and thus ensure a greater treasure for us all."

Angel saw her father mull that, then check Alex and Graham for their approval to proceed.

Graham, the youngest Montrose, rose to walk toward Nicholas. Angel felt shock to see how the two equaled each other in height and dark complexion, if not quite in broad build. "I would hear more of your thinking on this," he told Nicholas easily.

Angel smiled in satisfaction that the hope she and Nicholas, along with Allen and Geoffrey, had nurtured just before this meeting had borne such flower.

Now it was her duty to see if they could but pluck the fruit. She gazed at her father and two uncles in turn. "Ever have the three of you sought each other's help and support. What if I offered an alliance, based on your support of me in my endeavors? Would you favor me above all others?"

Her father cocked a pale brow. "What are these *endeavors?*"

Alex pursed his lips. "And who are these *others?*"

"I seek to rule my own lands and my treasury by myself."

Her father thought that very amusing. "What says your third husband to that?"

When no laughter nor verbal answer came to him, embarrassment did. He tried to cloak it in challenge. "I see. Your husband will spend his days counting his wealth, while you administer your estates. Including the Windom one? And what says Lord Devereaux to that?"

Geoffrey's brown eyes sparkled. "I say you need to hear the rest of Lady Forrester's offer."

"You can't tell me that as the rightful heir to Windom, you will allow her to take her dower *and* this castle and its environs as her own? What ails you, man?"

Geoffrey smiled into his cup. "*You* may value land highly, but it is not the only treasure, Lord Montrose. As for me, I do not wish to lose good men over such a dispute. I have my own estates to administer and villeins to aid, and I value peace for them and me. Extending my power is not as important to me as keeping the tranquility of my days. And these past few years with King John have been far from that. Life is hard enough than to ask for more troubles. So in this matter with your daughter, I would rather align myself with her and her new husband to counter another man who seeks to take this domain from her."

Dunstan raked his hair. "And who might that be?" he roared.

"Roger Bartlett," Angel said quietly.

In horror, her father turned to her. "Bartlett? But he is John's confidant and main supporter in the north. Since when is Bartlett interested in you, Angelica?"

"Since Chretian's death. His chamberlain, Eugene Demere, has gone to bring him here and force me to marry him." She waited for her father to see the horror of this. And the illogic.

He narrowed his eyes at her and then surveyed Nicholas. "Since, when Bartlett arrives, he will find you already *married,* where is the threat you seek to enlist me to combat?"

Dropping words like hot coals into his lap, she told him of Chretian's murder.

He sat, consumed.

So did his brothers.

Then she told him of Demere's threat.

Dunstan was shocked, but not enough to render him dumb or mute. "And you know not who did kill Chretian."

"I would to God I did. I have a few suspicions. A few indications of what may have happened, but no culprit."

That barely registering in Dunstan's brain, she moved forward relentlessly. Knowing paternal sympathy would never be the means to bring her father to her side, she chose instead the surer route to her father's compassion—greed.

"I need you and will see you well compensated for

it. The proceeds from my forests for this year perhaps might soothe your qualms about loss of my dowered Montrose lands? . . . I thought so. For certainly, you realize that once Bartlett realizes he is foiled and Demere does, too, they will both leave to try to gain King John's support to annul this marriage—or worse, take me to John and try me for murder."

Dunstan nodded. "And for treason. John will not take it lightly that you killed his man, but more, he will have to make a show of a woman who took another to husband against his will. Particularly a wealthy widow who wed a man of whom no one seems to have heard anything before this. And how, I ask myself, can that be?" He peered at Nicholas.

Allen Gainsbridge, who had sat as quietly through this as the cowed Hugh Lambert, now rose to refill his cup with wine. In deference he hoisted the flagon toward Dunstan and said, "More, my lord? You will need it, I wager, for this next. You see, I know a thing or two about Bartlett and his ambitions." Allen did the round to empty the jug, then resumed his chair next to Nicholas. All eyes stayed on him.

He recounted Roger Bartlett's befriending of the willful John. How Bartlett had prospered from it in land and offices and power. How he never abandoned support of the king whom many would see clipped of his aggression. "All to Bartlett's own ends, of course. And now that John faces invasion by Philip of France and so much opposition from his own barons—"

"—Led by you," said Dunstan.

"And by others near and dear to us. Now that that is so, if you come to your daughter's assistance in this matter, the odds are we would have John doing our will."

"Perhaps to you this looks advantageous, my Lord Gainsbridge. But if we support Angelica and we fail, we could *all* be tried for treason."

"True. But I doubt we could fail."

"How so?" Dunstan chuckled ruefully. "Are you a lunatic or a magician?"

"It helps when I am some of both."

"Explain yourself."

"Perhaps you have not counted us, but we are many and outnumber any Demere sympathizers left in this castle. In fact, his three most loyal guards occupied your good daughter's dungeon until this morning, when she cast them out. Outside, we have others who support us."

"Hah! Who? I saw no one. Lord Tremaine says only that two of John's knights have come lately to report back to the king of rebellious barons in the area. But I have heard that you, my Lord Gainsbridge, do continue your opposition to John. It is even rumored you do keep company with the Devil of Midnight."

Allen lifted an open palm. "Believe as you will."

Dunstan snorted. "Next you'll tell me his disciples stand outside the gate." When Gainsbridge did not disabuse her father of the statement, he sputtered, "Nay. You *are* a lunatic." Still, his brow furrowed and his eyes strayed—as did those of his brothers, Lambert and Geoffrey, one by startled one—toward Nicholas.

Dunstan was the first to recover. *"Nay,* I cannot believe that."

A shiver of despair that anyone might discern her Nicholas's true identity and take him from her made Angel rise and put this matter to the final test. "What you think is irrelevant, Sire. What you *do* is more

225

important to me. Will you or will you not help us with Demere and Bartlett?"

Dunstan stared at her.

Alex rose to his feet. "I will."

"So, too, will I," echoed Graham. "Dunstan?"

A scrambling on the stairs made many of the noblemen turn. From the corner of her eye, Angel saw Nicholas raise a hand and beckon someone forward.

"My lord and lady," panted Tom Carter, "a party of five, including Demere, stands outside the gate. Do we lower the drawbridge?"

Nicholas took her cold hand into his warm one. "What say you, sweet wife?"

"Let them in and strip them of their arms inside the gatehouse—but before you go, Tom," she considered the proud man who was her parent and who had never tasted of the dungeon, "you may do me one other service. First, I need only know one thing from this man. Tell me, Sire, what is your decision?"

"Angelica," Dunstan acceded to circumstances he could not control. "I would offer you my help, Daughter."

Like a phalanx of a heavenly host, the men surrounded Angel as she sat her chair, centered as it was before the great hall's fire. Her husband stood to her right, and as the sound of tramping feet upon the stairs announced the coming of the two she feared to meet, she reached for Nicholas's hand. He took hers, kissed it, and returned it to her lap. The act gave her serenity to glove her quaking courage.

Led by Tom Carter, Eugene Demere and Roger Bartlett walked the stairs shoulder to shoulder.

Demere, whose surly attitude the night he had accused her of murder would ever burn in her brain, appeared nonchalant.

The shock rocked her confidence. Once again, she feared the outcome here because Demere had always been a man to show his emotions on his face.

The sight of Roger Bartlett drove that thought away.

Here stood the man whom all these others wished to thwart. Here was the confidant of the king whom these wise men behind her could finally challenge because of her and her boldness to seize a Devil and make a bargain with him.

She thrilled and shuddered.

He was a big man, used to leading, succeeding in his every quest. With noble head framed by black hair and a pointed beard salted in gray, he was a comely man. Though he reminded her of her Devil in demeanor, he never could equal him for height or handsomeness or majesty.

"My Lady Forrester," Bartlett inclined his head in deference.

She knew at once he had heard from somewhere that she was married, else would he have used the title of Carlisle.

Her skin prickled. Another signal of an aspect awry. What was it?

"I am pleased to be welcomed into your presence." Bartlett cast a casual glance over her male company, stalling at Nicholas, who stood closest and obviously dearest. He moved on, unaffected. "I must say I expected fewer guests. I also expected a more cordial welcome."

"Circumstances have changed, my Lord Swansdown." She saw Nicholas's hand clench, the only sign he observed this man's presence. "You were summoned here by one who was less than kind to me."

Bartlett's tawny eyes ran to Demere's black ones. "Is that so?" He turned to Angel and smiled without a trace of guile. "I never knew."

"There is much to tell. The most important of it is that I am already married, sir."

"So I understand from rumor at Tremaine Castle. We hastened here as soon as we learned of it. A woman married so quickly—even before her late lord is cold—seems suspect. And you do have a history of marrying in haste," he said with a hint of snideness she resented. "We did not want you taken against your will."

Laughter bubbled in her throat. "Absurd."

"Oh, how so?"

"Really, my lord, you cannot feign such innocence with me. Nor with these men who support me. They know *all,* Swansdown."

"Perhaps, then, you should tell me *all.* I do not take lightly the stripping of arms from me and my men. Such vulnerability demands the satisfaction of at least an explanation."

As she related the story of Demere's threat to make her marry him, Bartlett arched a brow and calmly said, "How interesting. And I thought, my lady, that my proposal would find your favor because I brought you wealth and position and further blessings from our king." He sighed. "Frankly, Demere, I did not know you possessed the boldness. Chretian Forrester underestimated you, didn't he? Tell us what you know of this."

Demere, ever the gaunt look of a fox upon his features, shifted black eyes from Angel's assembly to his cohort. "Only as she has told you, my lord."

"Did you ever try to find the one who did it?"

"No."

"But simply used the ploy to intimidate her." Bartlett shook his head. "Not wise of you, Demere. Not to let a murderer run free. Nor to have a care for a lady who by her looks and bearing could never kill a fly. No wonder she sought aid—and quite a bit of it."

Bartlett examined a rigid Nicholas, and she could have sworn he sought some sign of a proclivity to interfere. When nothing came, he focused once more on Angel.

"Very well. I see you mean to keep your sanctity and your estates for yourself and your new husband. Since I assume you have documents to prove the union legally, and because I would lay down gold coins the sacrament has been blessed and consummated, I cannot quarrel with what is fact. Would you then permit me a night's hospitality under your roof so that I might return to my king tomorrow with the interesting confirmation of your marriage?"

"He knows already?"

"I sent a messenger with news of the rumor when first I heard it from Lord Tremaine."

So, it was done. She struggled mightily not to look too pleased. Instead, she considered his request.

She saw no problems with lodging him for the night. He had no arms. Neither did his knights. Until they left, Bartlett and his men would remain unarmed and separated. Furthermore, she wished to make no everlasting quarrel with the earl of Swansdown. After all, he was her neighbor to the south. And as a friend of John, Roger Bartlett could be a valuable ally as any of these men arrayed at her side.

"On two conditions, sir."

"Name them."

"You tell King John what you have said here about me. That I could never kill any living creature."

His oddly light eyes sparked with an emotion she likened to kindness. "'Twill be my pleasure, madam, to tell him how the woman fits the perfection of her name."

Nicholas stiffened.

She smiled. "Thank you."

"And the second?"

"Demere goes with you."

The chamberlain opened his mouth to object, but Bartlett said, "Done. Although I would not put him in my service, considering his perfidy to you, he may ride with me as far as Nottingham, where I meet the king for Christmas revels. There, I assure you, I will tell John of Demere's activities, and then"—he sized Demere for a coffin—"this man may wish to offer his services elsewhere." Bartlett grinned at Angel, all polite rectitude. "Perhaps now, my lady, you will do me the courtesy to introduce me to your guests."

She began with Hugh Lambert, who said nothing. Then she brought forth her father and uncles with whom Bartlett exchanged pleasantries of little consequence, other than to say he understood they were far from home in such a perilous time.

Her father eyed him. "We rushed to see to my daughter's welfare when we knew she was once more widowed and needed her family's support."

"Aye, so understandable. Though we have never

met, my Lord Montrose, I have heard of you and your brothers' independent stance in the northwest. You and yours do not always favor John. Sometime, over wine, I hope we can discuss our differences like rational men."

At her father's noncommittal response, she introduced Bartlett to Geoffrey Devereaux.

"How interesting you are here," Bartlett said. "For such circumstances, I should have expected it." To him, he made no sign he wished to talk, for the look on Geoffrey's face precluded it.

Before Allen Gainsbridge, he smiled lopsidedly. "We meet again, Gainsbridge. This time, as at Runnymede, the advantage is yours."

"I shall attempt to make it thus always."

Bartlett smiled with vacant eyes. "I never doubted it. Nor does our king."

"Then he is wise . . . in some things."

Bartlett faced Nicholas, who had not moved one muscle since the party had entered.

"This is my husband, Lord Nicholas Forrester."

The two men stared at each other, eye to eye. No smiles, no nods, no sign of any deference to social form crossed between them.

"I wish you well of your new wife, my lord," Bartlett finally broke the silence. "She is lovely in person and in heart. Any man would be honored to claim her."

"I will be all the more honored when you leave us on the morrow, Bartlett."

The lack of a polite citing of his nobility affected Bartlett not in the least. Angel frowned, recalling with what virulence Nicholas declared he knew the earl and hated him. While that might have been so, she saw here that Roger seemed a reasonable man. Smart enough to know when he had lost a battle, and intelligent enough to retire from the field when the day was so handily won by a larger force.

Though she had prepared to send Roger and Demere to the dungeon with the others, she was relieved she needn't.

"We have supper ready, my Lord Swansdown. I would see you well cared for under my roof. Come, you will dine heartily before we send you off to John with our good news."

The table laid, the two young squires, Gil and Jack, came forth with Kate the kitchen maid to serve the meal. Nell followed, her blue eyes on Demere, her smile for him alone. But he did not return it.

Instead, the chamberlain chose to take a place at the far end of one long table. His black eyes, which once had bored holes into Angel's heart with their accusations of murder, now rushed over her in simple hatred. To make it all the more potent, he refused to talk, even when a disturbed Michael Ross entered and attempted it.

Angel could never have been more shocked. Or more happy.

Nicholas could not have been more wary.

She put a hand to his forearm as Gil and Jack brought forth a rack of ribs. She whispered so that Bartlett, who sat at her other hand, would not hear. "Nicholas, you need not be so troubled now. All is done."

"Be not so certain. I do not like the looks of him."

"Obviously. But you can be civil."

"Never to him."

"I will not have you alienate him."

"He has me, long ago."

Undone, she sat back in her chair and watched with dead eyes the communion of her allies with each other. The Devereauxs with the Gainsbridges, the Montroses and Windoms, and even Roger Bartlett. She watched them accept food from Gil and Jack's platters and quaff her wine. Their actions soothed some of her worries, but Nicholas's silent anger ate at her own blossoming good humor.

She picked at her food.

"You keep a good table, madam," said Bartlett, as if he were an ordinary guest. A friend.

She smiled at him for the first time. "Thank you. I try to keep it so."

"Chretian allowed you control over your household."

"You knew him well?"

"Aye. Very. He was a kind man. John liked him, too."

"Why, then, have we not seen you here before this?"

"I have been with John, who is assailed on all sides. By his own barons and by the French who seek to take his crown from him. John is not an evil man, though many would paint him thus. He is prone to rages and revenge, which persuade some he is not worthy to be king."

"You support him and you seem rational to me, my lord."

"Dear lady, I try to be. As I do try to temper his rages. And John does get better at self-control. I think Chretian helped in that regard as well."

"Really. I am interested in how that occurred."

"Chretian was soft-spoken, mild mannered. A perfect opposite of John. When one was in Chretian's presence, one naturally turned more moderate. To do otherwise seemed . . . brutish. Wouldn't you agree?"

Her skin iced. What did Bartlett know of Chretian's true nature? "Aye. My Lord Carlisle was . . . sweet to me, to anyone. I often wondered that he had been King Richard's chamberlain and hardy compatriot in so many battles."

"A man can be kind, even gentle, to his fellow men and a hound of hell in combat. Richard was. Did you not know?"

Bartlett, she could have sworn, peered into her mind, searching for . . . what? . . . Things she would not want any to know. "Nay. I knew nothing of Richard. Only his fame as a handsome and erudite man, who by all bards' accounts was predestined to wear a crown."

"He was a good king if an absent one. He left much to be accomplished, he was so oft on crusade or at war in France. John inherited from his brother many troubles, not the least of which was to correct wrongs Richard began. That is why John has had to raise such monies by taxing. John tries to do his duty, though sometimes he fails to see the kindest way to accomplish that."

"Is that why you uphold him? Because you find his nature a challenge to tame?"

"Nothing so ethereal. I support John because he is the king. And I can assist him. As he once assisted me."

Relieved to discuss someone other than Chretian and eager to know more of Bartlett, she asked, "How so?"

"He affirmed my right to my inheritance."

"Swansdown?"

"Aye." He sat back in his chair and gazed out into the hall. "I was granted my earldom by order of John. There was a controversy over its lawful ownership and John resolved the matter in my favor. I owe much to him. Chretian never told you this, then?"

"Nothing of Swansdown." Behind her, she heard Nicholas take in air like bellows. "Should he have?"

"As your neighbor, I thought he would have found it an interesting tale, particularly because it fosters rumors that the previous heir still lives."

"Chretian did not deal in rumors. 'Twas one of the things I loved about him. But you can tell me now." She felt an odd curiosity and an even odder pull to know why Bartlett led her to this tale.

"The St. Cyr family—"

"St. Cyr?" Her head rang with echoes of another voice and tones unspoken.

"Aye. The St. Cyrs came from Normandy with William the Conqueror. They were granted the earldom by William and expanded their territory with service to his family. The St. Cyrs prospered in fortune but, save for one male heir, brought forth mostly girls. Since the estate was to go only to the surviving male line, no women could inherit. My mother was a St. Cyr. A cousin to the last male heir. And when that heir returned from crusade with Richard, my mother was a widow with lands and wealth of her own. I was orphaned, my father dead years before. The Bartlett domain was one King John wished to have in his camp, and so when the St. Cyr heir asked to marry the Bartlett widow, John agreed."

"I see. There were no offspring from your mother and the last St. Cyr's marriage, so you then became the acknowledged heir."

He barely moved his lips. But his words sank into her like stones. "By decree of church and king."

"And you tell me this now because . . . ?"

"Rumors run of how I do not rightfully own the estate. Tales say other claimants wish to take it from me."

She sat frozen. Did this not sound too familiar? Was this not a story of heritage and honor challenged? For lack of facts to do more than imagine parallels between this tale and her Devil's, she was lost. "Why tell me this? I do not take issue with you."

"Nay." He reconsidered his impassioned speech. "Forgive me. I do become adamant, even after all these years. I meant only to relate to you how important Chretian was to Richard, John, and me. Instead, I have told you my life history when I merely attempted to compliment you, your table, and your hospitality."

Bartlett's eyes defined Angel's face, and then he smiled. "I would say you are the supreme benefit Chretian could ever have gained for his years of loyal service to Richard's person." He brought her hand to his too-wet mouth, halting momentarily to gaze at her wedding ring, then placing a kiss to the back of her hand. Without letting go, he caressed her eyes with his. "I envy this new husband."

She smiled. Beside her, Nicholas pressed his leg to hers.

Roger leaned closer. "If he is not all you would hope, I invite you to come to me."

She stared at him, outraged at his proposal to satisfy her if Nicholas could not.

He smiled, a suitor's regard appearing and making her still in her chair. "I could be useful to you, if not as a husband, then as an ally—and a friend—a close one." He reached for her hand and squeezed it, but so hard that his fingers made the gold ring gouge her flesh.

She sought to take her hand from beneath his when Nicholas snatched up her other one.

"We will retire, Wife."

Crushed by one man and ordered by another, she chose a middling course. "I will have my harp and stay to sing."

"Nay, dear heart," said Nicholas, staring at her with agonized eyes, "you must come with me *now*."

Chapter 12

Nicholas shut their door upon the world. Molten gold anger sparked in his eyes as he took her to the privacy of her solar and spun her to look at him. "Bartlett is a snake! He plans to hurt you!"

Her irritation rose to astronomical heights. "He seemed accepting—"

"What he *appears* is not what he *is.*"

"How do you—?"

"I know him well!"

"He knows you not!"

"All the better to take him down."

"He has conceded!"

"Like hell he has."

She clenched both hands to fists. "How do you know?"

"This is my concern."

"This *is* a matter of my concern. My home, my life are at risk. Why do you hate Bartlett? *Aye!* I can see it. Why do you condemn him? For the things you have heard him do in the name of John?"

"Aye!"

"What else?"

He stared at her.

She advanced. "What else? For things he did against you?"

He set his jaw.

"Why will you not tell me?" Tears rose to cloud her vision of him. That he might not trust her after all they had shared ripped her to shreds.

He caught her arms and searched her eyes. "The lessons of youth die hard."

"*Why?* Have I bought you? Sold you?" She tempted the worst of angers and she knew it. Welcomed it. "Have I enslaved you?"

He glared at her, his eyes golden flames of misery. "Only with tender snares." He took her by the shoulders, his eyes rabid. "I fear for you. He plans something. I know not what. But I do feel it." He cast his eyes about the solar with no relief. "Jesus, if I only knew what!"

"What can he plan? He is defenseless. He acknowledges our marriage. He will leave me to my own devices with you," she said, and knew she didn't believe that totally. Something bit at her, gnawing at the edges of her contentment with the day's events.

"I heard him. He wants you. Invites you—a married woman—to come to him should ever I fail you."

"I would not consider it. 'Twas supper prattle."

"Like hell it was! He justifies himself. Thinking he can acquit wrongs of years ago with words! Speaking of John as if he were a normal man and Swansdown as if he had every right to it."

Stunned at himself, he stared at her.

Astonished, she looked at him anew. Her logical

Devil had become an irrational man. The mention of John she could understand. Not Swansdown. "What has Bartlett's estate to do with you?"

"Nothing you need to know." He began to turn from her.

She caught his sleeve. "I think it does." She went to stand in front of him. "Swansdown is my southern neighbor. Do you tell me the man who controls it—and befriends John—is a usurper?"

"Aye! I tell you that." Nicholas struggled mightily with himself to come to some sanity. "Let us to our rest, will you? Much will occur on the morrow." He tried to leave her and she would not allow him.

"How do you know?"

"I have heard."

"What have you heard?"

"Much." He rounded her and made for the urn and the washbowl. "It is late. I am weary."

She was faster and picked up the urn to hug it to her chest. "It is past time for you to tell me all I need to know. For you see I, too, am tired of half tales."

"They will do you no good." He considered middle space while a muscle in his jaw flexed.

"It could perform a miracle for you, though." She said it so softly he had to peer at her.

"I doubt it."

She set the pitcher aside and curled her fingers around his upper arms. His face was set, his eyes dead. "It could relieve you of a burden you have too long carried alone."

"You have enough concerns—"

She placed two fingers over his lips. "You have shouldered mine, walked with me along desperate

240

paths I once trod alone. Won't you allow me the chance to do the same for you?"

"You can't."

"You doubt I am able?"

He gripped her arms. "Nay, my Angel, you are able to do anything."

"Tell me. Then your burdens shall be my burdens, your joys mine. Wherever you go, whatever you do, there I am—"

"Would that I could have you with me always! But such will never be!"

She drifted closer to him. His scent, his formidable aura filling her mind, her heart. "Until the end of time, I am yours."

He put up a hand. "I am not worthy of your sacrifice. I have lied, stolen—"

"The same as I. For reasons as explainable."

"You do not know!"

"But I would stake my life on it."

He ground his teeth. "I am nothing! I have nothing to give you! Money, jewels, aye! But nothing else! I am a man without name or home. Without heritage or future."

"What you have given me goes beyond such earthly measures. Comfort, support, courage need no name other than their own. Money, land, and power I have. All I have the more of, because of you. But what good are they to me if I may not share the benefits with you?" His eyes narrowed and his mouth tensed. "Let me." She pressed closer. "Let me." She kissed his throat, his jaw, his cheek.

His arms encircled her with the snap of steel bands and his lips nestled in her hair. His voice was hollow. "I have never told another living soul."

"Then do you think you might impart it to an angel?"

He drew away to look down at her with more love in his eyes than she had ever seen. It made her heart burn to soothe his own hurt.

"Aye, I think I might tell my special Angel."

She took his hand and drew him to her solar. There, she sat among her cushions. He stood, hands on his hips, staring at the floor.

His eyes—gold, cold, and vacant—met hers. "I am the earl of Swansdown."

She did not flinch. But watched and waited.

"I am the only son of James St. Cyr and his first wife, Constanza di Moro of Venice. And therein lies the crux of my story and dilemma. For you see, my father met my mother when King Richard sent him to the Orient to create allies for Richard's crusade. My parents married immediately, the union blessed by a Venetian cardinal and approved by Richard. I was conceived—so said my father—within a few days of their wedding night. For the first five years of my life, I lived with my mother and her family in Venice while my father traveled often for Richard in search of money and alliances. As a result, my father was more ghost than man to me. Fortunately, I had the di Moros.

"The di Moros were a large family. Unlike the St. Cyrs, the di Moros claim many sons who work with each other to build a business and a family community which surpasses anything I have ever seen among blood relatives here in England or even France. The di Moros also are a power in the city, owning one of the three largest shipping companies which import the goods of the Asian steppes to the shores of the Mediterranean.

"As a child, I was taken every morning by my mother to the factory on the docks. I grew up speaking my mother's language, but also those of the Holy Land and others farther east. I also learned much of the riches of the world, seeing them unloaded from the di Moro fleet. I knew well the man who ruled over the city—and all its important families like my mother's. He is called the Doge. A man who rules the city of Venezia with such an iron hand even John would envy him his power." Nicholas flexed his powerful shoulders, then began to pace.

"This Doge is supreme in the city. He makes alliances to better the trade. He also rules the politics. For years, to control the trade routes, he has sought to control what happens in the Holy Land. The di Moros did not always support him. In fact, they were often at odds. During one conflict, one of my mother's brothers died mysteriously and my uncles said it was the Doge's work. We never knew for certain.

"One day, my father returned to my mother and me. I was five years old and more my mother's than my father's child. James St. Cyr was not deterred. With leave from King Richard, my father renewed his relationship with my mother and began one with me. For three months, we were inseparable. Then as quickly as he came, he left. He met Richard in Sicily, from whence they went to Acre in the Holy Land. There they fought and won the city. It was two years before I saw my father again.

"This time he came within the dead of night. Richard's ship and his had foundered off the coast of

Venice and he sought refuge for his king—and for his friends, one of whom was Chretian Forrester. Aye, 'tis true, I met him then. The di Moros gave the party aid and spirited Richard to the northern mountains from whence he might return home. My father left with him. But soon after they crossed the Danube, they were taken prisoner by a German prince who had been Richard's sworn enemy. For two years, my father remained with his king, going from one castle to another, ever changed to ensure that no one could capture them.

"I was nine when next my father returned to us. He came riding into our piazza on the biggest brute I had ever seen. Christ, I shall never forget how he smiled at me that morning he returned. I thought he must be God. He was so large, so kind. His voice so soft, especially for my mother." He swallowed and swirled to pace again.

"Within two months, we sailed for England. My mother did not cry, but I did. I left my cousins, my friends, my uncles. The joys I knew were many—and I must have suspected then—gone forever from me. We came here. Cold, raining, dreary England and the castle my father called his own. And I hated it.

"Worse, so did my mother. Loving my father as she did, she tried to hide it. But over the years, as I grew I saw how she withered. The clime was too cold, too barren. Even though the di Moros sent the comforts of home—silks and lemons and gold plate—to ease her existence. Still, she pined for her former life as well as for my father, who was often gone with Richard to France to fight even more battles. My mother loved my father as he did her, and welcomed him with eager arms each time he returned. But there was no continuing joy in her life.

"Within a few years, she died of cold, of disease, of lack of attention from the man whom she adored. My father came home to find her on her deathbed. Afterward, he wailed like a banshee for days in his chapel, never letting the priest near her to shroud her for her coffin. Finally, my father's chamberlain convinced him to part with her body, and in the dark of night, when my father could not see, they buried her. I did not see my father for weeks, and when he did emerge from his confinement he was a different man.

"His black hair had turned to snow white. He was haggard, slow to move, slower to think. News came that Richard, too, was dead. My father took it with no surprise or show of emotion. Into this void came an edict from the new King John. A widow of some wealth and land required a new husband. She was a cousin to my father, a St. Cyr."

Angel stirred, remembering Roger's words. "And John commanded that your father marry her."

"Aye. For political alliance. What John really craved was control of the northeast of England. And Lady Bartlett brought lands along the perimeter of Swansdown to the match. She also brought her son, older than me."

"Roger."

"Aye. Roger, who sits downstairs as imperial as God. Roger, who sits in Swansdown as if he had been born to it."

"But you are your father's son."

"That was the issue. I could not prove I was the true heir."

"I don't understand! What of your father? He knew. He could have—"

"Two months after he was wed, he died."

Her mouth fell open.

"Though he had betrothed me to an heiress and written a will which stated I was heir, John ignored it."

"But why?"

He shook his head. "Stories abound. Allen Gainsbridge says his father told him Lady Bartlett was John's mistress and that Roger is really John's illegitimate son. Another friend of mine says it is John's simple revenge on my father, who was too much a friend to Richard, whom John hated. Others have said it is John's attempt to align the Bartlett lands with the larger Swansdown estate, and thus keep the north firmly with John against all challengers."

"What do you say?"

"I think it is most likely all three. Whatever his motive, John seized my heritage and before a court in my own great hall, he called me a bastard, saying there was no English record of my parents' marriage. I knew as he said that, he meant to kill me. And so with the help of a loyal servant, I escaped my own dungeon, took gold coins from a hidden source inside my father's solar, and escaped to buy passage back to Venice. I was determined to get a copy of my parents' marriage certificate and take it to John. More the fool, I thought the presentation of a paper could win me back my heritage. But when I arrived in Venice, the Doge—who had ever hated the di Moros—had done his work. He had imprisoned them for challenging his power and confiscated the family's possessions, including their fleet. When he found me, he did the same to me as he had done to most of my cousins. He sold me to an infidel trader, a Moslem whose caravans crossed from Jerusalem to the sands of Asia and beyond."

"And thus you lived along the routes to the East."

"Aye, until I came to the attention of the Genghis Khan, who wished to rule the world and do it swiftly. He bought me and treated me well—the first man in many years to treat me fairly. Using my skills, he at the same time returned to me my dignity. We respected each other, taking from the relationship those things that equals trade and returning to it the honor due each one. With time and friendship growing, the Khan saw to it I accumulated wealth, and so eventually he allowed me my freedom. Though he permitted me to purchase it, 'twas a paltry sum he took.

"When I returned to Venice, I had not only enough gold and jewels to make the Doge envious, but enough to make him have the cardinal hand over the marriage certificate I needed. I was able to purchase also freedom for my two remaining cousins, who had wallowed for years in the Doge's cells. Because I could offer the Doge the contacts he needed to secure safer caravan travel to the Mongols of Genghis, he assisted me in outfitting two ships with a crew.

"I returned to England with my parents' certificate, my wealth, and one old friend, Ibn Said, whom you met that morning in your solar. And I had the will to fight John. Of course, after all these years, Roger Bartlett had solidified his claim to Swansdown, and the papers I had in my possession were worthless scraps."

She bemoaned his losses with a whispered conclusion. "And so you took to the forests, gathered those dissatisfied with John, and hounded him and any who supported him."

"Nor was I alone. Allen, who had been my boyhood friend, allied with discontented barons against John. I went to Gainsbridge Castle one night, revealed my true identity, and Allen welcomed me. My role as the Devil of Midnight became a more potent one as more men joined me in spirit and flesh. The past year has seen John bow to the will of those who seek to curb his. His signing of the Magna Carta shows it."

"Still, he does attempt to levy taxes, imprison any nay-sayers at will, and—" She bit her lip.

"And force widows to remarry against their will. Against the very clause he signed in the charter that he would no longer do that. *Aye,* John is a devil." Nicholas drew her up and wrapped her close to speak against her temple. "If I ever had cause to fight the man before, I would battle him now to the end of time. John shall not use you. Bartlett will not have you. You are too precious."

She held her breath, waiting, hoping he might say, *You are mine.* But what he had implied for days with every look, every move, came now only by his touch. And so she took that which was offered and added her own.

She embraced him fervently and leaned back to look into his eyes. With this she committed her life, her very soul. "You are my love."

He cursed roundly. "You cannot say that! Think that!"

"But I do, my darling. I love you—" She placed her lips on his and whispered, "with all my heart."

"Ahh, Christ, you are my agony." He tore her from him, raked his hair, and paced to the wall and back again. "I am no man for you. I have no life to give you! You are a countess, landed, wealthy! A woman bent on peace without any man to harass you again! I *am* nothing. *Have* nothing!"

"Do you think I care about that?"

"You should! You must!" He strode to face her and gripped her arms, pressing her back against the copious draperies. "You chose a life without men! You were right to do so!"

"That was before I met you, my love." She managed to raise one hand to cup his cheek. "Let me help you."

"You can't! No one can! Only if John were dead, but he *lives*. Christ, he looks as if he'll live for decades. And by then, you and I will be old, sour with the fruitless years of wanting what we cannot have."

She inched closer. "We can have what we want."

"*Nay!* There is no eternity for us!"

"Then let there be now. Ever now."

"There is nothing."

"You said you would never tell me lies." She flowed against him. "And I know there is this. Now. We can create a lifetime of joys in moments. I want you. I love you." She let her mouth speak on his. "You told me once you would give me anything I desired. I desire you, my darling. Deny me and refuse yourself this which we can give each other." She opened her mouth and pressed the sweetest kiss she could create to his. He stood there, simply holding her, unmoving while she prayed he would respond before she lost her hope.

But his hand plunged into her hair at her nape, and his other hand sealed her lower body to him. And he took the kiss deeper. Bending her over his arm, he sent his tongue inside her mouth and tasted every essence of her. He took her breath, her mind, and in one blinding moment, he took her heart. "Ahh, God sent me an Angel and for the life of me, I can't refuse you! Or myself!"

He swept her up and kept kissing her as he took her to their bed. With a swiftness that made her head spin, he set her on her knees, yanked the curtains about the bed, and put reverent but determined hands to her clothes. In lightning speed, she was naked for him. In moments, he soon was, too.

He was beautiful, her Devil incarnate. His massive shoulders molded to perfection. His titanic corded arms. The thick black down on his chest that tapered to lean hips and the long, strong rod of his manhood that stood in upright, steely need. She adored the looks of him. The strength of him. She put her hands to him, cupped him, stroked him.

He inhaled, his eyes flew closed, and he arched. She trailed kisses along his square jaw, his long throat, his marvelous shoulders. And all the while, she prepared him with the pressure of her hand and the hope in her heart.

"You take my breath away, my darling." She put her thighs over his and slid his manhood along the entrance to her very core. He was so wide, so hot, so very rigid, she thought she'd die of lack of air before she felt him inside her. "Let me show you how I love you." She kissed his lips in desperate adoration and undulated against him, as he had so often taught her these past bliss-filled nights and days.

"You undo me," he muttered, his teeth clenched against what she knew was his desire.

For once, she was determined she would take him from his control and show him heaven. "Nay, my love. I will only make you stronger. Happier. I promise you. Come with me. I need you, my Devil, my Nicholas, my husband."

The last word crossed every barrier he'd ever erected. For he rose like a heathen inspired, like a god determined, and wrapped his hands around her arms, and slid into her flowing need of him. Like a man possessed, his eyes were closed, his body rapt.

Angel had never known delight like this. He came inside her so painfully sweet, she sank to his sword with the will of one dying to the inevitable. She felt him sure. She knew him hers. She understood when he arrived at the last divide that would make him completely so. And she sank lower with one lithe surrender.

He growled, captured her close. She cried out in a small pain and greater ecstasy, then moved closer to him.

To the quick she was his. To his agony he became hers. She understood it to be so when he groaned, and at that moment she loved him all the more.

He paused. His eyes flicked open and he stared at her. Knowing her secret now, he was caught between heaven and hell. He grit his teeth and glanced down, already removing his body from hers.

But she would not allow it. "You have loved me, my darling." She seated herself more securely on him, feeling her body take his huge one with an avid satisfaction, and he moaned his delighted agony. "Nay, I am yours. I know—for you have taught me—that there is more. Finish this." She kissed his stiff lips. "Take us both to paradise. The way it should be between a man and woman."

"I want you so," he confessed.

And then he caught her up, took her down, rolled

her beneath him and, as if a vast barrier had broken its confines, he flowed over her, around her, inside her. He tasted her earlobes and whispered mysterious words against her cheek. Kissed his way down her throat to suckle her breasts to aching points of need. Trailed his tongue around the circumference of her nipples, and all the while, he slid inside her, whirling their sea of desire into a torrent of boiling need.

Her fingers bit into his shoulders. Her back arched.

He urged her on with wicked words and wild thrusts that took her to a shore of violent desire. Sweet shudders began inside her like a ripple, surged to a tidal wave, and crashed over her time and again in some never-ending song of how she loved him, needed him, would never live without him.

He caught up her resounding joy with ravenous lips and encompassing body, with his own declarations of how he wanted her, craved her, and would have her now. Now. *Now.*

He pounded into her with a fury made of torment and ecstasy. She felt her body flood and sweep all doubts away. He was hers. And she was his as she had never been any other man's—or could ever be. For she belonged now and for all time to the Devil.

Chapter
13

She lay limp in his arms, her lips to his ear, making little noises of delight.

And he loathed himself.

He smoothed her hair, caressed the curve of her shoulder, and began to pull from her wet, warm body.

"Don't go." She drew him back and nestled nearer.

He closed his eyes, caught between the need to leave her and the desire to grant her wish. She moved against him, her sinuous grace an artless enchantment. Still hard inside her, his need to keep his seed consumed his every moment. She knew it and spread her legs wider to hold him.

"I can't," he objected, tortured and tempted. If he lost total control and allowed the dam to burst, the abstinence he had practiced would ensure a tidal wave that brought a child, but she kissed him, moved against him with determination.

"We have known so little love alone, let us have a few minutes of it now."

Her appeal drowned his pain. Killed his will. Filled his mind with her. Just as his heart would forever be devoted to her. This time, wanting to erase whatever physical hurt he may have caused her the first time, he showed her a demonstration of his love that was slow and sweet and deep. Each moment he possessed her, he prayed for the control to hold his seed within the reservoir of his determination. And he gave himself up to loving her.

He slid along the walls of her moist grotto and felt the waters of her passion drench them both. He moved like a dreamer in a passage of liquid joy. To give her greater ecstasy, he hooked his hands beneath her knees and brought them up. Her sounds of rapture were music to his ears.

He stroked her swift and hard, sure and tender, sweetly shallow or fully sheathed. She adored everything, whatever the tempo or the texture, whether they became steeds galloping or butterflies fluttering. Whether he put her ankles around his neck or her long legs about his waist or turned her on her knees to let him serve her with adoring fingers and an insatiable body, she cried her pleasure and her need of him. And when her surges came that she pulsed to overflowing, he enhanced them all for her with lips and hands and exultations. Her luscious gates clamped around him, pulling him in, urging him on to his own destination. But always, before his own, he would pause, collect himself for the twenty-one inhalations, and give her all of what she needed. So when she was quite mindless and he knew she reached the end of her desires for this night, he attempted to retreat. But she would not let him go.

"Stay. Let us see the stars together!"

"My darling," he moaned into her mouth, "I see all of heaven with you in my embrace."

She wrapped her arms about him and whispered, "You must have joy as well." She captured his refusal with an openmouthed kiss that enkindled a fresh fire of desire in his brain. Plunging her fingers into his hair, she pressed her breasts to him and tantalized him with the scrape of taut satin nipples that singed his skin and made his manhood stand taller to witness a growing conflagration.

He could not stop the need to thrust inside her and hold fast to the center of her. God above, if he could only stroke her fully, naturally, he'd show her worlds unknown.

"Oh, Nicholas," she crooned on an endless shudder. "This is the way I want you always, darling. Completely joined to me skin to skin, heart to heart." Her hand slid along his hips to press his buttocks and thereby seat him securely at the door to all creation. A thunderbolt struck his mind, seared his control. In a flash, the splendid white silence of their souls' mating blinded him to reason, ignited crimson passion, and drilled a breach into the wall of the reservoir he tended in her name.

He pressed her back, raised both breasts, and laved her nipples in a delicately ravenous prelude to his first strong lunge. She lolled her head and grasped fistfuls of the sheets. He gave her ripe reward as with measured power he let her feel the long brazier of his desire for her. Suddenly, once could never be enough. In a second, there was no time to think, assess, restrain, hold, only eternities to demonstrate his infinite love of her, joy in her, need for her to feel all the

255

emotion he bore her, now and forevermore. So as he thrust into her succulent body and gave to her every physical declaration of his adoration, he blasted the reservoir that had kept him from her. Girded by his love of her, he tended her as man was meant to pleasure woman. And he came with the force of ten creations, an explosion that jolted his body, destroyed his mind, raised up his heart. Awhirl in the chaos, he gave her a glorious coupling that drove her to raving cries of ecstasy and made him marvel at a new universe the two of them created.

Exhausted, exhilarated, he settled to her and crushed her close. She kissed him madly, acknowledging and exploring this new terrain they inhabited together, a pure and shining place where no one could ever go, save them, together, as it was ordained for them since time began.

He wrapped his arms about her slick body and rolled to his side. Greedy to keep her for as many seconds as he could, he buried his mouth in her silken hair. Ridiculing his lack of control, he reluctantly bid adieu and then mentally departed from this land they could inhabit for mere minutes of their lifetimes. He felt like a man with all of heaven in his arms—but knew it to be hell.

The time of his trial had arrived and he could not fail to meet it. He had committed a wrong and now must make amends, if he could.

He left her easily. This time, she was so languid from their mutual experience, she let him go with only a gentle hand trailing his chest, arm, and hand. He went to the urn and poured water into the washbowl. He splashed the cold water in his face and wished he had discovered such sanity minutes ago. He glanced down at his body, stains of her innocence marking him forever as a fiend. He washed it off, too, but knew he'd wear the stigma always.

Grabbing the toweling, he scrubbed himself dry. He'd need oil of acacia and lemons. Not that either of them could guarantee much good now. His seed, boundless from the days and nights of wanting her and denying them both, had flowed into her with long, full shots to ecstasy. If his Angel were fertile, she could be pregnant with his child from any of his wild emissions, and no contraceptive oils or juices could save her from the consequence he had set in motion. Still, he had to try.

He began to dress, and she roused herself to prop on one elbow. Joy lit her eyes. Even in candlelight minutes after he'd enjoyed her, she still looked delectable, delicate, divine. He grew stiff again, and he groaned, wishing he could turn away to feel the whip of all his self-anger lashing him to firmer resolve.

But she stopped him with a look and a question. "Where are you going?" She sat higher. The sheet he had drawn about her fell to her waist. Her hair, a mantle of pale gold, outlined her flowering pink breasts and he knew he could make love to her for hours, days—nay, decades—and never cease his want of her.

He could not help himself. He went to her, cupped her face, and bent to give her a swirling kiss of homage. "I want lemons from the kitchen."

"Lemons?"

"Aye. For you. Trust me."

She beamed. "I do."

He knew she did. And God help him, that was why he needed lemons or, barring that, oranges, certainly vinegar. And a bath for her.

He opened the door, saw one of Devereaux's men on guard, and bade him take vigilant care of Lady Forrester.

He returned in minutes, in his hands a tray with a flagon of wine, some cheese, a vial of vinegar, and two lemons. He opened the door quietly. She slept, exhausted.

He did not disturb her but went to the chest where he kept his clothes and medicinals. The oil of acacia, good for salving many wounds, was also used by the Khan for contraception for those women, his "precious pearls," who could not conceive lest they die.

His own Angel was such a one. For if Demere and Ross or any others who worked against her knew that she was pregnant, they would surely kill her. Nicholas knew from the past few days of discovering the insidious sins of this household that whoever had killed Chretian would not hesitate to do the same to Angel. That was why he had been thrilled when she sent Demere's men to the dungeon. Why he was overjoyed when she had cast out Demere. Once he left her, he wanted her to be free of fear, alone.

That made his heart burn. He did not really want his Angel alone. Truth to tell, he wanted to be alone with her. As they had been minutes ago. As they should be always. But certainly, those minutes would be all they would ever share. And as before, he would see to it that she walked in sanctity alone. Alone, God help him, as he would evermore feel without her.

A knock came at the door, and as Angel roused and tucked the sheet about her, Kate and a Windom guard entered with the tub, toweling, and buckets of steaming water. They cast careful eyes to their mistress and him, then discreetly backed out the way they'd come.

Nicholas tested the temperature of the water, wished it were cooler, and then dismissed the idea as too uncomfortable no matter how beneficial to his cause it might have been. Then he emptied the vinegar into the tub. He strode to Angel, drew away the sheet, and scooped her up into his arms. She pressed her breasts to him, wound her arms about his neck, and placed a kiss on his cheek. The musky fragrance of her, redolent of their mutual passions, floated into his head. The essence of her stopped his heart. He kissed her, his lips ravenously seeking more of that on which he could never fully feast again. He had to let her go.

She sank into the water with a sigh. He watched her a moment as she took the sponge and soap to lave the body he had so recently washed with his desire. In remorse, he turned his back on her and returned to his tray. No sounds came from her, and he knew she watched him closely. Undeterred, he split the lemons, crushed the halves, and squeezed the juice into a goblet. He opened the trunk, found the vial of acacia, and—

She stood before him, a towel around her wet torso, a question in her eyes.

Her eyes—those large windows to her heart—sorrowed for the lack of him. And in that second, he could do naught but take her to him.

Clamping his eyes shut, he held her close. "Darling, I want to help you. I hurt you."

"Nay. Never have you hurt me."

Avoiding the response that this was her initiation and he knew she must be sore, he suppressed that line of discussion until later. For now, speed was most important, lest an Angel bear a Devil's child.

Tugging her to their bed, he threw wide the covers and halted. As evidence of how completely he had loved her, dark red blood spotted the white linen. And not just one or two evidences existed, but multiple streaks declared that she had been his. Repeatedly, wildly, completely his.

She viewed it with calm. He saw it as his conviction to the lowest realms.

"Rest," he said, and she sat upon the edge, her eyes following him as he went to empty the oil into his palms, dip his fingertips in it, and return to her. Then to lead her to his purpose, he leaned over her, reclined with her to cover her supple body, and said, "Kiss me."

She came, as he knew she would, like sunshine after rain. Brushing her mouth to his, she pressed tiny little kisses along the seam of his lips. "I love your mouth," she murmured.

"Do you, darling?" he breathed and pressed her down to her pillow. He rose above her, kneeling between her elegant legs. Giving woman that she was, she writhed beneath him, her breasts budding of their own accord for him. But he knew what he must do and how he must have her. "Open for me, will you, sweet? I need to feel you once again."

She spread her pretty thighs and he swallowed hard at the glistening deep rose their love had colored her. His fingers traced a pattern along her fragile folds. She held her breath. He parted her wide, slipped one finger and another inside her. She was molten wet satin.

Arching. Undulating.

He thrust in farther and her muscles pulsed around him. He groaned and succumbed, stroking her gently, bathing her in the oil and his undying need to love her. Forgetting his purpose, remembering his ardor—

"Oh, Nicholas, my love—no, don't stop!"

He had to. She was killing him. Transforming what was to be an effort to save her into one in which she took him to her care once more. He began to take his hand away and she pressed her own atop his.

"My darling, let me do this. The oil will soothe you, help you." He extracted those fingers and inserted two of the other hand.

She caught her breath. "Oh, my heart, this is wondrous medicine."

He wanted to die. He pressed his forehead to hers and kissed her lips. "I wish to take all essence of our mating from you, if I can."

She clutched his arms. "But—"

"I'll not chance a child, my Angel." And with that, he cleansed her in the oil, then left her to return for the cup of lemon juice and a small cloth.

He doused the cloth with the juice and came once more to lay beside her. With fervent pain in her grass green eyes, she watched him. Without words, he urged her legs open and caressed her pale blond hair, her feverish plump lips, her plush contours. When he was done, he leaned over and kissed the smooth skin of her belly. *Please God, answer this man's prayer. Let there be no more evidence that I love this woman.*

As he left her this time, she curled into her pillow. When he began to wash his hands, he heard the first of her sobs. They tore his heart and he turned for her, his love for her as undeniable in torment as in joy.

He steeled himself for what he had to do now, what

he had to know now. With heavy heart, he returned and gathered her into his arms. For long moments he simply held her, and when she had quieted enough, he began.

"Were you afraid to tell me you were a virgin?"

She shook her head.

"I cannot believe that you planned not to tell me." He dipped his head and drew her face up with a finger beneath her chin. "Not when we were so intimate, my darling."

"I wished no one to know, ever. At first, not you, either. It was not important. But as time drew us closer together and I grew to love you so, it became even less important—"

"You thought Demere would say you had no right to inherit from Chretian because the marriage had never been consummated."

"Aye! For only three reasons can a marriage be annulled. Chretian was never cruel to me. Consent was not an issue after I agreed to my father's conditions. Only this . . . this lack of Chretian's to make me his wife." She lowered her eyes, began to leave him.

He caught her, raised her face. "Why did he not make the vows valid, darling? You liked him. He honored you. So why not take you to his care?"

She rolled her shoulders, cast her eyes about the room. "On our wedding night he brought me here after the revels and he tried to kiss me but . . . he couldn't. Not in the way you do. Not on the lips. He told me he liked me and thought I would make a wonderful wife, but that he . . . had other preferences."

Other preferences? "He liked—"

"Men."

Nicholas drifted back against the pillows. The air socked from him, he watched Angel leave him and don a white silk chainse. She turned to him, so ethereal in her beauty, so devastating in her regard of him, he knew she put distance between them to tell him things she could not say within his arms. He caressed her with his eyes and waited.

"At first, I had no idea what he was trying to say." She smiled wistfully. "He had to explain to me so completely that he was embarrassed as I was. I was so naive about what husbands did with their wives. Good God, my nurse at Montrose had told me not a week before my wedding to Chretian about what I might expect of him. How he would put his body inside mine, cause blood to flow . . . How could I know about a man's love for a man? I felt so ignorant. So . . . undone."

He rose, poured them wine, and went to offer her a cup. When she had drunk, he took the goblet and led her to her solar. There he stretched out a hand and enfolded her.

"Chretian told me he had known a few women once when he was young. That he liked women. That he liked *me,* even *loved* me as . . . a friend. But that he was not . . . interested in me as most men would be in their wives. Life on crusade had taught him to favor men. He even said King Richard was—"

"Aye. 'Twas one of the characteristics my father told me about his liege. Not one to ever condone it, my father said Richard tried very hard to prove otherwise. Even with his own wife. For Richard desperately wanted an heir so that his brother John might not inherit the crown."

"I thought—or so my father had said—Chretian

wanted an heir. When I asked Chretian if that was so, he smiled and said he did. He had hopes before the marriage that he might be able to take me to him as a true wife, but that . . . he had thought long about it and he could not bring himself to do it. Besides, his lover objected."

Nicholas's heart clenched in fear. "And did he say who this lover was?"

"Never. Nor did I ask. I did not wish to know. I was not jealous, for I did not love Chretian. Not the way I love you," she said, and gazed at him sweetly.

He smoothed errant curls from her cheek. "I know."

"It was a marriage of strong friendship, though. Made more vital by Chretian's regard of me. I knew it and told him I appreciated his care. He asked . . . and I told him about why I had agreed to marry him. He was furious with my father and promised to see that Dunstan never could claim any dower portion which was mine."

Nicholas nodded, satisfied that he, too, could like Chretian Forrester for his care of Angel. "He wrote a will, then?"

"Aye, he gave it to me weeks after we were wed. He said he wanted me to have it for safekeeping. That way, neither king nor commoner could rob me of my Carlisle or Montrose lands. Chretian feared for my ability to keep all the Windom lands, for he did hear of Geoffrey Devereaux's distant claim. But Chretian thought I had a right to inherit the dower portion."

Nicholas idly considered her. For Chretian Forrester to take such care that she keep her dowered lands must mean he had reason to think many might try to take them from her. Possibly, he had even heard someone threaten to hurt her—or him.

Nicholas forced his mind to Angel, who smiled at him forlornly.

"But it takes more to keep a king at bay than a piece of parchment signed by a lesser knight. And then others came to claim their right to me and I—oh, Nicholas, I hated the very idea! I wanted no other man! I could think only how to save myself, and then it was Leon who suggested I enlist the Devil. He said he knew how to ensure you would come to me. That he knew where you met your informants and that—"

"Hmmm, aye. I have a bone to pick with Leon. For he need not have trussed me up and hauled me before you. Had he explained, I would have come on my own."

"He said you never showed your face."

"Only to my band, but obviously, Leon has frequented the forests enough to come close and know which among us is the Devil." Nicholas shifted, uneasy with the greater problem. "Do you have any thoughts of who Chretian's lover might be?"

"None. He would have the man with him each night after supper. I sewed here. My door was always closed. And afterward . . . well, Chretian would come and say it was time for me to come to bed. So I would sew until I grew weary."

"There was never . . . an article of clothing . . . anything which might indicate . . . ?"

She shook her head.

"And of the six men-at-arms who were here with Demere, have there ever been any rumors about them?"

"Nothing. The first I knew of anything amiss was when Gil and Jack said what they did the other day. 'Tis one thing to make a choice as an adult, and another, viler one to seduce an innocent to your ways."

"Aye, my darling. But that wickedness is gone. We need to worry about Demere, Ross, and perhaps Bartlett. Thank God the three guards are gone."

"Demere loves Nell."

"From the looks of his reaction to her tonight, I'd say the man loves himself more than anyone."

"Possibly. But you know what I mean about him. . . ."

"Aye. I do. We'll have to watch and wait. Which leaves us with Ross. What do you know of him? Does he . . . care for women?"

Her eyes widened. "I never saw a woman care for him. Not in any way. So I cannot conclude."

They sat a long time, quietly embracing. His mind awhirl, Nicholas sought answers where none appeared. Soon, he felt Angel's even breathing and knew she slept. He arranged her close and drifted into the softness of her cushions. The joy of her and the horrors she had imparted had taken a mighty toll and he, too, closed his eyes.

He told himself he would rest but a minute until the tub water cooled. Then would he strip the bed and soak out the blood that proclaimed his Angel had been a virgin till her Devil took her. Then, he would take her to her bed again and never put a hand to her, but see her to her just place in the world.

But the sun beat softly against his face when he heard the pounding at her outer chamber door. He sat up, confused, numb, with Angel still within his grasp.

Settling her to her cushions, he stood, groggy, bleary-eyed.

"Open the door, my lord!" Kate called frantically.

Nicholas ripped open the door to see Kate crying, a knife to her throat. At once, he found himself engulfed —and shackled—by men he'd never met.

But from their fine chain mail and steely expressions, he knew who they were. The king's men. "How did you get inside the castle?" was what he didn't know.

"Demere showed us a trapdoor to a tunnel," gruffed one as he wrapped ropes around Nicholas's wrists.

"Sorry you cast us out now?" chuckled someone, and when Nicholas turned he saw one of Demere's three guards whom Angel had banished two days ago. This one glanced at Angel as she rose from her sleep. "Here's a sight! In her chainse, no less!" He went for her.

Nicholas bolted, but not strongly enough to counter ropes and the deterrent of two men-at-arms. "Leave her alone!"

Nell sailed forth, skirting Nicholas and guards, headed for their bedchamber—and their bed.

Nicholas tore from his captors' grasp, but all too soon was waylaid.

Demere came close behind to sneer at him. "Give over, man. The castle is ours. Taken by means of the tunnel in the dead of night. We came so silently upon it that even your friends outside could not catch us all. Meanwhile, your friends inside these walls are well guarded and cannot help you."

Approaching at a more leisurely pace was Roger Bartlett.

He came right up to Nicholas, looked up into his

eyes, and said, "Good morning, *brother*. Oh, *aye,* I do know who you are. I remembered your father's ring when I saw it on your lady's hand. Of course, I suspected long before that you were the heathen of these forests. No one else could have so many resources or know the land so well. But 'tis a good morning for me, as you can readily see. And do look at it, for it may be your last sight of the sun. You see, you go to a dark and deep cell which my kind friend John has prepared for you."

Nell strode forward, trailing wrinkled white linen from her fingers. "I told you both last night we were too late when he drew the bed hangings about their lusting bodies," she muttered. "I thought he would take her—true husband or not! You would not stop him. *Now* see here the evidence of your silliness."

She yanked wide the sheet that bore the red marks of Angel's purity.

Demere smiled, then checked Bartlett's grin.

The earl of Swansdown surveyed those assembled, then rested his salacious gaze on the rightful owner of that name. "How fortuitous. We'll use the sheets to show she was not Chretian's wife—and thus, we'll prove she had cause to murder him—shall we say, Demere—out of jealousy?" His expression became satanic as he appraised Angel and once again, Nicholas. "It seems I'll have Windom and Carlisle not as dowry, but as reward. What say you to that, Nicky? When John finishes with you, you'll wish you never showed your face in England. Soon, you well may wish you were in the hell of which you so suitably named yourself lord."

Chapter
14

Demere led the mounted procession through ice-covered hills and vales. The path, like the others they had taken this day, was narrow and treacherous. So similar to ones Nicholas knew well from his youth and from mountain passes ten times higher and far bleaker than these conditions.

He assessed conditions with a calmness borne of years of discipline and meditation.

Within another hour they would reach Castle Tremaine. Because of its command of the major byways, that Norman structure became the resting place of many a traveler.

Nicholas anticipated their approach with disdain—and pleasure. The facade was one he knew well, the interior keep even better. For the current lord's deceased father, Guy Tremaine, had often shown the Devil of Midnight hospitality. If since Guy's death his son Charles Tremaine was not as discriminating in his choice of friends, Nicholas attributed it to the man's desire to wed one of King John's daughters. When John had made Charles suffer with delays, the young Lord Tremaine only became more adamant.

No matter. To seek rest here made good sense. And an excellent opportunity.

Nicholas shifted in his saddle, touched his knees to his horse's sides, and smiled to himself when the animal whickered.

Nemesis—for four years used to his master's every mood—recognized this signal. The beast had been the Devil's saving grace before. So must he now. The woods, the night, and the circumstance were alive with the need for the great Saracen black and his rider to perform a feat most western knights would never attempt. But in these circumstances, with enemies about him, Nicholas had few choices.

Only one choice, in fact. And he meant to take it. For to choose the alternative—no action—would surely kill his Angel.

He sought a glimpse of her ahead of him in the middle of the procession. With her hands roped behind her, she sat astride her own palfrey. Though days ago she had appeared to be a proficient rider, this current posture to which her captivity forced her wearied her. Indeed, they had hauled her from Windom Castle long before him, making him wonder what they might do to her out of his sight. But they delayed him only to anger him, and were placing her on her palfrey when he was brought to the courtyard. He knew then that they seated her too far forward in her saddle, and he cringed at how uncomfortable that must feel. Yet for some reason, she could not right herself. And he could see her distress—more emotional than physical—whenever she glanced his way. Even from this distance, her green eyes were black with shades of fear. For him. For he was bound with chains.

He sent her a look of courage, then lost contact as Nell ordered her to do something. He snapped his head around and faced the wind that cut through his woolen cowl. On such a winter's night—in any clime —no chains could hold him, no act deter him from rescuing her.

He might be alone—or seem to be—but he would help her. Despite the fact that he had been separated from Allen Gainsbridge by an insistent Demere. Over the objections of Father Samuel, who pleaded to be taken to the king to give his testimony. And without the pleadings of Dunstan Montrose, who, in the horrible hour in which his daughter was taken from him by men no force could conquer, had begged that Bartlett show her mercy.

"For she is an innocent," Dunstan shouted, tears glistening in his eyes. "She was made to wed Chretian against her will. If she is guilty of anything, it is that she did not hate him—or me—but instead showed us succor and forgiveness!"

"A pretty speech, Montrose. Too late. Too little." Then Roger had ordered them all remain at Windom or return home at their will. "I have not enough men to guard all of you and your tricks on a long journey. I have only enough to deter you from trying to take her from me."

But Nicholas would.

He'd take her far from here. Far from John and his infernal rule. He'd take her to France. To his cousin, the count St. Cyr in Poitiers. There, Ramon would keep her safe while he himself finally destroyed the power of John.

For he would. He must. No one hurt his Angel without forfeit of every asset.

Then as a plain man, a free man, he would return to Poitiers and offer to return her to her rightful home. And if she wished to remain celibate, he would retire from this field of battle, the ordeal over, the prize won. But if perchance the years had shown her she were still enamored of him, he would finally give voice to his abiding love and ask her to become his wife.

If she agreed, he'd live as an ordinary mortal with a woman who was his own. He'd keep her, treasure her. He'd use his wealth and build a newer castle for her so intricate and impregnable no one would ever breach the walls to take her from him again. They'd have children. And for the rest of his days, he would forget Swansdown, his father and mother's misery—and all his hellish past. To have an Angel . . .

A lone bird called from the trees.

Among the evergreens a rustling reverberated in the still of the chilled night air.

Nicholas nudged his right toe at the belly of Nemesis. In acknowledgment, the horse sidestepped.

"Ho! Hey!" Michael Ross, who had ridden behind him all day, spurred his mount forward and grabbed Nicholas's reins. "Control this beast or I bind your hands behind you, whatever Lord Swansdown's objections."

Short of horses as they had been, the king's men—fifteen knights sent from John—needed to transport the brigand Devil of Midnight on his own steed. There had been no other choice, except the unacceptable one of allowing the Devil to walk to Nottingham, where the king declared he would meet with Bartlett and Demere. Nottingham was four days' hard journey on horseback from Windom Castle, and King John had decreed his knights bring him the rebellious bandit within that time. Roger Bartlett had let that information slip when they had gathered everyone in the courtyard, readying the procession to leave Windom Castle.

"Then we'll see how the Devil fares before the King of England." He came close to Nicholas to smile scornfully into his placid face, and at Roger's tone, Nemesis had suddenly reared. Roger's composure shattered as the black stallion sawed the air with mighty hooves.

It had taken three men to capture the reins. But frantic to be off, Roger had finally ordered Nicholas to calm the beast.

And in the end, Nicholas rode his own horse. With control of his own reins. Hands to the fore. Because Nemesis would never allow another man to mount him, much less restrain him.

Nicholas vowed the concession would be their undoing. For in the trees, among the brush, sat the Devil's disciples. Probably all twelve in force, if Nicholas knew his stalwart group. Not as many as this contingent of fifteen of the king's men, Demere's three, plus Roger and his lone man-at-arms, but enough to cause upheaval—and an abduction.

He found his chance when one of the horses lost its shoe and, tender-footed from the ice and stones, would not proceed. The guards took the opportunity to take turns relieving themselves in the deeper thickets. One by one, they left the road until the force was halved.

Nicholas strained to hear what he could of their actions. Footsteps, parted pine needles, trickling water . . . and when one man returned, he knew that man was a token offering to the disciples' favorite ploy. He knew his time was now.

"Demere," Nicholas called forward to where the chamberlain stood against a tree, arms crossed. "I must do the same as your men."

Demere flicked a hand at Ross. "Take him. Make it quick."

Nicholas shot a glance at Angel, sitting her saddle like a queen, and guarded by the witch, Nell. *Dismount,* he prayed. *Do it now.*

But she didn't. He closed his eyes, set his mind to touching hers, and tried again.

To his right, within the arms of one thick pine, Tall Vic brandished a dagger. Across the path, James pulled his bow into an arc.

"Get down." Ross tugged at Nicholas's chains.

"Wait." Nicholas struggled with his feet. "My leg's gone numb."

Ross cursed and crossed to the other side of the horse.

Nicholas shot a look at Angel and knew he had to try to extract her now, while the force was smaller, while no one suspected.

As Ross rounded Nemesis's flank, Nicholas dug his toe into the animal's belly and the horse kicked backward. The thud of hoof on flesh made Nicholas wince. He jabbed the horse to make him sprint the distance between him and Angel.

Surprise lit Nell's eyes.

Demere sprang forward.

Nicholas unwound the chains from his wrists and dropped them to the ground. He galloped to Angel and reached both arms to take her. Her palfrey bucked. Her eyes went wild.

Around him, Nicholas could hear the sound of daggers drawn, swords bared and crossed, bodies with air *whoofed* from their lungs.

His arms went round her waist. He pulled.

She would not budge.

She sat her saddle so firmly, he nearly bolted from his own.

Tears glistened in her eyes.

He found his balance and stared at her, stunned. They were surrounded, the bold maneuver lost to the cunning of Demere, who strode forward to stand next to a sneering Bartlett.

"We knew from the abduction of Lady Abbeville that you would try to take this woman from her saddle, as you had that lady. What is this? A heathen trick? Not to worry. We were prepared. We chained your precious lady to her saddle. Show him, Nell."

With a salacious smile, the maid flung back Angel's skirts to reveal the binding of her legs to the saddle with chains as strong as his.

"Come forth." Bartlett raised a hand and beckoned to men in the forest.

Nicholas sat while Tall Vic was dragged to Bartlett's feet by men whom he did not recognize.

Bartlett came up to him then and spoke into his face. "Did you dare to presume," he seethed with bared lips and unending glee, "that I would capture the Devil of Midnight and not take all precautions against his escape? I have studied you. Your tactics. Your successes. And I have learned. You have harassed me and mine for years. The king wants you dead, too.

With such motivation, how could I fail? Now I have outsmarted you at your game. I shall enjoy watching you hang, brother dear. 'Twill be my delight when we meet John."

He spun to Demere, who stood with arms crossed, a smile of satisfaction wreathing his face. "Fortunate you suggested we keep those other guards hidden. Can we claim here only two of the Devil's disciples?"

Demere preened.

One of his men took Tall Vic by the scruff of his black silk tunic and was surprised when Vic bested him by six inches. Another guard raised up Ibn Said.

"Two," said Demere. "But that is more than we had ever hoped to take. John will be pleased, I think. Especially with this little man." He went to peer down into Ibn's dark brown face and stuck one forefinger in the black fur vest and flicked it.

Ibn spit in his face.

Wiping his chin, Demere flung back his arm to hit him, and Ibn lashed out with a side kick that had the chamberlain sprawling on his back.

"Take him away!" Demere cried from his indignant position on the ground. "Bind him!"

Vic was chuckling.

Demere had the foresight not to go too near this disciple. "Take this one, too. Gag him. I'll have no more opposition. From anyone." He spun to Bartlett. "I want you to tell Tremaine we need the benefit of his deepest dungeon for these pests."

"Aye," said Bartlett softly, serenely. "Tremaine will do our will. He is too spineless to consort with this Satan and his converts."

But three guards who had relieved themselves did

not return. And when the wind whipped high and no further sounds came from the forest, Bartlett refused Demere's suggestion to search for them. "I want to be inside Tremaine before midnight."

Within minutes, the party had remounted. Vic rode behind a guard. Ibn did the same. Nicholas was seated on Nemesis, closely guarded by two more men as well as Michael Ross. Angel still rode in the middle of the procession, and she, too, merited two more men about her. But the wind picked up and the moon darted in and out from storm clouds.

A bird cooed.

Tall Vic, mounted behind a king's guard, turned, eyed Nicholas, and wiggled his cupped fingers at the Devil. Nicholas's gaze noted with a caught smile how Vic had unraveled the ropes that had so hastily bound him. His eyes flashed to Vic, who pursed his lips. The band's sign of their third disciple.

Mute Harry.

Nicholas understood—and almost laughed aloud.

Mute Harry was Swansdown's butcher's brother, expert in his craft. For this donkey-faced man, who had been silenced at six when Bartlett slit his tongue in two, possessed a skill of gutting beasts—or men— with an innovative eloquence that left one speechless.

So, further along the path, Nicholas knew no surprise when they slowed, then stopped and heard Demere call to the advance man, "What goes there? Why do we not proceed?"

Tall Vic rolled his shoulders and cast Nicholas a backward glance.

Unless Nicholas missed his guess, what went there was Mute Harry.

"Jesus save us!" yelped a guard and then another, as the procession clogged up the narrow road to Tremaine.

"We'll never get past this mess," moaned one man to another.

Demere moved forward, irritated. As he strode beyond the errant moonlight, Nicholas could still hear him as he cursed, then gagged.

"They slit their throats," one guard said.

"And this one's belly," mourned another.

From behind, Nicholas heard the brush part and brambles rustle, and the two guards who brought up the rear were in hand-to-hand combat with two more disciples clad in black, their faces the only sign they might be human.

Ross unsheathed his dagger, but he was too late.

Nicholas kneed his horse to ride past Vic, who took the opportunity to catch his leader by the waist and jump up behind him. The weight of such a big man landing behind him shook Nicholas.

And so, at first, he felt the thump in his side as just another blow.

Arrows whizzed, their *thwump* as they tore flesh making him rejoice . . . and try more desperately to clear the path before him to Angel.

But the king's men had surrounded her at the first stroke of the attack. And Nicholas could not even see her for the shields raised about her and the melee of guards and disciples before her.

Demere and Bartlett, swords and daggers gleaming, came for him, one at either side. But behind Nemesis, someone had put Demere on the ground while Vic sliced the air, holding off Bartlett.

"You'll not have her!" Bartlett bellowed as he parried with the mounted Vic.

"Watch me!" Nicholas vowed.

It was then he felt a wide, hot blade sink into his hip, and knew this one was an ax seated to its brace. It froze his breath and took all his strength to turn the horse about.

"Vic!" he seethed. "I—can't!" He sagged backward against his man, who contorted with his fight against Bartlett.

Vic caught one arm about Nicholas's chest and inadvertently drove the blade of the first knife further into screaming flesh and bone. In blinding agony, Nicholas opened his mouth and knew no sound came forth.

Vic cursed, grabbed the handle of the dagger, and pulled it free. With a cry, he flung it away, reached around, and seized the reins from Nicholas's lax fingers.

Nemesis circled, then churned the earth, and the last sight Nicholas knew was that of Angel, one hand over her mouth, Bartlett beside her, red with rage at his loss.

She took up a stone from the floor of her pit and marked against the age-old wall the eighteenth day of her imprisonment in a castle whose name she did not know. She took great care to chisel the small tally. It was the task by which she began each morn and by which she prayed each hour that Nicholas had survived this day to live another.

A wriggly creature slithered over her ankle and she brushed the thing away, as if it were a speck of dust, an insignificant element to a normal day. Since coming here, she had grown circumspect about her surroundings and knew it was because of the days she had spent with a man who engendered courage.

Having learned well from such a noble tutor, she found it was easy to bear her condition. Minor to note the impertinence of something so small as an insect to attack someone so much larger. For it was the nature of every living thing to attempt survival, no matter the cost. It was the arrogance of some to survive at the expense of others, no matter the morality.

She caught her lower lip with her teeth as she concentrated on the neatness of her day's mark. She made them sure and straight, as sure as her belief that God could not punish Nicholas. Despite the hideous memory of the dagger in his chest—and the sickening sight of the ax buried in his hip.

Nay, he could not die.

He must not.

It was her Devil's self-proclaimed duty to set all unjust counts aright and save those who could not save themselves from the predatory instinct of an unethical few.

For that alone, God had to allow Nicholas to survive.

He had to.

For that, she would gladly take the burden for both Nicholas and herself.

Compared to his survival, what was her own life? Unimportant in the order of the universe. Meager in the chaos John created here on earth.

Her titles? He could have them. Her lands? He would find a way to confiscate them, Great Charter or not. Of that she was sure.

She put down her stone, ran a reassuring finger over her wedding ring, and gathered her filthy but warm cloak about her. In the weak rays of sunlight through the latticed iron bars above this ancient pit, she huddled against the wall. She had no delusions that she might survive John's wrath. After all, Bartlett and Demere—with Nell's help at spying at the hole the night Nicholas had fully loved her—could prove she had not been Chretian's true wife. They had the sheets with dark red evidence. But that was the only thing they could prove.

Certainly, Demere could propose that she had opportunity to kill Chretian. And motive. Lord knew, Chretian often spoke in public of how his young wife would have taken a vow of celibacy if her father let her.

The only thing Demere did not have was a weapon. For that, he had assumed it was the pillow. Aye, *Demere* was the first one to state the pillow was the object used to suffocate Chretian. . . . Why?

Was it a good guess?

Or a conclusion based on other things?

That made her sit straighter, focus her gaze upon the snowflakes that now and then fluttered through the trapdoor. Each was intricate, floating to the ground and disappearing. As invisible as the evidence of a man's last breath upon a pillow cover.

Was the truth just as invisible?

Was there not a way to show the facts as only God knew them to be? Was there not a way to reveal them for mortals? For John?

She prayed that she might be given the chance to find those truths. Like her Devil, it satisfied her sense of justice.

281

But surely, with John's penchant to overlook whatever he must to gain his own way, Angel accepted the fact that this lack of particular weapon was one John would excuse in his own interest. Unless she could prove otherwise.

But how?

For if she could not, she would die.

Not here.

Not now.

Probably without a trial.

And soon. By means of a rope from a rafter, or swifter, by stroke of an ax. Either way, she cared not.

She could meet her God with a clear conscience.

For she had done most of her duty here on earth. She had been obedient, generous, and kind. True to herself and her God. Though in the past priceless days with the Devil she had come to know a life of celibacy was not one she needed to claim for fear of men, she hoped her God would excuse her shortsightedness. For never had she known the Devil's equal and never would she so again. Neither here on earth nor in realms beyond. She had loved him with every fiber of her being, with all her heart and soul.

And neither John nor Demere, Bartlett nor God Himself could ever alter her undying devotion to the one man who had shown her paradise on earth.

And at the memory, and with great hope, she rose to her feet. Before her suddenly appeared a vision. Shimmering in the frosty morning light was an iridescent figure that she recognized as her own guardian. The one who had stood with her inside another pit of degradation and promised her great love—if she would only endure. The radiance of this being surpassed her eyes' fragile abilities. Though she had to turn away, she spoke to it with her heart.

Tell me what to do, she pleaded.

And in the tongue of angels, she heard things she could never repeat. She could only don the mantle of courage they inspired and go forth to meet her next challenge.

Within seconds, she heard the guards approach as they usually did at this hour with what passed for her morning meal of watery gruel.

She smiled, serene.

The oubliette squeaked open.

One guard reached down an empty hand. "Come, my lady. The king arrived last night. He wants you in his hall within the hour."

Chapter

15

King John of England looked less a monarch than a sick man, older than his forty-eight years. Coughing, he slouched in a huge chair and dismissed the two guards who had escorted her from the kitchen. His dark gray-streaked hair scattered across his brow as if he'd not yet combed it this morning. He sat alone on the dais and brooded at Angel's approach like a raven over poor pickings.

"Come, come," he urged with a weary waggle of his fingers. "I wish to see this legendary Angel closely. You clean up nicely, I hear." His heavily lashed eyes ran down the peasant's gown, which a handservant had thrown at her after a warm and satisfying bath in the kitchen. "In fact, I appreciate women. Especially a lady who—my men have told me—shines like her name."

She strolled toward him, letting him feel her own indifference to his power, and stopped short to proclaim, "Mayhap. If she has not been starved or left to rot in a pit."

He slapped a palm to the armrest. "You should have thought of that when you defied me, lady!"

She took a step nearer this man whom many feared, but whose wrath meant nothing to her now. "You should have thought of that when you sent your curs, Bartlett and Demere, to do your bidding, my liege." She smiled humorlessly. "You sent me a good husband in Chretian Forrester, then waited too long to send me another. You cannot blame me for your tardiness."

"Or the icy weather?"

"Precisely."

"How could one know you would wed again so quickly? And so poorly?"

"You cared not for how quickly I wed Chretian. You and my father thought of that before my first husband cooled in his vault."

John stood, only by virtue of the dais standing taller than she. "You are a witch!"

"You should know."

His nostrils flared. "Women find me interesting. I could let you see how kingly I am and take you to bed." His black eyes examined her in the rough wool as if he would strip it away.

"You could try to put me there, I suppose. But would you not wonder, my liege, when the night might come with me in your bed, that you would die in it?"

"*You* will die for that impertinence."

"Better than a living hell with Bartlett. But then, when I am gone, I leave him to you. We'll see if *you* survive him—and his aspirations." She bared her teeth in glee as John took the implication to heart.

Beset as this king had been for years with rebellious barons—and now a French invasion—any indication that yet another man proved traitorous hit a sad but reminiscent note of outrage. One eye twitched. "Bartlett petitioned me to marry you before Chretian."

"That is a new piece of information. But I must offer you my thanks at your selection, for I am still alive because you chose Chretian."

"Bah! You think to sway me here from charges of treason and murder by casting aspersions on Bartlett."

"Think what you will, my liege. Don't you always?"

"By God's blood, you wag a sharp tongue. No wonder your first two husbands died."

She cocked a brow at him.

"Or should I say, no wonder your second died by your hand?"

She moved closer to this man who, rumor said, liked women all too well in the flesh, but never enough in the spirit to honor them as equals. One step from him, she drew nearer and nailed him with her eyes. If—after eighteen days in a cold pit—she still had her wits.

"You may say whatever you like, sir. You are the king. But I will tell you I did not kill Chretian. *Why* would I? Oh, *please,*" she waved a hand, "tell me not this old reply about my wish to become celibate. Of course, I said it. But never after I married Chretian! Never!"

He roared in laughter, his eyes rolling to the ceiling. "Why not?"

"I wanted a husband, children, a happy home. And Chretian was a kind man!"

"He was a sodomite!"

She gasped as if he'd hit her. "You *knew* this?"

286

"Christ! Who in hell did not?"

"*I* didn't!" She thumped her chest. "No one told *me* his preference for partners!"

"But who are you that we should bother to tell you? You are just a woman."

"If you thought this woman had never been Chretian's wife, why bother to wait for proof? Why not come immediately at his death and confiscate all my possessions based on Chretian's failure to take me to his care?"

"At the time of Chretian's death, it was immaterial to me whether Chretian had forced himself upon your virginity. I merely wanted to ensure your extensive lands remained within my realm of control and marry you to one of my own. When suspicions arose that you had killed Chretian, then had I cause to wonder if the consummation had occurred. But again I had no need to fear as long as I sent you a new bridegroom of my choosing. With your defiance of my wishes and your unapproved marriage, I have now developed a taste for compensation." He licked his lower lip in consideration of her breasts. "And vengeance."

"Then find the real murderer and satisfy your hunger by punishing the right person."

"But I have." He smiled at her, placid in his power.

"Really? And what is my motive?"

"Your maid, Nell, Demere, and a few of your men-at-arms tell me you show a very passionate nature."

Memories came to her of how she had caressed and kissed Nicholas in their sight these past days. Those scenes joined with ones of how she and Chretian had been jovial friends. She glared at John, defying him to make of such tenderness a reason for a sin against man and God.

The king leaned down. "So when your husband—despite his oft-proclaimed desire to deflower you and make you a true wife—would not bed you, you killed him."

She laughed, incredulous. "Now *that* makes very little sense. Why would I kill the only man—from king to father and father-in-law—who had ever treated me kindly? Tell me, my noble liege, why *did* you make me marry him?"

John resumed his chair. A tirade of coughing wracked his chest, and when it was finished he frowned at her. "Chretian was a good and loyal man," he said finally. "He wanted to retire from court. The constant troubles there upset him and he thought he would die soon. He wanted an heir. And I thought to reward him for his service to me—his loyalty to the Crown, even if he had once been Richard's lover."

"No wonder Chretian spoke so well of him," she whispered, and remembered Nicholas's mention of Chretian's and Richard's fondness for each other—and the rumored hatred John had for his older brother. "Why would you be so kind to Chretian, then, if he had once cared so well for Richard?"

John struggled with a liquid cough and twisted his mouth as he contemplated her question. "Because Chretian came to me soon after Richard's death and swore his allegiance. I took him at his declaration and placed him in my household. Looking always for subterfuge, I saw none from him. And so, at his plea after all these years to have a domain and take a wife and find peace, I took pity on him. I gave him a widow whose lands were vast—and unless a distant Windom relative could prove his heredity, she would inherit all of rich Windom in the north. I needed you and yours to be aligned with me. Even now, once Christmas is ended, I go north to fight the Scots. I shall probably continue to fight my own countrymen along the way as well." He stared into space. "I wished to reward Chretian for his allegiance to me. So few had given me that. . . . So few of Richard's friends . . . I needed that."

She felt his misery, but sympathized not in the least for the man who had bought and sold women and abducted some for others and even for himself. A man whom many said was an obsessive husband of a pretty girl twenty years his junior. A jealous mate, who—when the girl was unfaithful—took her lover, split his belly, and hung him by the heels over her bed to let him die there before her eyes.

He was a fiend who by perverse chance had come to rule a kingdom.

How could she touch him, except by summoning his own sympathy for someone misused and misunderstood?

"My liege, I have accepted that you may very well kill me for failure to get your approval before I wed."

"Aye," he growled, "you wed the Devil of Midnight. The churl who eats up my forests with his discontented crew and snarls my shipping with his corsairs! I cannot forget that you would do this!"

"Then, why do we talk, my liege? Why waste our breaths? Kill me and have done. I am resigned."

For what she said was true. She knew it. He could kill her—could have her axed here, now or yesterday.

There was a reason why he hadn't. And she exulted that she had this chance to speak with him, but feared the reason that had stayed his hand.

"I want you dead, 'tis true. I want you as an example to all who would defy me."

Her heart pounded with what she instinctively knew. "But you want something else *more.*"

"Aye, my Angel. Do you know what they call you? These past weeks you have sat that pit?"

She shook her head, afraid to know, wild with the need of it. "What?"

"The Angel of Midnight."

She shivered. "How could the common folk know I married their bandit?" she whispered.

"The Devil's disciples tell tales abroad. Rumors reach us here and all are reported to me."

"What do they say?" *Does he live?*

He chuckled, all the more sardonic with the sound of his infernal rasping. "They say the Devil's wounds are deep, but with his heinous determination he recovers."

Her eyes shut in ecstasy, her lips moved in silent thanks.

"Lady, I want him."

Her eyes flew open, and she knew what it felt like to be gutted. For she remembered the scene wherein Nicholas had been saved by his own disciples as they assaulted Bartlett's contingent. That they could not take her with them, chained as she was to her horse, was a sorrow compared to the joy of seeing Nicholas go free. Now she could not bear the thought that that would be reversed. Yet she voiced her knowledge. "And so you will trade me to gain him."

"Actually, 'twas the Devil's suggestion," John oozed. "Come forth, Lord Montrose!"

Expecting John's summons meant her father, Angel turned to see her uncle Graham emerge from the shadows of a pillar. As weary as the king, her kinsman offered a small smile of compassion.

"Why have you come, Uncle?"

"I volunteered. I am the least important of my friends. Should I be seized, not many would mourn me. No lands would fall to brigands. All would revert to your father. Of my allies, I am the most . . . expendable."

"All in my interest. Uncle, I am not worth this risk."

"I represent both my brothers as well as a united group of Geoffrey Devereaux, Allen Gainsbridge, and the Devil of Midnight when I say you are worth this. We seek to see you from here."

"But I do not."

Graham ignored her and pleaded with her by using other means. "I bring you word the Devil lives. He wishes to see you do the same."

She narrowed her eyes at him. "Not at such a high price."

"He is determined to ransom you."

"I am of another mind. For me this bargain is none." Her eyes flew to John, who examined his nails while she probed his evil intentions. She faced her uncle with fury in her soul. "In exchange for me, the Devil will deliver himself up to this fiend?" She pointed at the man on the dais. "Nay. I will not allow it."

"You have no choice!" John bellowed, then went still. "An Angel ransomed for a Devil. I like the whole idea. I really do. It smacks of a certain justice, wouldn't you say?"

Wincing with the pull of young skin over an ugly hip wound, Nicholas turned on his straw pallet toward Graham Montrose. "How is she?"

Graham looked at his two brothers, then Gainsbridge and Devereaux. All of these men in the past few weeks had formed a fond friendship built of mutual goals, respect, and hatred of one king's injustice. Nicholas knew Graham pondered what he might say that would convey the truth of Angel's horrid circumstances without arousing his own devilish anger.

But Nicholas had learned more about patience in the last weeks. While these men strengthened their bond, in his well-concealed and guarded forest cottage, Nicholas had tossed wildly upon this rough bed in fevered delirium, consumed not only with his mortal pain but his mental one. For although his agile band of disciples had saved him from Demere's and Bartlett's hands, they could not rescue Angel, and her fate became his greatest agony.

He knew they had taken her to John. The king at most would kill her without a hearing, and at the very least would throw her in a dungeon, in some stinking pit that would challenge her courage and hope until he was ready to dispense his brand of justice. But now, as in that treasured week Nicholas had spent with her, he would ensure an Angel a bright future. Even if he had to buy it with his own.

"She appears healthy, vigorous even." Graham sat beside Nicholas to relate his news of his audience with

John. "When she entered, I swear to you I hardly recognized her."

"John has starved her?" Nicholas's fear recurred that she suffered now as she had in the past. He could endure any ordeal in this life, except that she should be hurt again, and this time because of another man—him. His eyes ran to her father, the first man who had abused her, and who now stood at the foot of the pallet, head bowed. Dunstan Montrose became a different man these last weeks of his daughter's imprisonment by John of England. Dunstan was morose, troubled in his soul with the sins he had committed against his own flesh and blood. Now, he joined with Nicholas, Allen, and Geoffrey to offer recompense to the offspring he had so wronged. Nicholas prayed they might succeed.

Graham shook his head. "She looks thinner, aye. Paler. No wonder. John told me with great glee that his men had kept her in a pit."

Nicholas cursed. "Bartlett and Demere's doing, no doubt, until John arrived from his battles to the south. I wonder—" He did not want to know but had to ask, "Did they beat her?"

"I saw no evidence of that. She moves with ease, like one graced. Somehow, with all of this, I would vow on a Bible, she looks stronger, placid even. Naturally, she objected to the ransom. She told him— before she knew I was there—that she was ready to die. She is. It's as if she has no quarrel with anyone— except now, of course, with you."

Allen Gainsbridge pushed away from the wall of the forest hut and peered at Graham. "And the condition of his troops? Are they as bedraggled as our reports?"

"Weary. Sick from the cold, but more ragtag because of the endless struggle they have had to fight their way north. The English hate the foreign mercenaries John hired, and the foreigners hate John for not paying them. They all mutter of desertion and rebellion. If John had half an ounce of sense, he'd give up this campaign."

Geoffrey Devereaux grinned at Allen. "And begin to live a more agreeable life?"

Allen smiled. "So by our alliance of Gainsbridge, Devereaux, and Montrose lands and men here in the north, we offer the king a good strategic advantage. If we agree to lay down our arms—in exchange for how we want the Devil kept alive and treated well in captivity—John can move north to fight the Scots with no one to harass him at the rear of his battle lines."

Nicholas cocked a brow. "Meanwhile, he'll have much needed money to pay his mercenaries and his English men-at-arms."

"Aye," said Allen. "Your logic there is sound."

Nicholas frowned. "But has John agreed to all our stipulations?"

Graham nodded slowly. "He wants the Devil badly."

"Even the release of Ibn?" Nicholas asked.

"Aye. Your friend is included in the bargain."

Dunstan Montrose came from his reverie. "Did you see Bartlett?"

"Briefly. John brought him forth after he returned Angel to her cell. John told him how we demand the public exchange of Angel for you and how he must be present. Bartlett did not like it and claimed Demere and his three guards from Windom would hate to attend such an inquisition. But I think John enjoyed seeing Bartlett squirm."

Allen snorted. "John is so accustomed to duplicity that he uses it against his own supporters. He doesn't see how it eats at the fabric of everything he does."

Nicholas agreed. "His loss is our gain."

Allen inhaled, jammed his hands to his hips, and considered the roof. "I pray God our friends arrive in time."

Nicholas gave a painful smile. "The other northern barons will come. They have said they would support us in this, and all of them have always kept their word to me."

Alexander Montrose shook his head. "Our ploy must not be bluff."

"Fear not," offered Father Samuel. "The host of heaven is on our side. The plan is perfect."

Nicholas remained silent, keeping his worries to himself. John Plantagenet of England, who had stolen many men's and women's dignity and rights, yielded to no one easily. He had hated his older brother and schemed against him. He had sold his own first wife and intimidated his second. His actions had brought some nobles to heel, sent others to horse, and driven many to oppose him entirely. Now, even his cousin the French king saw an opportunity to take the crown from him. But through it all, John had survived. By dint of will. And cunning.

Thus, Nicholas knew one truth. It took a devil to best one.

Chapter
16

The sun sank low in the winter sky when next her guard reached down a hand to help her up into the courtyard. Without words, he bid her follow him.

Past men-at-arms whose numbers ran to at least one hundred, Angel walked with head held high and anguish in her heart for them. Whether English or foreigners, they seemed miserable. Coughing much like their leader, threadbare and huddled together, they looked at her with vacant eyes.

This afternoon, unlike yesterday morning, her guard took her beyond the kitchen up into the keep. On winding stairs, they climbed until they stood outside a huge oak door.

"You are to bathe and dress. There are ribbons to braid your hair and a clean gown. The king says you will do this or he will not allow you to see the Devil of Midnight."

"Can I trust John?" she blurted more to herself than to him.

"Will you take the chance and defy him?"

She shook her head and walked past him when he opened the door. As he closed it behind her, she balked. There stood Nell. Alone. Towels in her hand. A smile upon her face.

"Welcome, my lady. I'm sure you'll enjoy this bath."

Angel wanted to scream at her and refuse this, yet another degradation. But she knew it was John's eternal perversity to offer Nell for the element he required. Compared to the sight of her Devil once more, what was it then to allow Nell to see the flesh that she already knew so well? Meaningless.

For compensation, there was no denying that Nell, who knew her duties well and who evidently wished to please the king, proved useful when it came to washing and drying her waist-length hair and twining ribbons in the loose braid. It was true, the gown Angel had been given was a luxuriant burgundy baudekyn with warp of gold and woof of silk, the belt an intricately wrought golden chain. Even her shoes of padded red satin felt rich. And suddenly she knew her Devil had sent these here for her.

When she was ready, she spun for the door, flung it wide, and nodded to her guard to lead her down. Behind her, she could hear Nell's foot upon the stairs. Angel thought that odd, for would Nell not remain to clean the room? Was she coming to this exchange of an Angel for a Devil?

That this irreverent maid should witness the downfall of a Devil pained her greatly. Her guard had his cohorts open the door to the great hall where yesterday she had stood before John alone. She surveyed the crowded room with feigned equanimity. Amazingly, all her foes were assembled. Bartlett, Ross, Demere, and his six Carlisle guards. And on the dais, John. Alone. Pensive. Resplendent in sapphire velvet. Evil in his smile.

Eager to have done with this, Angel stepped over the threshold and paused to take a fuller view of those present. This second look told her neither Bartlett nor Demere were entirely happy with these circumstances, and she wondered why when John had been their protector—or so they said and thought. But even Michael Ross, who never claimed John as lord, stared at her bitterly. Meanwhile, the Carlisle guards either did not know enough to care or simply couldn't. Nor were they armed with swords. A good sign. Unless, of course, beneath their tunics hung their daggers.

She walked to John and met him eye to eye. "I am ready. Do what you will."

He liked her courage—and despised it. Grinding his teeth, he bellowed to her guard, "Bring the Saracen!"

In minutes, Ibn Said was thrust to his knees before John. Angel stood aside and watched with abject horror, for the little man was just as filthy as she had been and even thinner than she remembered him. But certainly—as he raised his smiling face, his white teeth brilliant against the bronze of his skin—she knew he had not suffered.

John leaned forward in his chair. "We have a duty for you, dog."

Ibn's answer was the usual. He spit on the floor.

John was not affected. "We want you to run to your master."

Ibn's eyes, adjusting to the light of day, finally

opened wider. "I know not where to find him," he said, while his white smile flashed.

"He will find you."

Ibn knit his brows. "These are doubtful orders. My Devil is specific in all things."

John shook his head. "These are my orders. We cast you outside the curtain wall. You will walk the main road toward London, where your Devil will meet you along the way."

Ibn crossed his arms. In his black silk tunic and odd flowing breeches, he looked exotic, rigid, proud, and immovable.

John stood. "Go! If you defy me, just think on this—this lady dies."

Ibn blanched.

"Your master would not like that. You tarry and the Devil says this must be done before nightfall. I wish it ended myself for I grow bored."

With bewildered eyes and reluctant body, Ibn was escorted from the hall.

Within the hour, her guard returned, approached John, and said, "Sire, the Devil and his friends are here. The Infidel is not among them."

John waved a hand. "I care not for that one, only the Devil. But first, bring his gold."

From the maw beyond the hall door came forth a group of seven men, all deeply cowled—save for Father Samuel—all moving slowly, surveying those in the hall for their numbers and their readiness to combat. Two carried between them a chest, which they laid before John.

"Open it," he said, his eyes on the wooden casket as large as a small stool.

The guard came forth and popped the hinge, and everyone gasped. Inside the coffer was gold coin to the brim.

Angel took a step forward, but with a flick of John's hand Nell restrained her with a grip on her arm. Her eyes confirmed her hope—they meant to pay for her with money! Nicholas would go free!

John sighed. "I like the looks of this. But I object to the hoods. Which of you is the man I want?"

"We will speak of that when all else is revealed to our satisfaction." One man stepped forward who certainly had the height, the arrogance—but not the voice—of her Devil.

"Let us see your face."

"When we are ready." At John's glance at his guard, the one who took the lead of the cowled group continued, "You promised not to touch us. All our stipulations must be satisfied or we withdraw our offer."

"You have taken your little Moslem dog. I have the specific group of men assembled as you stipulated, even to the handmaiden you required be present. We are not armed, and only one guard walks the room. You see the lady. She lives. Yet you come to me draped so that no man may see your face. *Why?*"

"*You* did not so require," came the reply.

Across the room, one of the Carlisle guards made the bad choice of snickering.

"Remove that cretin!"

Demere winced as the guard took the Carlisle man by his scruff and escorted him to the door.

Angel turned her attention to the six men whose hoods hid their visages. And by the scan, she knew instantly who her Devil was. He was the tall one, as tall as the man who proclaimed he was the Devil of Midnight, but who really was—by his matching height and breadth—her uncle Alex. Her Devil was the one nearest her, the one whose whole being seemed focused on hers. Though she could not see his eyes, she caught the line of his mouth, the one she had kissed—the one that now was so pained with concern for her—and surely for two wounds that even now could be barely healed.

My darling, she said to him with her entire heart, *how can you stand here and do this?*

His lower lip jutted out.

She took his reply for what it was. *Never will I leave you.* How many times had he said that to her before? And so, even now, was it true.

"Remove your cowl!" John said with solemnity.

"Not until we remove the hood from your eyes, Sire. We wish to show you true maliciousness in the guise of a real murderer and accomplices."

"Bah! Take them off, I say!"

The seven glanced about them, hands up as if to ward off an attack. Yet none of the Carlisle guards moved. Nor did Ross, Bartlett, or Demere.

Alex stepped forward toward Angel and John. "We are pleased they are not armed, as we demanded. So now we give you what you need to feel safe. The proof to take the traitor from your midst."

"I am the king. I need no proof."

"The Great Charter which you signed declares there must be judgment by an accused's peers. No imprisonment, exile, or death sentence can occur without it."

"What means that charter to me?"

Nicholas's deep bass voice filled the hall. "Obviously it has meant little these last six months, but now it means the difference between gaining what you want and need. A Devil for an Angel."

"I did not promise a trial. But in the interest of your . . . generosity, you may proceed."

Across the room, Demere looked to Bartlett, who closed his eyes in denial.

"We wish," said Nicholas, "that as you allow this lady to leave us you will see her go with pardon for her arrest—and clear her name of murder and treason."

"That requires a miracle, for she is guilty of both."

"How do you know unless you ask all involved?" Nicholas persisted.

"Why should I take the time?"

"Because if you do not, you will wonder till the end of your days if I spoke an iota of truth. Risk it if you will, but I would say you have too many troubles to take on one more. Your soldiers are ill and tired. I saw them in the courtyard. Yet you prod them on in work they hate. No Englishman likes killing Englishmen. As to the foreigners, they grumble because you have not paid them."

"That will end this day with your help." John smiled like a snake. "Then will I have more choices! If only I had fewer factions."

One man swept off his hood. John sucked in his breath as Allen Gainsbridge strode forward. "Then allow me, Sire, to offer you one faction's agreement to a truce, if you will but hear this man out."

"Gainsbridge! God, man, you try me ever."

"But I will let you cross through my lands and assure you the cooperation of my neighbors to the north as you pass to meet the Scots, if you do this good turn."

"Why, Gainsbridge? You have nothing to gain from this."

"Nothing you would value, Sire. But to save an innocent person from your wrath, I would do this, and more."

"This lady is far from innocent."

"How do you know? Only by word of Chretian Forrester's chamberlain."

"And the earl of Swansdown."

"And isn't that odd? Because, of course, that man was not there the night Chretian died."

John's left eye twitched.

"Sire, for all the years when you have betrayed those to whom you gave your word of honor, this hour's work will be recompense. You suspect me of some ruse. I swear I do not have one. And you know me to be a man of my word."

John nodded. "Gainsbridge, you and your kind are a plague on me." He turned to Angel. "Tell us, lady, what happened the night your second husband died."

She told it all and said it quickly. Her need to sew. Her knowledge that Chretian took a lover to his bed, and her usual practice of remaining in her solar with the door closed until Chretian would come to call her to their bed and her rest.

Perverse in his interest, John clung to every word while a smile broke upon his mouth. "And did you not wonder who this man was? Did you not ask?"

"No," she said flatly. "'Twas not my right to know."

"But if you did, we'd have someone else on whom to hang the blame. Were you not angry, jealous?"

She glared at John. "I was angry that I had been

made to marry to suit others' conditions, but *jealous?* Nay. I liked Chretian, but I did not love him. Not as you mean."

John's eyes cut to Nell. "Why do you smile? You were the chambermaid there. Do you know differently?"

"Nay, Sire," Nell purred with a satisfaction that made Angel turn to watch her. "I know there was not love between Lord Carlisle and his wife. Not carnal love."

Gainsbridge narrowed his eyes at the maid. "Do tell us what there was between them."

She smiled a cloying look of supremacy. "Kindness. He was oh-so-sweet to her. Rubbing her back or bringing her cold hands to warmth. He was so polite with her. Always calling her *my lady* or *my angel,* as if she were some priceless thing. I hated it. It made me sick."

John shifted impatiently. "This woman is but a maid. An imbecile. Her word—"

Nell took umbrage at that. Her silver blue eyes flamed. "Chretian Forrester was a simpering fool! Yet many men liked him. It made me turn my stomach."

Gainsbridge strode to face her. "Many men, eh?"

"What?" In her confusion, she realized she had given something away. "Aye. Aye, many men. And I am a woman."

"And you like a good tumble, eh?"

She crossed her arms and avoided his eyes. "I am a woman. I like men. That's the way it's supposed to be. Not like Chretian Forrester! Seducing men to his bed, doing unnatural things with them night after night."

Allen Gainsbridge studied Nell until she writhed. "How did you know that?"

Her face fell. "What?"

"That he performed those acts."

"I . . . I just knew."

"Were you there when they did them?"

"No! I wouldn't—"

"Well, then, how can you know?"

"I *saw* them!"

"If you were not there, *how* did you see them?"

Trapped, she bit her lip and glanced about her and over to the Carlisle contingent. "Through the squint hole." At Gainsbridge's urging, she said, "Aye! There's a squint hole into the master bedchamber. I have used it, looked through it! What more do you want from me?"

"The name of the man who was Chretian's lover."

"Why?" She slivered her eyes.

"Why not? Does he mean anything to you?"

"Nay," she blustered. "He is less than nothing to me."

Seconds slid by.

"We await you, Nell."

Her eyes went across the hall. "Ross. Michael Ross."

Even Angel gaped. She would have suspected one of the six Carlisle guards—certainly, one of the perverse three who had beset the two squires. Not Ross.

Not burly, morose Michael Ross who set his jaw, flung out his arm, and pointed at Nell. "What would you know of kind affection? You are but a slut, spreading yourself for every animal that walks with a third leg!"

"Not for you!" she shot back.

"Christ, who'd want you? You were too busy chasing Demere to see what was happening."

Nell clamped her lips and grew beet red.

Ross whirled to face the king. "She does not tell you of the others Chretian took to his bed."

John licked his lower lip, enjoying this. "Do tell us."

"This man!" Ross thumped one of the Carlisle men on the arm. "And I think that man, too." He nodded to another, the breath and the life draining from him fast. "I loved Chretian. I was faithful to him. But he was not so to me." He bit back a sob.

"Think you," whispered John with a malevolent gleam in his eye, "that a man like Chretian could be true to any man after he had lost the greatest love of his life?"

"He didn't have to lose me!" Ross wailed. "I loved him! I was faithful! It was he—"

John threw back his head and roared in laughter. Wiping tears from his eyes, he struggled to look at a wild Michael Ross. "Oh, you are a fool. The love of Chretian's life was my brother, Richard. Never *you*. Christ, you bloated frog, who are *you* that you could begin to compare to the mythic Richard?"

Angel felt ill. John loved the brother he also dearly hated.

Broken, Michael Ross lunged forward, and it was Allen Gainsbridge who restrained him. With the move, so, too, had the cloaked party surrounded her. By her side now stood Nicholas, his body heat offering the only warmth to this chilling confrontation.

John stood and hovered over Ross. "So you killed Chretian."

"No!"

"In a jealous rage!"

"No! I would never hurt him, no matter whom he

306

took to his bed. I loved him." Tears rolled down his pockmarked cheeks. "'Twas Demere who put the pillow to his face! I know it!"

Angel shuddered with the force of the knowledge. But bracing one shoulder behind her, Nicholas supported her for the next shock.

John blossomed in wild rage. *"How do you know?"*

"I went to Chretian that night, but he dismissed me. I—I *was* jealous because I had long suspected someone else took my place in Chretian's affections. I hid within a huge cupboard. Soon, someone mounted the stairs. Demere had always had women, so I never thought it might be him. But there he came, sure and bold. I could not believe my eyes."

"And he entered?" John asked, a hand flicking to the guard to catch Demere, who had begun to make for the door.

"Aye. And did not come out."

"How do you know that? Did you remain there?"

"Aye. The next thing I knew, Lady Carlisle came to the door and began crying for someone to help her. When a guard climbed the stairs in response, he left and returned with Demere."

"How could that be?"

"There are winding corridors within the castle. They lead in many directions. He must have left through one of those."

"Aye!" shouted Demere, flinging off the restraint of John's man and walking forward to face the king. "I left by the secret corridor, but I did not kill him!"

"So . . . we have only your word, Ross. We have witnesses—or have you forgotten the guard can testify he brought Demere to Lady Carlisle?"

"I have not forgotten. But I tell you, when I left the cupboard and went inside the chamber, Chretian was dead and *I did not kill him.*"

"And neither did I!" Demere objected.

John scanned the group against the wall. "So who else knew of what went on in that room? In that bed?" His nostrils widened. "And who else had a fond desire to see Chretian dead? Hmmm?" He brought forth the two guards whom Ross had named as lovers of Chretian. "What say you?"

When they did not reply, John chose one to harass. "Then you'd prefer your guilt put to a trial by ordeal?"

Angel moaned. To have one's innocence tested by putting a hand into a fire to see if flesh burned a guilty person struck fear into her heart. Nicholas stepped nearer.

"Nay," whimpered the guard. "I did not kill him. But I know who else had good cause and a chance."

"Is that so?" sneered John. "And who might that be?"

He turned, a look of glory on his features. "Nell."

"He lies. I was nowhere near Chretian that night."

"She was! I saw her come through the passage from the corridor."

Nell flushed and went for the guard with both hands. This time, another cowled man caught her. In the fracas, Geoffrey Devereaux was revealed. But none paused to register his presence because the frightened guard continued.

"The corridor they speak of leads to the guards' chamber. I was amazed when I saw her sail through. She never saw me, for I was so far in a corner. I never thought the one who killed him might have been her. I only thought she'd been at the squint again."

"Were you at the squint?" John asked.

"No!"

"But then," said Demere as he turned slowly to her, "if you did not, how could you know enough about Chretian's death to come to me almost minutes before the alarmed guard arrived to take me to Lady Carlisle?" He blinked and stared at John. "She told me Lady Carlisle had killed her husband with a pillow."

"And you believed her?" John was now incredulous.

"Aye. I was panicked. Confused. Thrilled. The guard was banging at my door. And I—I wanted to believe Lady Carlisle had killed her husband."

Nell snorted. "He had wanted to be rid of her from the start. He was afraid she'd turn Chretian's mind to taking a woman as a lover."

"Oh, you *are* vile," he snarled.

She curled her mouth up viciously. "Not as much as you, you snake." She looked at John. "Demere was thrilled that night that Chretian was dead and his wife the cause. And do you know why, Sire? Because it meant he would not have to do the deed which his other lover set for him months ago."

"Other lover?" John asked.

"Aye!" Nell ranted now, oblivious to care. "It meant he would not have to kill Chretian himself! Aye, instead, I did it for him! Like a fool, *I* did it for him. I did it to have him totally to myself." She moved forward and stared at John. "But I found he loved another more than me."

"So take your revenge and tell us who that man is."

"Roger Bartlett."

John sank in his chair.

Bartlett had not moved. "What silliness is this, Sire? Would you take a maid's word over mine? We are here to see the Devil of Midnight ransom a woman, a murderess. Surely, you cannot believe this —this pack of lies!"

"I think I have heard enough in the heat of passion to know truth when it stands before me," John said nonchalantly. "Ever have I wondered that you pandered to me so."

"You *fault* me for my loyalty? Absurd!"

"I like loyalty. But not too much of it. It builds men whose power can rival mine. Besides, becoming so loyal to another for political reasons"—he shifted in his chair—"makes my skin crawl."

"I am your flesh! My mother told me! You affirmed it!"

"Did I? I cannot recall that conversation."

"You promised me control in the north!"

"Ah, but if you had continued to rely on me—and not on chamberlains—we might have gone on together."

"This is ridiculous! You will take the word of an outlaw?"

"Certainly. I always know what his loyalties are. Whereas I may not with yours."

"You are a bastard."

"So—supposedly—are you. Guard, take this rabble away, will you? The air grows fetid. We will deal with each in turn. Later. For now, let's see them attired in chains and put into the pits."

It took minutes of shouting and wrestling to clear

the room of Nell, Demere, Ross, Bartlett, and the Carlisle guards.

Angel watched them go and knew her ordeal was only half over.

Allen Gainsbridge turned to John, who fought a spasm of coughing. "So thus you see we have cleared Lady Carlisle of the charge of murder."

"The greater one of treason is not one I am likely to absolve. She took a man to husband of whom I—even by rights of the Great Charter which you love to quote—and only I have the right to approve. You, lady," he shook a weary finger at her, "conspired against me."

She may have been cleared of murder, but still the issue remained of the ransom and exchange. She would best Nicholas at this round by disclosing all.

"Sire, I sought to foil you and did not conspire with anyone. I thought of the idea of a false marriage on my own."

"False marriage?" he bellowed.

"Aye. I needed a man who would help me, quickly. A man I could trust to help someone in distress. There was only this outlaw, whose reputation said he would assist the despairing. So I made imitations of documents and had my loyal servants capture the Devil of Midnight. Never did I think they would be able to take him—but they did."

Her father and Uncle Graham flung back their hoods.

Dunstan Montrose spoke. "Sire—"

"Nay, Father, I need to tell him all." Angel searched John's face for his mood and thankfully found him disposed to logic. "I made the offer. I made the bargain. I was terrified of Demere and his threats. And I was still grieving for Chretian and wanted no other husband. Can't you see, Sire, I wanted to be free—not bound to yet another man who did not want me, but my money and lands?"

Dunstan blinked back tears. "She had good cause here, Sire. For years she had been beset by me, making her marry her first husband, and then with your consent, I forced her to wed Chretian."

Geoffrey Devereaux stepped near John. "Sire, I wished to wed her, too, and take my family's lands back into one unit. But when I arrived and she told me she had married, I was not inclined to fight to gain Windom for me."

"Why not, Devereaux? Land is almost as good as money."

"The land I own is enough money for me, Sire. I wish a peaceful life. And I would do much to gain it, even avoid war with my neighbors. For I have had enough of war with you for my sovereign."

John smacked his lips. "What is your price, Devereaux?"

"I will join with Allen Gainsbridge and his allies to see you through the north without incident if you will let this lady go."

"This is bribery on bribery!"

Allen extended a hand. "Merely another name for political expediency, Sire. What will you?"

John wagged a finger at Dunstan. "I wish to know this man's price as well."

"My alliance with you for the northwestern portion of England. My brothers join me in it. For this, you will free my daughter of the charge of treason."

"And you swear you will do this, hold loyally to me until I die—and then to my son?"

"Aye, my liege. I will do it," said Dunstan.

"So, too, I," said Graham as he flung back his hood.

"And I," offered Alex.

John examined them each in turn. "I need the proof."

Allen smiled. "Have you ever known any of us to promise so much before, Sire?"

"Nay. That is why I require proof."

Nicholas removed his cowl. His bronze skin pale, his golden eyes dim from exertion, he nonetheless challenged his king. "You may come to the parapet, then, and gaze out upon the land surrounding this castle, Sire. There you will see that a combined force of all our men have stood at the ready to raze this castle should we not emerge within the hour. The number of this group is—to the best of our hurried calculations—over three hundred men strong. When we retire, Sire, with Angel in our midst, those men become your safeguard north to Berwick."

Angel recoiled. "Nay, you must not do this."

John ignored her. His mouth must have watered with the offer, for he rolled his tongue around his mouth. "You are shrewd, Devil. That is quite an impressive number."

"Aye. They are the bowmen and mounted knights from the coalition which demanded you go to Runnymede."

"A noble lot, they think themselves. Are you not also afraid what others will say of this?"

"They will say we saved an innocent from John's wrath."

John inhaled and considered the priest. "You come to verify there was no real ceremony?"

Samuel, who had listened to all with a cocked ear, came forward with a pastoral smile. "Aye. This lady went through a ceremony, Sire. Performed by me, it was. But it was not a valid sacrament."

"Why not, Father? Demere, Ross, and even the maid were convinced the ceremony was a true one."

"I did my best to make it appear so. But I did not take their vows or bless the union with the proper words. I mixed their order and substituted new words."

"Why?"

"Well, Sire, I must tell you, I can give confession and perform absolutions, but never for myself! Why would I wed a man and woman who wished only to use the sacraments of the church to their own ends? I could not do that."

"But you are an outlaw in this band?"

"That does not make me less a man of God's—only less a man of yours."

"You are right." John turned to Angel. "So, lady, your supporters have won the day for you. You may go."

"I go nowhere."

John gave a short laugh. "This is no game. I said—"

"I'm going nowhere." She stepped away from Nicholas, who had gone rigid at her words. She faced the seven. "Do you think I will allow all of you to side with him, to help him, only to save me? I can't believe it. I am not worth all this."

Nicholas spoke to her with a rasping voice. "You are worth everything. You must go."

She shook her head. "I'd rather die and give his subjects some other injustice to add to their list!"

"Daughter—"

"*Nay*. You are worth more. He will kill you, no matter that you offer him the world!" Seeing she made no point with Nicholas, she shrugged off her father's hand and looked at John. "I will not do this. You may not have this. Send me back to your pit. Kill me. I care not. You are not worthy of the life of my Devil, let alone gold *and* the combined force of his friends."

"You, madam, have no choice!"

"*No-o-o!*" To be made once more to do a man's will, even if to save her own life, killed her hope, her everlasting belief that all things came aright with faith and perseverance.

John struggled to his feet and shot a hand toward the door. "All of you, get you gone from me, *now*. All of you, save this one! Out! And take her with you!"

"For Christ sake, Allen!" Nicholas said under his breath. "Leave while you can."

Her father took one of her arms and Allen Gainsbridge the other. Both pleaded that she leave now.

"No!" She wrestled to be free of their steely hold. But it was useless.

Never had she been free, save for a few blissful days and nights when she had been married to a Devil.

And now, wed to him only in the eyes of God, she would at the insistence of her king become once more a widow.

The pain of watching her go was a torment greater than Nicholas had ever known. Once more she was required to do men's will. This time, she went because she did his. And like the Devil who had been cast out from Heaven, this Devil's punishment would be the same. To see no more the visage of the one he adored the most.

Even if he did survive John's wrath and cunning, Nicholas was certain Angel would never look upon him with any favor again. For he had promised never to treat her as all those other men had done. Yet he, like all those others who had used her to their ends, had ordered her life and made her act against her will.

For that he would dwell in hell for long eternities.

John's punishment would be slight compared to that.

He turned to the inevitable and the man who now controlled his every breath. "Now to the final act." He faced John fully. "We are agreed that you will never touch her, cross her land, accost her villeins."

"Aye. Your money and your allies have paid fully for her. Now I need my satisfaction, Devil. I cast you out of England." John grinned. "Fitting for a Devil to be exiled, eh? 'Tis a far trip to the bleak Irish island I have chosen for you, Devil. There may you sit for the rest of your days and ponder the sea and the surf, while the woman you have loved and lost damns your name for all eternity."

Chapter

17

The first news he had of her was in February.

Graham Montrose had traveled to the rocky isle along the southwest coast of Ireland as the first appointed emissary from Allen Gainsbridge and their allies. Nicholas was not allowed to write letters or in any way communicate with the outside world save for this occasional visitor John permitted him. So, coming to check that the Devil of Midnight still lived—and therefore that the alliance would continue as they promised—Graham trudged up the stone path to the crumbling wattle and daub hut Nicholas knew as exile.

The two friends, guarded by Nicholas's two jailers, sat before the best small fire one could build in such a forsaken place and drank their wine in companionship. But there was only one topic Nicholas wished to discuss.

"How is she?"

Graham swirled his wine. "She retired to her

Windom Dower House last month after giving over her rights to Windom Castle to Geoffrey. He did not want to take the castle, said it was her home and she should remain. But she ignored him. Days later, she wrote him a letter, acknowledged his rights—and simply left." Graham stared at him, biting his lower lip.

"What else is wrong?" Nicholas clutched his goblet.

"She will not speak to any of us. Her servants fear for her sanity. She has put guards to her doors and will not let us in."

Weeks later, when Geoffrey Devereaux arrived with the meager supplies John sent for his famous prisoner, Nicholas wasted even less time. As sharp clouds scudded across the crisp blue spring sky, Nicholas walked his friend to the dreary cottage and asked the most vital question.

"She has left Windom Dower House," Geoffrey replied with sorrow. "I learned it as I set sail last week. I had a message from her father. He is mad to find her."

"You mean he does not know where she is?"

"No one knows. She left in the dead of night. Not even her servants have clues."

"Her steward, Peter, nor Edwin? Leon. *Leon* has resources, ways. He would know."

"I think not, Nicholas. We asked him. He would have said, I think, because he is so loyal to her."

"All the more reason to keep silent. You *must* find her."

"Aye, we will." Geoffrey glanced at the two guards, who took more care investigating the barrels of wine he had brought with him than in listening to their prisoner's conversation. Still, he lowered his voice.

"But we will do better when we are assured you are once more free of this oppression."

"Just get me home so that I can find her," he shot back.

"I have a plan," Geoffrey whispered. "One guard will fall ill with some bad wine I seem to have brought with me." His eyes twinkled. "We have another man eager to fill this one's shoes and do the English king's will." He raised his brows.

"How accommodating. I assume he is Irish."

"To the bone."

A month later, courtesy of the Irish guard and his family, Nicholas was free of his rocky isle—but far from home. Smuggled into the Welsh hills by a band of outlaws so reminiscent of his own disciples, and hidden by a princely opponent of John, Nicholas paced the hall of his host's castle with foreboding. He was not wrong to feel that way. For when news came the morning after his arrival, it was a brief note from Dunstan Montrose, and its words resounded like a death knell in his heart.

"Angelica has retired to the Dominican Abbey of St. Anne in York. It is the one she lived in as a girl. When I requested to see her, the reverend mother refused me. Angel cannot speak with anyone, for she has taken a vow of silence."

Nicholas balled the parchment in his fist. In his heart, he knew the other vow she'd taken was one engendered by her distrust of men. The one that she had longed to take before she met him. The one of celibacy.

All his hopes to return one day a free man to his home, to declare his love for her and ask her to marry him, were for naught.

For this—above all else—he burned to be back in England, fighting against the man who had taken all that was good in the world and destroyed it.

When the messenger returned to Dunstan the next morning, he had in his keeping the confirmation that Nicholas had been safely brought to freedom in this Welsh sanctuary. He also carried to Dunstan a plan to destroy John of England forevermore.

Summer came into the abbey walls but brought little warmth into Angel's heart. Beneath it rested the substance of her agony. She spanned her hands over the huge swell of her stomach and straightened her back. With this child so great, her body had suffered. But not half as much as her mind.

She had feared this child's father a dead man. Knowing John's inability to make a promise and keep it, Angel had assumed that soon, no matter the wealth of gold or number of allies offered, John would see her Devil killed.

In her anger at what men had made her do, she swore she did not care what happened to Nicholas, but knew she lied. Under her bravado lived her unending love of him, just as her manifestation of it lived under her heart. And she had to give up the pretense. She wanted her Devil alive and free and hers, but knew that never would be so.

In her wild temper last winter, she had refused to speak to any of the men who had aided Nicholas in his exchange. From her family to Geoffrey and Allen, she blamed them all for her misery—and whatever horrors her Nicholas suffered in her name.

She claimed she'd taken the vow of silence. It was such a simple way to avoid them all. And then, when her suspicion that she carried a Devil's child became a fact, she knew she had not only to refuse the men any audience, but to turn away anyone who would carry tales to John. For if the king knew she carried the Devil's baby, she would die. And while she still had not recovered enough of her objectivity to say she forgave her Devil his bargain, she adored this baby within her body and would allow no one opportunity to kill the only expression of her one week within her loved one's arms.

Then, as July became August and numerous kicks and jolts declared this child imitated his father in power, her viewpoint began to change. Afraid of any communication being intercepted by the king, she wrote to no one outside the abbey, but waited for rumors to drift in. She was left to wonder if Nicholas lived. Soon, she prayed it was so. Suddenly, her guardian angel appeared to her to tell her it was. And her hope revived.

From beyond the convent's walls came whispers, then bold tales that the Devil of Midnight lived, that he had been exiled and had returned to deliver them from evil. And inside the serene walls of St. Anne's, Angel sewed tiny garments and prayed for swift deliverance for them all.

In mid-October, the news that the king of England was nigh unto death in Newark went round the abbey with as many prayers and signs of the cross as any monarch with such a reputation could hope for from women who had abandoned the world at a young age.

But Angel laid her precious burden in a huge oak cradle, went to the chapel, and fell to her knees, thankful. Tears in her eyes, she admitted sinfully that she was grateful the wretched man would now cease his earthly woes. For so would all his subjects.

In the past months, they had all suffered. John and his army filled with English and foreign mercenaries had scourged the countryside. Burning out those who could not afford to pay John a hefty bribe, his soldiers had met little resistance from the Scots. But that was poor solace when John had once more to turn south and put his attentions to the rebellious in his kingdom. For whether he besieged them or starved them, they opposed him all the more.

And since the summer, when the French armies began a greater siege of John's castles in England, the king had suffered serious losses at the hand of the Devil of Midnight. That outlaw now led not merely his own band of disciples but also Gainsbridge, Devereaux, her kinsmen, and the rebellious English barons who had opposed John for more than a year.

Angel thrilled to each exploit she heard. More fearsome and more ruthless now, her Devil took no prisoners and gave no shelter to any who were the king's. John was once more beset and bested. While John burned and looted, bribed and slaughtered any who tried to oppose him, the Devil of Midnight and his friends won victory after victory. She had thought for so long that Nicholas was dead at the hand of John that she smiled every time she knew her Devil won. But as the tales continued, her hope soared that Nicholas might defeat the one who kept them from each other.

This time, Angel knew John could not stop the Devil. Surrounded, hounded, John took ill and now faced God's decree that he return to his Maker.

Serene as she had not been in many months, Angel

rose from her knees and returned to her cottage, where she sewed for the nuns and prayed for the man she adored to free them all from the terrors of their existence.

As soon as John's son was proclaimed king and the countryside was calm once more, she would return to Windom Dower House. For she had two good reasons to go home. One was to give the Devil his due—her undying love. The second was to present him with her physical evidence of it.

"The stubborn man will not come!" Allen muttered into his wine. "In the past two weeks, I have sent two invitations."

"And I one," said Geoffrey. "He does not write in return, but sends word by his guard."

"I thought surely," Angel mourned, "that he would come for Advent revels."

"He sees no one," Geoffrey explained. "I asked his gatehouse guard why I was being refused even the courtesy of a personal greeting. He told me the earl of Swansdown had given strict orders no one was to enter. Christ's bones, the poor man looked as riddled as we and said the former Devil of Midnight does not eat well or sleep, but roams the castle night and day like a dreamer. He says he fears for his new lord's mind. He asked me if the young king knows that this new earl of Swansdown is a madman."

Recognizing many of the characteristics she herself had displayed when first she was taken from the Devil, Angel thrust down her sewing. It was to be a tunic of ruby velvet, a Christmas present for Nicholas. "Yet he sends gifts often. This length of velvet. Lemon candies. Last week, I received a gold chain girdle. He knows we are here, waiting for him." *Does he know how much I want him?*

Geoffrey smacked his lips. "He sent me a present of gold coin last week. Just the coin, no letter."

Allen scratched his beard. "He's stripping himself of everything valuable. He has been in that castle for less than a fortnight. At the rate he goes, I fear for what tomorrow brings."

"Mayhap," Geoffrey pointed a finger, "he knows not how to live with all the wealth his years have brought him."

"Or all the peace," concluded Angel.

"Whatever the cause of his brooding, I do not like it," Allen said. "He must come out and live a normal life."

"But how? If invitations do not work—"

"I know another way," said Angel.

Chapter
18

York Shire, England
November 1216

Prayers came true.

She knew they did the minute they rolled him from the winnowing sheet.

He was everything she remembered. A big man. A virile man.

An angry one.

As he cursed and fought to uncoil himself from the tangle of the sheet, he rose to his feet and, struggling with the ropes, he glared at Peter and Leon.

But then his eyes fell upon her . . . and he stopped.

He'd lost some weight. His skin was paler. His golden eyes dimmer, sparking only now with surprise. But he was still so heartbreakingly handsome that her breath left her as she gazed at him. Would that she might do so for long years.

She waved a hand in dismissal to Peter and Leon, her eyes never straying from the gold ones that poured into hers like liquid flame. She let him satisfy himself and stood stark still, her heart aching for him.

Presently, he glanced about him, narrowing his gaze on the chairs, her pile of sewing, her roaring chamber fire. She went to him and unwound the ropes from his wrists. Circling both with her fingers, she brought them to her mouth and placed one tender kiss in each palm. He made some soundless objection like an animal wounded, roiled by succor he dared not believe.

She winced and looked up into his pain-filled eyes with tears in her own. Swallowing hard all the agony she needed to forget here, she concentrated on ridding him of his. One torment at a time.

She swirled for her table and the wine she meant to share with him. With shaking hands, she managed to pour some of it into a golden goblet—one of the treasures he had sent last week—and returned to him. Unlike that unforgettable night when she had first captured him and had him brought before her here in this room, he was not on his knees and his hands were not bound.

But his mind was.

And as he had freed her from all her horrors, so would she now do the same for him.

She offered him the cup but he did not see it. His eyes—oh, God, his eyes that many said stopped evil in its track—fell over her like a starving man's at a feast. While she wondered if he noted the changes in her breasts and waist, she felt her body respond as it always had, and took the scintillating feeling to nourish the other sustenance she needed to provide for him. Taking his hands, she molded them around the cup and put her fingers beneath it.

He let it fall to the floor. Snatching up her hand, he stared at the ring of onyx, gold, and pearls.

"I have worn it all these months," she told him finally, breaking their silence and the mystic spell that held him rigid.

He spun away and went to face her fire.

She took his rejection for what it was—confusion. And outrage.

"You speak? How is that?" he asked in no kind tone.

"'Twas a ploy to make your friends leave me alone. I hated them for what they'd done."

"Let—us—be—frank. You hated *me!"*

"Aye. That was true, too." She bit her lip. This was more difficult than she expected. "But only for a while. At first, when my father and Allen took me from you, I thought John would hang you."

"Christ, I paid him enough to keep ten armies alive!"

"Aye! But I did not trust him, nor did I know how badly he needed money. Nor could I have known how you stipulated that you be exiled and that your friends be given leave to call on you to assure themselves of your existence! You did not tell me!"

He whirled on her. "Damn it, how could I?"

She swallowed back her fear, for never had she seen this Devil's anger so wild and so focused on her alone. "I know. I came to realize that."

"I thought you trusted me!" he seethed, taking a menacing step toward her.

She held her ground. "I know. And I did. But I didn't trust completely at the end, did I?"

He clamped his jaw and glared at her for answer.

"I thought John so perverse. I had known men to be devious, cruel, greedy, but never had I seen such a potent combination of it in one man until I was put before him. Will you fault me that I thought his power so great not even the Devil of Midnight could deter him?"

"Nay. That would not be fair." He gnawed at the inner flesh of his cheeks. "And I have always been fair."

"I know," she whispered.

"So tell me why am I here?" He sank his hands on his hips and stared at her. "I wish to know, and quickly, so that I may return to my own home."

"Why?"

"Why what? That I wish to go home? Well, I would think that would be obvious. It is so grand. Swansdown Castle has been well preserved by the previous lord, or did you not know? Until Bartlett's death by John's henchman the castle was well provisioned with every luxury the man could afford. Last week, I ordered all the furnishings burned. All the plate melted."

"I know. I heard of the bonfires you built." It was the incident that made her fear for the total loss of his mind and the reason she had given the final order to Leon to insinuate himself into the earl of Swansdown's presence and bring him here to her. Leon, true to form, had told a lie to gain entry. He said that he had news of Angel, and that brought forth the Devil with speed. That Leon had been faster and tied him was apparent.

Nicholas snorted. "I thought of putting a torch to the interior as well. I might yet."

"Oh, but why?" Her heart was breaking for him.

"Why not? What means that place to me? I lived there only a few years. 'Tis not my home."

"It is your inheritance. You are the rightful earl of Swansdown. Why not keep it?"

"Why," he blurted, "would I keep the hellish place? Have you ever seen it?" She shook her head and kept her place as he stalked her. His nostrils flared as he loomed over her. "It is a palace," he breathed. "Bartlett fancied himself a prince. I haven't seen so much finery since once my uncles took me to the Doge's palace in Venice. Like that tyrant, Bartlett was a glutton. Swansdown Castle reeks of him and his indolence. I love gutting the place."

"But you'll have nothing left. And it once was everything you wanted."

"Not everything," he murmured. His eyes, now so close, delved into hers with hurt pride and ravenous need. "Once, long ago, I wanted it because it was mine and it had been taken from me unjustly. Then, later, I wanted it because it would give me leave to have the greater joys I desired. But that was taken from me, too."

"By circumstances."

"It matters not the way I lost them. I have. That is all I know. All I *feel."* His hand came up and he would have put it in her hair, against her cheek, but he caught himself and stepped toward the door.

"Wait!" She hastened after him and grabbed his arm. "You can't go!"

"Jesus, woman!" He turned on her and grasped her shoulders so hard she felt her bones begin to bend. "What do you think I'm made of!" He shook her.

That brought forth tears. "Flesh!" she cried. "And bone! Blood and iron!" She struggled to place one hand against his heart as he backed her to the cold stone wall. "You're made of tender love and care. . . . Oh Nicholas, my darling," she pleaded with him, his eyes wide with his turmoil, "you're made of all the things I want and need. Don't leave, my darling. Stay, stay. I need you!"

"You're mad!"

"Aye!" she admitted. "Mad to have you out of that castle. Wild to have you here. To tell you, darling, that I love you and I can't forget you."

"You should have thought of that before you brought yourself to the abbey in York and took those vows!"

"I took no vows. I told you. It was a ploy to—"

"Do not do this!" He pressed her to the wall so forcefully she felt each ridge, each hard, cold truth. Yet, tears misted his eyes. "You cannot lie to me. I *never* lied to you!"

"I know," she murmured. "But you must believe me: I never took a vow of silence."

"How could I care about the silence!" he bellowed. "I care only that you vowed to stay away from *me!* From men!"

"What are you saying?"

In his agony, he drew in air with a hiss. His body crushed hers to the wall. She reveled in the joy of having him so close after all these long and lonely months—and knew he did it more in anguish than in love.

"Did you take a vow of celibacy, or not?"

Her mouth dropped open. "Who told you that?"

"What is this?" He wrapped his arms around her, still in anger. "What are you doing to me?" He brought her from the stones and more securely against the hot wall of his chest. His mouth spoke above hers. "When I need you so, what right have you to send your men to take me from my home? Is it not enough," he rasped, his lips a whisper away, "that I yearn for you night and day? That I can't forget your smile or your body or your innocence you gave so freely. Why can't you leave me in peace?"

She would have kissed him then. It would have been so simple, so fulfilling. So final—and yet not. For still she would have to rid him of his false notion that she had taken a vow of celibacy. And she would rather show him the evidence of her own aspirations for them before she showed him her never-ending desire for him. So she pushed away, her body screaming for the lack, and spoke the truth.

"Because you're not in peace, my love. And neither am I."

His features contorted. "Such was the life I was meant to live. Ever has it been so." He made to turn again.

Once more, she waylaid him. "Nay. You will not go until we have settled this. I—I have some things to say, and two to show you. Then, if you wish, you may leave. And I promise you," she faltered for a moment at the thought of losing him again, "this time, I will let you go and never seek to bring you back."

Avoiding looking into his face, she crossed to her table and poured a cup of wine for herself. She needed the fortitude, because if she failed to say it all, tell it accurately and well, he would be lost to her. He had been dead to her for so many months that to even broach that thought made her head pound.

"I loved you from the start, you know. You were so

very different for me. Kind, honest. Gentle with me. More than Chretian, you offered me support and equality. Even when you took me to bed, you were so sweet, so careful of me as if I could break. And so it was that in your care, you helped make me stronger. I needed to be, didn't I? For all of the men and women who had plotted against me were a dastardly lot, weren't they? And we had no idea how much so." She took another drink, the vapors of the wine hitting her senses and loosening her tongue.

"Certainly, by the time I was brought before John, I had met the worst of men—and the best. As I rode home with my father and Allen, I knew it to be so. And I grieved for you. Though they told me of your exile, not your death, I did not believe them because I could not trust John. I went inside Windom Castle, took the oaths of fealty from those remaining whom I could trust, and retired to my solar." She turned to face him. "Like you now, I was despondent with my loss. Angry with my God who had deserted me, just as you think now He has deserted you."

"I am no concern of God's."

"But you are."

"I have no evidence."

A smile of serenity spread across her mouth. "But I do, my darling. I do." Placing the cup down, she went to him then and wound her arms around him. He shuddered to have her there, but he did not pull away. "I never took a vow of celibacy. I couldn't. I went to the abbey in February of last year, my love, because I needed sanctuary from John. He pillaged the land, burned out many. His mercenaries roamed at will, raping and ransoming any and all for what money they could get. I feared to stay here, even with the serfs so loyal. I feared because I thought if John wished to take me, if he knew how much you still meant to me, he would come for me and then kill me."

"Nay, my Angel, if John so much as came within twenty miles of Windom, I told him my allies would take revenge and see him die." This time when his hand rose, he threaded it through her hair to cup her cheek. "I would never let him have you."

"And I never wanted him to have any part of you."

He shook his head. "For as soon as I knew you had left here and gone to the abbey, when I learned you took vows and were in a place where he could not take you for fear of God and country, I made one of my own vows to return and fight him till the end."

"And so did you do, my love." She let her pride shine in her eyes.

He traced her chin and her lips with the backs of his fingers. "But these past two weeks, to regain my title and my home and return to peace was different. To be no longer at war with him—with anyone—for the first time in my life—" He licked his lips. "I do not know what to do. How to live. My allies have gone home to their wives and their families. And my band is dispersed. Some of them were Swansdown retainers and came home with me."

"And Ibn and Father Samuel?"

"Both remain with me, yet is my castle like a tomb. Filled to the rafters of my mind with the sound of your voice as you sing or laugh, the memory of your lips as you kiss and your words as you make love. I cannot live like this. I cannot get away from the emptiness. The endless stream of people who wish me to come out." His eyes flowed into hers. "But oh, I cannot. For the one I wanted most in all the world is not with me and *God, my darling, how I hunger for you.*"

Tears flowed like a river now. She wiped them away and stepped backward. Biting back a sob, she told him not to move, and she turned for the door.

Blinking away the remnants of her sorrow, she made for the hall and the far chamber. Within moments, she bade Leon open the door for her and she strode inside her solar once more to face a Devil.

He had his back to her, considering her fire, when he turned to her and swayed with the force of what she held in her arms.

Two babies wrapped in swaddling clothes slept there peacefully. She smiled down at their perfect cherubs' faces and then up at their stunned father, and walked forward.

"Here," she said as if this were a regular occurrence, "do take James. He is so much heavier than his sister that my arm grows weary already."

Unaccustomed as he was to holding his son, Nicholas reached out his hands and experimented with positions before he held him finally clutched close to his heart. He stared at the child for long minutes and then reached over to push his sister's blanket from her face.

"And her name?" he asked with a quivering voice.

"Constance."

"Of course, you would name her for my mother and him for my father and give me a complete family," he murmured as he put one large finger into his daughter's clenched palm and examined the tiny hand with teardrops in his eyes. "When?" he asked, choked.

"The first of September. 'Twas a lovely day. The sky

was clear blue, the sun as gold as your eyes. That I shall always remember. The nuns were a consolation, if not very helpful with the birthing. We were very surprised when there were two."

"*Aye*," he ground out.

"Come," she whispered, and took him to her solar, where they both sat side by side, their children in their arms.

As she smoothed the blanket under Constance's chin, Angel said, "Now you see why I went to the abbey and why I stayed. I heard of your escape from the island and that you went to Wales. My father brought me news by way of writing. I would not speak with him, you see. I was too afraid to let anyone see me . . . for I"—she chuckled through fresh tears—"I was very great with these children. They were not easy to carry and—" She broke down then at the memory of all the lonely months when she feared for him and wanted him with her to share this joy.

She felt his arm go around her. "Oh, my darling Angel," he whispered into her hair, "what you have suffered at all our hands. I would never see you hurt."

Arms full of slumbering babies, it was difficult to embrace. She could only press her lips against his throat. "I love you so."

"I know," he said.

"Then, tell me, my lord, at long last what I need to know."

"Aye, I will. But look at me."

She raised her face and it was like staring into the sun. "I love you, my Angel. I knew it from the moment they unwound me from that filthy winnowing sheet. I have loved you for so long and so badly, I am not certain I can make the kind of husband a lady of your consequence and"—he glanced down at his children—"and of your power may need." She clutched his tunic and he smiled brilliantly, obliterating all their wretched pasts. "But oh, my sweet love, I will spend eternity trying to make you as happy as you deserve."

"You make all of England happy, darling. For what you won is peace for us all. Now lay down your sword, your cares, and let me make you happy. Marry me."

"Aye, this time with all the right words." He kissed her lips with joy and promise. "I adore you, my Angel. I will forevermore."

And so it passed into local legend that the fifth earl of Swansdown added to his crest of black swan upon a field of gold the symbol of his wife, an angel. Their children and their children's children, unto the eighteenth generation, still use the heraldry to mark the family estates.

The ancient twelfth-century Swansdown Castle still bears the splendid inheritance of that earl and his beloved wife: his bow and one battered golden wine goblet. Her harp and a length of priceless ivory silk, which still holds her needles. The place is world renowned, so much so that each year hundreds tour the well-preserved fortress to see the glories that the earl brought to his home decades before routes to the land of Kublai Khan became a regular occurrence. Inside the richly appointed solar, the visitors ooh and ah over the finest gold necklaces from India. The first Chinese porcelains ever to reach the shores of England. A treasure trove of rubies and emeralds. Vials of powder labeled Dragon's Bones and Tiger's Teeth. And one long strand of perfect pearls.

Inside the Swansdown family chapel, a statue of a carved life-size Angel and her Devil embrace for eternity above an inscription, which reads:

"Herein stands the Devil of Midnight, who fought that freedom might survive.

"Here stands the Angel of Midnight, who endured that love might conquer all."

Author's Notes

Opposition to the unscrupulous King John of England forms the stuff of western legends. Though the tale of a certain Robin Hood takes precedence in folk-lore, historians think many bands of men—not only the most famous set of so-called Merry Men of Lincolnshire—removed themselves from the power of the Crown into many forests. From all accounts, John's disregard of what the English were fast coming to value as certain inalienable rights—particularly the abuse of marriage rights of rich widows—merited such rebellion. In fact, one historian claims that John's rebellious barons grouped together demanding a certain Great Charter of rights after John had illegally seized a comely widow and forced her to his bed.

While John was the West's personification of the Devil, another simultaneously appeared in the East. This Scourge of God, who called himself the Genghis Khan, led a fearsome group of men—thousands strong, hordes from the bleak Mongolian landscape, where winters ensured only the strong survived and the only human right was to comply with the will of the clan's leader.

Decisive in battle, leading his cavalry attired in black silk upon their black horses, Genghis was circumspect in treatment of his friends—and brutal to his enemies. Word of his draconian methods spread to the princes of feudal Europe, and the very thought of such power shook their imaginations. Yet, Europeans benefited from Genghis's unparalleled achievement of opening a path across the rugged terrain of Asia: They traveled that open route to the wonders of India, the southeast ports, and the glories of the Chinese Empire. Every schoolchild knows the results—trading companies, ventures like that of Marco Polo, the rush to find quicker routes to the ecstasies of the Orient, the urge to exploration. The list never ends.

I hope you enjoyed my rendering of the period and the issues western women dealt with during it.

Watch for my next Pocket release in mid-1996. *Treasures* tells the tale of a young Victorian woman whose only desire is to restore her reputation after her fiance leaves her waiting at the altar. When he suddenly reappears with apologies and a new proposal, she wonders if she dares flaunt propriety and trust him again.

Write to me and let me know how you liked *Angel of*

Midnight. A self-addressed, stamped envelope is appreciated. My address is:

13017 Wisteria Drive, #384
Germantown, MD 20874

Happy Reading!

Jo Ann Power

Pocket Star Books
Proudly Presents

TREASURES

JO-ANN POWER

Coming from
Pocket Star Books
Spring 1996

The following is a preview of
Treasures. . . .

**Kent, England
Friday, March 27, 1874**

If money could buy what she wanted, she'd gladly squeeze stones—she'd even bleed turnips—to get what she needed.

But since you've already hit the bottom of your bank account, you can't do either, now can you, Cat?

Her problem was she knew she could make matters worse.

With what she faced downstairs in that receiving line and ballroom, she knew she could do more than suffer—she could die. And in more dire ways than financially.

Suppose she went downstairs, waltzed into that ballroom, and no one waltzed with her? What happened to a twenty-three-year-old jilted spinster who tried to open a school for girls and couldn't enroll enough students to meet the monthly butcher's bill?

Idleness. Frosted with poverty. And more ostracism.

She would change that. Her own self-respect depended on it. These past three years, she'd come to know *that* was more valuable than any other prize on earth.

Cat squeezed her eyes shut and summoned courage. Tonight, she needed every ounce. For weeks, Cat had debated, demurred, and finally accepted her friends' invitation to this house party. Then, she'd removed the purples of her mourning and packed them away with her memories of her doting father. Cheered, she'd taken herself off to Paris and ordered a new Worth wardrobe. When she returned, she replaced the fading Farrell family brougham with a black lacquered coach fit for a duke, and practiced quadrilles and waltzes with her cousin Jessica in the morning room until she dropped. Now she stood here, in this flurry of iris silk, hoping someone—please God, *anyone*—would deign to smile at her, talk with her, ask her to dance just one time. Only help her slightly, politely recover that elusive, priceless commodity—respect.

Cat sailed down the vacant hall to the main staircase. Below in the foyer she knew the cream of London would soon assemble for the last country event before the launch of the Annual Season in London. She'd assist Dorrie and Blanding with the receiving line, hope no one fainted dead away at the sight of her, and pray she could survive the ball with at least one man—other than Blanding—to dance with her. . . .

That her wish came true made her want to hug a footman! Instead she smiled at him and took a champagne flute from his tray, then sank to a chair behind a fat fern. The rest of the world could waltz past while she recovered and began the illusion of that public persona she longed to cultivate. To those who mattered, she would now become that venerable oddity—The School Headmistress. To her students, she would become The Battle-ax. The Harpie. The Prune.

Ugh. Just her image.

"The champagne *is* reviving, isn't it, Cat?"

She halted, mid-daydream, mid-nightmare.

The sound of his voice sank into her bones.

"Then again, you always did adore the stuff."

No, no, no. Her eyes fell closed as a bass voice brushed across her senses, stirring to life memories of passionate moments. *This cannot be happening.*

"Of course, I much prefer something stronger. Like the way brandy tastes from your lips."

She clutched the flute so hard that she stared at it, amazed it didn't shatter. She strangled a gasp. "Oh, God in Heaven, Spence, go away!" It was a whisper, an order, a horror that he—of all people—should be here now.

She glanced about the room. Courtesy of the fern, no one seemed to notice that Spencer Lyonns stood behind her, spoke to her, conversed with her as if . . . as if this were a normal occurrence, as if nothing had ever passed between this woman and this man. "How did you get in?"

"Dorrie and Blanding invited me."

"You *can't* be serious." She swallowed painfully, knowing she had to temper the outrage in her voice. If she weren't careful she'd be seething, and that wouldn't win her any friends or any students.

"I am quite honest with you, darling."

"Oh, please," she groaned in abject terror. "Go away, Spence. Don't do this to me. *Why* do this to me? Why would Dorrie and Blanding—"

"I'll tell you everything, Cat. Just dance with me."

She caught herself before she hooted. Petrified, she scanned the room like a trapped animal. "I *can't* dance with you. Not ever. You're mad."

"Yes, *very*. I never knew just how far gone I was until I looked at you a few minutes ago. Dance with me, Cat."

"No. You know what they'll say."

"I know what they're beginning to say now as they see us talking."

She set her shoulders, dug her nails into her skirts. "They're saying what a curious sight. Isn't that Spencer Lyonns trying to speak casually to the woman he left at the altar? I do wonder that the man has the nerve, don't you? He must be ready to be committed."

"Ah, yes, Cat. He is *that.*"

"Walk away from me, Spence. Now."

"Or you'll do what? Deliver me the telling blow? By all social rules, I admit I deserve it. But the truth is, you can't do it. It's not your nature to be cruel, darling. And it's not theirs to think beyond what you show them. Tonight, everything you want depends on you acting according to code."

"Yes! How could you come here, knowing that? How could Dorrie and Blanding do this when they understood that I needed respectability so much?"

"Don't castigate your friends. They have your best interests at heart. Mine, too. They knew so much. More than I gave them credit for." She felt his hand on her bare back, discreetly restraining her from rushing from her chair. *"No!* God, Cat, don't leave me looking furious. This crowd would gobble it up. You've got to calm yourself, please. I knew there was no easy way to do this. So did Dorrie and Blanding. But we're here, so are all of the people who matter to you and me, and I'm asking you to wipe the past from both our lives. Dance with me."

She took another drink, but frozen terror far surpassed cold alcohol for raw power. "I cannot imagine how waltzing with you could possibly help me."

"It would show the world we are friends."

"But we're not."

"We could be."

"We won't."

"We should."

"We can't ever be friends."

"How do you know if you've never tried, darling?"

"I don't *want* to know, Spence. And I don't want to be called 'darling.'"

"But you *are* mine."

"Do you mind if I laugh hysterically?" She shook her head in disbelief. "You come to me in a room jammed to the chandeliers with English society, shock me, regale me with simple arguments to supposedly, *blithely* end three years of—of ostracism by *dancing* with me?"

"It's impulse, born of watching you. As before, you create a violent compulsion in me. Besides, you know I never enter those bloody receiving lines." He took a step to her side and dropped his hand from her fevered skin. "And I knew you'd never come if you thought I'd be here. So did the Billingtons. You *must* listen to me. In the meantime, please take that startled look from your face. Despite this obliging potted forest we have about us, people are beginning to notice and whisper. Smile, will you?"

She ground her teeth. "Why don't *you?*"

"I am. I have been all this while. You should, too."

How could she? Instead, she forced herself to notice how others perceived this encounter between the notorious two whom London's *Tatler* dubbed "The Cat and the Lyonn." Some stared. One openly. Others intermittently.

She turned her face and saw the precise black crease of his trousers. She need never look at him to recall the man who made her heart skip and her mouth water and her eyes hurt for all his blinding handsomeness.

Till the second she died, she would recall his every feature. His blond hair as pale as the noon sun, with platinum streaks as dazzling as a solar glare on swirling desert sands. His green eyes, dark and moist as jungle foliage. His mouth, with its deep bow in the upper lip and the pouting wealth of the lower. His broad, bronzed face. His skin, smooth as a god's. His body, big and bold and brawny. His heart, which he had said was hers, only hers. His life, his happiness, which he said he would surrender to her keeping. Until the one day when he would have given all and vowed his troth forever—and instead he had disappeared.

"You return so easily, Spence. Wanting things I can't give you. You ruined me once. You won't again."

Then despite what all the world might rumor, she left him.

God, what had he done? Gone and ruined her again?

He couldn't stand it if he had. The first time had nearly killed him, exactly as it had destroyed their happiness. If he had done it again here tonight, he couldn't know how he'd retrieve the situation. Just when he had arranged everything so that he wouldn't fail, couldn't fail!

What had he said? That he wanted to dance with her?

He did. He shouldn't have. Convention didn't condone a jilted woman waltzing with the man who had shamed her.

But he couldn't help himself, couldn't drown his remorse or strangle his compassion and his need to put his hands on her. Place his arms around her. Pull her close. Move with her across this floor, across the years, take her back to what they might have been, should have been. Draw her forward to what they could be again.

That made him freeze in his tracks.

Could they recapture what they had felt for each other?

His mind whirred. Why would he think that absurdity?

Because you want her.

Because he had never really enjoyed any other woman. Because she was the first woman he found totally unpredictable. The only woman he had ever trusted.

But he hadn't gauged how much his betrayal had cost her. Spence's gaze trailed off in the direction she'd gone.

She had vanished.

He cursed and spun for the French doors to the garden. Jamming his hands into his trouser pockets, he strolled the terrace past Dorrie's roses across the grass to the rambling gazebo that glistened black in the moonglow.

Marching up the steps, he reached into his tuxedo jacket for a cigar and realized he'd forgotten to put any there. Hell, he'd been so eaten alive by the jitters at seeing Cat again, he would have been fortunate to remember how to spell his name.

The sound of someone whispering and then sucking in her breath made him stop. In the shadows, he spied the hem of a gown and the toe of a woman's shoe. Had he intruded on a lovers' rendezvous? He began to bow in apology and would have left had the color of the lady's gown not sent sparks to his brain. He straightened and stared into the void.

She did not even breathe.

"Cat?" he whispered, delighted at such good luck.

"You followed me," she groaned. "I wanted a few moments alone."

He took a step forward. He heard her fall back against the chaise's cushions.

A fierce growl made him freeze. From the shadows emerged a black animal, teeth bared, ready for attack.

"Bones! Be good. Sit," Cat ordered the Labrador.

"Bones?" Spence asked on a lilt of laughter. "Well now, where did you get—?" He felt teeth pierce his trouser, graze his left ankle—and hold. Spence grimaced. "I say, old man, could you possibly unclamp your jaws?"

"Bones! Let him go!" Cat demanded, then in a normal tone explained, "He's mine. He used to be the game dog for the Ashford village butcher, but he pointed at everything, living or dead. Mr. Torrence was forever confused by his actions and said Bones was too old to track properly."

"Ah. The butcher was going to put the poor old fellow out of his misery, I bet. And you couldn't hear of it."

"Yes. Now Bones lives at Farrell Hall."

"Tracking no one but you, I see." Spence felt the animal give him an unnecessary nip as a warning before he did as his mistress asked. Freed, Spence stepped forward but Cat shrank away. "I'm so glad you're here. I—"

She rose on a whoosh of silk skirts.

He grew frantic. "I came out for air and—"

"A cigar?" she asked in an incredulous tone.

"Among other things."

"Allow me to leave you to it."

"You could share it with me," he said, recalling the time he'd handed one over for her education and they had both been startled when she loved it—before she'd coughed herself blue. Clearly, she remembered none of that, only her intent to get away from him. But he caught her arm just as she would have flown around him toward the entrance.

The dog grumbled low in his throat.

Spence ignored him.

Cat stood paralyzed as Spence moved closer, pressing her back, feeling every tremor through her terrified body. "Let me go, Spence. I don't want what you're offering."

"Not air?" he mused, his mouth trailing her temple and ear, loving her personal musk, which not even roses could rival.

"Not even a cigar," she confirmed with that hushed voice that spoke to him in his dreams.

He noted her wry humor. "Honestly, Cat, I didn't know you came out here. I came for the same reason you did. To escape a stifling room." *And boiling desire for you.*

She strained away from him, shivering as if she'd heard that last. "I'm cool now."

"Yes, cold, I'd say. Here—" He shrugged out of his swallowtail cutaway and swirled it over her bare shoulders before she had taken two more steps. "Stay," he pleaded, while he told himself he must remove his hands. "Remain and talk to me. I promise I won't be brash or forward. I was before. I apologize."

Slowly she turned in his arms, and within the silver rays of gathering night, he could see on her exquisite face utter surprise. "You astonish me."

Not half as much as you do me. He narrowed his eyes to examine what he thought he saw in her own. He called it curiosity and gave thanks it wasn't indifference. "I am pleased to elicit more from you than the anger of before. How is it that I can do that?"

"You once told me you never apologized to anyone for anything you did. It was beneath your dignity."

"Even a Lyonns learns how to deal with failure. And mistakes."

Her shivers became tremblings. "I must go." She tried to spin away.

He tightened his grip on her. And though the dog objected again, Spence said, "Won't you stay and let me explain more?"

"No." She tugged.

He couldn't let her go. His superior strength meant he could so easily keep her body. But he needed to capture her mind, and his voice dropped to a desperate urgency. "I could tell you how a Lyonns tries very hard to understand his short-comings. How he wants to change—"

"Oh, Spence, *please.*" Her eyelashes drifted down in agony. "That's irrelevant now."

He stepped nearer, close enough to draw the roses from her hair, let down her curls, sink his hands into the thick golden red mass that twined into his every memory of her. "I do want to make it all up to you." He'd almost called her "darling." He wouldn't make that mistake again. "Cat, I need to talk with you. Let me. That's the primary reason I'm here this weekend."

"Talking with me won't change anything, Spence. You know it won't. I don't want to be seen with you. I don't want to remember." She stared at him with a determination drawn in every elegant line of her heart-shaped face. "I came here thinking I could reingratiate myself into society. I cannot do that if you persist in this—this masquerade of caring for me."

He could tell her that was no ruse, but she wouldn't believe him. He said the only thing that might make a difference. "Cat, I want to help you."

She gaped, but recovered admirably. "I don't want your help."

"But if you have it, you'll be accepted much faster." That was true in one respect: They'd show society they were rational people who could approach each other with civility. It was also not exactly true. For if indeed he did find in her father's effects the item he needed to satisfy the Government, he would condemn her father on many counts. In his grave over a year, Walter Farrell would not be here to defend himself, which meant, of course, that Spence had to tread very carefully for all concerned. Compelled as he was by duty, Spence could only brave the winds of fortune and hope he could protect Cat from any storm.

What a gargantuan task he had set himself.

Cat frowned. She was considering his words, he knew. What he couldn't fathom was what her decision was when finally she raised her eyes to his. "Very well, since I can't escape you or snub you these next few days without damage to my own dignity, I suppose I could consent to a practical measure. We'll pretend we accept each other."

For the first time in years, he grinned and felt it to his fingertips. "It's a beginning."

"No. It's the end."

He'd change that, make it more than she expected. "You won't be sorry."

"Where you are concerned, I have ceased to be sorry."

That subdued him. "Good. You never did anything wrong."

"Spence, as absolution, your words are a little late."

"But true."

"Now, will you remove your hands from me?"

"If I do, will you stay?"

"You haven't anything more you could say to me that would interest me."

His hope fell at his feet. *What if I told you I have wanted you every day of the past three years?* He couldn't say that. But how the deuce was he supposed to get her to listen to him?

"What if I said I was saddened to hear of your father's death? How sorry I am he's gone. He was a great man, a noted scholar, and we are all the poorer for his passing."

Her eyes, which she had closed at the mention of her father, opened now, and when she looked at him again, tears dotted her lashes. She stroked the lapels of his jacket absently. "You can say you admired him in spite of his behavior toward you?"

"He came to like me as I did him."

"He thought you'd make a worthy member of the family."

"I am certain when he died, he had changed his mind."

"He decried the day he ever met you—or your brother."

"I wish he were here now so that I might tell him I never meant to harm you."

"He'd say to believe that would take an awful stretch of the imagination."

"Perhaps. But it is true."

From the look on her face, she wanted to accept that as gospel. She bent her head, pressed her cheek to his jacket, and inhaled. Her eyes grew dreamy and sad. She jerked her head up. "If you'll excuse me, I want to go inside."

For a second he could have sworn he'd rekindled embers. All right, she wouldn't dance with him, but maybe—

He caught up to her as she made her way down the path, with one hunk of canine flesh separating them. "You're not going in the hunt tomorrow morning, are you?"

"You know I can't bear those horses and hounds rabid to tear at one little fox."

"Come riding with me then."

She choked out a strangled sound of surprise as they reached the terrace steps, and the music floating out about them seemed less sweet than the tones of her amusement, rueful though it was. "I will *not* ride with you anywhere, least of all alone at a house party while the others are off traipsing about the countryside!"

"Then stay here and meet me in the morning room *for newspapers and coffee and good conversation.*"

"Spence, no."

"I promise to begin your day brightly with me about."

For a second, she looked tempted—and God above, with the stars in her eyes, so very tempting.

"*No*. We will appear congenial, but we will never take coffee and conversation together. I couldn't bear— I just couldn't."

He watched her walk away for a moment with her faithful canine escort plodding along at her skirts. Her head high.

He caught up to her, taming a knowing smile to one less irritating to her. "There is one thing you could do, though."

She spun so abruptly he walked right into her. As he stood flush to her warm torso, his hands steadied them both as he felt her body's instant sizzle.

Irritated probably as much with herself as with him, she tilted her head and whispered, "And *what* might that be?"

He let his eyes dance to her shoulders. "You could return my jacket to me so they won't think we were standing out here conversing like any loving couple would do."

She ground her teeth, whirled off the offending garment, and thrust it at him as if it were a monster. "Take it."

He put his hand to hers.

She yanked away. "Spence, do me one service only."

"Anything."

"Leave me alone."

In a furl of her skirts and rose attar, she opened the door and disappeared.

Her Cerberus plunked himself down to face Spence.

He grinned at the glowering dog. "Well, old man, I see your position in this matter. But you'd save yourself a lot of trouble if you just accepted conditions as they are."

The dog shook his head, flews wobbling, spittle flying. Then he smacked his gums as if to say, *We are not dissuaded.*

"No? But neither am I, because, you see, leaving your lady alone is the one thing I will never do again."